G. Cain del. Gery Bichar

Cousin Bette

Honoré de Balzac

Translated by George Burnham Ives

Book-of-the-Month Club
New York

Cousin Bette was first published in 1846.

Printed in the United States of America

TO DON MICHELE ANGELO CAJETANI, PRINCE OF TEANO:

It is not the Roman prince, nor the heir of the illustrious house of Cajetani, which has given popes to Christendom, to whom I dedicate this small fragment of a long story, but the learned commentator of Dante.

To you I owe my comprehension of the marvelous framework of ideas, whereon the greatest of Italian poets constructed his poem, the only poem that the moderns have to offer in emulation of that of Homer. Until I had heard your voice the *Divina Commedia* seemed to me a stupendous enigma, to which no one had been able to find the key, the commentators least of all. To understand Dante thus is to be great like him; but all forms of greatness are familiar to you.

An intelligent Frenchman might build up a reputation for himself, might earn a professorship and many a decoration, by publishing, in a dogmatic volume, the improvisation with which you assisted us to while away the hours of one of those evenings when we were resting from the fatigue of a day of sight-seeing in Rome. Perhaps you are not aware that most of our professors live upon Germany, England, the Orient or the North, as insects upon a tree ; and, like the insect, they become an integral part of their subject, borrowing their value from its value. Now, Italy has not yet had justice done her from the professor's chair. I shall never receive the credit due to me as a man of letters for my self-restraint. I might, by appropriating your ideas, have become a learned man with the authority of three Schlegels ; whereas I am content to remain a simple doctor of social medicine, the veterinary surgeon for incurable diseases, were it only that I might bear witness to my gratitude to my cicerone, and add your illustrious name to the names of Porcia, San-Severino, Pareto, Di Negro and Belgiojoso, which represent, in the *Comédie Humaine*, the close and enduring alliance between Italy and France, which Bishop Bandello, author of divers extremely amusing tales, perpetuated in the same way, in the sixteenth century, in that magnificent collection of novels, whence several of Shakespeare's plays were derived, in some cases entire rôles *verbatim et literatim*.

The two sketches which I dedicate to you constitute the two ever-enduring faces of the same fact. *Homo duplex*, our great Buffon has said ; why not add : *Res duplex?* Everything is two-fold, even virtue. So Molière always presents both sides of every human problem ; and in imitation of him Diderot wrote one day : *Ceci n'est pas un conte*, which may perhaps be considered Diderot's masterpiece, wherein he presents the sublime figure of Mademoiselle de Lachaux sacrificed by Gardanne, in contrast to the figure of an unexceptionable lover slain by his mistress. My two novels are placed together, therefore, like twins of different sexes. It is a literary caprice which one may gratify once in a way, especially in a work wherein one seeks to portray all the forms in which thought may be clothed. Most disputes among men, are due to the fact that there are people, learned and ignorant alike, so constituted that they can see but one aspect of a fact or an idea, and invariably claim that the one they have seen is the only true, the only sound one. So it was that the Holy Book prophetically announced: "God will give the world over to dissension." I confess that that single passage of Scripture should lead the Holy See to bestow upon you the government of the two Chambers, in obedience to the sentence expounded in 1814, by the ordinance of Louis XVIII.

May your intellect, may your poetic nature, vouchsafe their patronage to the two episodes of the *Poor Relations*

Of your affectionate servant,

DE BALZAC.

Paris, August-September, 1846.

THE PRODIGAL FATHER

*

Toward the middle of the month of July, 1838, one of the public carriages called *milords*, then a novelty in the streets of Paris, passed along Rue de l'Université, containing a stout man of medium height, in the uniform of a captain in the National Guard.

Among the good Parisians, who are commonly accused of being so very clever, there are those who fancy themselves infinitely more attractive in uniform than in their ordinary garb, and who credit the fair sex with so depraved a taste as to be favorably impressed by a bearskin cap and regimentals.

The physiognomy of this captain in the Second Legion exhaled a smug self-satisfaction which imparted an additional glow to his fat, ruddy cheeks. By the halo which wealth acquired in business binds around the brow of retired shopkeepers, it was easy to identify him as one of the chosen public servants of Paris,—at the very least a former deputy of his arrondissement. In like manner you may be sure that the ribbon of the Legion of Honor was not lacking on his chest, ostentatiously inflated *à la*

Prussienne. Planted proudly in a corner of the milord, this decorated personage allowed his glance to stray from one to another of the passers-by, who very often in Paris are thus made the beneficiaries of genial smiles intended for absent bright eyes.

The milord stopped in that portion of the street which lies between Rue de Bellechasse and Rue de Bourgogne, at the door of a large house newly built upon part of the courtyard of an old family mansion with a garden. The mansion itself had been spared, and still stood in its original shape at the end of the curtailed courtyard.

Simply by the way in which the captain accepted the services of the driver in descending from the milord, one could recognize the quinquagenarian. There are movements of the body whose artless heaviness is as outspoken as a certificate of birth. The captain drew his yellow glove on his right hand, and without pausing to question the concierge, directed his steps toward the entrance to the ground-floor of the mansion with an air which said: "She is mine!" Paris concierges have a knowing eye; they never interfere with decorated individuals dressed in blue, with a heavy tread; in short, they know a rich man when they see him.

The whole ground-floor was occupied by M. le Baron Hulot d'Ervy, who had been commissary-in-chief under the Republic, formerly intendant-general of the army, and was at this time at the head of one of the most important departments of the Ministry of War, Councilor of State, grand officer of the Legion of Honor, etc., etc. Baron Hulot had taken the surname of Ervy, his birthplace, to distinguish himself from his brother, the famous General Hulot, colonel of the grenadiers of the Imperial Guard, created by the Emperor Count de Forzheim after the campaign of 1809. The count being the elder brother and responsible for the welfare of his junior, procured for him with fatherly good judgment a place in the War Department, where, thanks to their united services, the baron earned and obtained the favor of Napoleon. As early as 1807 Baron Hulot was intendant-general of the armies engaged in Spain.

Having rung the bell, the citizen captain made divers violent attempts to re-adjust his coat, which was badly wrinkled, as well behind as in front, by the action of his pear-shaped paunch. Admitted as soon as a liveried domestic caught sight of him, this important and imposing personage followed the domestic, who announced, as he threw open the door of the salon:

"M. Crevel!"

Upon hearing this name, admirably adapted to the bearing of the man to whom it belonged, a tall, fair, well-preserved woman seemed to experience something like an electric shock, and sprang to her feet.

"Hortense, my love, go out into the garden with your Cousin Bette," said she hastily to her daughter, who sat at her embroidery a few steps away.

With a graceful courtesy to the captain, Mademoiselle Hortense Hulot left the room through a long window, taking with her a thin, meagre old maid, who looked to be older than the baroness, although she was five years younger.

"Your marriage is the matter in hand," said Cousin Bette in the ear of her little Cousin Hortense, with no sign of offence at the unceremonious fashion in which the baroness dismissed her, as if she were of no account whatever.

The general appearance of this cousin would have afforded, at need, a sufficient explanation of the lack of ceremony.

She wore a currant-colored merino dress, the cut and trimming of which dated from the Restoration; an embroidered neckerchief, which might have been worth three francs; a straw hat covered with shell-shaped pieces of blue satin edged with straw, like those worn by the old-clothes women at the Market. At sight of the goatskin shoes, the style of which pointed to a shoemaker of the lowest order, a stranger would have hesitated to salute Cousin Bette as one of the family, for she much resembled a dressmaker on day wages. Nevertheless the old maid did not leave the room without a little friendly nod to M. Crevel, to which that personage replied by a sign of intelligence.

"You will come to-morrow, won't you, Mademoiselle Fischer?" said he.

"You are to have no company?" asked Cousin Bette.

"My children and yourself, no one else," replied the visitor.

"Very well, then, you may count upon me."

"I am at your service, madame," said the captain of militia, bowing once more to Madame Hulot.

As he spoke he bestowed upon the baroness such a glance as Tartuffe bestows upon Elmire when, at Poitiers or Covtances, a provincial actor feels called upon to bring out the real meaning of the part.

"If you will come this way with me, monsieur, we can talk business much more conveniently than in this salon," said Madame Hulot, indicating an adjoining room, which, in the division of the suite, was known as a card-room.

This apartment was separated by only a thin partition from the boudoir, the window of which looked upon the garden, and Madame Hulot left M. Crevel alone for a moment, deeming it advisable to close the door and window of the boudoir, so that no one could come there to listen. She also took the precaution to close the long window of the large salon, smiling as she did so at her daughter and her cousin, who had established themselves in an old pagoda at the end of the garden. As she returned she left the card-room door open, so that she could hear if anyone should open that of the salon. As she went and came the baroness, being unobserved, allowed her features to express her real thoughts; and anybody who had seen her would have been almost terrified by her agitation. But as she returned across the large salon to the card-room her face assumed that mask of impenetrable reserve which all women, even the most ingenuous, seem to have at command.

During these preliminaries, which were, to say the least, singular, the national guardsman examined the furnishings of the room in which he found himself. As his eyes fell upon the silk hangings, once red, now faded to pale violet by the action of the sun, and worn threadbare at the folds by long use, a carpet whence the color had vanished, chairs on which the gilding was worn away, and the stained and spotted silk coverings worn out in strips, expressions of disdain, satisfaction and hope succeeded one another upon his vacant, parvenu shopkeeper's face. He was looking at himself in the mirror, which hung above an old Empire-clock, passing himself in review, as it were, when the rustling of her silk dress announced the baroness, and he at once struck an attitude.

Having thrown herself upon a little couch, which must have been very beautiful about 1809, the baroness, pointing to an armchair, the arms of which were terminated by bronzed sphinxes heads, from which the paint had fallen off in scales, leaving the wood bare in spots, motioned to Crevel to be seated.

"These precautions you are taking, madame, would be of most delightful augury for a—"

"For a lover," she suggested, interrupting the national guardsman.

"That is a weak word," said he, placing his right hand upon his heart, and rolling his eyes in a fashion that almost invariably makes a woman laugh when in cold blood she sees them assume such an expression: "lover! lover! say rather one bewitched."

"Listen, Monsieur Crevel," rejoined the baroness, whose mood was too serious to admit of laughter, "you are fifty years old; ten years younger than M. Hulot, I know, but at my age a woman's folly should be justified by good looks, youth, celebrity, merit, or some other of the brilliant qualities which dazzle us to the point of making us forget everything, even our age. If you had an income of fifty thousand francs your age would outweigh your fortune, so that of all that a woman demands you possess nothing at all."

"And what of love?" said the national guardsman, rising and walking toward her; "a love, which—"

"No, monsieur, obstinacy!" said the baroness, interrupting him to put an end to the absurd scene.

"Very true, obstinacy and love," he retorted, "but something better, too; rights—"

"Rights?" cried Madame Hulot, rising to a sublime height of scorn, defiance and wrath. "But," she continued, "at this rate we shall never have done, and I didn't ask you to come here to talk upon the subject which caused your banishment, notwithstanding the close connection between our families."

"I thought—"

"Again!" she exclaimed. "Can you not see, monsieur, by my cool and unconcerned way of speaking of lovers and love and of every subject most dangerous for a woman to talk about, that I am perfectly sure of retaining my virtue? I have no fear, not even of arousing suspicion, by closeting myself with you. Is that the conduct of a weak woman? You are well aware why I asked you to come !"

"No, madame," rejoined Crevel, assuming a frigid manner. He pursed up his lips and again struck an attitude.

"Very well; I will be brief in order to abridge our mutual discomfort," said the baroness, looking him in the face.

Crevel executed an ironical salute, in which one of the guild would have recognized the airs and graces of a former traveling salesman.

"Our son has married your daughter—"

"And if it were still to be done!"—said Crevel.

"The marriage would not take place, I strongly suspect," retorted the baroness hastily. "However, you have no reason to complain. My son is not only one of the leading advocates of Paris, but he has been deputy for a year past, and his début in the Chamber was brilliant enough to make it reasonable to suppose that he will be a minister before long. Victorin has twice been selected to report important bills, and if he wished, he might even now be avocat-général of the Court of Appeal. So that if you mean to insinuate that you have a son-in-law without fortune—"

"A son-in-law whom I am obliged to support, madame," rejoined Crevel, "which to my thinking is even worse. Of the five hundred thousand francs which constituted my daughter's dowry, two hundred have gone God knows where !—to pay the debts of monsieur, your son, to furnish the house in a way to make people stare ; a house that cost five hundred thousand francs and yields scarcely fifteen thousand, as he occupies the best part of it himself, and upon which he still owes two hundred and sixty thousand francs.—The income barely covers the interest on the debt. This year I give my daughter twenty thousand francs to enable her to make both ends meet. And my son-in-law, who was earning thirty thousand francs at the Palais, they say, is neglecting the Palais for the Chamber."

"This is also a side issue, Monsieur Crevel, and keeps us far away from the subject. But, to have done with it, if my son becomes a minister, if he makes you an officer in the Legion of Honor and Councilor of the Prefecture of Paris, for one who once dealt in perfumery you will have no cause to complain."

"Ah ! there we are, madame. I am a shopkeeper, a grocer, a dealer in almond paste and Portugal water and cephalic oil, and I should esteem myself highly honored to have married my only daughter to the son of M. le Baron Hulot d'Ervy ; my daughter will be a baroness. 'Tis the Regency come again ; 'tis Louis XV.; 'tis the *Œil-de-bœuf !* That's all very fine.—I love Célestine as a man loves his only daughter ; I love her so dearly that, in order that she might have no brother or sister, I resigned myself to all the inconvenience of widowerhood in Paris—in the prime of life, too, madame !—but understand that, for all my insensate love for my daughter, I will not cut into my fortune for your son, whose expenses seem rather mysterious to me, a former tradesman."

"Monsieur, there is M. Popinot, once a druggist on Rue des Lombards, now Minister of Commerce."—

"My friend, madame!"—said the retired perfumer, "for I, Célestin Crevel, formerly chief-clerk to Père César Birotteau, purchased the business of said Birotteau, Popinot's father-in-law, Popinot being then a simple clerk in the establishment; and he himself reminds me of it, for he is not proud—I must do him that justice—with people who have attained a good position, and have an income of sixty thousand francs."

"Ah, well, monsieur, the ideas that you suggest by the word 'regency,' are not in fashion at a time when men are accepted for their personal qualities, and that is what you did when you married your daughter to my son."

"You have no idea how that marriage came about!"—cried Crevel. "Ah! this accursed bachelor life! Except for my misbehavior my Célestine would be Viscomtess Popinot to-day!"

"But, once more, let us not indulge in recriminations as to things that are passed and gone," rejoined the baroness with energy. "Let us talk of your extraordinary conduct, which gives me just cause for complaint. My daughter Hortense had an opportunity to marry, her marriage depended entirely upon you; I believed you to be of a generous disposition, I thought you would do justice to a woman who never admitted any other than her husband's image in her heart, that you would realize how necessary it was for her to refuse to receive a man whose visits might compromise her, and that you would be only too willing, out of regard for the family with which you are allied, to forward Hortense's union with Councilor Lebas.—But you caused the marriage to fall through, monsieur—"

"Madame," replied the quondam perfumer, "I acted as an honest man should. I was asked the question whether the two hundred thousand francs supposed to constitute Mademoiselle Hortense's marriage-portion would be paid. I replied in these exact words: 'I would not vouch for it. My son-in-law, to whom the Hulot family allotted that sum as his marriage-portion, had debts, and it is my opinion that, if M. Hulot d'Ervy were to die to-morrow, his widow would be without a crust.' That's the whole of it, dear madame."

"Would you have used that language, monsieur," demanded Madame Hulot, gazing fixedly at Crevel, "if I would have consented to be false to my vows for your sake?"

"I should have had no right to say it, dear Adeline," cried this singular lover, cutting the baroness short, "for you would find the marriage-portion in my portfolio."

And, to add the greater force to his words, the corpulent Crevel dropped upon one knee and kissed Madame Hulot's hand, attributing to hesitation her speechless horror at his words.

"Buy my daughter's happiness at the price of—? Oh! monsieur, rise, or I will ring—"

The former dealer in perfumery rose with great difficulty. This state of affairs so incensed him that he again struck his favorite attitude. Almost every man is particularly given to some posture which he deems best calculated to show off all the advantages with which nature has endowed him. This posture, in Crevel's case, consisted in folding his arms *à la Napoléon*, turning his head three-fourths around, and looking in the direction in which the artist made him look in his portrait, that is to say, toward the horizon.

"To remain faithful," he exclaimed, with well simulated rage, "to remain faithful to a libert—"

"To a husband, monsieur, who is worthy of my fidelity," retorted Madame Hulot, interrupting Crevel in order not to allow him to utter a word she did not choose to hear.

"Look you, madame, you wrote me to come, you wish to know the explanation of my conduct, you drive me to extremities with your imperial airs, your disdain, your—contempt! Would not one say that I was a blackamoor? I say again, and mark my words! that I have a right to—pay my court to you—for— But no, I love you enough to hold my tongue—"

"Go on, monsieur; I shall be forty-eight years old in a few days; I am no silly prude and I can listen to anything—"

"Give me your word then as a virtuous woman—

for, unluckily for me, you are a virtuous woman—never to mention my name, or to say that I told you the secret."

"If you make that a condition of the disclosure, I swear that I will name to no one, not even to my husband, the person from whom I learned the enormities you are about to confide to me."

"I believe you, for only you and he are concerned—"

Madame Hulot turned pale.

"Ah! if you love him still, prepare to suffer! Do you wish me to hold my tongue?"

"Say on, monsieur, for, according to your own account, it is for you to justify in my eyes the extraordinary statements you have made, and your persistence in tormenting a woman of my age, who would like to see her daughter well married, and then—die in peace!"

"You see, you are unhappy—"

"I, monsieur?"

"Yes, lovely and noble creature!" cried Crevel, "you have suffered only too much—"

"Monsieur, be silent and go! or address me properly."

"Do you know, madame, how Monsieur Hulot and I became acquainted?—through our mistresses, madame."

"Oh! monsieur—!"

"Through our mistresses, madame," repeated Crevel in a melodramatic tone, and abandoning his attitude to make a gesture with his right hand.

"Well, what then, monsieur?"—said the baroness calmly, to Crevel's unbounded amazement.

Petty seducers never understand noble hearts.

"Five years a widower," resumed Crevel, in the manner of a man about to tell a story, "and not caring to marry a second time for the sake of my daughter, whom I idolize, nor to form liaisons in my own establishment, although I had at the time a very pretty cashier, I furnished apartments, as they say, for a little seamstress of fifteen, of marvelous beauty, and with whom, I confess, I fell head over ears in love, and so, madame, I begged my own aunt, whom I had sent for from my native place—my mother's sister—to make her home with the charming creature and keep an eye upon her, so that she might remain as virtuous as possible in that—what shall I say?—*chocnoso*—no, illicit situation!—The little one, whose vocation for music was very apparent, was supplied with teachers and received an education—it was necessary to keep her mind occupied!—Furthermore, it was my purpose to be at one and the same time her father, her benefactor, and, let us say the word, her lover: to kill two birds with one stone, do a kind action, and make sure of a kind friend. I was happy for five years. The little one had one of those voices which make the fortune of a theatre, and I can not better describe her than as a Duprez in petticoats. It cost me two thousand francs a year, simply to cultivate her talents as a singer. She made me mad over music, and I had a box at the Italiens for her and my daughter. I used to go there one day with Célestine, the next with Josépha."—

"What, the famous singer?"—

"Yes, madame," responded Crevel, proudly, "the renowned Josépha owes everything to me.—At last, in 1834, when she was twenty years old, thinking that I had bound her to myself forever, and having become as wax in her hands, I wished to afford her some little distraction, and allowed her to make the acquaintance of a pretty little actress, one Jenny Cadine, whose lot in life bore some resemblance to hers. This actress also owed everything to a protector, who had bestowed great care upon her bringing up. This protector was Baron Hulot."—

"I know it, monsieur," said the baroness in a calm, unmoved voice.

"Eh! the deuce!" cried Crevel, more and more taken aback. "Very good! But do you know that your monster of a man *protected* Jenny Cadine at the age of thirteen?"

"Well, monsieur, what of it?" said the baroness.

"As Jenny Cadine," resumed the former tradesman, "was twenty, Josépha's age, when they became acquainted, the baron must have been playing the rôle that Louis XV. played with Mademoiselle de Romans from 1826, and in that case you had for at least twelve years—"

"Monsieur, I had my reasons for allowing M. Hulot his liberty."

"That falsehood, madame, will suffice no doubt to atone for all the sins you have committed, and will open the gate of Paradise to you," retorted Crevel with a cunning leer, which made the baroness blush. "Tell that to others, sublime and adorable woman, but not to Père Crevel, who, you must know, has made one of a party of four with your villain of a husband too often not to be fully aware of your worth! He sometimes reproached himself, between two glasses, as he dilated to me upon your perfections. Oh! I know you well: you are an angel. Between a young girl of twenty and yourself a libertine might hesitate: I do not."

"Monsieur!"—

"All right; I will stop at that.—But understand, O saintly and dignified woman, that husbands, once in their cups, tell many tales of their wives to their mistresses, who laugh without stint at them."

Tears of shame, which trickled from between Madame Hulot's lovely eyelashes, brought the national guardsman to a halt, and he no longer thought of assuming his favorite attitude.

"I resume," said he. "We were brought together, the baron and myself, by our rascalities. The baron, like all men of vicious habits, is very attractive, and a downright good fellow. Oh! the rascal won my heart! He was a man of expedients.—But a truce to these reminiscences.—We became like two brothers.—The villain, for all the world like the Regent, did his best to lead me astray, to preach Saint-Simonism where women were concerned, to fill me with the ideas of a great lord, of a thoroughbred aristocrat; but, mark you, I loved my little one well enough to marry her, if I had not dreaded having children. How do you suppose that two old papas, such friends as—as we were, could fail to think of marrying our children? Three months after your son's marriage to my Célestine, Hulot—I don't know how I can pronounce his name, the traitor! for he deceived us both, madame—well, the traitor spirited my little Josépha away from me. The villain knew that he was supplanted by a Councilor of State and an artist—save the mark!—in the heart of Jenny Cadine, whose vogue increased most prodigiously, and he took from me my poor little mistress, a love of a woman; but you certainly must have seen her at the Italiens, where his influence secured her an engagement. Your man is not as prudent as myself, who am as regular as a sheet of music—he had already been well cut into by Jenny Cadine, who cost him well nigh thirty thousand francs a year. Well, you must know he ruined himself utterly for Josépha. Josépha, madame, is a Jewess; her name is Mirah—an anagram of Hiram—an Israelitish device intended as a means of identification, for she was abandoned as a child in Germany—my investigations prove that she is the natural daughter of a wealthy Jew banker. The stage, and, above all, the lessons she learned from Jenny Cadine, Madame Schontz, Malaga and Carabine, as to the method of handling old men, developed in this child, whom I maintained in a virtuous and inexpensive life, the instinctive thirst of the first Hebrews for gold and jewels, for the golden calf!

The celebrated cantatrice, having acquired a fierce greed for gain, is determined to be rich, very rich. And so she squanders not a sou of all that is squandered upon her. She tried her hand upon Monsieur Hulot, and plucked him clean. Oh! she *shaved* him, as the saying is! The poor fellow, after contending with one of the Kellers and the Marquis d'Esgrignon, both mad over Josépha, to say nothing of her unknown idolaters, will soon see her taken from him by that enormously wealthy duke, who patronizes the arts. What's his name?—a dwarf?—ah! yes; the Duke d'Hérouville. This great nobleman proposes to have Josépha all to himself; the whole courtesan world is talking about it, and the baron knows nothing of it; for it is the same in the thirteenth arrondissement as in all the others: the lover, like the husband, is the last to find out what is going on. Now do you understand my rights? Your husband, fair lady, has robbed me of my happiness, of the only joy I have had since I lost my wife. Yes, if I had not had the ill-luck to meet that old spendthrift, Josépha would still be mine; for you see I would never have put her on the stage; she would have remained obscure, virtuous and all my own. Oh! if you had seen her eight years ago; slender and lithe, with the golden complexion of an Andalusian, as they say; black hair that shone like satin, eyes with long brown lashes, whose glances were like flashes of lightning, the distinction of a duchess in her gestures, and as modest in her poverty, her unassuming grace and loveliness, as a wild deer! By the fault of Monsieur Hulot her charms, her purity, everything has become a trap for wolves, a hole to catch hundred-sou pieces. The little one is the queen of demi-reps, as the saying goes. Last of all, to-day she *blagues*, she who used to know nothing at all, hardly the meaning of the word!"

At this juncture the quondam perfumer wiped his eyes, in which a few tears had gathered. The evident sincerity of his grief had its effect upon Madame Hulot, who roused herself from the fit of abstraction into which she had fallen.

"Well, madame, can one find such another treasure at fifty-two years? At that age love costs thirty thousand francs a year; I have the figures from your husband, and I am too fond of Célestine to ruin her. When I first saw you at the first evening party you gave us, I could not understand why that villain Hulot should keep a Jenny Cadine.—You had the bearing of an empress.—You are less than thirty years old, madame," he continued; "to me you seem young; you are beautiful. On my word of honor I was touched to the heart that day, and I said to myself: 'If I had not my Josépha, as Père Hulot neglects his wife, she would fit me like a glove.' Ah! pardon me, that is an expression of my former trade. The perfumer will peep out from time to time, and that is what prevents my aspiring to be a deputy. So it was that when I was betrayed in such dastardly fashion by the baron, for, among old sinners like us, our friends' mistresses should be held sacred, I swore to take his wife away from him. It's no more than fair. The baron would have nothing to say, and we are sure of impunity. You turned me out of doors like a mangy dog at the first words I let fall as to the state of my heart; thereby you redoubled my love, my obstinacy, if you please, and you shall be mine."

"How, pray?"

"I don't know, but it shall be. Look you, madame, an idiot of a perfumer—retired!—who has but one idea in his head is more formidable than a man of intellect who has thousands of them. I am clean gone over you, and you are my revenge! it is as if I were in love twice over. I speak frankly to you, like a determined man. Just as you say to me: 'I will not be yours,' so I talk coolly with you. In short, I play with my cards on the table, according to the proverb. Yes, you shall be mine, and before long, too. Oh! if you were fifty, still you should be my mistress. It shall be, I say, for I expect every assistance from your husband—"

Madame Hulot fixed her eyes upon the scheming tradesman in such a terrified stare, that he thought she had gone mad, and he checked himself.

"You would have it so, you poured out your scorn on me, you defied me, and I have spoken!" he said, feeling the necessity of justifying the brutality of his last words.

"Oh! my child! my child!" cried the baroness in a voice like a dying woman's.

"Ah! I no longer care for anything!" rejoined

Crevel. "On the day Josépha was taken from me, I was like a tigress whose whelps have been stolen.—In short, I was as I see you now. Your daughter! she is the means by which I obtain you. Yes, I put a stop to your daughter's marriage!—and you can not find a husband for her without my help! Beautiful as Mademoiselle Hortense is, she must have a dot."

"Alas! yes," said the baroness, wiping her eyes.

"Very well, try asking the baron for ten thousand francs," said Crevel, striking his attitude once more.

He waited a moment, like an actor marking time.

"If he had them he would give them to the one who takes Josépha's place," said he, pitching his voice in a higher key. "Does a man ever stop on the road he has taken? He is too fond of women!—There is a golden mean in everything, as our king has said.—And then vanity takes a hand! He's a fine man! He'll ruin you all for his own gratification. Indeed you're on the road to the poor-house even now. See, since I ceased my visits you haven't been able to re-furnish your salon. The words *straitened circumstances* are belched out at one by every lizard on yonder hangings. What son-in-law would not be dismayed by such thinly disguised evidences of poverty in its most horrible form, the poverty of people of fashion? I have been a shopkeeper and I know what I'm talking about. There's no eye so keen as a Paris tradesman's to discover the difference between real and apparent affluence.—You haven't a sou," he said in a low voice. "That is visible in everything, even in your servant's coat. Do you want me to disclose to you certain frightful mysteries of which you know nothing?"

"Monsieur," said Madame Hulot, whose handkerchief was saturated with her tears, "Enough! Enough!"

"But my son-in-law supplies his father with money, and that is what I intended to tell you at the outset as to your son's proceedings. But I have an eye to my daughter's interests—never fear."

"Oh! to marry my daughter and die!"—cried the wretched woman, fairly beside herself.

"Very good, this is the way to do it!" rejoined the former perfumer.

Madame Hulot looked up at Crevel with a gleam of hope, which transformed her features so swiftly, that that single movement might well have softened the man's heart and induced him to abandon his absurd project.

"You will be beautiful for ten years to come," resumed Crevel, posing; "be kind to me, and Mademoiselle Hortense is married. Hulot has given me the right, as I told you, to make the bargain without scruple, and he won't be angry. For the last three years I have put my capital to good use, for my follies have been few and far between. I am three hundred thousand francs to the good over and above my fortune, and they are yours."

"Go, monsieur," said Madame Hulot; "go and never show your face to me again. Except that you made it necessary for me to know the secret of your cowardly conduct in the matter of Hortense's marriage—yes, cowardly"—she repeated, in response to Crevel's gesture, "how can you vent your spleen upon a poor girl, a lovely, innocent creature?—Except for that necessity which tore my maternal heart, you would never have spoken to me again, you would never have put foot inside my door. Thirty-two years of honor, of wifely loyalty, shall not go for nothing under the attacks of M. Crevel—"

"Former dealer in perfumery, successor to César Birotteau, sign of *La Reine des Roses*, Rue Saint Honoré," said Crevel, in a mocking tone, "ex-deputy mayor, captain in the national guard, chevalier of the Legion of Honor, just as my predecessor was."

"Monsieur," continued the baroness, "M. Hulot after twenty years of constancy may have grown weary of his wife; that concerns nobody but me; but, you see, monsieur, that he has made a great mystery of his infidelities, for I was unaware that he had supplanted you in Josépha's heart."

"Oh!" cried Crevel, "by the use of money, madame!—The nightingale has cost him more than a hundred thousand francs within two years. Ah! you are not yet at the end."

"A truce to all this, Monsieur Crevel. Not for you will I renounce the happiness a mother feels when she can kiss her children without a pang of remorse at her heart, and feel that she is respected and loved by her family, and I will give back my soul to God without stain."

"*Amen!*" said Crevel with the diabolical sneer in which people of extravagant pretensions indulge when they are thwarted anew in such enterprises. "You are unacquainted with poverty in its last stages—shame, dishonor. I have tried to enlighten you, for I would have been glad to save you and your daughter!—but you shall spell out the modern parable of the *prodigal father*, from the first letter to the last. Your tears and your pride touch my heart, for it is a terrible thing to see a woman one loves weep!" continued Crevel, taking a seat. "All that I can promise you, dear Adeline, is to take no steps against you or your husband; but never send to me for information. That's all!"

"What shall I do, pray?" cried Madame Hulot.

Hitherto the baroness had borne up bravely under the threefold torture which this explanation inflicted upon her heart, for she suffered as woman, as mother, and as wife. Indeed, as her son's father-in-law became more arrogant and aggressive, she had found strength in her very resistance to the shop-keeper's brutality; but the touch of good nature he exhibited in the midst of his exasperation as a re-jected lover, as a humiliated national guardsman, relaxed the extreme tension of her nerves; she wrung her hands, burst into tears, and was in such a state of prostration that she allowed Crevel, on his knees, to kiss her hands.

"My God! what will become of us?" she cried,

wiping her eyes. "Can a mother look on unconcernedly and see her daughter pine away before her eyes? What will be the fate of such a superb creature, as strong in her virtuous life by her mother's side, as in her richly-endowed nature? Some days she walks in the garden, sad at heart, without knowing why. I find her with tears in her eyes."

"She is twenty-one years old," said Crevel.

"Should I put her in a convent?" asked the baroness, "for at such crises religion is often powerless against nature, and the girls who have been most piously brought up lose their heads!"

"But rise, monsieur, I pray you; do you not see that everything is now at an end between us, that you fill me with horror, that you have crushed a mother's last hope!"

"And what if I should raise it again?" he said.

Madame Hulot gazed at him with a frenzied expression, which touched him, but he forced back his compassion because of that phrase: *you fill me with horror!* Virtue is always a little too unkindly and takes no account of the devices and expedients by which people extricate themselves from a false position.

"In these days men don't marry, without *dot*, a young woman as lovely as Mademoiselle Hortense," continued Crevel, resuming his affected manner. "Your daughter is one of those beauties who frighten husbands; she is like a thoroughbred horse which requires too expensive care to find many buyers. Walk about with such a woman on your arm? Every one will stare at you, follow you, covet your wife. Such good luck is disquieting to many men, who don't thirst for lovers to kill, for, after all, one never kills but one. In your present situation you can provide a husband for your daughter only in one of three ways: by my assistance, but you'll have none of it! And, again: by hunting up an old man of sixty, very rich, one who has no children, but would like to have; such a man is hard to find, but they do exist; there are so many old men who take Josephas and Jenny Cadines, why shouldn't you find one who would make as big a fool of himself legitimately?—If I hadn't my Célestine and our two grandchildren I would marry Hortense. Two! The last way is the easiest."—

Madame Hulot raised her head and looked anxiously at the perfumer.

"Paris is a city where all the enterprising fellows who sprout like wild shrubs on French soil come together; talent of all kinds swarms there, without hearth or home, and courage capable of anything, even of rising in the world.—Well, these fellows—your humble servant was one of them in his day, and knows whereof he speaks!—What had Du Tillet or Popinot twenty years ago?—They were both plodding along in Papa Birotteau's shop with no other capital than the wish to succeed, which, in my opinion, is worth all the capital in the world!—You can eat up your capital, and you can't eat up your moral strength!—What had I myself? desire to succeed and courage. Du Tillet to-day is on a par with the greatest personages. Little Popinot, the richest druggist on Rue des Lombards, became a deputy and is now minister. Very well, one of these *condottieri*, as they say, of the Stock Exchange, the pen or the brush, is the only being in Paris, capable of marrying a lovely young girl without a sou, for they have all sorts of courage. M. Popinot married Mademoiselle Birotteau without the slightest hope of a liard of *dot*. Those people are mad! They believe in love, as they believe in their luck and their talents!—Find some enterprising fellow who will fall in love with your daughter, and he will marry her without a care for the present. You must agree that, for an enemy, I am not ungenerous, for this advice is against my own interest."

"Ah! Monsieur Crevel, if you really mean to be my friend, give up these absurd ideas!"—

"Absurd? Madame, do not rush on your own destruction in this way, pray,—I love you, and you will come to me! I mean to say some day to Hulot: 'You took Josépha from me, and I have taken your wife!' —It's the old law of retaliation! And I will follow out my plan to the end, unless you become excessively ugly. I shall succeed, too, and for this reason," he added, striking his attitude and looking Madame Hulot in the face,—"You will not fall in with an amorous old man or an amorous young man either," he resumed after a pause, "because you love your daughter too dearly to abandon her to the devious ways of an old rake, and because you, Baroness Hulot, sister of the old lieutenant-general who commanded the old grenadiers of the Old Guard, will never resign yourself to take up with the man of enterprise in the place where you will find him; for he may be a simple artisan, just as the millionaire of to-day was a simple mechanic ten years ago, a simple overseer of workmen, a simple foreman of a factory. And then, when you realize that your daughter, with the spirit of her twenty years, is capable of dishonoring you, you will say to yourself: 'It's much better that I should be the one to dishonor myself; and if M. Crevel will keep it secret, I will earn my daughter's dowry, two hundred thousand francs, by ten years' devotion to the former glove merchant—Père Crevel!'—I bore you, and what I say is shockingly immoral, is it not? But if you were consumed by an irresistible passion you would resort to such arguments, as women who are in love use, to justify you in yielding to me.—Hortense's interests will suggest to your heart these methods of compounding with your conscience."—

"Hortense has another uncle."

"Who? Père Fischer?—He is winding up his affairs, by the baron's fault also, for his rake spares no cash-box within its reach."

"Count Hulot—"

"Oh! your husband, madame, has already squandered the savings of the old lieutenant-general—he used them to furnish his songstress's house.—Come, will you allow me to go away without hope?"

"Adieu, monsieur. One is easily cured of a passion for a woman of my age, and Christian thoughts will gain the upper hand. God protects the unfortunate—"

The baroness rose to compel the captain to withdraw, and forced him back into the large salon.

"Ought the lovely Madame Hulot to pass her life amid such rubbish as this?" he said.

And he pointed to an old lamp, a chandelier of which the gilding was worn off, the threadbare carpet; in fine, all the rags and tatters of opulence which made of that white and red and gold salon a ghastly spectre of the festivities of the Empire.

"Virtue, monsieur, sheds its lustre over everything here. I have no desire to acquire a magnificent establishment by making of this beauty which you attribute to me *a trap for wolves, a hole to catch hundred-sou pieces!*"

The captain bit his lips as he recognized the epithets with which he had inveighed against Josépha's greed.

"For whose sake is all this perseverance?" he asked.

At that moment the baroness had escorted him as far as the door.

"For a libertine!"—he added, with the smug expression of a virtuous man and a millionaire.

"If you were right, monsieur, there would be some merit in my constancy, that's all."

She left the captain after she had bowed to him as one bows to rid one's self of a bore, and turned her back too quickly to see him for the last time in his favorite pose. She set about opening all the doors she had previously closed, and did not notice the threatening gesture with which Crevel said adieu. She walked with the proud and noble bearing of a martyr at the Coliseum. Her strength was exhausted, nevertheless, for she dropped upon the couch in her blue boudoir as if she were ready to faint, and lay there with her eyes fixed upon the ruined kiosk where her daughter was chattering with Cousin Bette.

*

From the first days of her married life up to that moment the baroness had loved her husband as Joséphine finally came to love Napoléon, with an admiring, motherly, unreflecting affection. Even if she did not know all the details Crevel had given her, she was very well aware that for twenty years past Baron Hulot had been guilty of acts of infidelity, but she drew a veil of lead over her eyes and wept in silence, and never a reproachful word escaped her lips. In return for this angelic sweetness of temper she had gained the veneration of her husband, and was worshipped as a divinity by those about her. A wife's love for her husband, and the respect with which she hedges it about, are contagious in a family. Hortense believed her father to be a flawless model of conjugal affection. As for Hulot, the son, he had been brought up to admire the baron, in whose person everyone recognized one of the titans who sustained Napoléon, and he knew that he owed his position to the paternal name, rank and importance; moreover the impressions of childhood retain their influence for a long while, and he still feared his father; so that even had he suspected the irregularities disclosed by Crevel, he was too respectful to complain, and would besides have excused them for reasons based upon the way in which men look at such matters.

It becomes necessary at this point to explain the extraordinary devotion of this beautiful and noble-hearted woman; this, in a few words, is the story of her life:

In a village on the extreme frontier of Lorraine, at the foot of the Vosges, lived three brothers, named Fischer, simple laborers, who left their homes, by force of the republican conscription, to join the army called the Army of the Rhine.

In 1799, André, the second brother, a widower, and father of Madame Hulot, left his daughter in charge of his elder brother, Pierre Fischer, who was rendered incapable of further service by a wound received in 1797, and engaged in certain enterprises in the way of military transportation, being indebted for the opportunity to the patronage of the commissary-in-chief, Hulot d'Ervy. It happened, naturally enough, that Hulot, who paid a visit to Strasbourg, made the acquaintance of the Fischer family. Adeline's father and his younger brother were at that time bidders for the contract to furnish forage in Alsace.

Adeline, then sixteen years old, might be compared to the famous Madame du Barry, like herself a child of Lorraine. She was one of those perfect, bewildering beauties, one of those women like Madame Tallien, upon whose moulding nature bestows especial care; upon them she lavishes her most precious gifts: distinction, nobility, grace, refinement, elegance, flesh unlike other flesh, and coloring compounded in that undiscovered workshop where Chance is the workman. Those lovely creatures all resemble one another. Bianca Capella, whose portrait is one of Bronzino's chefs-d'œuvre; the Venus of Jean Goujon, the original of which was the celebrated Diane de Poitiers; Signora Olympia, whose portrait is in the Doria Gallery; Ninon, Madame du Barry, Madame Tallien, Mademoiselle Georges, Madame Récamier, all those women, who retained their beauty despite their years, their passions, or the excessively dissipated lives they led, have points of striking similarity in their shape and build, and in the character of their beauty; so striking as to lead one to believe that there exists in the ocean of the generations of mankind an Aphrodisian current whence issue all these Venuses, children of the same briny wave.

Adeline Fischer, one of the fairest of the divine race, possessed the sublime characteristics, the serpentine outlines, the poisonous fabric of those women who are queens from their birth. The fair hair which God's hand bestowed upon our mother Eve, the figure of an empress, a majestic bearing, a stately profile, the modesty of a village maiden, caused all men to stop and look as she passed by, charmed as amateurs in art are charmed by a Raphael; and so it was that the commissary, having seen her, took Mademoiselle Adeline Fischer to wife, to the unbounded amazement of the Fischers, who had been brought up in awe of their superiors.

The elder, a soldier of 1792, and severely wounded in the attack upon the lines at Wissembourg, adored the Emperor Napoléon and everything connected with the Grande Armée. André and Johann spoke with respect of Commissary Hulot, the Emperor's protégé, to whom, moreover, they owed their prosperity, for Hulot d'Ervy, finding them to be intelligent and honest, took them from the provision train of the army to place them at the head of a special commissary-department. The brothers Fischer made themselves useful in the campaign of 1804. Hulot, at the peace, obtained for them the contract to furnish forage in Alsace, not knowing that he should be sent to Strasbourg later to make preparations for the campaign of 1806.

To the young peasant girl this marriage was like an Assumption. The fair Adeline passed without transition from the mire of her native village to the paradise of the imperial court. About that time the commissary, who was one of the most upright and untiring officials of his corps, was created a baron, summoned to attend upon the Emperor, and attached to the Imperial Guard. The lovely village maiden had the courage to educate herself for love of her husband, with whom she was nothing less than madly in love. Indeed the commissary-in-chief was as a man, the counterpart of Adeline as a woman. He was one of the chosen few among handsome men. Tall, well-built, fair, with sparkling blue eyes full of fire, of irresistible variety of expression, and a graceful figure, he attracted attention among the D'Orsays, the Forbins, the Ouvrards; in a word, in the battalion of the handsome men of the Empire. A man made for conquest, and imbued with the theories in vogue under the Directory in respect to women, his licentious career was interrupted for a considerable time by his attachment to his wife.

In Adeline's eyes the baron was, from the beginning, a sort of god who could do no wrong; she owed everything to him: fortune,—she had a carriage, a house in town, and all the luxuries of the time; happiness,—she was loved in sight of all the world; a title,—she was a baroness; celebrity,—she was known at Paris as lovely Madame Hulot; in fact, she had the honor of repelling the homage of the Emperor, who presented her with a diamond necklace, and continued to confer distinction upon her in his thoughts, for he would ask from time to time: "What of lovely Madame Hulot, is she still virtuous?" in the tone of a man capable of wreaking vengeance upon him who should succeed where he had failed.

Not overmuch intelligence is needed, therefore, to distinguish, in a simple, innocent, spotless heart like Madame Hulot's, the causes of the fanatical adoration which was mingled with her love. Having said to herself that her husband should never have ground for complaint against her, she became, in her inmost heart, the humble, devoted, blind servant of her creator. Take note, however, that she was endowed with great good sense, with the good sense of the common people, which gives solidity to their education. In society she talked but little, spoke ill of no one, and did not seek to shine; she reflected deeply upon every subject, listened closely and modeled herself upon the most virtuous women and those of most eminent birth.

In 1815 Hulot followed the line of conduct adopted by the Prince of Wissembourg, one of his most intimate friends, and was one of the organizers of that improvised army, whose defeat at Waterloo brought the Napoléonic cycle to a close. In 1816 the baron became one of the bugbears of the Feltre ministry, and was not reinstated in the commissary department until 1823, when his services were needed for the Spanish war. In 1830 he reappeared in the government as *quart de ministre,* at the time of the species of conscription undertaken by Louis-Philippe among the old adherents of Napoléon. After the accession of the younger branch, of which he was a zealous supporter, he remained at the Ministry of War, an indispensable fixture. He had obtained his marshal's baton, however, and the king could do nothing more for him, unless it were to make him a minister or peer of France.

Being without occupation from 1818 to 1823, Baron Hulot became most assiduous in his attentions to the gentler sex. Madame Hulot fixed the date of her Hector's earliest infidelities about the time of the grand *finale* of the Empire. At that time the baroness had played the rôle of *prima donna assoluta* in her household for twelve years. She still possessed the time-honored, deep-rooted affection which husbands feel for their wives when they have resigned themselves to play the part of sweet-tempered and virtuous companions; she knew that no rival could hold the field two hours against a word of reproach from her, but she closed her eyes and ears, and chose to know nothing of her husband's conduct away from home. She treated her Hector in short as a mother treats a spoiled child. Three years prior to the conversation we have described, Hortense espied her father in a proscenium box at the Variétiés, with Jenny Cadine, and exclaimed:

"There's papa!"

"You are mistaken, my dear, he is at the marshal's," the baroness replied.

The baroness had seen Jenny Cadine, but, instead of feeling a pain at her heart when she saw how lovely she was, she said to herself: "That rascal Hector ought to be very happy." She suffered none the less, and in secret abandoned herself to frightful paroxysms, but when she saw her Hector again she always saw in him her twelve years of unalloyed happiness, and lost the power of uttering a single complaint. She would have been glad to have the baron make her his *confidente*, but she had never ventured to hint to him that she knew of his vagaries, out of respect for him. Such excessive delicacy is never found save in the noble daughters of the people who know how to receive blows without returning them: in their veins flows the blood of the first martyrs. Young women of good family, being the equals of their husbands, feel the need of tormenting them: and of marking their acts of toleration by biting words, as one marks up points at billiards, all in a diabolically revengeful spirit, and to make sure of gaining a hold upon them, or of the right to take their revenge in kind.

The baroness had a passionate admirer in her brother-in-law, Lieutenant-General Hulot, the venerable commander of the foot grenadiers of the Imperial Guard, upon whom a marshal's baton was to be bestowed in his last hours. This old man, having from 1830 to 1834 commanded the military division which included the Breton departments, the scene of his exploits in 1799 and 1800, had taken up his abode in Paris, near his brother, whom he always loved with the love of a father for his son. The old soldier's heart sympathized with that of his sister-in-law; he admired her as the noblest, the most saintly of her sex. He had never married because it was his ambition to fall in with a second Adeline, whom he had sought to no purpose through twenty provinces and as many campaigns. Rather than lose caste in the heart of this old republican without reproach and without stain, of whom Napoléon said: "My gallant Hulot is the most stiff-necked of republicans, but he will never betray me," Adeline would have endured much more cruel suffering than that imposed upon her. But the old man, seventy-two years of age, broken down by thirty campaigns, wounded for the twenty-seventh time at Waterloo, was an object of admiration to Adeline, and not a protector. The poor count, among his other infirmities, could hear only with the aid of an ear trumpet.

So long as Baron Hulot d'Ervy was a handsome man his *amourettes* had no perceptible effect upon his fortune: but at fifty years he was obliged to reckon with the Graces. At that age love changes to vice; a most absurd vanity becomes mingled with it. And so, about that time, Adeline noticed that her husband became wonderfully particular touching his toilet, dyeing his hair and whiskers, and wearing belts and corsets. He was determined to remain handsome at any price. This excessive care for his person, a fault of which he formerly made great sport, he carried to the smallest details. At last Adeline discovered that the Pactolus which flowed to the dwellings of the baron's mistresses took its rise beneath her roof. Within eight years a considerable fortune had been squandered, and so effectually that, at the time of the younger Hulot's marriage, two years before, the baron was forced to confess to his wife that his salary constituted their entire fortune.

"Where will this lead us?" was Adeline's answer.

"Never fear," replied the councilor of state. "I will turn over to you the emoluments of my office, and provide for Hortense's marriage and our future by going into business."

Her profound faith in the power and great merit, in the capabilities and character of her husband, allayed her momentary anxiety.

Now, the nature of the baroness' reflections and her tears after Crevel's departure should be perfectly understood. The poor woman had known for two years that she was at the bottom of an abyss, but she believed herself to be alone there. She did not know how her son's marriage was brought to pass, nor was she aware of Hector's liaison with the covetous Josépha: in short, she hoped that no one on earth knew of her sorrow. Now, if Crevel spoke so freely of the baron's extravagant courses, Hector must be in a fair way to forfeit the consideration in which he was held. From the irritated perfumer's vulgar talk she obtained a clear idea of the hateful bargaining which resulted in the young advocate's marriage. Two courtesans had been the high priestesses of that union, suggested in some debauch amid the degrading familiarities of two tipsy old men!

"So he forgets Hortense!" she said to herself, "and yet he sees her every day; will he seek a husband for her in his harlots' circle?"

The maternal instinct alone, more powerful than the wifely loyalty, spoke at that moment; for she saw Hortense, with her cousin Bette, laughing the unrestrained laughter of heedless youth, and she was well aware that that nervous laughter was a no less ominous symptom than the tearful reverie of a solitary walk in the garden.

Hortense resembled her mother, but her hair was of the hue of gold, naturally wavy, and grew in astonishing profusion. Her complexion was like mother-of-pearl. In her could be seen the fruit of an honest marriage, of a pure and noble love in all its intensity. There was a glowing animation in her expression, a mobility of feature, a youthful impulsiveness, a freshness of life, an overflowing store of health, which created an atmosphere about her, and generated electric currents. Hortense compelled attention. When her deep-blue eyes, swimming in the fluid in which innocence immerses them, rested upon a passer-by, he started involuntarily. Moreover her complexion was not marred by a single one of those red blotches, which are the price commonly paid by golden blondes for their milk-white skins. Tall, plump, without stoutness, endowed with a beautiful figure, which equaled her mother's in distinction, she well deserved the title of goddess so lavishly bestowed by the ancient authors. So it was that no one who saw Hortense on the street could forbear to exclaim: "Great heaven! what a lovely girl!" She was so innocent that she would say, on returning home:

"Why, what do they all mean, mamma, by crying out: 'What a lovely girl!' Weren't you with me? Aren't you lovelier than I?"—

And in very truth, although she had passed her forty-seventh year, the baroness might well have been preferred to her daughter by those who love sunsets, for she had as yet lost nothing *of her advantages*, as the ladies say, by one of those phenomena seldom seen, especially in Paris, where Ninon caused much heartburning in that particular, to such an extent did she seem to usurp the prerogatives of the ugly in the seventeenth century.

As she thought of her daughter, the baroness' mind reverted to the father; she fancied him falling lower and lower day by day, until he reached the very mire of society, and perhaps dismissed some fine day from the ministry. The idea of the downfall of her idol, accompanied by an indistinct vision of the misfortunes predicted by Crevel, caused the poor woman such torture that she lost consciousness after the manner of ecstatics.

Cousin Bette, with whom Hortense was talking, looked up from time to time to see when they might return to the salon, but her young cousin was plying her so closely with questions just when the baroness reopened the long window, that she did not notice her.

Lisbeth Fischer, who was five years younger than Madame Hulot, although she was the daughter of the eldest of the brothers Fischer, was far from being as beautiful as her cousin: and so she had been prodigiously jealous of Adeline. Jealousy was the fundamental quality of this *eccentric* character, a word invented by the English to designate the follies, not of commonplace people, but of great families. A peasant of the Vosges, in the fullest meaning of the term, thin, dark, with glossy black hair, heavy eyebrows joined by a tuft, long, powerful arms, large feet, a mole or two on her long, apelike face—such was this maiden's portrait in a few strokes.

The family, who made one household, sacrificed the commonplace girl to the beauty, the acrid fruit to the brilliant flower. Lisbeth worked in the fields while her cousin was petted at home; and it occurred to her one day, when she found Adeline alone, to try and pull out her nose, a pure Greek nose such as old ladies admire. Although she was whipped for this transgression she continued none the less to tear the favorite's dresses and spoil her neckerchiefs.

At the time of her cousin's extraordinary marriage, Lisbeth bent her head before that freak of destiny as Napoléon's brothers and sisters bent before the splendor of the throne and the all-powerful word of command. Adeline, who was kind-hearted and sweet-tempered to excess, bethought herself at Paris of Lisbeth, and sent for her about 1809, with the purpose of rescuing her from poverty by arranging a marriage for her. As it was impossible to find a husband as soon as Adeline could have wished, for this black-eyed damsel, with the coal-black eyebrows, who could neither read nor write, the baron began by giving her a trade. He apprenticed Lisbeth to the court embroiderers, the famous brothers Pons.

The cousin, called Bette for short, having become a worker in gold and silver lace, and being of the energetic temperament common to mountaineers, had the courage to learn to read, write, and cipher; for her cousin, the baron, had impressed upon her the necessity of possessing so much learning in order to conduct an embroidery establishment. She was determined to make her fortune; in two years she metamorphosed herself. In 1811 the peasant girl had become a rather pleasing, clever and intelligent forewoman.

The product called gold and silver lace-work included epaulets, shoulder-knots and sword-tassels; in short, that numberless variety of gorgeous objects which glisten upon the rich uniforms of the French army and upon civilian costumes. The Emperor, with an Italian fondness for dress, lavished gold and silver embroidery upon all the seams of his retainers' garb, and his Empire comprised one hundred and thirty-three departments. The furnishing of these decorations, generally supplied to the tailors, who were men of wealth and substance, or directly to the great dignitaries, was in itself a lucrative business.

At the very moment when Cousin Bette, the most skilful workwoman in the Pons establishment, where she was entrusted with the superintendence of the manufacture, might have settled herself for life, the Empire fell with a crash. The olive-branch of peace in the hands of the Bourbons alarmed Lisbeth; she feared a falling off in that line of business, which would have henceforth but eighty-six instead of a hundred and thirty-three departments to look to for support, to say nothing of the enormous reduction of the army. Taking fright at the uncertain prospects of the industry, she refused the offers of the baron, who thought her mad. She justified his opinion by breaking with M. Rivet, the buyer for the Pons establishment, with whom the baron proposed that she should wed, and so became once more a a simple work-girl.

The Fischer family thereupon fell back into the

precarious situation from which Baron Hulot had extricated it.

Ruined by the catastrophe of Fontainebleau, the three brothers Fischer in desperation took service in the free companies of 1815. The eldest, Lisbeth's father, was killed. Adeline's father, sentenced to death by a court-martial, fled to Germany, and died at Trèves in 1820. The youngest, Johann, came to Paris to implore the aid of the queen of the family, who was said to be eating from gold and silver, who never appeared at receptions without diamonds upon her head and neck, as large as walnuts, and presented by the emperor.

Johann Fischer, at that time forty-three years of age, received from Baron Hulot a sum of ten thousand francs with which to start a small enterprise in the way of forage, at Versailles, a privilege obtained from the Ministry of War through the secret influence of friends whom the former intendant-general still possessed there.

These family reverses, the disgrace of Baron Hulot, the certainty of counting for very little in that vast upheaval of men, interests and affairs, which made Paris a hell and a paradise, were too much for Cousin Bette. She thereupon abandoned all thought of contest or comparison with her cousin, after she had felt her superiority in so many different directions; but envy still lay hidden at the bottom of her heart, like a pestilential germ which may come to the surface and lay waste a city, if one opens the fatal bale of wool in which it is confined. From time to time she would say to herself:

"Adeline and I are of the same blood, our fathers were brothers, she lives in a fine house, I in an attic."

But year after year, on her birthday, and on New Year's Day, Lisbeth received gifts from the baron and baroness; the baron, who was most kind to her, paid for her winter's supply of wood; old General Hulot received her once a year at dinner, and a cover was always laid for her at her cousin's table. They laughed at her, but they never blushed for her. In short, they had provided her with her independence at Paris, where she lived in her own way.

The young woman was, in truth, afraid of every sort of restraint. Her cousin offered to take her to live with her—Bette detected in the offer the halter of a state of servitude; many a time the baron solved the difficult problem of finding a husband for her; but, though attracted at first, she would soon refuse in fear and trembling lest her lack of education, her ignorance, and her poverty should be cast in her face; lastly, if the baroness suggested that she should live with their uncle and keep house for him, in the place of a hired housekeeper, who must necessarily be a great expense, she would reply that she was much less inclined for a marriage of that sort.

Cousin Bette's ideas presented that strange aspect which is noticeable in natures that have developed very late in life, in savages, who think much and speak little. Her peasant intelligence, moreover, had acquired, in the conversations of the workshop, through constant association with the artisans of both sexes, a touch of Parisian keenness. This girl, whose character strikingly resembled that of the Corsicans, and who was animated to no purpose by the impulses common to strong natures, would have loved to protect a man of feeble character; but since she had lived in the capital, the capital had changed her on the surface. The Parisian polish made that stout-tempered soul liable to rust. Endowed with a ready wit that had become profound, as always happens with those who have taken a vow of true celibacy, she would have been in any other situation a woman to be feared, with the stinging fashion in which she expressed her thoughts. If evil-minded, she would have sown discord in the most united family.

In the early days, when she cherished certain hopes, the secret of which she shared with no one, she had decided to wear corsets and conform to the fashion, and she thereby achieved a momentary splendor, during which the baron deemed her a marriageable subject. Lisbeth was at that time the piquant brunette of the old French romances. Her piercing glance, her olive complexion, her willowy figure, might have tempted a major on half-pay; but she was content, she laughingly said to herself, with her own admiration. She ended by enjoying her life, after she had pruned it of all material cares, for she dined out every day, after working from sunrise. She had therefore to provide only her breakfast and her rent; her employers dressed her and gave her many acceptable articles of food, as sugar, coffee, wine, etc.

In 1837, after twenty-seven years of life, during half of which she had been supported by the Hulot family and her uncle Fischer, Cousin Bette, resigned to the fate of being nobody, allowed herself to be entertained without scruple; she voluntarily declined to attend grand dinner-parties, preferring the more intimate society where she would count for what she was worth, and avoid blows to her self-esteem. Everywhere, at General Hulot's, at Crevel's, at the younger Hulot's, at Rivet's, the successor of Pons—to whom she had become reconciled, and at whose house she was a welcome guest—at the baroness', she seemed one of the family. She had the knack of propitiating the servants everywhere, by giving them small *pourboires* now and then, and by always chatting with them a few moments before entering the salon. This familiarity, by which she frankly put herself on a level with them, won for her their humble good-will, a very essential thing for a parasite.

"She's a kind-hearted, excellent woman!" was the universal verdict concerning her. Her willingness to oblige, which was unlimited when it was not exacted, was, as was her false good-comradeship, a necessity of her position. She had come at last to a true comprehension of life when she saw herself at everybody's mercy; and, as she was determined to make herself agreeable to everybody, she laughed with the young people, with whom she put herself in sympathy by a sort of wheedling manner which always attracts them, she divined and espoused their wishes, she made herself their interpreter, she seemed to them to be a safe confidant, for she had not the right to scold them. Her unvarying discretion won for her the confidence of those of mature years, for, like Ninon, she possessed divers manly qualities. As a general rule, confidences are made below rather than above. One employs one's inferiors much more frequently than one's superiors in secret affairs; thus they become the accomplices of our inmost thoughts, for they are present at their deliberations; Richelieu looked upon himself as a made man when he acquired the right to be present at the council. The poor girl was supposed to be so dependent upon everybody that she seemed to be condemned to absolute dumbness. She dubbed herself the family confessional. The baroness alone, who did not forget the harsh usage she had received in childhood at the hands of her more powerful, though younger cousin, still retained a measure of distrust. Nor would she, for very shame, have confided her domestic grief to any but God.

At this point it is necessary perhaps to call attention to the fact that the baroness' establishment had lost none of its magnificence in the eyes of Cousin Bette, who was not impressed, like the parvenu dealer in perfumery, by the distress written upon the worm-eaten arm-chairs, the discolored draperies and the torn silk. It is with the furniture amidst which we live as with ourselves. As we look ourselves over every day, we end, as the baron did, by believing ourselves little changed, still youthful, when others see the hair turning gray on our heads, circumflex accents on our brows, and huge pumpkins in our bellies. These apartments, in Cousin Bette's eyes still illuminated by the Bengal fires of the imperial victories, were therefore still magnificent to her.

As time passed Cousin Bette had contracted divers eccentric habits peculiar to old maids. For example, instead of following the fashion, it was her good pleasure that the fashion should adapt itself to her peculiarities, and abide by her whims, always in arrears. If the baroness presented her with a pretty new hat, or a dress cut in the prevailing style, Cousin Bette would immediately make everything over to suit herself, and as surely spoil it, producing a costume which reminded one of the fashions in vogue under the Empire, and of her old Lorraine costumes. The hat that cost thirty francs was ruined, and the dress became a shapeless rag. In this respect Cousin Bette was as obstinate as a mule; she chose to please herself and nobody else, and deemed herself charming thus arrayed; though this process of assimilation which had a certain harmony in it that made her an old maid from head to foot, it made her at the same time so ridiculous that nobody, no matter how well disposed, could receive her on great occasions.

This restless, capricious, independent spirit, the inexplicable shyness of the girl, for whom the baron had four times found eligible *partis*—an employé of his department, a major, a contractor for provisions and a retired captain—and who had refused the hand of a lace-maker, since become wealthy, earned for her the sobriquet of "Nanny-Goat," which the baron laughingly bestowed upon her. But this sobriquet applied only to superficial peculiarities, to those variations which all of us offer to one another's sight in society. This young woman, who, under careful observation, would have exhibited the fierce side of the peasant disposition, was still the child who tried to tear out her cousin's nose, and who would perhaps, if she had not become reasonable, have killed her some day in a paroxysm of jealousy. Only by knowledge of the laws and of society did she overcome the natural tendency which peasants have in common with savages, to pass instantly from impulse to action. Therein it may be consists all the difference between man in his natural state and civilized man. The savage has impulses only, the civilized man has impulses and ideas. So it is that in the savage the brain receives, so to speak, few impressions, it is entirely at the mercy of the impulse which takes it by storm; whereas in the civilized man ideas descend from the brain to the heart, which they transform; it is swayed by innumerable interests, innumerable impulses, while the savage admits but a single idea at one time. This is the cause of the momentary ascendency of children over their parents, which ceases when the wish is gratified, while, in the case of the man who lives close to nature, this cause acts continuously. Cousin Bette, the Lorraine savage, although a bit treacherous, belonged to this category of characters, more common among the people than is generally supposed, which fact may serve to explain their conduct during revolutions.

At the time when this episode begins, if Cousin Bette had chosen to allow herself to be dressed fashionably, if she had accustomed herself, as the Parisian women do, to follow every new style, she might have been both presentable and acceptable; but she remained as stiff as a poker. Now, if she have no charm of person a woman does not exist in Paris. So it was that the black hair, the fine but stern eyes, the rigid outlines of the face, the rough complexion of a Calabrian, which made of Cousin Bette a copy of one of Giotto's figures, and which a true Parisian would have turned to good account, above all else her extraordinary raiment, gave her such a fantastic appearance, that she sometimes resembled the monkeys, dressed as women, carried about by the little Savoyards. As she was well known in the households united by family ties, in which she passed her time, as her social evolutions were restricted to that circle, and as she loved her home, her eccentricities no longer surprised anybody, and disappeared out of doors in the ceaseless motion of the Paris streets, where no one looks at any save pretty women.

Hortense's laughter at that moment was caused by a victory she had won over Cousin Bette's obstinacy; she had surprised her into making a confession demanded for three years past. However clever at concealment an old maid may be, there is one sentiment which will always make her break her tongue's fast, and that is vanity! For three years Hortense, who had developed excessive curiosity in a certain direction, had been assailing her cousin with questions, propounded with the breath of perfect innocence be it said; she wished to know why her cousin had never married. Hortense, who knew all about the five rejected aspirants, had constructed her little romance, she attributed to Cousin Bette an affair of the heart, and a war of pleasantries was the result. "We young girls!" Hortense would say, speaking of herself and her cousin. On several occasions Cousin Bette had replied jokingly: "Who says that I haven't a lover?" Cousin Bette's lover, real or imaginary, thereupon became the theme of much harmless banter. At last, after two years of this petty warfare, Hortense's first word, the last time that Cousin Bette came to the house, was:

"How's your lover?"

"Oh! pretty well," was the reply; "he's a little out of sorts, poor boy."

"Ah! is he delicate?" asked the baroness, with a laugh.

"I should say so; he's very light.—A coal-black creature such as I am can love no one but a moon-colored blonde."

"But what is he? What does he do?" said Hortense. "Is he a prince?"

"Prince of the hand-tool, as I am queen of the bobbin. Can a poor girl like me win the love of a landed proprietor with a house of his own and money in the funds, or of a duke and peer, or of some Prince Charming out of your fairy tales?"

"Oh! I would like to see him!"—cried Hortense, with a smile.

"To see what sort of a looking creature it is who can fall in love with an old nanny-goat?" rejoined Cousin Bette.

"It must be some old monster of a clerk with a long goatee!" said Hortense, glancing at her mother.

"That's where you're wrong, mademoiselle."

"Then you have a lover?" queried Hortense, with an air of triumph.

"As truly as you have none!" retorted Cousin Bette with an offended air.

"Very well, Bette, if you have a lover why don't you marry him?"—said the baroness, making a sign to her daughter. "For three years now you have been talking about him, you have had time to study him, and, if he has remained true to you, you ought not to prolong a situation so irksome to him. Besides it is a matter of conscience, and then, even if he is young, it's high time for you to take some one to be the staff of your old age."

Cousin Bette gazed earnestly at the baroness, and seeing that she was laughing, she replied:

"It would be hunger marrying thirst; he's a workman, I a workwoman, if we had children they would be workmen too.—No, no, we love each other with the heart—it's less expensive."

"Why do you keep him out of sight?" Hortense asked.

"He wears a jacket," laughingly replied the old maid.

"Do you love him?" queried the baroness.

"Ah! I should think so. I love him for himself, the cherub. For four years I have been carrying him in my heart."

"Very good, if you love him for himself," said the baroness gravely. "If he really exists, you are doing him a great wrong. You don't know what it is to love."

"We all know that trade when we are born," said the cousin.

"No; there are women who love and remain selfish, and that is your case!"—

The cousin hung her head; her look would have made the person shudder upon whom it might have fallen, but she looked at her bobbin.

"If you would present your love-lorn suitor to us, Hector might find a place for him and put him in a position to make his fortune."

"That cannot be," said Cousin Bette

"Why not, pray?"

"He is a Pole or something of the sort, a refugee."—

"A conspirator?"—exclaimed Hortense. "Aren't you lucky!—Has he had thrilling adventures?"—

"Why, he fought for Poland. He was a professor

in the college where the students began the revolution, and as he was put there by the Grand Duke Constantine he has no hope of pardon."—

"Professor of what?"

"Fine arts!"

"And he came to Paris after the failure of the uprising?"

"In 1833 he made his way to Germany on foot."—

"Poor boy! He is—?"

"He was barely twenty-four at the time of the insurrection, he is twenty-nine now."—

"Fifteen years younger than you," said the baroness.

"What does he live on?"—asked Hortense.

"On his talents."—

"Ah! he gives lessons?"—

"No," said Cousin Bette, "he receives them and harsh ones, too!"—

"And his name? Is it pretty?"—

"Wenceslas!"

"What imaginations old maids have!" cried the baroness. "By your way of speaking any one might believe you, Lisbeth."

"Don't you see, mamma, that he's a Pole so used to the knout that Bette reminds him of that charming little emblem of his fatherland."

All three began to laugh, and Hortense sang: *Wenceslas! idole de mon âme!* instead of *O Mathilde.*—And for a few moments there was something like an armistice.

"These little girls," said Cousin Bette, with a

glance at Hortense when she returned to her side, "think that no one can love but themselves."

"Come," said Hortense, when she and her cousin were alone, "prove to me that Wenceslas isn't a *conte,* and I'll give you my yellow cashmere shawl."

"But he is a *comte!*"

"All Poles are *comtes!*"

"But he's not a Pole, he's from Li—va, Lith—"

"Lithuania?"

"No."—

"Livonia?"

"That's it."

"But what's his name?"

"Look you, I want to know if you are capable of keeping a secret."—

"Oh! cousin, I will be dumb—"

"As a fish?"

"As a fish!"

"By your eternal life?"

"By my eternal life!"

"No, by your happiness on earth?"

"Yes."

"Well, then, his name is Wenceslas Steinbock!"

"There was one of Charles the Twelfth's generals who bore that name."

"That was his great-uncle! His father settled in Livonia after the death of the King of Sweden, but he lost his fortune at the time of the campaign of 1812, leaving the poor child penniless at the age of eight. The Grand Duke Constantine, on account of his name of Steinbock, took him under his patronage and put him at school."—

"I don't take back what I said," replied Hortense, "give me a proof of his existence, and you shall have the yellow shawl. Ah! that color takes the place of paint for brunettes."

"You will keep my secret?"

"You shall know mine."

"Very well; the next time I come I will bring the proof."

"But the best proof is the lover himself," said Hortense.

Cousin Bette, who had upon her arrival at Paris fallen a prey to a fervent admiration for cashmeres, was fascinated by the thought of possessing the yellow shawl given by the baron to his wife in 1808, and which, in accordance with the custom of some families, had passed from mother to daughter in 1830. For ten years the shawl had been well worn; but the precious material, which was always carefully laid away in a sandal-wood box, was still new in the old maid's eyes, like the baroness' furniture. So she had brought in her reticule a gift which she intended to present to the baroness on her birthday and which, in her opinion, should demonstrate the existence of the eccentric lover.

This gift consisted of a silver seal, composed of three figures standing back to back, surrounded by foliage and holding up the globe. The three figures represented Faith, Hope and Charity. Their feet rested upon monsters which were tearing one another to pieces, and among which the symbolic serpent crawled. In 1846, after the tremendous impulse given to the art of Benvenuto Cellini by Mademoiselle de Fauveau, Wagner, Jeanest, Froment-Meurice, and wood-engravers like Liénard, this masterpiece would surprise no one; but at the time of which we are writing a young girl, and a connoisseur in such matters, might well have been thunderstruck upon examining this seal when Cousin Bette handed it to her, saying:

"Look, what do you say to this?"

The figures, in design, in their drapery, and in their attitudes, belonged to the school of Raphaël; by the manner in which they were executed they recalled the school of the Florentine bronze-workers, the school founded by Donatello, Brunelleschi, Ghiberti, Benvenuto Cellini, John of Bologna, etc. The French Renaissance could show no distorted monsters more fantastic in design than those which symbolized the bad passions. The palms, the ferns, the reeds and rushes which surrounded the Virtues were grouped so effectively and with such good taste as to drive the ordinary craftsman to despair. A ribbon joined the three heads together, and upon the vacant spaces between each two heads, was a W, a chamois and the word *fecit.*

"Who engraved this?" Hortense asked.

"My lover, to be sure," replied Cousin Bette. "There is ten months' work in that; so I earn more making sword-tassels.—He told me that Steinbock means, in German, *animal of the cliffs*, or chamois.

He proposes to sign his works in this way.—Ah! I shall have your shawl—"

"How so?"

"Can I buy such a trinket? or order it? it's impossible; so it must have been given to me. Who could make such presents? a lover!"

Hortense, with a capacity for dissimulation at which Lisbeth Fischer would have been dismayed had she detected it, carefully avoided expressing all her admiration, although she felt that thrill which all people feel whose souls are susceptible to the beautiful when they see a perfect, flawless and unexpected masterpiece.

"Really," she said, "it's very pretty."

"Yes, it is pretty," rejoined the old maid, "but I prefer an orange cashmere. You see, little one, my lover passes his time working at that sort of thing. Since his arrival in Paris he has made three or four stupid little things like this, and that's the result of four years of study and labor. He has served as apprentice to founders, moulders and jewelers—bah! hundreds and thousands have gone the same way. Monsieur tells me that in a few months now he will be famous and rich—"

"Why, do you see him?"

"See him! do you think it's a fable? I told you the truth jokingly."

"And he loves you?" asked Hortense, eagerly.

"He adores me!" replied her cousin, with a serious expression. "You see, little one, he has never known any but pale, insipid women, such as they all are in the North; a dark, graceful young girl like me warms his heart. But not a word of this! You promised me."

"It will be with this one as with the other five," said the young girl with a bantering air, as she looked at the seal.

"Six, mademoiselle; I left one in Lorraine who would unhook the moon for me to this day."

"This one does better than that," rejoined Hortense, "he brings you the sun."

"Where can you have that coined into money?" asked Cousin Bette. "One must have a lot of land to get the benefit of the sun."

These jocose remarks on one side and the other, followed by others no less absurd, which the reader can imagine, gave rise to the laughter which had redoubled the agony of the baroness by forcing her to compare her daughter's future with the present, when she saw her yielding freely to the joyous impulses of her age.

"But if he gives you jewels that require six months' work, he must be under great obligations to you?" queried Hortense, in whose mind the seal gave rise to profound reflections.

"Ah! you want to know too much at one time," replied Cousin Bette.

"But, listen,—I am going to let you into a conspiracy."

"Shall I be associated with your lover in it?"

"Ah! you would like to see him! But you must understand that an old maid like your Bette, who has succeeded in keeping a lover for five years, keeps him well hidden.—So let me alone. I am not a cat, you know, nor a canary, nor a dog, nor a parrot; an old nanny-goat like me must have some little thing to love and fondle, so I take a Pole."

"Has he moustaches?"

"As long as these," said Bette, pointing to a shuttle filled with gold threads.

She always carried her work with her, and worked while waiting for dinner to be served.

"If you keep asking me questions, you shall know nothing," she resumed. "You are only twenty-two and you are more of a chatter-box than I who am forty-two, yes, forty-three."

"I am made of wood and I listen," said Hortense.

"My lover has made a bronze group ten inches high," continued Cousin Bette. "It represents Samson tearing a lion to pieces, and he has buried it and rusted it so that he can make people believe now that it is old as Samson. This chef-d'œuvre is on exposition at one of the bric-à-brac shops on the Place du Carrousel, near my house. If your father, who knows M. Popinot, the Minister of Commerce and Agriculture, and the Comte de Rastignac, could say a word to them about this group as a fine piece of antique work he had seen in passing! It seems that great personages devote themselves to such matters instead of interesting themselves in our sword-tassels, and that my lover's fortune would be made if they would buy or even go and examine that wretched bit of copper. The poor boy insists that they would take the trifle for a real antique, and pay a big price for it. Then if it is one of the ministers who takes the group, he will go to him, prove that he is the maker of it and be awarded a triumph! Oh! he fancies himself on the pinnacle of fame; he has as much pride, has the youth, as two new counts."

"He is Michael Angelo born again; but, for a lover, he doesn't lack shrewdness,"—said Hortense. "How much does he want for it?"

"Fifteen hundred francs!—The dealer ought not to sell the bronze for less than that, for he must have his commission."

"Papa is the king's commissioner at this moment," said Hortense; "he sees the two ministers every day at the Chamber, and I will see to it that he does the business for you. You will be a rich woman, Madame la Comtesse Steinbock!"

"No, my man is too lazy; he does nothing for whole weeks but play with red wax, and nothing goes forward. Bah! he passes his life at the Louvre and the Bibliothèque, looking at engravings and sketching them. He's an idler."

The two cousins continued their conversation in a jocose vein. Hortense laughed as one does when one forces one's self to laugh, for she was assailed by a passion which all young ladies have experienced, the love of the unknown, the vague love in which the thoughts take shape about any image which chance throws in their way, as the frost collects upon the bits of straw left hanging by the wind upon the window-sill. For ten months she had transformed into a real being her cousin's imaginary lover, believing, as did her mother, in her cousin's vow of perpetual celibacy; and within a week the phantom had become Count Wenceslas Steinbock, the dream had a certificate of birth, the vapor condensed and became a young man of thirty years. The seal she held in her hand, a sort of Annunciation, in which genius burst forth like a ray of light, had the power of a talisman. Hortense was so elated by her good fortune that she began to suspect that the fable was true; her blood was in a state of fermentation, and she laughed like a mad woman to throw her cousin off the scent.

"Ah! I think the door of the salon is open," said Cousin Bette; "let us go and see if M. Crevel has gone."—

"Mamma has been very sad for two days; the marriage that was suggested is broken off, no doubt."—

"Pshaw! it can be arranged; the man in the case—I may tell you so much—is a councilor of the royal court. Would you like to be Madame la Présidente? Well, if it rests with M. Crevel, he will say something to me about it, and I shall know to-morrow whether there is any hope!"

"Cousin, leave the seal with me," said Hortense; "I won't show it.—Mamma's birthday is within a month, and I will give it back to you that morning."

"No, give it to me now,—I must have a case for it."

"But I will let papa see it so that he can speak to the minister with some knowledge of what he is talking about, for the authorities will not take any risks," said she.

"Very well, but don't show it to your mother, that's all I ask of you; for if she should know that I have a lover, she would laugh at me."—

"I promise."—

*

The two cousins reached the door of the boudoir just as the baroness swooned, and the cry uttered by Hortense sufficed to bring her to herself. Bette ran to fetch the salts. When she returned she found the mother and daughter in each other's arms, the mother soothing her daughter's fears, and saying:

"It's nothing; a mere nervous attack.—Here's your father," she added, recognizing her husband's ring; "on no account say a word to him of this."

Adeline rose to go and meet her husband, with the purpose of taking him to the garden until dinner, of speaking to him of the abandoned marriage, of forcing him to an explanation concerning the future, and of trying to give him a little advice.

Baron Hector Hulot made his appearance clad in parliamentary and Napoléonic garb, for it is easy to distinguish the imperialists—those who served under the Empire—by their military carriage, their blue coats with gilt buttons, buttoned to the throat, their black silk cravats, and by the authoritative manner growing out of the habit of despotic command which was made a necessity by the swiftly moving events amid which their lot was cast. In the baron's appearance there was nothing, we must confess, that savored of the old man; his sight was still so good that he read without glasses; his handsome oval face, framed by black whiskers—too black, alas!—presented its natural color, enlivened by the delicate veining which denotes a sanguine temperament; and his paunch, confined by a belt, was nothing less than majestic, as Brillat-Savarin says. A most aristocratic air and extreme affability were the outer envelope of the libertine with whom Crevel had taken part in so many parties under the rose. He was one of those men whose eyes glisten at the sight of a pretty woman, and who smile at all the lovely creatures, even at those who pass them on the street, and whom they are not likely to see again.

"Did you speak, my dear?" said Adeline, seeing that his face wore a thoughtful expression.

"No," Hector replied; "but I am tired to death listening to others speak for two hours without reaching a vote.—They fight battles with words, in which the speeches are like cavalry charges that don't scatter the enemy! They have substituted talk for action, to the disgust of people who are used to marching, as I said to the marshal when I left him. But it's quite enough to be bored to death on the ministerial benches; let's enjoy ourselves here.—Good afternoon, Nanny-goat!—good afternoon, my little kid!"

He put his arm about his daughter's neck, kissed her, fondled her, took her upon his knee, and placed her head upon his shoulder so that he might feel the soft golden locks against his face.

"He is bored and tired out," thought Madame Hulot, "and I shall weary him still more,—I will wait. Do you remain at home this evening?"—she asked aloud.

"No, my children. After dinner I must leave you; and had it not been the nanny-goat's day, and my children's and my brother's, you would not have seen me."—

The baroness took up the newspaper, glanced over the theatrical announcements, and laid the sheet down, for she had seen *Robert le Diable* announced at the Opera; Josépha, whom the Italian Opera had ceded to the Opéra Français six months before, was to sing the rôle of Alice. This pantomime did not escape the baron, who gazed fixedly at his wife. Adeline lowered her eyes, and went into the garden, whither he followed her.

"What is it; tell me, Adeline?" he said, putting his arm about her waist and drawing her to his heart. "Don't you know that I love you more than—"

"More than Jenny Cadine and Josépha!" she replied desperately, interrupting him.

"Who told you that?" demanded the baron, releasing his wife and drawing back a few steps.

"Some one wrote me an anonymous letter, which I burned, and which said, my dear, that Hortense's marriage fell through on account of our poverty. Your wife, my dear Hector, would never have mentioned it; she has known of your liaison with Jenny Cadine, and has she ever complained? But Hortense's mother must tell you the truth."

Hulot, after a moment's silence most painful to

his wife, the beating of whose heart could be heard, unfolded his arms, seized her, strained her to his heart, kissed her on the forehead, and said with the exaltation born of enthusiasm:

"Adeline, you are an angel, and I am a miserable wretch."

"No! no!" replied the baroness, quickly placing her hand upon his lips to prevent his speaking ill of himself.

"Yes; I haven't a sou at this moment to give Hortense, and I am very wretched; but since you have opened your heart to me thus, I can pour into it the sorrow which is stifling me.—If your uncle Fischer is in embarrassed circumstances, I am the cause of it, for he indorsed my notes to the amount of twenty-five thousand francs! And all for a woman who deceives me, who laughs at me when I am not there, who calls me an old *dyed cat!* Oh! it's a frightful thing that it should cost more to gratify a vice than to support a family!—and yet she's irresistible.—I might promise you at this moment never to go back to the abominable Israelite, and if she should write me two lines I should go, as we used to go into action under the emperor."

"Don't worry, Hector," said the poor woman in despair, forgetting all about her daughter at sight of the tears welling up in her husband's eyes. "I have my diamonds, you know; before everything, save my uncle!"

"Your diamonds are worth barely twenty thousand francs to-day. That wouldn't suffice for Père

Fischer, so keep them for Hortense. I will see the marshal to-morrow."

"Poor dear!" cried the baroness seizing her Hector's hands and kissing them.

That was the whole of the lecture. Adeline proffered her diamonds, the father turned them over to Hortense, she looked upon that as a sublime effort, and she was helpless.

"He is the master, he can take everything here, he leaves me my diamonds; he is a god!"

So ran the thoughts of the poor woman, who had certainly gained more by her gentleness than another would have done by an outbreak of jealous wrath.

The moralist would in vain deny that, generally speaking, persons well brought up and very vicious are much more amiable than virtuous persons; having crimes to purchase pardon for, they solicit indulgence provisionally by dealing very leniently with the faults of their judges, and they acquire the name of being very kind. Although there are delightful people among the virtuous, virtue deems itself sufficiently estimable in itself to dispense with any outlay; then, too, the truly virtuous, for we must leave out the hypocrites, almost always have some slight suspicion of their situation; they fancy that they are cheated in the great market of life, and they indulge in sharp speech after the fashion of people who think themselves misunderstood. Thus the baron, who blamed himself for the ruin of his family, exerted all the resources of his wit and of his power to charm, upon his wife, her children and her cousin Bette. When his son arrived and Célestine Crevel, who was nursing a little Hulot, his manner to his daughter-in-law was charming, and he overwhelmed her with compliments, a species of nourishment to which Célestine's vanity was not accustomed, for never was the child of mere wealth so vulgar or so utterly insignificant. The grandfather took the little monkey in his arms, kissed him, declared that he was delightful and enchanting; he talked baby-talk to him, prophesied that the youngster would be taller than himself, aimed a flattering speech or two in the direction of his son Hulot, and handed the child back to the stout Norman girl whose duty it was to hold him. Whereupon Célestine exchanged with the baroness a glance which said: "What an adorable man!" Naturally she would defend her father-in-law against the assaults of her own father.

Having exhibited himself in the guise of affable father-in-law and indulgent grandpa, the baron took his son into the garden to offer some observations full of common sense as to the attitude he should assume in the Chamber in reference to a delicate question which had arisen that morning. He filled the young man with admiration by the depth of his views, he touched his heart by his friendly tone, and especially by the deferential way in which he manifested his purpose to consider him thenceforth as upon his level.

M. Hulot, the younger, was a perfect type of the young men produced by the Revolution of 1830; his mind saturated with politics, respectfully silent in regard to his aspirations, concealing them beneath an assumed gravity, very envious of established reputations, uttering vague phrases instead of incisive words, the diamonds of French conversation, but well supplied with manner, and mistaking stately bearing for dignity! Such people are walking coffins, which contain Frenchmen of other days; the Frenchman stirs uneasily from time to time, and beats against his English envelope; but ambition holds him back, and he resigns himself to suffocate therein. This coffin was always draped in black cloth.

"Ah! here's my brother!" said Baron Hulot, going to the door of the salon to welcome the count.

Having embraced the probable successor of the late Marshal Montcornet, he took his arm and led him into the room with every mark of affection and respect.

This peer of France, who was excused from attending the sessions of the legislature because of his deafness, possessed a noble head frosted by time, with gray hair still abundant enough to be smoothed down by the pressure of his hat. Short, thick-set, but of late years somewhat spare, he wore his green old age with a sprightly air; and as he was still extremely active, though condemned to a life of repose, he divided his time between reading and walking. His gentle manners were visible upon his white face, in his bearing, in his straightforward speech, overflowing with sensible ideas. He never talked of war or campaigns; he was too great to have need of assuming airs of greatness. In a salon he confined his rôle to untiring attention to the desires of the ladies.

"You are all in high spirits," he said, as he observed the animation which the baron instilled into the little family reunion. "Hortense isn't married yet, however," he added, as he detected traces of sadness on his sister-in-law's face.

"That will come soon enough," cried Cousin Bette in his ear in a deafening tone.

"Ah! there you are, bad seed that refused to sprout!" he retorted with a laugh.

The hero of Forzheim was very fond of Cousin Bette, for he detected certain points of resemblance between her and himself. Without education, sprung from the common people, his courage had been the sole artisan of his military fortune, and his common sense took the place of intellect. Full of honors, and with unsullied hands, his noble life was drawing happily to its close in the midst of the family upon which all his affections were centred, without a suspicion of the vagaries, still secret, of his brother. No one enjoyed more than he the lovely spectacle of these reunions, where no subject of discord ever arose, where brothers and sisters were equally devoted to one another, for Célestine had been instantly adopted as one of the family. From time to time the gallant little Count Hulot would inquire why Père Crevel did not come.

"My father's in the country!" Célestine would

shout in reply. On this occasion they told him that the quondam dealer in perfumes was traveling.

This true union of hearts in her family caused Madame Hulot to reflect:

"This is the most stable of all forms of happiness, and who can deprive us of it?"

When he saw the baron devoting himself to Adeline, the general joked him about it to such an extent that the baron, dreading ridicule, transferred his devotion to his daughter-in-law, who, at these family dinner-parties, was always the object of his flattery and attentions, for he hoped through her to bring Père Crevel around and induce him to abjure his resentment. Anyone looking in upon this family party would have found it difficult to believe that the father was on the verge of ruin, the mother in despair, the son in the last stage of anxiety concerning his father's future, and the daughter engaged in stealing a lover from her cousin.

At seven o'clock the baron, seeing that his brother and son, with the baroness and Hortense, were absorbed in a game of whist, took his leave, to go and applaud his mistress at the Opera, taking with him Cousin Bette, who lived on Rue du Doyenné, and who made the lonesomeness of that deserted neighborhood a pretext for always going home immediately after dinner. All Parisians will agree that the old maid's prudence was quite rational.

*

The existence of the cluster of houses which skirt the old Louvre is one of those demonstrations against common sense which the French people love to indulge in, so that Europe may take comfort as to the modicum of wit with which they are to be credited, and may cease to stand in awe of them. It may be that we have unknowingly given voice to a profound political reflection. It certainly will not be out of place to describe this corner of the Paris of to-day, for hereafter it will be impossible to imagine it; and our nephews, who will doubtless see the Louvre completed, will refuse to believe that such a bit of barbarism endured for thirty-six years in the very heart of Paris, in front of the palace wherein three dynasties have received during those thirty-six years, the élite of France and of Europe.

Every man who comes to Paris, though it be for a few days only, notices between the wicket leading to the Pont du Carrousel and Rue du Musée, some half-score houses with dilapidated façades, which the disheartened proprietors make no attempt to repair, the remnant of an old quarter which has been falling into decay from the time that Napoléon determined to complete the Louvre. The Rue du Doyenné and the cul-de-sac of the same name are the only thoroughfares of this gloomy and deserted neighborhood, where the inhabitants are probably ghosts, for no living person is ever seen there. The pavement, which is much lower than the roadway of Rue du Musée, is on the same level with Rue Froidmanteau. Partly buried already by the grading up of the square, these houses are enveloped in the perpetual shadow cast by the lofty galleries of the Louvre, blackened on that side by the north wind. The darkness, the silence, the chilly atmosphere, the cavern-like excavation of the ground, all concur to make of these houses something very like crypts, living tombs. When one drives in a cab along the outskirts of this dead quarter and casts a glance down the Ruelle du Doyenné, a cold chill strikes one's heart, and one wonders who can live in such a place, what probably takes place there at night, at the hour when that lane becomes a fitting resort of cut-throats, and when the vices of Paris, wrapped in the mantle of darkness, throw off all restraint. This problem, terrifying in itself, becomes appalling when one sees that these so-called houses are enclosed by a swamp on the side toward Rue de Richelieu, by an ocean of billowy heaps of paving-stones on the side toward the Tuileries, by small gardens and hovels of forbidding appearance on the side toward the galleries, and by plateaus of hewn stone and rubbish on the side toward the old Louvre. Henri III. and his minions looking for their stockings, Marguerite's lovers in search of their heads, might be expected to dance sarabands by moonlight on that deserted spot, overlooked by the walls of a chapel which is still standing, as if to prove that the

Catholic religion, so firmly rooted in France, outlives everything. It will soon be forty years that the Louvre has been crying through all the mouths cut in its walls, through all its yawning windows: "Pluck out these warts from my face!" Doubtless the authorities have realized the utility of this cut-throat place, and the necessity of symbolizing, in the heart of Paris, the close alliance between misery and splendor which characterizes the queen of capitals. So it may be that these repellant ruins, in whose bosom the journal of the legitimists contracted the disease of which it is dying, the impure hovels of the Rue du Musée, and the boarded booths of the hucksters who frequent that thoroughfare, will enjoy a longer and more prosperous life than the three dynasties!

As early as 1823 the modest rent of lodgings in these houses, doomed to destruction, led Cousin Bette to install herself there, despite the necessity of going home before nightfall imposed upon her by the dangerous condition of the quarter. This necessity was in accord, however, with the provincial custom to which she adhered of retiring and rising with the sun, a custom which enables country people to effect a noteworthy saving in the way of fuel and light. She lived, then, in one of the houses which gained a view of the square by the demolition of the celebrated mansion formerly occupied by Cambacérès.

Just as Baron Hulot set his wife's cousin down at the door of her abode, saying to her: "Adieu, cousin!" a young woman of small stature, graceful and pretty, dressed in the height of fashion, and exhaling the choicest of perfumes, passed between the carriage and the wall on her way into the house. This lady, without the slightest premeditation, exchanged a glance with the baron, solely to have a look at the lodger's cousin; but the old rake felt that sudden thrill which all Parisians feel when they fall in with a pretty woman who realizes, as the entomologists say, their *desiderata*, and, with cunning moderation, he drew on one of his gloves before returning to the carriage, in order that he might be able, without embarrassment, to look after the young woman, whose dress was most attractively adjusted over something very different from the abhorrent and deceptive hoopskirt.

"There's an attractive little woman," he said to himself, "whom I would be very glad to make happy, for she would do the same by me."

When the stranger had reached the landing of the staircase which led to the portion of the house fronting on the street, she glanced back at the porte-cochère out of the corner of her eye, without actually turning around, and saw the baron rooted to the spot by admiration, consumed with desire and curiosity. Such episodes are like flowers which all Parisian women delight to smell when they find them in their path. Some women, devoted to their duties, virtuous and attractive, return home in ill-humor when they have failed to gather such a little nosegay during their walk.

The young woman swiftly ascended the stairs. Soon a window of the apartment on the second floor was thrown open, and she appeared thereat, but accompanied by a gentleman, whose bald head and by no means wrathful eye betrayed the husband.

"How sly and clever these creatures are!—" said the baron to himself; "that's her way of showing me where she lives. She's a little too eager, especially for this neighborhood. I must look out."

He raised his head when he had entered the *milord,* whereupon the lady and her husband swiftly drew back, as if the baron's face had produced upon them the effect of the fabled head of Medusa.

"One would say that they know who I am," thought the baron. "In that case everything is explained."

In fact, when the carriage had driven up into the Rue du Musée, he leaned out to catch another glimpse of the stranger, and found that she had returned to the window. Ashamed at being caught gazing at the capote which sheltered her admirer, the young woman hastily drew back.

"I will find out who she is from the Nanny-goat," said the baron to himself.

The features of the councilor of state had produced, as we shall see, a profound impression upon the couple.

"Why it's baron Hulot, in whose department my office is!" cried the husband as he left the balcony.

"True, Marneffe, the old maid of the third floor at

the end of the courtyard, who lives with that young man, is his cousin, isn't she? How strange that we should not find it out until to-day, and then by chance!"

"Mademoiselle Fischer live with a young man!—" repeated the clerk. "That's mere concierge's gossip; we mustn't speak so lightly of the cousin of a councilor of state, who has great influence with the ministry. Come, let's have dinner, I have been waiting for you since four o'clock!"

Lovely Madame Marneffe, a natural daughter of Count Montcornet, one of Napoléon's most celebrated lieutenants, had been married, through the instrumentality of a dowry of twenty thousand francs, to an under clerk at the War Department. By the influence of the illustrious lieutenant-general, marshal of France, during the last six months of his life, this knight of the pen had attained the unhoped-for dignity of chief clerk in his bureau; but just as he was on the point of being appointed deputy chief of the bureau, the marshal's death nipped the hopes of Marneffe and his wife in the bud. The slender proportions of Monsieur Marneffe's income—Mademoiselle Valérie Fortin's marriage-portion having already disappeared, partly in payment of the clerk's debts, partly in the necessary outlay of a young man beginning housekeeping, but principally in satisfying the requirements of a pretty woman, accustomed under her mother's roof to luxuries which she did not choose to forego,—had compelled the young couple to economize in the matter of rent. The location of the Rue du Doyenné, near at hand to the Ministry of War and the centre of Paris, suited Monsieur and Madame Marneffe, who had occupied an apartment in Mademoiselle Fischer's house for some four years.

Sieur Jean-Paul-Stanislas Marneffe belonged to that class of clerks who steer clear of downright brutishness by the species of force which depravity bestows. A lean little man, with thin hair and beard, an unhealthy pallor on his cheeks, more faded than wrinkled, eyes with slightly-reddened lids and adorned with glasses, a shambling gait and a still more shambling carriage, he realized the type which every one sketches in his own mind of a man arraigned at the assizes for a crime against public morals.

The apartment occupied by this family, a type of many Parisian families, presented the misleading aspect of pseudo luxury which characterizes so many interiors. In the salon, the furniture covered with worn cotton-velvet, the statuettes of plaster counterfeiting Florentine bronze, the wretchedly-carved chandelier, merely painted over, with sconces of imitation crystal, the carpet of which the low price was explained too late by the quantity of cotton woven in by the manufacturer, and now visible to the naked eye; everything, even to the curtains which would have demonstrated to your satisfaction that the splendor of woolen damask does not endure three years; everything sang of poverty as loudly as a ragged beggar at a church door.

The dining-room, ill-cared for by a single servant,

presented the disgusting appearance of the dining-room in a country hotel; everything was greasy and untidy.

Monsieur's chamber, not unlike the chamber of a student, was furnished with the bed and belongings of a bachelor, decayed and worn-out like himself, and made up once a week. This horrible chamber, where everything was in confusion, where old stockings hung upon the backs of horsehair chairs, on which the flowers were outlined in the dust, proclaimed the man who cares little for his home, who lives abroad, at the gaming-house, in the cafés or elsewhere.

Madame's chamber was an exception to the disgraceful slovenliness which dishonored the principal apartments, where the curtains were everywhere yellow with smoke and dust, and where the child, evidently left to shift for itself, left its toys lying around on all sides. Situated in the wing which connected, on one side only, the building on the street with the main building constructed at the rear of the courtyard close against the adjoining property, Valérie's bedroom and dressing-room, with dainty chintz hangings, violet-wood furniture and a moquette carpet, had a savor of the pretty woman, and, let us say it, almost of the kept mistress. Upon the velvet-covered mantelpiece stood a clock of the prevailing fashion. There was a little cabinet well supplied, and jardinières in Chinese porcelain upon handsome stands. The bed, the toilet-table, the wardrobe with a long mirror, the tête-à-tête, the indispensable knick-knacks, were in accord with the taste or the caprice of the day.

Although it was third-rate in point of richness and elegance, and although everything was three years old, a dandy would have found nothing to carp at, except that the splendor smacked of the bourgeoisie. Art, and the air of distinction resulting from the little things which good taste makes its own, were wholly lacking. A professor of social science would have recognized the lover in certain of those useless trifles in the way of rich bijouterie, which can come only from that demi-god, who is ever present, though ever absent in the apartment of a married woman.

The dinner of which the husband, wife and child partook, and which had been delayed since four o'clock, would have betrayed the financial crisis through which the family was passing, for the table is the most unerring thermometer of income in Parisian households. A soup made of herbs and bean-water, a bit of veal with potatoes, swimming in reddened water in the guise of gravy, a plate of beans and cherries of inferior quality, the whole served and eaten upon dishes and plates chipped along the edges, and ware having the non-resonant sound of German silver. Was that a *menu* worthy of that charming creature? The baron would have wept to witness it. The dingy carafes did not cloak the shocking color of the wine, bought by the litre at the corner wine-shop. The napkins had been in use for a week. In short, everything was eloquent of poverty without dignity, of the indifference of husband and wife alike, to their home. The most superficial observer would have said, upon seeing these two beings, that they had reached that deplorable stage where the necessity of living sets one's wits at work to invent some successful fraud.

The first remark made by Valérie will explain the delay inflicted upon the dinner, due in part, probably, to the selfish assiduity of the cook.

"Samanon will not take your notes except at a discount of fifty per cent., and he insists upon an assignment of your salary as security."

Thus we see that poverty, still unsuspected by the head of the department, and which was screened behind a salary of twenty-four thousand francs, without counting perquisites, had reached its last stage with the clerk.

"You have *made* my chief," said the husband with a glance at his wife.

"I think so," she replied, with no sign of alarm at the word, borrowed from the slang of the green-room.

"What will become of us?" continued Marneffe. "The landlord will seize our goods to-morrow. And your father must go and die without making a will! Upon my word these people of the Empire all think they're immortal like their Emperor."

"Poor father," said she; "he had no child but me, and he loved me dearly! The countess must have burned the will. How could he have forgotten me, when he used to give us now and again three or four notes of a thousand francs at one time?"

"We owe for four terms, fifteen hundred francs! Is our furniture worth it? '*That is the question!*' as Shakespeare says."

"Well, adieu, my boy," said Valérie, who had swallowed only a few mouthfuls of the veal, from which the cook had abstracted the gravy for a gallant soldier just returned from Algiers. "For great ills, heroic remedies!"

"Where are you going, Valérie?" cried Marneffe, barring his wife's path to the door.

"I am going to see our landlord," she replied, adjusting her English curls beneath her dainty hat. "You must try and get into that old maid's good graces if she is really your chief's cousin."

The ignorance of the various lodgers in the same house concerning one another's social standing, is one of the constantly-recurring phenomena which best depict the headlong whirl of life in Paris; but it is easy to understand that a clerk who goes early every day to his office, returns home to dinner, and goes out every evening, and a woman addicted to the diversions of Paris, are not in a way to know anything of the life of an old maid who lodges on the third-floor-back of their house, especially when that old maid has such habits as Mademoiselle Fischer.

Lisbeth was always the first person in the house to go out for her milk and roll and her hot coals; she spoke to no one, and retired with the sun; she never received letters or visits, and was not inclined to be neighborly. Hers was one of those anonymous insect-like existences, such as are to be found in certain houses, where one learns after four or five years that there is an old gentleman on the fourth floor who knew Voltaire, Pilâtre de Rozier, Beaujon, Marcel, Molé, Sophie Arnould, Franklin and Robespierre. What M. and Madame Marneffe had said concerning Lisbeth Fischer they had learned on account of the isolation of the quarter, and the relations which their pecuniary embarrassment had established between themselves and the concierges, whose good-will was too necessary to them not to have been zealously cultivated. Now the pride, the reticence, the reserve of the old maid had engendered in the concierges the exaggerated respect, the aloofness which betokens the unavowed ill-will of inferiors. The concierges, furthermore, deemed themselves, in a measure, as they say at the Palais, the equals of a lodger whose rent was two hundred and fifty francs. The confidences of Cousin Bette to her second-cousin Hortense being true, every one will understand that it was quite possible that the concierge, in some confidential gossip with the Marneffes, had slandered Mademoiselle Fischer when she thought that she was simply backbiting her.

When the old maid received her candle from the hands of the respectable Madame Olivier, the concierge, she stepped forward to see if the windows of the attic above her apartment were lighted. At that hour, in July, it was so dark at the end of the court-yard that the old maid could not go to bed without a light.

"Oh! never fear, M. Steinbock is at home, he

hasn't even been out," said Madame Olivier maliciously to Mademoiselle Fischer.

The old maid vouchsafed no reply. She was still the peasant in so far that she scorned the "what they will say" of people far removed from her; and, just as the peasants see nothing outside their village, she was mindful only of the opinion of the little circle in which she lived. So she unhesitatingly went up, not to her own apartment, but to the attic in question. And for this reason. At dessert she had stowed away in her bag divers fruits and sweetmeats for her lover, and she went to give them to him, for all the world as an old maid would take a tidbit to her dog.

She found, working by the light of a little lamp, of which the brilliancy was increased by its passing through a globe filled with water, the hero of Hortense's dreams, a pale young man of fair complexion, seated at a sort of bench covered with sculptor's tools, red wax, moulding-sticks, rough-hewn pedestals and models cast in copper; he was dressed in a blouse and held in his hand a little group in modeling wax, at which he was gazing with the absorbed air of a poet in the throes of composition.

"Here, Wenceslas, see what I have brought you," said she, placing her handkerchief on a corner of the bench.

She thereupon carefully extracted from her basket the sweetmeats and the fruit.

"You are very kind, mademoiselle," replied the poor exile in a melancholy voice.

"They will refresh you, my poor boy. You heat your blood working so; you weren't made for such hard work.—"

Wenceslas Steinbock looked at the old maid in amazement.

"Eat them, pray," she continued abruptly, "instead of staring at me as at one of your figures when it pleases you."

Upon receiving this spoken blow the young man's amazement ceased, for therein he recognized his female mentor, whose tenderness always surprised him, so accustomed was he to be scolded by her. Although Steinbock was twenty-nine years old, he seemed, as many blondes do, five or six years younger; and one would have thought, at sight of that youthful countenance, whose freshness had vanished by stress of the fatigues and miseries of exile, beside that other thin, harsh face, that nature had gone astray in the distribution of sexes. He rose, threw himself upon an old Louis XV. couch covered with yellow Utrecht velvet, and seemed disposed to rest. The old maid thereupon took a green-gage and gently offered it to her friend.

"Thank you," said he, taking the fruit.

"Are you tired?" she asked, giving him another.

"I am not tired with work,—but tired of life," was the reply.

"What an idea!" said she sharply. "Haven't you a good genius who looks after you?" she continued, handing him the sweetmeats, and watching him eat them all with evident pleasure. "You see, when I was dining at my cousin's I thought of you—"

"I know," said he, bestowing upon Lisbeth a glance that was at once caressing and plaintive, "that but for you, I should have died long ago; but, my dear girl, artists require distraction—"

"Ah! there we are!—" she cried, interrupting him, putting her arms akimbo, and fixing a pair of flashing eyes upon him. "You would like to go and ruin your health in the unspeakable dens of Paris, like so many workmen who end their days in an alms-house! No, no, make your fortune, and when you have money in the funds you shall amuse yourself, my child; then you will have the wherewithal to pay for your dissipation and your doctor's bills, rake that you are."

Wenceslas Steinbock, upon receiving this broadside, accompanied by glances whose magnetic flame penetrated his whole being, hung his head. If the most ill-natured gossip could have witnessed the opening of this scene, he would have realized at once the falsity of the slanders set afloat concerning Mademoiselle Fischer by the Oliviers, husband and wife. Everything in the tone, the actions, and the glances of these two beings demonstrated the purity of their secret life. The old maid exhibited a brutal but sincere maternal affection. The young man submitted as an obedient son submits to a mother's tyranny. This strange alliance seemed to be the result of a powerful will acting incessantly upon a weak character, endowed with the inconsistency peculiar to the Slavs, which, while it leaves them capable of heroic courage on the battle-field, imparts an incredible lack of coherence to their acts, and gives them a moral flabbiness, the causes of which should give food for thought to the physiologists, for the physiologists are to politics what the entomologists are to agriculture.

"And what if I die before I get rich?" queried Wenceslas, dolefully.

"Die?—" cried the old maid. "Oh! I won't let you die. I have life enough for two, and I'll give you an infusion of my blood, if need be."

As he listened to that frank, impetuous outburst, tears gathered in Steinbock's eyes.

"Don't be downhearted, my little Wenceslas," continued Lisbeth, deeply moved. "Look you, my cousin Hortense thought your seal very pretty, I am sure. Come, I will help you to sell your bronze group, then you will be out of my debt; you shall do what you please, you shall be free! Come, laugh a little!—"

"I shall never be out of your debt, mademoiselle," replied the poor exile.

"Why not, pray?—" demanded the peasant from the Vosges, taking the Livonian's part against herself.

"Because you have not only supported me, lodged me and taken care of me in poverty, but more, you have given me strength! You have made me what I am, you have often been harsh to me, you have made me suffer—"

"I?" said the old maid. "Are you going to begin again your nonsense about poetry and the arts, and make your fingers crack and twist your arms talking about the beau ideal and the rest of your Northern idiocy? The beautiful isn't worth as much as the substantial, and I am the substantial! You have ideas in your brain? A fine thing, no doubt! And I have ideas, too.—Of what use is what one has in his brain, if he gets no good from it? Those who have ideas aren't so far ahead as those who have none, if they know how to bestir themselves.—Instead of thinking of your dreams, you must work. What have you done since I went away?—"

"What did your pretty cousin say?"

"Who told you she was pretty?" demanded Lisbeth quickly, in a tone in which roared the jealousy of a tiger.

"Why, you yourself."

"I did it to see the face you would make! Do you want to run after the petticoats? You love the ladies; very well, mould them, express your aspirations in bronze; for you will have to get along for some time yet without love affairs, and especially without my cousin Hortense, my dear. She's not the fish for your hook; that young woman must have a man with an income of sixty thousand francs,—and he is found.—Well, well, the bed's not made!" she added, looking through into the other room. "Oh! my poor boy! I forgot you—"

The active creature at once removed her gloves, her cape and her hat, and like any maid, quickly made up the little cot-bed upon which the artist slept. This mixture of roughness, harshness even, and kindness will explain the empire Lisbeth had acquired over this man, whom she treated as something belonging to herself. Does not life bind us to one another by its alternations of good and bad? If the Livonian had fallen in with Madame Marneffe instead of Lisbeth Fischer, he would have found in his protectress a complaisance which would have led him into some filthy, dishonoring path, where he would have been ruined. He certainly would have done no work, the artist would not have broken his shell. And so, while he deplored the old maid's fierce cupidity, his reason bade him prefer that arm of iron to the slothful and perilous existence which some of his compatriots led.

The alliance between this female energy and this masculine weakness, a sort of contradiction not uncommon in Poland, it is said, came about in this way.

In 1833, Mademoiselle Fischer, who sometimes worked at night when she had much work on hand, was conscious, about one o'clock one morning, of a strong smell of carbonic acid, and heard the groans of a dying man. The odor of charcoal and the death-rattle proceeded from an attic above the two rooms which composed her suite, and she concluded that a young man who had recently come to the house and hired the attic, which had been to let for three years, was taking his own life. She ran swiftly up-stairs, burst in the door with her Lorraine muscle with such leverage as she could get, and found the lodger writhing upon a pallet, in the convulsions of the death-agony. She extinguished the fire in the brazier, with the opening of the door the air rushed in and the exile was saved; and when Lisbeth had put him to bed like a sick man, and he had gone to sleep, she was able to detect the causes that led to the suicide in the absolute nudity of the two attic rooms, where there was nothing but a wretched table, the pallet, and two chairs.

Upon the table lay this writing, which she read:

"I am Count Wenceslas Steinbock, born at Prelie in Livonia.

"Let no person be accused of my death; the reasons for my suicide are to be found in these words of Kosciusko: 'Finis Poloniæ!'

"The great-nephew of one of Charles the Twelfth's gallant generals did not choose to beg. My weak constitution debarred me from military service, and yesterday I saw the last of the hundred thalers with which I came from Dresden to Paris. I leave twenty-five francs in the drawer of this table to pay the rent I owe the landlord.

"Having no relations, my death concerns no one. I beg my compatriots not to blame the French government. I have not made myself known as a refugee, I have asked for nothing, I have not made the acquaintance of any exile, and no one in Paris knows of my existence.

"I shall die in the faith of Christ. May God forgive the last of the Steinbocks!

'WENCESLAS.'

Mademoiselle Fischer, profoundly touched by the dying man's honesty in paying his rent, opened the drawer, and found therein five pieces of one hundred sous.

"Poor young man!" she cried. "And no one on earth to take an interest in him!"

She went down to her room, took her work, and returned to the attic, where she watched the Livonian nobleman as she worked. When the exile awoke, his astonishment at finding a woman at his bedside can be imagined; he thought that he was still dreaming. As she sat making gold shoulder-knots for a uniform, the old maid had made a vow to look after the poor child, whom she gazed upon in admiration while he lay asleep. When the young count was fully awake, Lisbeth spoke encouragingly to him, and questioned him in order to ascertain how he could earn his living. Wenceslas, having told her his story, added that he owed his present condition to his pronounced vocation for art; he had always felt an inclination for the sculptor's profession; but the time necessarily devoted to study seemed to him too long for a penniless man, and at that moment he felt much too weak to follow a manual trade, or to undertake to learn sculpture. This was all Greek to Lisbeth Fischer. She answered the poor fellow by saying that Paris offered so many opportunities, that any man who really wished to do so ought to be able to make a living. Stout-hearted people need not die there if they possessed a good stock of patience.

"I am only a poor girl myself, a peasant, and yet I have succeeded in making myself independent," she added in conclusion. "Listen to what I say. If you choose to go to work in good earnest, I have some small savings, and I will loan you from month to month such money as you need to live, but to live simply, not to go about drinking and running after women! One can dine at Paris for twenty-five sous a day, and I will get your breakfast with mine every morning. Then I will furnish your rooms, and pay such apprenticeship fees as you think necessary. You will give me an acknowledgment in proper form for the money I lay out for you; and when you are rich you can pay it all back. But if you don't work I shall consider myself pledged to nothing, and I shall give you up."

"Ah!" cried the unfortunate youth, who still felt the bitterness of his first contact with death, "the exiles of all countries are very wise to look toward France as the souls in purgatory look to Paradise. What a country is that where one finds help and noble hearts everywhere, even in an attic like this! You will be everything to me, my dear benefactress, and I will be your slave! Be my mistress," he added, with one of those caressing demonstrations so characteristic of the Poles, and which cause them to be most unjustly accused of servility.

"Oh! no, I am too jealous, I should make you wretched; but I will gladly be a sort of comrade to you," Lisbeth replied.

"Oh! if you but knew how fervently I prayed for some human being, even a tyrant, to care about me when I was struggling in the wilderness of Paris!" said Wenceslas. "I sighed for Siberia, where the Emperor would send me if I should return!—Be my Providence—I will work, I will be better than I am, although I'm not a bad sort of fellow."

"Will you do whatever I tell you to do?" she asked.

"Yes!"—

"Very well; then I take you for my child," she said, gayly. "Here I am with a boy just out of his coffin. Come! let us begin. I will go down and make things ready; do you dress, and come and share my breakfast when I knock on the ceiling with my broom-handle."

The next day Mademoiselle Fischer made inquiries as to the sculptor's trade from the dealers to whom she carried her work. By dint of much questioning she succeeded in discovering the workshop of Florent and Chanor, a concern specially engaged in casting and in fine chased work in bronze and silver-plate. She introduced Steinbock there as a would-be apprentice in sculpture, a proposition which seemed peculiar, for their business consisted in casting the models of the most celebrated artists, and they did not give instruction in sculpture. The old maid's

G. Cain del. Gaujean sc.

obstinacy and persistence finally prevailed and she secured a position for her protégé as designer of ornaments. Steinbock very quickly learned the art of modeling ornaments, and invented new ones; he had the aptitude. Five months after he had finished his apprenticeship as carver he became acquainted with the famous Stidmann, the principal sculptor of the house of Florent. After twenty months Wenceslas knew more than his master; but in thirty months the savings amassed by the old maid bit by bit, during sixteen years, were all gone. Two thousand five hundred francs in gold! a sum which she intended to invest in an annuity, and represented by what? By the note of hand of a Pole! Thus Lisbeth still worked, as in her younger days, to defray the Livonian's expenses. When she saw in her hands a bit of paper instead of her gold pieces, she lost her head, and went to consult M. Rivet, who had been for fifteen years the friend and adviser of his chief and most skilful workwoman. When they knew what had happened M. and Madame Rivet berated Lisbeth, treated her as a lunatic, reviled the refugees, whose manœuvres to become a nation once more, endangered the prosperity of our commerce, and the peace-at-any-price policy, and they urged the old maid to take what is called in business, security.

"The only security that rascal can offer you is his freedom," said M. Rivet.

M. Achille Rivet was a judge at the Tribunal de Commerce.

"And that's no joking matter for foreigners," he continued. "A Frenchman remains five years in prison, and then goes free without paying his debts, to be sure, for he is no longer subject to any law but his conscience, which never troubles him; but a foreigner never gets out of prison. Give me the note of hand; you must indorse it over to my book-keeper, who will have it protested, sue you both, and obtain, after hearing, a judgment for arrest, and, when all is in order, he will execute a defeasance to you. In this way your interest will run on, and you will always have a loaded pistol at your Pole's head!"

The old maid allowed this course to be adopted, and told her protégé not be disturbed by the lawsuit, the only purpose of which was to furnish security to a money-lender who agreed to make them an advance. This shift was due to the inventive genius of the judge of the Tribunal de Commerce. The unsuspecting artist, with blind confidence in his benefactress, lighted his pipe with the stamped documents, for he was a smoker, like all men who have disappointments or superfluous energy to overcome. One fine day M. Rivet showed Mademoiselle Fischer a bundle of papers, and said to her:

" You have Wenceslas Steinbock bound hand and foot, and so effectively that in twenty-four hours you can shut him up at Clichy for the rest of his life."

The upright and worshipful magistrate experienced that day the satisfaction which should follow the certainty of having committed a bad action for a good purpose. Good-will wears so many guises at Paris, that this singular expression is consistent with one of its variations. Once the Livonian was entangled in the meshes of commercial procedure, payment of the debt was the next thing to be thought of, for the eminent tradesman looked upon Wenceslas Steinbock as a swindler. The heart, probity, poetry, were in his eyes, in matters of business, horrors. In the interest of poor Mademoiselle Fischer, who had, to use his expression, been *plucked* by a Pole, Rivet called upon the wealthy firm with whom Steinbock served his apprenticeship. Now Stidmann, who, seconded by the notable artists among Parisian goldsmiths already named, raised the art in France to its present state of perfection which enables it to contend with the Florentines and the Renaissance,—Stidmann happened to be in Chanor's office when the lace-maker called in quest of information concerning one Steinbock, a Polish refugee.

"Whom do you call 'one Steinbock?'" cried Stidmann ironically. "Can it be by any chance a young Livonian I had for a pupil? Understand, monsieur, that he is a great artist. They say that I think I'm the devil; but that poor boy doesn't know that he may become a god—"

"Aha!" exclaimed Rivet with satisfaction.

"Although," he continued, "you spoke rather cavalierly to a man who has the honor of being a judge of the Tribunal of the Seine—"

"Your pardon, consul!—" interposed Stidmann, putting the back of his hand to his head.

"I am very glad to hear what you say," continued the magistrate. "This young man is able to earn money, then?—"

"To be sure," said old Chanor, "but he must work; he might have saved a deal already if he had remained with us. What can we do? Artists have a horror of dependence."

"They have due regard for their worth and their dignity," rejoined Stidmann. "I don't blame Wenceslas for starting out alone to try and make a name and become a great man; it's his right! And yet I lost much when he left me!"

"There you have it," cried Rivet; "that's the ambition of the young men just hatched from the university egg.—For heaven's sake begin by saving money and seek glory afterwards!"

"One spoils his touch picking up crowns!" replied Stidmann. "It is for glory to bring us fortune."

"What would you have?" said Chanor to Rivet; "one can't tie them—"

"They would gnaw through the halter!" retorted Stidmann.

"All these gentry," said Chanor, with a glance at Stidmann, "have as much caprice as talent. They are terribly extravagant, they have *Lorettes*, they throw money out of the window, and they have no time to attend to their work; they thereupon neglect their orders; we have recourse to workmen who are not their equals, but who make money; then they complain of the hard times, whereas if they had attended to business they would have mountains of gold—"

"You remind me, old papa Lumignon," said Stidmann, "of that ante-revolution bookseller, who said: 'Ah! if I could have Montesquieu, Voltaire and Rousseau, poor as church-mice, in my loft, and keep their breeches in my closet, what nice little books they should write for me, with which I would make my fortune!' If one could forge great works like nails, the errand-boys would make them—Give me a thousand francs and hold your tongue!"

The excellent Rivet returned home delighted for poor Mademoiselle Fischer, who dined with him every Monday, and whom he was sure to find there.

"If you can make him work hard," said he, "you will be more lucky than wise, for you will be repaid, principal, interest and costs. This Pole has talent and can earn his living; but you must conceal his trousers and his shoes, keep him from going to the Chaumière and to the Quartier Notre-Dame de Lorette,—hold him in leash. Unless you take these precautions, your sculptor will be a *flâneur*, and you know what artists understand by that! Horrible things, I tell you! I have heard that a thousand franc note is gone in a day."

This incident had a tremendous effect upon the home life of Lisbeth and Wenceslas. The benefactress dipped the exile's bread in the absinthe of reproaches, when she saw that her funds were endangered, and she very often believed them lost. The doting mother became a cruel step-mother, she scolded the poor child, worried him, blamed him for not working rapidly enough and for choosing such a difficult trade. She could not believe that models in red wax, tiny figures, sketches for ornaments, mere experiments, could have any value. In another moment, sorry for her harshness, she would strive to do away with its effects by soft words and little attentions. The unfortunate youth, after groaning to find himself dependent upon this fury, and under the domination of a Vosges peasant, would be overjoyed by her wheedling ways and the maternal solicitude of one who cared for naught but the physical, the material side of life. He was like a wife, who forgives the brutal treatment of a week for the sake of the caresses of a momentary reconciliation. Mademoiselle Fischer thus acquired absolute dominion over this life. The love of domination, which lay dormant in germ in the old maid's heart, developed with great rapidity. She was able to satisfy her pride and her need of action; had she not a being all to herself, to scold and guide and flatter and make happy, without fear of a rival? The good and the evil traits of her character came into play equally. If she sometimes made a martyr of the poor artist, she lavished upon him as a recompense, delicate attentions as refreshing as the fragrance of wild flowers, she enjoyed seeing him want for nothing; she would have given her life for him; of that Wenceslas had no doubt. Like all noble hearts, the poor fellow forgot the harshness, the failings of this woman, who, moreover, had told him the story of her life, by way of apology for her barbarity, and he remembered only her benefactions.

One day the old maid, exasperated because Wenceslas had gone out to lounge about the streets instead of working, made a scene.

"You belong to me!" said she. "If you are an honest man, you should do your best to pay what you owe me as soon as possible—"

The young nobleman, in whose veins the blood of the Steinbocks took fire, turned pale as death.

"My God!" she continued, "before long we shall have nothing to live on but the thirty sous that I, a poor girl, earn—"

The two paupers, losing their tempers in the duel of words, waxed hot against each other; and the unhappy artist thereupon, for the first time, reproached his benefactress for having rescued him from death to make him lead the life of a galley-slave, far worse than nothingness, where one might at least find repose, he said. And he spoke of going away.

"Go away!—"cried the old maid—"Ah! M. Rivet was right!"

And she thereupon categorically explained to the youth that in twenty-four hours she could put him in prison for the rest of his days. It was a knock-down blow. Steinbock fell into a condition of black melancholy and absolute silence. The next night Lisbeth, overhearing preparations for suicide, went up to her boarder's room, and handed him the bundle of papers with an acquittance in due form.

"Here, my child," said she, with tears in her eyes, "forgive me! Leave me, and be happy; I torment you too much; but tell me that you will sometimes think of the poor girl who put you in a way to earn your living. What would you have? You are the cause of my ill-humor; I might die, and what would become of you without me?—That's the reason of my impatience to see you in a position to make things that can be sold. I don't ask for my money for myself, not at all!—I am afraid of your laziness, which you call reverie, of the many hours you consume forming your great conceptions, during which you gaze at the sky, and I would like to have you contract the habit of working."

This was said with an accent, a look, an attitude, and tears, which touched the noble artist to the heart; he threw his arms about his benefactress, pressed her to his breast, and kissed her on the forehead.

"Keep these papers," he said, almost gayly. "Why should you send me to Clichy? am I not imprisoned here by gratitude?"

This episode in their secret life together had happened about six months before, and had caused Wenceslas to produce three pieces of work: the seal which Hortense retained, the group placed with the dealer in bric-à-brac, and a beautiful clock, which he was just on the point of finishing, for he was putting the last screws into the model.

This clock represented the twelve Hours, admirably delineated by twelve female figures whirling around in such a mad, swift dance, that three Loves, clinging to a mass of flowers and fruit, were unable to stop any of them save Midnight, whose torn chlamys remained in the hands of the boldest of the three. The group rested upon a round pedestal, beautifully ornamented with figures of fantastic animals. The Hour was indicated in a monstrous mouth opened in a yawn. Each Hour presented special devices, most happily conceived to indicate the customary pursuits of mankind at that hour.

It will be easy now to understand the extraordinary attachment Mademoiselle Fischer had conceived for her Livonian; she wished him to be happy, and she saw that he was wasting, pining away in his attic. The cause of this lamentable situation is plain. The Lorrainer watched over this child of the North with the affection of a mother, the jealousy of a wife, and the cunning of a dragon; she so arranged matters as to make every species of folly or dissipation impossible, by keeping him always without money. She would fain keep her victim and her comrade to herself, virtuous as he was perforce, and she did not understand the barbarity of this insane desire, for she had become accustomed to privations of every sort. She loved Steinbock enough not to marry him, and she loved him too much to give him up to another woman; she could not resign herself to be to him a mother simply, and she deemed herself a madwoman when she thought of any other rôle. These contradictory feelings, this ferocious jealousy, this joy in possessing a man for her own, all combined to excite the old maid's heart beyond measure. Having been really in love for four years, she cherished the mad hope that this inconsequent, purposeless life, her persistence in which was likely to cause the ruin of him she called her child, might last indefinitely. The struggle between her impulses and her common sense made her unjust and tyrannical. She revenged herself upon the young man for her own lack of youth, beauty and wealth; and, after each revengeful outburst, her innate consciousness that she had done wrong led her to acts of humility and infinite tenderness. It did not occur to her to sacrifice to her idol until she had written her power upon his body with an axe. It was, in a word, Shakespeare's *Tempest* reversed, Caliban, master of Ariel and Prospero. As for the unhappy, meditative, slothfully inclined youth of lofty ideals, there opened to his eyes, as to those of the caged lions at the Jardin des Plantes, a glimpse of the desert which his heart had become under the hand of his protectress. The forced toil which Lisbeth exacted from him did not fulfil the demands of his heart. His ennui became a physical disease, and he was dying by degrees, unable to ask, and helpless to procure the requisite money for a transgression which is often a necessity. On certain days of reviving energy, when a realizing sense of his misery increased his exasperation, he would glare at Lisbeth, as a thirsty traveler, traversing an arid waste, might glare at a pool of brackish water. These bitter fruits of poverty and of this hermit's life in Paris were keenly relished by Lisbeth. And yet she foresaw with dismay that the first symptom of a real passion would deprive her of her slave. Sometimes she blamed herself for having furnished this poet with the means of doing without her, in forcing him, by her tyranny and her reproaches, to become a great sculptor of trifles.

On the morrow these three lives, so truly wretched, and in such diverse ways: the life of the despairing mother, of the Marneffe family, and of the unhappy exile, were destined all to be affected by the innocent passion of Hortense, and by the strange termination of the baron's ill-fated passion for Josépha.

*

As he was about to enter the Opera, the Councilor of State was attracted by the somewhat sombre appearance of that temple of art on Rue le Peletier. where he saw neither gendarmes, nor lights, nor attendants, nor barriers to keep the crowd within limits. He looked at the bill-board, and saw thereon a white band, in the centre of which appeared in staring letters this decisive phrase:

CLOSED ON ACCOUNT OF ILLNESS.

He rushed off incontinently to the abode of Josépha, who lived near at hand, on Rue Chauchat, as did all the artists engaged at the Opera.

"Monsieur, whom do you wish to see?" inquired the concierge, to his unbounded amazement.

"Do you no longer know me, pray?" rejoined the baron with some inquietude.

"On the contrary, monsieur, it is just because I have the honor to recognize you, that I say: 'Where are you going?'"

A deathly chill froze the baron's blood.

"What has happened?" he demanded.

"If Monsieur le Baron should go to Mademoiselle Mirah's apartment he would find there Mademoiselle Héloïse Brisetout, M. Bixiou, M. Léon de Lora, M. Lousteau, M. de Vernisset, M. Stidmann, and a number of ladies redolent of patchouly, having a house warming—"

"Very good, but where is—?"

"Mademoiselle Mirah?—I am not sure that I ought to tell you."

The baron slipped two hundred-sou pieces into the concierge's hand.

"Oh! well, she is now on Rue de la Ville-l'Évêque, in a house the Duc d'Hérouville has given her, so they say," said the porter in an undertone.

Having inquired the number of the house, the baron took a milord and was set down before one of the pretty little modern houses with double doors, in which everything, from the lantern without to the gas within, betokened luxurious living.

The baron, in his blue broadcloth coat, white cravat, white waistcoat, linen trousers and varnished boots, with plenty of starch in his shirt front, was taken for a belated guest by the concierge of this new Eden. His portliness, his gait, everything about him, tended to justify that opinion.

In answer to the bell rung by the concierge, a footman appeared in the vestibule. This footman, who was new, like the house, admitted the baron, who said to him in a commanding tone, accompanied by an imperial gesture:

"Give this card to Mademoiselle Josépha—"

The dupe mechanically looked about the room in which he found himself, a reception room, filled with rare flowers, and of which the furnishings must have cost four thousand crowns. The footman returned and begged monsieur to wait in the salon until they left the table to take their coffee there.

Although the baron had been familiar with the luxury in vogue under the Empire, which was certainly most prodigious, and the manifestations of which, if not enduring, none the less cost fabulous sums, he stood like one dazzled, struck dumb, in that salon, whose three windows opened upon a fairy-like garden, one of the gardens which are manufactured in a month with artificial soil, transplanted flowers, and turf which seems to have been obtained by chemical process. He marveled not only at the display of wealth, the gilding, the most costly sculptures of the so-called Pompadour style, and the marvelous materials which any parvenu tradesman might have ordered and secured with oceans of gold, but those other things which none but princes have the faculty of finding, of selecting, of paying for and of giving away: two pictures by Greuze and two by Watteau, two heads by Van Dyck, two landscapes by Ruysdael, two by Guaspre, a Rembrandt and a Holbein, a Murillo and a Titian, two Teniers and two Metzus, a Van Huysum and an Abraham Mignon—in a word, two hundred thousand francs in pictures beautifully framed. The settings were worth almost as much as the canvases.

"Ah! now do you understand, my bonhomme?" queried Josépha.

Over heavy Persian carpets she had stolen, on tiptoe into the room, through a door that opened noiselessly, and surprised her adorer in one of those periods of stupefaction when the ears ring so that one can hear nothing but the knell of disaster.

This word *bonhomme*, addressed to this high administrative functionary, a word which portrays to admiration the audacity with which such creatures drag the greatest lives through the mire, left the baron rooted to the spot where he stood. Josépha, all in white and yellow, was so magnificently arrayed for the festal occasion that she shone, even in the midst of this insensate luxury, as the rarest jewel of all.

"Isn't it fine?" she continued. "The duke laid out on it all the profits of a little investment in stocks which he sold at an advance. Not a bad fellow, my little duke, eh? Only the great lords of the old days know how to change coal into gold. The notary brought me, before dinner, the contract for the purchase of the house to sign, and it contains a receipt for the price. What fine fellows all the great lords yonder are: D'Esgrignon, Rastignac, Maxime, Lenoncourt, Verneuil, Laginski, Rochefide, La Palférine, and, for bankers, Nucingen and Du Tillet, with Antonia, Malaga, Carabine and La Schontz, are all sorry for your hard luck. Yes, my old friend, you are invited to join us, but on condition that you drink at once the worth of two bottles of champagne, Hungarian and Cape wine, to put yourself on a level with them. We are all too full here, dear boy, not to close the Opera; my manager is as tipsy as a cornet-à-piston, he's in the *cackling* stage!"

"Oh, Josépha!—" cried the baron.

"What a bore it is to have an explanation!" she

interrupted with a smile. "Tell me, are you worth the six hundred thousand francs that this hotel and its furnishing cost? Can you bring me a paper good for an income of thirty thousand francs, such as the duke gave me in a horn of white paper filled with sugar-plums? That was a sweet idea!"

"What perversity!" exclaimed the Councilor of State, who, in that moment of frenzy, would have pawned his wife's diamonds to replace the Duc d'Hérouville for twenty-four hours.

"It's my trade to be perverse!" she retorted. "Ah! so that's the way you take it! Why didn't you organize a company? Bless my soul, my poor *dyed cat*, you ought to thank me! I leave you just when, if I had stayed with you, you would have devoured your wife's future, your daughter's dowry, and—Ah! you are weeping. The Empire is dying out!—I salute the Empire."

She assumed a tragic pose, and declaimed:

"Your name is Hulot! I no longer know you!—"

and returned to the dining-room.

Through the half-opened door came a flash of light, accompanied by a burst of sound betokening the increasing wildness of the revel, and laden with the odors of a banquet of the first order.

The cantatrice came back and looked through the door, and when she saw Hulot standing on the same spot as if he were made of bronze, she stepped forward and reappeared.

"Monsieur," said she, "I turned over the rubbish in Rue Chauchat to little Héloïse Brisetout de Bixiou; if you choose to ask for your nightcap, your boot-jack, your belt and the wax for your whiskers, I stipulated that they should be returned to you."

The effect of this horrible banter was to drive the baron from the house, as Lot was driven from Gomorrah, but without turning to look back like Madame Lot.

Hulot returned home, striding along like a madman, talking to himself, and found his family calmly playing whist for two sous a point, as when he left them. When she saw her husband's face, poor Adeline thought that some terrible disaster had occurred, that he was dishonored; she gave her cards to Hortense and led Hector to the same little room where, five hours earlier, Crevel had predicted for her the most degrading tortures of poverty.

"What's the matter?" said she in deadly terror.

"Oh! forgive me; but let me tell you the infamous story."

For ten minutes he gave vent to his fury.

"Why, my dear," said the poor woman heroically, "such creatures don't know what love is! Such pure, devoted love as you deserve; how could you, with your good sense, undertake to contend with a million of money?"

"Dear Adeline!" cried the baron, throwing his arms about his wife, and pressing her to his heart.

The baroness had poured a soothing balm upon the bleeding wounds of self-esteem.

"To be sure," said the baron, "take away the Duc d'Hérouville's fortune, *she* would not hesitate between us."

"My dear," continued Adeline, making one last effort, "if you really must have mistresses, why don't you do as Crevel does and take women who are not so expensive, and who belong to a class likely to be happy with a little for a long time to come? We should all be the gainers. I can understand the need, but I cannot understand at all the vanity—"

"Oh! what a dear, noble woman you are!" he cried. "I am an old fool, and I don't deserve to have an angel like you for a helpmeet."

"I am simply my Napoléon's Joséphine," she replied, with a shade of melancholy.

"Joséphine was not your equal," said he. "Come, I will have a game of whist with my brother and my children; I must stick to my trade of paterfamilias, find a husband for Hortense, and bury the libertine.—"

This benignity touched poor Adeline so deeply that she said:

"That creature has wretched taste to prefer anybody in the world to my Hector. Ah! I would not give you up for all the gold on earth. How can any one let you go when she has the good fortune to be loved by you!—"

The glance with which the baron requited his wife's fanatical adoration confirmed her in the opinion that gentleness and submission are a woman's most potent weapons. She was wrong in that. The noblest sentiments carried to extremity produce results like those of the greatest vices. Bonaparte became Emperor because he shot down the populace within two steps of the spot where Louis XVI. lost the monarchy and his head because he would not allow the blood of one M. Sauce to be shed.

The next morning Hortense, who went to bed with Wenceslas' seal under her pillow, so that she might not be separated from it while she slept, was dressed betimes, and sent a message to her father, begging him to come to the garden as soon as he rose.

About half-past nine, the father, in compliance with his daughter's request, gave her his arm, and they walked together along the quays and by the Pont Royal to the Place du Carrousel.

"Let us pretend to be out for a saunter, papa," said Hortense as they passed through the wicket to cross the vast square.

"Out for a saunter here?—" queried her father jocosely.

"We are supposed to have gone to the Museum, and down there," said she, pointing to the booths against the walls of the houses that stood at right angles to Rue du Doyenné, "see there are dealers in bric-à-brac and pictures.—"

"Your cousin lives down there."—

"I know it; but we mustn't let her see us—"

"What do you propose to do?" said the baron

finding himself within thirty yards of the window at which he had seen Madame Marneffe, who suddenly came to his mind.

Hortense had led her father in front of the window of one of the shops at the corner of the cluster of houses which skirt the old Louvre and face the Hôtel de *Nantes*. She entered the shop; her father remained outside, busily engaged in gazing at the windows of the charming little lady who had left her image on the old beau's heart the evening before, as if to soothe the wound he was so soon to receive in that organ, and he could not refrain from putting his wife's advice in practice.

"I must fall back on the little bourgeoises," he said to himself, recalling Madame Marneffe's adorable charm. "This woman will speedily make me forget the grasping Josépha."

This is what took place simultaneously inside the shop and outside the shop.

As he scrutinized the windows of his latest charmer the baron spied the husband, who, while brushing his own overcoat, was evidently on the watch, and seemed to be awaiting some person's appearance on the square. Fearing lest he should be seen and afterwards recognized, the amorous baron turned his back upon Rue du Doyenné, but so placed himself that he could glance in that direction now and then. This manœuvre brought him almost face to face with Madame Marneffe, who, coming from the quay, was doubling the headland of houses on her way home. Valérie felt something like a shock as she received the baron's astonished gaze and she replied to it with a prudish simper.

"Pretty creature," cried the baron, "for whom one would do many a foolish thing!"

"Eh! monsieur," she replied, turning about like a woman who has resolved upon a desperate course, "you are M. le Baron Hulot, aren't you?"

The baron, with increasing amazement, nodded his head assentingly.

"Very well, since chance has brought our eyes together twice, and I am fortunate enough to have aroused your curiosity or your interest, I will tell you that instead of doing foolish things you ought to do justice.—My husband's fate depends upon you."

"How so?" queried the baron gallantly.

"He is a clerk in your department at the Ministry of War, M. Lebrun's division, M. Coquet's bureau," she replied with a smile.

"I am inclined, Madame—Madame—?"

"Madame Marneffe."

"My dear Madame Marneffe, to do injustice for the sake of your lovely eyes—I have a cousin who lives in your house, and I will call on her one of these days, as soon as possible; come there and prefer your request."

"Pardon my boldness, Monsieur le Baron; but you will understand how I ventured to speak as I did; I have no protector."

"Aha!"

"Oh! monsieur, you misunderstand me," said she, lowering her eyes.

The baron thought the sun had disappeared.

"I am in despair, but I am a virtuous woman," she continued. "Six months ago I lost my only protector, Marshal Montcornet."

"Ah! you are his daughter?"

"Yes, monsieur, but he never acknowledged me."

"So that he could leave you part of his fortune."

"He left me nothing, monsieur, for no will was found."

"Oh! poor little woman, the marshal was taken off suddenly by apoplexy.—But don't lose hope, madame; we owe something to the daughter of one of the Chevaliers Bayard of the Empire."

Madame Marneffe bowed gracefully, and was as proud of her success as the baron of his.

"Where the devil was she coming from so early?" he asked himself, while he watched the undulating movement of her dress, to which she imparted a somewhat exaggerated grace. "Her face is too tired to be returning from the baths, and her husband is waiting for her. It's very puzzling and furnishes much food for thought."

When Madame Marneffe was safely housed, the baron desired to know what his daughter was doing in the shop. As he entered, still gazing at Madame Marneffe's windows, he very nearly collided with a pale-faced youth, with sparkling gray eyes, dressed in a summer coat of black merino, trousers of coarse ticking, and with gaiters of yellow leather over his shoes, who darted out like a wild man; and he watched him run toward Madame Marneffe's house, and go in.

As she glided into the shop, Hortense had immediately distinguished the famous group in a prominent position on a table placed in the centre of the floor within range of the door. Even without the circumstances to which she owed her foreknowledge of it, this masterpiece would in all probability have attracted the girl's attention by virtue of what we must call the *brio* of great things, for it is sure that, in Italy, she might have posed for the statue of *Brio.*

All the works of men of genius do not possess in the same degree the brilliancy, the splendor visible to the eyes of all, even of the ignorant. For example, certain of Raphaël's pictures, such as the famous *Transfiguration*, the *Madonna di Foligno*, the frescoes of the *Stanze* in the Vatican, do not compel instant admiration, as do the *Violin-Player* in the Sciarra gallery, the portraits of the Doni and the *Vision of Ezekiel* in the Pitti gallery, the *Bearing of the Cross* in the Borghèse gallery, the *Wedding of the Virgin* in the Bréra Museum at Milan. The *Saint John the Baptist* in the Tribune, and *Saint Luke Combing the Virgin's Hair* in the Academy of Rome, have not the fascination of the portraits of Leo X., and of the *Virgin* at Dresden. Nevertheless all are equally meritorious. More than that: the *Stanze*, the *Transfiguration*, the Cameos, and the three easel pictures at the Vatican represent the highest degree of sublimity and perfection. But these masterpieces demand from the most appreciative admirer intense application and study to be understood in all their details; while the *Violinist*, the *Wedding of the Virgin*, and the *Vision of Ezekiel* enter your heart at once through the double door of the eyes, and make a place for themselves there; you love to receive them thus without exertion; it is not the acme of art, but it is true pleasure. This fact proves that the element of chance enters into the production of artistic works, just as in some families there are beautiful children who come into the world without causing their mothers to suffer, and upon whom everything seems to smile, with whom everything succeeds; there are, in a word, flowers of genius as there are flowers of love.

This *brio*, an untranslatable Italian word which we are beginning to adopt, is the characteristic of first works. It is the fruit of the eager, daring impetuosity of youthful talent, a quality which manifests itself later at certain propitious moments; but then it does not come from the artist's heart; and instead of throwing it into his work as a volcano emits flame, he suffers it, he owes it to circumstances, to love, to rivalry, often to hatred, and more than all to the requirements of a reputation to be maintained.

Wenceslas' group was to his future works what the *Wedding of the Virgin* is to Raphaël's complete work, the first step of his talent, taken with inimitable grace, with the enthusiasm and fascinating exuberance of childhood, with its innate force concealed beneath pink and white flesh, dotted with dimples, like echoes of a mother's laughter. Prince

Eugène, they say, paid four hundred thousand francs for this picture, which would be worth a million to a country where there are no Raphaels, but no one would give that sum for one of the frescoes, which are, however, much superior as mere works of art.

Hortense restrained her admiration as she thought of the amount of her savings, but assumed an expression of indifference and said to the dealer:

"What is the price of this?"

"Fifteen hundred francs," he replied, glancing at a young man sitting on a stool in a corner of the shop.

This young man was struck dumb as he looked upon Baron Hulot's living masterpiece. Hortense, thus warned, recognized the artist by the flush which suffused his pale, pinched face, and she saw a spark set alight by her question gleaming in his gray eyes; she looked at his face, which was as thin and drawn as that of a monk immersed in asceticism, and she admired the well-shaped, rosy lips, the small, graceful chin, and the silky, chestnut locks of the Slav.

"If it were twelve hundred francs," said she, "I would tell you to send it to me."

"It's an antique, mademoiselle," observed the dealer, who believed, like all his brethren, that this *ne plus ultra* of bric-à-brac expressed all there was to be said.

"Excuse me, monsieur, it was done this year," she replied gently, "and I have come for the express purpose of asking you to send the artist to us, if he agrees to the price, for we may be able to secure some valuable orders for him."

"If the twelve hundred francs are for him, what will there be for me? I am a dealer," was the good-natured rejoinder.

"Ah! to be sure," said the girl in a disdainful tone.

"Oh! mademoiselle, take it! I will arrange matters with the dealer," cried the Livonian, beside himself with excitement.

Fascinated by Hortense's sublime beauty, and by her manifest love for the arts, he added:

"I am the maker of that group, and for ten days I have come here three times a day to see if any one would recognize its merit and make an offer for it. You are my first admirer, so take it!"

"Come with the dealer, monsieur, an hour from now—Here is my father's card," said Hortense.

Then, as the dealer went into an adjoining room to wrap the group in cloth, she added in an undertone, to the unbounded astonishment of the artist, who thought he must be dreaming:

"Out of regard for your future, Monsieur Wenceslas, do not show this card, or mention the name of your customer to Mademoiselle Fischer, for she is our cousin."

The words "our cousin," made the artist's head swim; he caught a glimpse of Paradise as he looked upon an Eve come thence to earth. He had dreamed of the lovely cousin of whom Lisbeth had spoken to him, as constantly as Hortense had dreamed of her cousin's lover, and when she entered the shop he thought:

"Ah! if she could be like this!"

The glance which the lovers exchanged can be imagined; it was a glance of flame, for virtuous lovers have not the least hypocrisy.

"Well, well, what the devil are you doing in here?" the father asked his daughter.

"I have spent the twelve hundred francs I had saved; come."

She took her father's arm, as he repeated:

"Twelve hundred francs!"

"Yes, thirteen hundred!—but you will lend me the difference."

"For what, pray, could you spend that amount of money in this shop?"

"Ah! that's the question!" replied the happy maiden; "if I have found a husband, it won't be a high price."

"A husband, my child, in this shop?"

"Tell me, father dear, would you forbid me to marry a great artist?"

"No, my child. A great artist in these days is a prince without a title; he has glory and fortune, the two greatest social advantages, after virtue," he added, pharisaically.

"Of course," said Hortense. "And what do you think of sculpture?"

"It's a very poor game," said Hulot, shaking his head. "One must have powerful patronage, in addition to great talent, for the government is the only customer. It is an art without a market; to-day there are no great people, nor great fortunes, nor entailed palaces, nor heirlooms. We can only find room for small pictures and small figures, so the arts are threatened by the *little.*"

"But a great artist who should find a market?—" queried Hortense.

"That would solve the problem."

"And who is powerfully supported?"

"Better still!"

"And noble?"

"Nonsense!"

"A count?"

"And a sculptor!"

"He has no fortune."

"And he reckons upon Mademoiselle Hortense Hulot's?" said the baron sarcastically, fixing his eyes searchingly upon his daughter's.

"This great artist, a count, and a sculptor, has just seen your daughter for the first time in his life, and for five minutes, Monsieur le Baron," retorted Hortense calmly. "Yesterday, you must know, my dear, good, little father, while you were at the Chamber, mamma fainted. This fainting, which she laid to her nerves, was caused by some disappointment connected with the breaking off of my marriage, for she told me that, to rid yourself of me—"

"She loves you too dearly to use an expression so—"

"Unparliamentary," laughed Hortense; "no, she didn't use those words; but I know myself that a marriageable daughter who doesn't get married is too heavy a burden for honest parents. Very well, she thinks that, if a man of energy and talent, who would be satisfied with a *dot* of thirty thousand francs, should make his appearance, we should all be very lucky! In short, she thought it advisable to prepare me for the modesty of my destiny, and to prevent my indulging in too splendid dreams.—Which means that I have no *dot* and that my marriage is broken off."

"Your mother is a dear, good, noble woman," replied the father, deeply humiliated, although well pleased with this disclosure.

"Yesterday she told me that you would allow her to sell her diamonds in order to find a husband for me; but I prefer that she keep her diamonds, and I would like to find a husband for myself. I think I have found the man, the suitor who comes up to mamma's programme—"

"Here!—on the Place du Carrousel!—in one morning?"

"Oh! papa, the trouble dates from further back than that," she retorted slyly.

"Come, my little girl, let us tell our dear father the whole story," said he coaxingly, concealing his uneasiness.

Under a promise of absolute secrecy, Hortense related the substance of her conversations with Cousin Bette. Then, when they reached home, she showed her father the famous seal as a proof of the sagacity of her judgment. The father in his inmost heart marveled at the profound address displayed by young women acting by instinct alone, as he realized the simplicity of the plan which this imaginary passion had suggested to the innocent girl in a single night.

"You shall soon see the *chef-d'œuvre* I have bought; the dealer is going to bring it and dear Wenceslas will come with him—The designer of such a group should make his fortune; but you must obtain for him, by your influence, an order for a statue and a room at the Institute—"

"How you go on!" cried the father. "Why, if we let you have your way, you would be married before the legal time, within eleven days—"

"Must we wait eleven days?" she replied with a laugh. "Why, in five minutes I loved him as you loved mamma when you first saw her! and he loves me as if we had known each other two years. Yes," she continued, in reply to a gesture from her father, "I read ten volumes of love in his eyes. And will not you and mamma accept him for my husband when he has proved to you that he is a man of genius? Sculpture is the foremost of the arts!" she cried, clapping her hands and dancing up and down. "Listen, I will tell you everything—"

"Is there something more, pray?"—queried her father with a smile.

Her absolute, prattling innocence had altogether reassured the baron.

"A confession of the greatest importance," said she. "I loved him before I knew him, but I have gone mad over him since I saw him an hour ago."

"A little too mad," commented the baron, delighting in the spectacle of this outspoken passion.

"Don't punish me for confiding in you," she rejoined. "It is sweet to cry into a father's heart: 'I love him, I am happy in loving him!' You are going to see my Wenceslas! Such a melancholy brow!—gray eyes in which the sun of genius shines!—and such a distinguished air! What do you think, is Livonia a beautiful country?—The idea of my Cousin Bette marrying that man, when she's old enough to be his mother!—Why it would be downright murder!—I am so envious of what she must have done for him! I fancy that she won't look with pleasure upon my marriage."

"We must conceal nothing from your mother, my angel," said the baron.

"I must not show her this seal, and I promised not to betray my cousin, who is afraid of mamma's raillery, so she says."

"You are very scrupulous about the seal, but you steal your Cousin Bette's lover!"

"I made a promise about the seal, but I made no promise about the man who made it."

This incident, patriarchal in its simplicity, was curiously in touch with the secret position of this family; and the baron, while applauding his daughter for her frankness, told her that henceforth she must leave the affair to the prudence of her parents.

"You understand, my little girl, that it is not for

you to ascertain whether your cousin's lover is a count, whether he has the proper papers to establish it, and whether his conduct offers guarantees of his nobility—As for your cousin, she refused five offers when she was twenty years younger, and I will undertake to say that she will be no obstacle."

"Listen to me, father, if you want me to be married don't mention our lover to my cousin until the moment has come to sign my marriage-contract—For six months I have been questioning her on this subject!—Somehow there's something inexplicable about her—"

"What is it?" said her father curiously.

"Well, her look is not pleasant when I go too far, even in a joking way, concerning her lover. Make your investigations; but let me sail my own boat. My frankness ought to set your mind at rest."

"The Lord said: 'Suffer little children to come unto me!' and you are one of those who are coming," rejoined the baron, with a slight infusion of irony.

After lunch, the dealer, the artist and the group were announced.

The sudden blush which overspread her daughter's face made the baroness anxious at first, then watchful, and Hortense's embarrassment, her flaming glance, soon revealed the mystery so poorly concealed in that youthful heart.

Count Steinbock, dressed in black from head to foot, seemed to the baron a very distinguished young man.

"Could you make a statue in bronze?" he asked, as he held the group in his arms.

Having admired it with a knowing air, he passed the bronze to his wife, who was not a connoisseur in sculpture.

"Isn't it lovely, mamma?" whispered Hortense in her mother's ear.

"A statue! monsieur, it is not so hard to do, as to arrange the figures in a clock like this one, which monsieur was kind enough to bring," was the artist's reply to the baron's question.

The dealer was engaged placing upon the buffet in the dining-room the wax model of the twelve Hours, whom the Loves were trying to catch.

"Leave that clock with me," said the baron, dumfounded by the beauty of the work, "I would like to show it to the Ministers of the Interior and of Commerce."

"Who is this young man you're so interested in?" the baroness asked her daughter.

"An artist rich enough to make the most of this model might make a hundred thousand francs out of it," said the dealer in curiosities, assuming a knowing and mysterious air, as he detected the good understanding between the maiden's eyes and the artist's. "To do it you would only have to sell twenty copies at eight thousand francs, for each copy would cost a thousand crowns to cast; but, if you number each copy and destroy the model, you would easily find twenty amateurs delighted to be the only ones to own the work."

"A hundred thousand francs!" cried Steinbock, looking from the dealer to Hortense, and from her to the baron and baroness.

"Yes, a hundred thousand francs!" the dealer repeated, "and if I was rich enough, I'd buy it of you myself for twenty thousand francs; for by destroying the model it becomes a valuable piece of property.—But one of the princes ought to pay thirty or forty thousand francs for this *chef-d'œuvre*, and adorn his salon with it. A clock has never been made, by an artist, which pleases the bourgeois and the connoisseur at the same time, and this one, monsieur, solves that difficulty—"

"Take this, monsieur," said Hortense, giving six gold-pieces to the dealer, who thereupon withdrew.

"Do not mention this visit to any one on earth," said the artist to the dealer, following him to the door. "If any one asks you where we carried the group, say to the Duc d'Hérouville, the famous collector who lives on Rue de Varenne."

The dealer nodded his head assentingly.

"Your name?" the baron asked the artist when he returned.

"Count Steinbock."

"Have you papers to prove your identity?"

"Yes, Monsieur le Baron, they are in the Russian and German languages, but without authentication—"

"Do you feel that you are capable of making a statue nine feet high?"

"Yes, monsieur."

"Well, if the persons whom I propose to consult

are pleased with your work, I can obtain for you the statue of Marshal Montcornet, which is to be erected over his tomb at Père-Lachaise. The Minister of War and the former officers of the Imperial Guard have given a large sum, in order to have the privilege of selecting the artist."

"Oh! monsieur, my fortune would be made!—" said Steinbock, overwhelmed by so much good luck at one time.

"Have no fear," replied the baron, graciously, "if the two ministers to whom I propose to show your group and this model, are well pleased with your work, your fortune is in a fair way—"

Hortense squeezed her father's arm so that she made him wince.

"Bring me your papers, and say nothing of your hopes to anyone, not even to our old Cousin Bette."

"Lisbeth!" cried Madame Hulot, arriving at some understanding of the end, but unable to guess at the means.

"I can give you proof of my skill by making a bust of Madame—" Wenceslas added.

Struck with Madame Hulot's beauty, the artist had been comparing the mother and daughter for some moments.

"Well, monsieur, life bids fair to become bright for you," said the baron, completely won by the refined and distinguished exterior of Count Steinbock. "You will soon learn that in Paris no one can possess talent without soon paying the penalty, and that all faithful work finds its reward here."

Hortense blushingly handed the young man a pretty Algerian purse containing sixty gold-pieces. The artist, always the gentleman, replied to Hortense's blush with a modest change of color easy to interpret.

"Can it be, by any chance, that this is the first money you have received for your works?" asked the baroness.

"Yes, madame, for my works of art, but not for my labor; for I have been a workman—"

"Very well, let us hope that my daughter's money will bring you good luck!" rejoined the baroness.

"And take it without scruple," added the baron, noticing that Wenceslas still held the purse in his hand without putting it in his pocket. "This sum will be made good by some great nobleman, by a prince, perhaps, who will surely return it to us with interest to possess this lovely work."

"Oh! I think too much of it, papa, to give it up to anybody in the world, even the Prince Royal!"

"I can make another group prettier than this for mademoiselle—"

"It wouldn't be this one," she replied. And, as if abashed at having said too much, she went into the garden.

"Then I shall break the mould and the model when I return home!" said Steinbock.

"Well, bring me your papers, and you will soon hear from me, if you realize my expectations, monsieur."

After this sentence the artist felt obliged to take

his leave. Having saluted Madame Hulot and Hortense, who returned from the garden expressly to receive his salute, he went and walked about in the Tuileries gardens, without the power or the courage to return to his attic, where his tyrant would plague him with questions and wrest his secret from him.

Hortense's lover imagined himself the producer of groups and statues by the hundred; he felt in himself the power to chisel marble with his own hand, like Canova, who was once as weak as he and was near dying of his weakness. He was transfigured by Hortense, who had become for him a living, visible inspiration.

*

"Well," said the baroness to her daughter, "what's the meaning of this?"

"It means, dear mamma, that you have seen our Cousin Bette's lover, who, I hope, is now mine.—But close your eyes, feign ignorance. Good heavens! I intended to conceal it all from you, and here I am telling you everything—"

"Adieu, my children," cried the baron, kissing his wife and daughter; "I may go and see the Nanny-goat, and I shall learn many things from her about the young man."

"Papa, be prudent," urged Hortense.

"Oh! my dear girl!" cried the baroness when Hortense had concluded the recital of her poem, the last stanza of which was the adventure of that morning, "my dear, little girl, Innocence will always be the greatest rake on earth!"

Sincere passions have an instinct of their own. Put a gourmand where he can take fruit from a plate, he will make no mistake, but will take the best, even without looking. In like manner, leave young women, well brought-up, absolutely unfettered in their choice of husbands, and if they are in a position to secure the ones they select they rarely go astray. Nature is infallible. The work of Nature, in this regard, is called Love at first sight. In love the first sight is second sight, pure and simple.

The baroness' satisfaction, although concealed beneath her maternal dignity, was no less great than her daughter's; for of the three methods of marrying Hortense, of which Crevel had spoken, the one most to her liking seemed in a fair way to succeed. She saw in this incident the response of Providence to her fervent prayers.

Mademoiselle Fischer's galley-slave, being compelled at last to return to his lodgings, conceived the idea of concealing the joy of the lover behind the joy of the artist in ecstasies with his first success.

"Victory! my group is sold to the Duc d'Hérouville, who is going to give me orders for more," he said, throwing down the twelve hundred francs in gold on the old maid's table.

He had, as we can imagine, put Hortense's purse in a safe place; he had it against his heart.

"Well," replied Lisbeth, "it's very lucky, for I am killing myself with work. You see, my child, money comes very slowly in the trade you have chosen, for this is the first you've received, and it's nearly five years that you've been digging! This is hardly enough to repay what you have cost me since you gave the note of hand that stands me instead of my savings. But don't be alarmed," she added, after counting the money, "it will all be used for you. We have here enough to make us secure for a year. In a year from now, you can pay your debts, and have a round sum of your own, if you go on in this way."

Seeing that his ruse was successful, Wenceslas told the old maid some wonderful tales about the Duc d'Hérouville.

"I mean that you shall dress all in black, in the fashion, and have a new stock of linen, for you ought to make a good appearance when you call upon your patrons," said Bette. "And then, too, you must have a larger and more suitable apartment than your horrid attic, and furnish it in good shape—how gay you are! You are not the same man," she added, eyeing Wenceslas keenly.

"Why they said that my group was a masterpiece."

"Very well, so much the better! Make more of them," retorted the old maid sharply, matter-of-fact to the last degree, and incapable of comprehending the joy of triumph, or beauty in art. "Think no more about what is sold, but make something else to sell. You have spent two hundred francs in cash, without counting your labor and your time, over that infernal *Samson*. It will cost you more than two thousand francs to have your clock cast. Look you, if you take my advice, you will finish those two little boys crowning the little girl with blue-bells; that will take the fancy of the Parisians! I am going to call on M. Graff, the tailor, before I go to M. Crevel's. Go up to your own room and let me dress."

The next day the baron, who had gone mad over Madame Marneffe, went to see Cousin Bette, who was vastly amazed, when she opened her door, to find him before her, for he had never paid her a visit.

She at once said to herself: "Can Hortense have designs on my lover?"—for, the night before, she had learned at M. Crevel's of the rupture of the marriage with the councilor of the royal court.

"What, cousin, you here? You come to see me for the first time in your life; surely it's not on account of my lovely eyes?"

"Lovely! they are indeed," replied the baron; "you have the loveliest eyes I have seen—"

"Why have you come? Really, I am ashamed to receive you in such a hovel."

The first of the two rooms comprised in Cousin Bette's suite served as parlor, dining-room, kitchen and work-room. The furniture was such as one finds in the houses of well-to-do mechanics: walnut chairs stuffed with straw, a small walnut dining-table, a work-table, colored engravings in frames of stained wood, little muslin curtains at the windows, a large walnut wardrobe, the floor well scrubbed and fairly shining with cleanliness; all without a speck of dust, but cold to the last degree, a perfect picture by Terburg in which nothing was lacking, not even the gray effect produced by a wall-paper once of a bluish tint and faded to the color of flax. As for the bedroom, no one had ever entered there.

The baron took it all in at a glance, saw the sign manual of slender circumstances upon everything, from the cast-iron stove to the cooking utensils, and was taken with nausea as he said to himself:

"So this is virtue!—Why have I come," he answered aloud. "You are too shrewd a girl not to end by guessing, and so it's much better to tell you," he cried, seating himself and drawing aside the plaited muslin curtain to look across the courtyard. "There is in this house a very pretty woman—"

"Madame Marneffe! Oh! I see!" said she, grasping the whole affair. "And Josépha?"

"Alas! cousin, there is no Josépha—I was turned out of doors like a lackey."

"And you would like?—" queried the cousin, regarding the baron with the dignity of a prude taking offence fifteen minutes too soon.

"As Madame Marneffe is a lady of very good position, the wife of a clerk, and as you can associate with her without compromising yourself," continued the baron, "I would like to see you on neighborly terms with her. Oh! never fear, she will show the very greatest consideration for the cousin of M. le Directeur!"

At that moment they heard the rustling of a dress on the staircase, accompanied by the footsteps of a lady in the daintiest of boots. The sounds ceased upon the landing. After two taps on the door Madame Marneffe made her appearance.

"Pardon me, mademoiselle, for this intrusion upon you, but I failed to find you yesterday when I came to pay you a visit. We are neighbors, and if I had known that you were the cousin of Monsieur the Councilor of State, I should, long ago, have asked you to use your influence with him. I saw him come in, and thereupon I took the liberty of coming;

for my husband, Monsieur le Baron, spoke to me of a report on the *personnel* of the department which will be submitted to the minister to-morrow."

She seemed to be agitated, and to be trembling; but she had simply run up the stairs.

"You have no need to play the petitioner, fair lady," replied the baron; "it is my place to ask the favor of an interview with you."

"Very well, if mademoiselle agrees, come!" said Madame Marneffe.

"Go, cousin, I will join you later," said cousin Bette prudently.

The lady relied so confidently upon M. le Directeur's visit, and upon the understanding between them, that she had not only made her own toilet with an eye to such an interview, but had made the toilet of her apartment as well. Early in the morning the rooms were filled with flowers purchased on credit. Marneffe had assisted his wife to scrub the furniture, and to restore lustre to the smallest objects by washing with soap, and brushing and dusting everything. It was Valérie's aim to be surrounded by an atmosphere of freshness in order to gratify M. le Directeur, and to gratify him sufficiently to earn the right to be cruel, to hold the sugar-plum out of reach, as for a child, by employing all the resources of modern tactics. She had taken Hulot's measure. Give a Parisian woman, who is driven to extremities, twenty-four hours, and she would overturn a ministry.

This man of the Empire, accustomed to the style

of love-making in vogue under the Empire, was sure to be absolutely ignorant of the modern style, the new-fashioned scruples, the different style of conversation invented since 1830, in which the *poor, weak woman* ends by causing herself to be looked upon as the victim of her lover's desires, as a Sister of Charity who dresses his wounds, as a ministering angel. This *new art of love* consumes an enormous number of pious words in doing the devil's work. Passion is a martyr. One aspires to the ideal, to the infinite; on one side and the other the lovers seek to become better through love. All these fine phrases are a mere excuse for displaying still more ardor in practice, more frenzy in the downfall than in the old days. This hypocrisy, the characteristic of our time, has infected the art of love-making with gangrene. The lovers deem themselves a pair of angels, and they act like a pair of devils, if they can. Love had not time to indulge in analysis of this sort between two campaigns, and, in 1809, it achieved successes as rapidly as the Empire. Under the Restoration, Hulot, the well-favored, becoming a ladies' man once more, had in the first place played the part of consoler to a few former lady friends, at that time fallen, like burned-out stars, from the political firmament, and subsequently, no longer young, allowed himself to be led captive by the Jenny Cadines and Josépha s.

Madame Marneffe had trained her batteries on learning the baron's antecedents, as narrated at length to her by her husband, on the strength of certain information gleaned at the department. As the comedy of modern sentiment might have for the baron the charm of novelty, Valérie's plan was formed, and, let us say at once, the test that she made of her power during that morning call fulfilled all her expectations. Thanks to her sentimental, capricious, romantic manœuvres, Valérie, without making any promises, obtained the post of deputy chief of bureau, and the Cross of the Legion of Honor for her husband.

This little warfare did not go forward without dinners at the *Rocher de Cancale*, theatre parties, and an abundance of gifts in the way of mantles, scarfs, dresses and jewels. The apartment on Rue du Doyenné was not satisfactory; the baron formed a plot to furnish a suite magnificently for her in a charming modern house on Rue Vanneau.

M. Marneffe obtained leave of absence for a fortnight, to be taken at any time within a month, to go to his province to settle some business matters there, and he also received an honorarium. He promised himself to take a little trip to Switzerland to study the fair sex.

While Baron Hulot's mind was thus occupied with his *protégée*, he did not forget his *protégé*. The Minister of Commerce, Comte Popinot, loved the arts; he gave two thousand francs for a copy of the *Samson* group, on condition that the mould should be broken so that there should be no *Samsons* in existence save Mademoiselle Hulot's and his own. This same group aroused the admiration of a prince, to whom the model of the clock was exhibited, and who ordered a copy of it; but his must be the only copy and he offered thirty thousand francs for it. The artists consulted, among whom was Stidmann, declared that the designer of those two works of art could be trusted to make a statue. Immediately the Maréchal Prince de Wissembourg, Minister of War, and president of the subscription committee for the monument to Maréchal Montcornet, called a meeting of the committee, by whom the execution of the statue was entrusted to Steinbock. Comte de Rastignac, then Under-Secretary of State, desired to have a specimen of the work of the artist whose fame was waxing great amid the acclamations of his rivals. He obtained from Steinbock the charming group of the two little boys crowning a little girl, and promised him a studio at the government marble warehouse, situated, as every one knows, at Gros-Caillou.

This was success, but such success as comes to one at Paris; that is to say, unreasoning, and likely to be the undoing of those whose shoulders and loins are not fitted to bear it, as, by the way, is often the case. Count Wenceslas Steinbock was talked of in the newspapers and reviews, but neither he nor Mademoiselle Fischer had the slightest suspicion of it. Every day, as soon as Mademoiselle Fischer went out to dine, Wenceslas called upon the baroness. He passed an hour or two there, except on the day on which Bette dined with her cousin Hulot. This state of affairs lasted for some days.

The baron, assured as to the rank and civil status of Count Steinbock; the baroness, delighted with his disposition and his morals, and Hortense, proud of her sanctioned love, of the celebrity of her suitor, no longer hesitated to speak of the marriage; lastly, the artist himself was at the summit of bliss, when Madame Marneffe's indiscretion put everything in jeopardy. It happened in this way.

Lisbeth, between whom and Madame Marneffe Baron Hulot was desirous to arrange an intimacy, so that he might have an eye in that household, had already dined with Valérie, who, for her part, wishing to have an ear in the Hulot family, treated the old maid with great kindness. It occurred to Valérie to invite Mademoiselle Fischer to the house-warming in the new apartment in which she was to be installed. The old maid, overjoyed to find another house at which to dine, and fascinated by Madame Marneffe, had become very fond of her. Of all the persons with whom she had been on friendly terms, not one had expended so much for her. In fact, Madame Marneffe, outdoing herself in little attentions to Mademoiselle Fischer, was in much the same position, so to speak, in respect to her, that Cousin Bette occupied in respect to the baroness, M. Rivet, Crevel, all those in short with whom she was accustomed to dine. The Marneffes aroused Cousin Bette's especial sympathy by allowing her to see the extreme destitution of their household, and painting it, as always, in its most vivid colors; friends who were in their debt but had proved ungrateful; sickness; a mother, Madame Fortin, from whom they had concealed her straitened circumstances, and who died in the belief that she was still wealthy, thanks to superhuman sacrifices, etc.

"Poor people!" she said to her cousin Hulot. "You are quite right to take an interest in them, they deserve it, for they are so brave, so kind. They can barely live with the thousand crowns salary of the office of deputy-chief, for they have run in debt since the death of Marêchal Montcornet! It's downright barbarism for the government to expect a clerk who has a wife and children, to live in Paris on a salary of twenty-four hundred francs."

In this way a young woman, who made a show of friendship for her, who told her everything, consulting her, flattering her, and apparently proposing to be guided by her, became in a short time dearer to eccentric Cousin Bette than any of her relations.

Meanwhile the baron, discovering, to his admiration, in Madame Marneffe a modesty, an education and manners which neither Jenny Cadine nor Josépha nor their friends had ever exhibited, had fallen in love with her within a month, with an old man's passion, an insensate passion which seemed reasonable enough. Indeed he saw no signs of mockery, no taste for revelry, no mad extravagance, no depravity, no contempt for social amenities, nor that absolute independence, which in the case of the actress and the singer, had caused all his woes. He was free likewise from the rapacity characteristic of courtesans, which may be compared to the thirst of the sand.

Madame Marneffe, who had become his friend and his confidante, made an extraordinary ado about accepting the least thing from him.

"It's all right so far as offices are concerned and gratuities, and anything you can obtain for us from the government; but do not begin by dishonoring the woman you claim to love," Valérie would say; "otherwise, I shall not believe you—and I love to believe you," she would add with a glance à la Sainte Thérèse taking a peep at heaven.

With every gift there was a fortress to be carried, a scruple of conscience to be overcome. The poor baron resorted to stratagem to offer her a trifle, very costly by the way, congratulating himself on having at last fallen in with a virtuous woman, on having found the realization of his dreams. In this primitive household, as he styled it, the baron was as much a god as in his own home. M. Marneffe seemed to be a thousand leagues from entertaining a thought that the Jupiter of his department purposed to descend upon his wife in a shower of gold, and he made himself the footman of his august chief.

Madame Marneffe, aged twenty-three, a pure and timorous bourgeoise, a lovely flower hidden in Rue du Doyenné, could know nothing of the dissipation and demoralization of courtesans, which were now disgusting beyond measure to the baron, for he had never yet known the charm of the virtue which resists, and the shrinking Valérie made him taste that charm, as the song has it, *the whole length of the river.*

When matters had once arrived at this stage between Hector and Valérie, no one will be surprised to learn that Valérie soon knew from Hector the secret of the approaching marriage of Steinbock, the great artist, with Hortense. Between a lover without privileges, and a wife who does not readily make up her mind to become a mistress, oral and moral conflicts take place wherein the word often betrays the thought, just as, in a fencing match, the foil becomes as active as the sword in a duel. At such a time the most prudent man imitates M. de Turenne. So it was that the baron had hinted at the entire freedom of action which his daughter's marriage would give him, in reply to the loving Valérie, who had more than once cried:

"I cannot understand how one can commit a sin for a man who is not wholly one's own!"

Already the baron had sworn a thousand times, that, *for twenty-five years*, everything had been at an end between Madame Hulot and himself.

"They say she is so lovely," Madame Marneffe replied; "I must have proofs."

"You shall have them," said the baron, overjoyed at this demand, whereby his Valérie seemed to compromise herself.

"And how? You must never leave me," rejoined Valérie.

Hector was thereupon compelled to disclose his

plans then in process of execution on Rue Vanneau, to prove to his Valérie that it was his purpose to give to her that half of life which belongs to a lawful wife, assuming that the day and night divide equally the lives of civilized people. He spoke of leaving his wife without scandal by leaving her alone as soon as his daughter was married. The baroness would then pass all her time with Hortense and the young Hulots; he was certain of his wife's submission.

"And then, my little angel, my real life, my true home will be on Rue Vanneau."

"Lord, how coolly you dispose of me!—" said Madame Marneffe. "And my husband?—"

"That ragamuffin!"

"Indeed beside you he is just that—" she answered with a laugh.

Madame Marneffe had a frantic longing to see the young Count Steinbock after she had heard his story; it may be that she desired to obtain some specimen of his handiwork while they still lived beneath the same roof. Her curiosity displeased the baron to such a degree that Valérie swore that she would never look at Wenceslas. But, after she had secured her reward for abandoning this whim, in the shape of a complete tea-service in old Sèvres pâte tendre, she retained the desire at the bottom of her heart, as if written upon a memorandum. And so, one day, when she had asked *her* Cousin Bette to come and take coffee with her in her apartment, she led the conversation round to her lover, in order to ascertain if she could see him without risk.

"My darling," said she, for each called the other "my darling," "why have you never introduced your lover to me?—Do you know that he has lately become famous?"

"He, famous?"

"Why, everyone is talking about him!—"

"Nonsense!" cried Lisbeth.

"He is to make the statue of my father, and I could help him materially to make his work a success, for Madame Montcornet can't, as I can, loan him a miniature by Sain, a chef-d'œuvre done in 1809, before the Wagram campaign and given to my poor mother; in short, a youthful, handsome Montcornet—"

Sain and Augustin together held the sceptre of miniature-painting under the Empire.

"He is going to make a statue, do you say, my dear?—" asked Lisbeth.

"Nine feet high, ordered by the War Department. Well, well, where have you been? I have to tell you the news! Why the government is going to give Count Steinbock a studio and apartments at Gros-Caillou, at the marble warehouse; your Pole may be the director there, a post worth two thousand francs, a ring on his finger—"

"How do you know all this, when I know nothing of it?" said Lisbeth at last rousing from her stupor.

"Tell me, my dear little Cousin Bette," said Madame Marneffe, graciously, "are you capable of a devoted friendship that will stand every test? Do you wish that we should be to each other like sisters? Will you swear to have no more secrets from me than I have from you? to be my spy as I will be yours?—Above all, will you swear never to sell me either to my husband or to M. Hulot, and never to confess that it was I who told you—"

Madame Marneffe paused in this *picador's* work, for Cousin Bette frightened her. The Lorrainer's face had become terrible to look upon. Her piercing black eyes glared like those of a tiger. Her expression resembled that we imagine the pythonesses to have worn; she ground her teeth together to prevent them from chattering, and a terrible convulsion caused her whole frame to tremble. She had thrust her claw-like hand between her cap and her hair, to grasp it and so sustain her head, which had become too heavy; she was in a raging fever! The smoke of the fire which consumed her seemed to find vent through her wrinkles, as through so many crevices plowed by a volcanic eruption. It was a sublime spectacle.

"Well, why do you stop?" said she, in a hollow voice; "I will be to you all that I was to him. Oh! I would have given my blood for him!—"

"You love him then?—"

"As if he were my child!—"

"Oh well," rejoined Madame Marneffe, breathing more freely, "if you love him in that way, you will soon be very happy, for you wish him to be happy, do you not?"

Lisbeth replied with a nod as swift as a mad-woman's.

"He is to marry your second cousin in a month."

"Hortense?" cried the old maid, beating her brow and rising.

"Aha! then you do love this young man?" queried Madame Marneffe.

"My dear, we are friends for life and death," said Mademoiselle Fischer. "Yes, if you have an attachment for anybody it shall be sacred to me. In short, your vices will become virtues in my eyes, for I shall stand in need of your vices, myself!"

"So you are living with him, are you?" cried Valérie.

"No, I would have been a mother to him—"

"Oh! then I don't understand it at all," said Valérie; "for in that case you are neither fooled nor deceived, and you ought to be very happy to see him make a good marriage; that gives him a fair start. Besides all is over so far as you're concerned. Our artist goes to Madame Hulot's every day, as soon as you go out to dinner—"

"Adeline!—" muttered Lisbeth. "Oh, Adeline, you shall pay me for this, I'll make you uglier than I am!—"

"Why, you're as pale as a corpse!" cried Valérie. "Is there something then, that ?— Oh! what an idiot I am! the mother and daughter must suspect that you would put obstacles in the way of this love affair, as they conceal it from you," cried Madame Marneffe; "but if you are not living with the young man, my darling, all this is more incomprehensible to me than my husband's heart—"

"Oh! you don't know," rejoined Lisbeth, "you don't know what an underhand business this is! it's the last blow that kills! I have received blows that wounded me to the very soul! You don't know that ever since I was old enough to feel I have been sacrificed to Adeline! They beat me, and fondled her! I went about dressed like a scullery-maid, and she was rigged out like a lady. I dug in the garden, I picked beans; and she, why her ten fingers never moved except to arrange her gewgaws!—She married the baron, she came to the Emperor's court to shine, and I remained in my village till 1809, waiting for a suitable match, four years; then they brought me here, but only to make a work-girl of me, and offer me husbands in the shape of clerks, and captains who looked like porters!—I have lived on their leavings for twenty-six years—And now it happens just as in the Old Testament, the poor man owns a single lamb which is his only treasure, and the rich man who has whole flocks covets the poor man's lamb and steals it—without warning, without asking for it, Adeline filches my happiness!—Adeline! Adeline! I shall see you in the mire, lower down than I!—Hortense, whom I did love, has deceived me—The baron—No, that isn't possible. Come, tell me again the things that may be true in all this."

"Be calm, my darling—"

"Valérie, my dear angel, I will be calm," replied the strange creature, seating herself. "There is only one thing that will restore my reason; give me a proof !—"

"Why, your Cousin Hortense owns the *Samson* group, and here is a lithograph of it published by a review; she paid for it out of her savings; and it's the baron who, in his future son-in-law's interest, is pushing him ahead and obtaining all these commissions for him."

"Water!—water!" exclaimed Lisbeth after a glance at the lithograph, beneath which she read: *Group belonging to Mademoiselle Hulot d'Ervy.* "Water! my head's on fire; I am going mad!"

Madame Marneffe brought water; the old maid removed her cap, took down her black hair, and dipped her head in the basin which her new friend held for her; over and over again she deluged her forehead, and checked the inflammation that had begun. After this immersion she recovered her self-control completely.

"Not a word," said she to Madame Marneffe, as she wiped her head, "not a word of all this.—Look at me!—I am perfectly calm, and it is all forgotten! I am thinking of something very different!"

"She will be at Charenton to-morrow, that's certain," said Madame Marneffe to herself, with a glance at the Lorrainer.

"What shall I do?" continued Lisbeth. "Look you, my little angel, I must just hold my tongue, bow my head, and go straight to the tomb as the water goes to the river. What could I attempt? I should like to grind them all to dust, Adeline, her daughter and the baron! But what can one poor relation do against a whole rich family?—It would be the story of the earthen pot and the iron pot over again."

"Yes, you are right," Valérie replied; "you must simply look out and pull all the hay you can out of the manger.—Such is life in Paris."

"And I shall die very soon," said Lisbeth, "if I lose that child, to whom I thought I should always be a mother, with whom I expected to pass my whole life—"

Tears were in her eyes, and she stopped. This exhibition of feeling on the part of this woman of fire and brimstone made Madame Marneffe shudder.

"After all, I have found you," she said, taking Valérie's hand; "that's a consolation in this great disaster—We will love each other dearly; and why should we part? I shall never poach on your preserves. No one will ever fall in love with me!—every one of those who proposed to me would have married me because I was under my cousin's protection.—To have the energy to carry Paradise by storm, and to waste it in grubbing for bread, water, rags and an attic! Ah! that's true martyrdom, my dear! I have withered away under it."

She paused abruptly and darted into Madame Marneffe's blue-eyes a lowering glance which pierced that charming creature's soul, as a dagger-blade might have pierced her heart.

"But why talk about it?" she cried, reproaching herself. "Ah! I never said so much before, not I!—

"*The trick will come back to its master!*"—she added, after a pause, quoting an expression children use. "As you wisely suggest: I must sharpen my teeth and pull all the hay I can out of the manger."

"You are right," said Madame Marneffe, so alarmed by this outburst that she no longer remembered having uttered that apothegm. "I think you have the right idea, my love. Life's none too long, you know, and we must get as much as we can out of it, and use others for our own ends.—I have come to that already, young as I am! I was brought up as a spoiled child, my father made an ambitious marriage and almost forgot me, after making me his idol and bringing me up like a queen's daughter! My poor mother, who fed me on the loveliest dreams, from my cradle, died of disappointment when I married a paltry clerk on twelve hundred francs salary,—a cold-blooded old rake of thirty-nine, corrupt as a whole bagnio, and who saw in me only what your suitors saw in you, a means of helping on his fortunes!—Well, I ended by finding out that that beast of a man is the best of husbands. As he prefers the dirty street-walking trulls to me, he leaves me free. If he takes all his salary himself, he never asks me to explain the source of my income—"

At that point she paused, like one who feels that she is being carried too far by the torrent of confidence, and, impressed by the attention with which Lisbeth was listening to her, she deemed it necessary to make sure of her, before disclosing to her the inmost secrets of her heart.

"You see, my love, what confidence I have in you!—" continued Madame Marneffe, and Lisbeth replied with a most reassuring gesture.

One often swears with the eyes and with a movement of the head, more solemnly than at the Assizes.

"I have all the externals of virtue," Madame Marneffe resumed, laying her hand upon Lisbeth's as if to accept her pledge; "I am a married woman, and I am my own mistress, to such a point that if Marneffe takes a fancy to say good-bye to me when he starts for the office in the morning, and finds my chamber-door locked, he goes his way quite undisturbed. He cares less for his child than I care for one of the marble children playing at the foot of one of the *Fleuves*, at the Tuileries. If I don't come home to dinner, he dines very pleasantly with the maid, for the maid is everything to monsieur, and after dinner he goes out, not to return until twelve or one o clock. Unfortunately, for a year I have had no maid, which means that I have been a widow for a year—I have had but one passion, one stroke of luck—that was a rich Brazilian, who went away a year ago, all through my fault! He went to sell his property, turn everything into money, so that he could settle in France. What will he find left of his Valérie? a dust-heap. Pshaw! it will be his fault and not mine, why didn't he come back sooner? Perhaps he has been shipwrecked too, like my virtue."

"Adieu, my dear," said Lisbeth abruptly; "we

won't live apart any more. I love you and esteem you, and I am yours! My cousin has been tormenting me to go and live in your house that is to be, on Rue Vanneau; I wouldn't do it, for I guessed the cause of his sudden kindness—"

"Yes, you were to keep an eye on me, I know that," said Madame Marneffe.

"That's just the reason of his generosity," rejoined Lisbeth. "In Paris most benefactions are speculations, just as most ingratitude is revenge! —One treats a poor relation like the rats to whom one gives a bit of bacon. I will accept the baron's offer, for this house has become hateful to me. Surely we both have wit enough to know how to hold our tongues as to what would injure us, and to say what ought to be said; so, no indiscretion, and a friendship—"

"That will stand any test!—" cried Madame Marneffe joyfully, delighted to have a defensive weapon, a confidante, a sort of virtuous aunt. "Look you! the baron is doing things handsomely on Rue Vanneau—"

"I should say so," replied Lisbeth, "he has laid out thirty thousand francs! Deuce take me, if I know where he got them, for Josépha, the singer, drained him dry. Oh! you have fallen on your feet," she added. "The baron would steal for the woman who holds his heart between two little soft, white hands like yours."

"Well, then, my love," rejoined Madame Marneffe, with the courtesan's sense of security, which is but recklessness, "just take everything here that will look well in your new lodgings—the commode, the mirrored-wardrobe, the carpet, the hangings—"

Lisbeth's eyes dilated with frantic delight; she dared not believe in the reality of such a gift.

"Why, you do more for me in one moment than my rich relations in thirty years!—" she cried. "They never so much as asked me if I had any furniture! At his first visit, a few weeks since, the baron made a rich man's grimace at sight of my poverty.—But, I thank you, my love, I will be worth all this to you; later you will see how!"

Valérie accompanied *her* cousin Bette to the staircase where the two women kissed each other.

"How her breath smells!—" said the pretty creature to herself when she was alone; "I'll not kiss *my* cousin very often! However, I must take care and humor her, and she'll be very useful to me, she'll put me in a way to make my fortune."

Like a true Parisian Creole, Madame Marneffe abhorred exertion; she was as easy-going as a cat, an animal that never runs or hurries, unless driven to it by necessity. In her eyes life should be all pleasure, and the pleasure obtainable without trouble. She loved flowers, provided that someone sent them to her. She could not conceive of a theatre party without a good box all to herself, and a carriage to go and come. These courtesan's tastes Valérie inherited from her mother, who was overwhelmed with presents by General Montcornet during his sojourns at Paris, and who had seen all the world at her feet for twenty years; being very extravagant she squandered everything, consumed everything, in the luxurious mode of life of which the secret has been lost since the fall of Napoleon. The grandees of the Empire rivaled, in their vices, the great noblemen of a former time. Under the Restoration the nobility never forgot that they had been whipped and despoiled; and so, barring two or three exceptions, they had become economical, virtuous, provident, commonplace in a word, and utterly devoid of grandeur. Later, 1830 consummated the work of 1793. In France, henceforth, there will be great names, but no more great families, except in the event of political upheavals, difficult to forecast. Everything bears the stamp of personal character. The fortune of the wisest is ephemeral. The family has been destroyed.

The powerful embrace of the distress which was gnawing at Valérie's heart on the day when, according to her husband's expression, she *made* Hulot, had determined that young woman to use her beauty as a means of making her fortune. So it was that she had felt for some days the necessity of having with her, in her mother's place, a devoted friend to whom she might confide what she ought not to confide to her maid, and who might go and come, and act and think for her, an *âme damnée* in short, who would consent to an unequal division of the good things of life. Now she had divined, as had Lisbeth herself, the baron's purpose in concluding an alliance between them. Being counseled thereto by the redoubtable wit of the Parisian Creole, who passes her time lying at full length upon a couch, turning the lantern of her observation into all the dark corners of men's hearts and emotions and schemings, she had conceived the plan of making an accomplice of the spy. Probably her appalling candor was premeditated; she had detected the real nature of this excitable old maid, so passionate over trifles, and wished to make a friend of her. Thus this conversation was like the stone the traveler throws into a chasm to ascertain its depth. And Madame Marneffe was dismayed to find an Iago and Richard III. combined in this apparently weak, humble, and by no means alarming, person.

*

In an instant Cousin Bette was herself once more; in an instant that wild Corsican nature, having broken the feeble bonds which held it down, once more stood threateningly erect, as the branch of a tree escapes from the hands of the child who pulls it down to him to steal the green fruit.

To every student of social questions, the abundance, the perfection and the rapid succession of ideas in virgin natures will always be objects of admiration.

Virginity, like all abnormal things, has a special richness, an absorbing grandeur of its own. Life, the forces of which are expended economically, has taken on in the virgin nature a quality of incalculable resistance and endurance. The brain is enriched in the sum total of its reserved faculties. When undefiled creatures have occasion to call upon their bodies or their minds, when they resort to action or to thought, they find at such times that their muscles are of steel, that their intellects are infused with sagacity, and they are conscious of a diabolic strength or the black magic of will.

In this view the Virign Mary, considered for a moment simply as a symbol, by her grandeur casts in the shade all the Hindoo, Greek, or Egyptian types. Virginity, mother of great things, *magna parens rerum* holds in her lovely white hands the key to the worlds above. In short, this grand and exalted exception deserves all the honors which the Catholic Church has conferred upon it.

In a moment then, Cousin Bette became the Mohican, whose snares cannot be avoided, whose dissimulation is impenetrable, whose swift decision is based upon the incredible perfection of his organs. She was the personification of uncompromising hate and revenge, as they exist in Italy, in Spain and the East. These two emotions, which have twice the force of friendship, or of love in their most extreme form, are known only in countries bathed by the sun. But Lisbeth was first of all a child of Lorraine, that is to say, bold in deception.

She did not willingly assume this last part of her rôle; she attempted to do a singular thing, the result of her profound ignorance. She had the same idea of a prison that all children have, she confounded solitary confinement with imprisonment. Solitary confinement is the superlative degree of imprisonment, and is a prerogative of the criminal tribunals.

When she left Madame Marneffe, Lisbeth hurried to Monsieur Rivet's and found him in his office.

"Well, my dear Monsieur Rivet," said she, after she had turned the key in the office-door, "you were right; these Poles! they're *canaille*—faithless, lawless people, all of them."

"People who would like to set Europe on fire," said the pacific Rivet, "ruin all sorts of trade and traders for a country which is all swamp, they say, and filled with disgusting Jews, to say nothing of the Cossacks and peasants, varieties of wild beasts wrongly classed with the human race. These Poles misunderstand the present age. We are no longer savages! War is dying out, my dear young lady, it vanished with the kings. Our time is the triumph of commerce, industry and the middle-class shrewdness which made Holland what she is. Yes," he continued, warming to his subject, "we live in an age when the nations are sure to obtain everything by the lawful development of their liberties, and by the *pacific* working of constitutional institutions; that's just what the Poles know nothing about, and I hope—You were saying, my dear?" he added, breaking off his sentence, as he saw by his workgirl's expression that his lofty political flights were beyond her comprehension.

"Here are the papers," said Bette; "if I don't want to lose my three thousand two hundred and ten francs I must put that rascal in prison.—"

"Aha! I told you so!" cried the oracle of the Saint-Denis quarter.

The Rivet establishment, successor to Pons Brothers, was still located on Rue des Mauvaises-Paroles, in what was once the Langeais mansion, built by that illustrious family in the days when the great noblemen were grouped about the Louvre.

"For that reason I blessed you as I came along!—" replied Lisbeth.

"If he has no suspicion he'll be in limbo at four

o'clock in the morning," said the magistrate, consulting his almanac to ascertain the hour of sunrise; "but not until day after to-morrow, for we can't imprison him without notifying him that application has been made for a warrant of arrest, with extra-judicial notice of the time fixed. And so—"

"What an idiotic law," said Cousin Bette, "for the debtor will run away."

"He has a right to do so," said the magistrate with a smile. "So, look, this is the way—"

"As for that, I will take the paper," said Bette interrupting him. "I'll hand it to him and say that I have been compelled to raise money and that the lender demanded that formality. I know my Pole; he won't even unfold the paper, but will light his pipe with it!"

"Ah! not bad! not bad, Mademoiselle Fischer! Very well, don't be afraid; the affair will be put through in haste. But one moment! to shut a man up isn't the whole of it; that judicial luxury is only resorted to in order to get at his money. Who will pay you?"

"They who give him money."

"Oh yes! I forgot that the Minister of War has commissioned him to make the monument to be erected to one of our customers. Ah! the house has furnished many a uniform for General Montcornet, he soon blackened them in the smoke of the cannon! What a gallant fellow! and he paid promptly!"

Though a marshal of France may have saved the Emperor or his country, " he paid promptly " will always be his warmest eulogy in the mouth of a tradesman.

"Well, Monsieur Rivet, on Saturday you shall have your flat tassels. By the way, I am leaving Rue du Doyenné, and am going to live on Rue Vanneau."

"You are doing wisely, it has pained me to see you in that hole, which dishonors, yes! notwithstanding my distaste for anything resembling opposition, I dare to say that it dishonors the Louvre and the Place du Carrousel. I adore Louis-Philippe, he is my idol, he is the august and perfect type of the class upon which he has founded his dynasty, and I shall never forget what he has done for the gold-lace trade by reorganizing the National Guard—"

"When I hear you talk in that way," said Lisbeth, "I wonder why you aren't a deputy."

"They distrust my attachment to the dynasty," rejoined Rivet, "my political foes are the King's. Ah! he's a noble character, it's a fine family; in short," he continued, resuming his argument, "he's our ideal; morals, economy, everything! But the "completion" of the Louvre was one of the conditions on which we gave the crown, and the Civil List, to which no limit of time was fixed, leaves, I admit, the heart of Paris in a shocking state.—Just for the reason that I am *juste milieu* myself I would like to see the middle of Paris in a different condition. Your neighborhood makes one shudder.—You'd have been murdered there some day

—By the way, your Monsieur Crevel is appointed major of his legion; I hope we shall furnish his new epaulettes."

"I dine there to-day, and I will send him to you."

Lisbeth thought that she would have her Livonian all to herself, flattering herself that she was about to cut off all communication between him and the world. The artist, as he would cease to work, would be forgotten, like a man buried in a cavern, where she alone would go to see him. She had two days of bliss before her, for she hoped to deal a deadly blow at the baroness and her daughter.

To reach Monsieur Crevel's house on Rue des Saussayes, she went by the Pont du Carrousel, Quai Voltaire, Quai d'Orsay, Rue Bellechasse, Rue de l'Université, Pont de la Concorde, and Avenue de Marigny. This illogical route was marked out for her by the logic of the passions, which are always bitterly hostile to the legs. So long as she was on the quays Cousin Bette walked very slowly, gazing at the right bank of the Seine. Her reckoning was accurate. She had left Wenceslas dressing, and she reasoned that as soon as he was rid of her, the lover would go to the baroness's by the shortest road. Indeed, just as she was walking along the parapet of Quai Voltaire, devouring the stream with her gaze, and walking in imagination on the other bank, she recognized the artist as he came through the wicket of the Tuileries garden on his way to the Pont Royal. She overtook her faithless one there, and was able to follow him unseen, for lovers rarely turn; she followed him as far as Madame Hulot's house and saw him go in like a frequent visitor.

This last proof, which confirmed Madame Marneffe's confidential statements, drove Lisbeth to frenzy.

She reached the abode of the newly-chosen major, in that state of mental irritation which leads to murder, and found Père Crevel in his salon, awaiting the arrival of his children, Monsieur and Madame Hulot junior.

But Célestin Crevel is so perfect and outspoken a representative of the Parisian parvenu, that it is difficult to enter the dwelling of this fortunate successor of César Birotteau without some ceremony. Célestin Crevel is a whole world in himself; and he deserves, more than Rivet, the honors of the palette, because of the important part he plays in this domestic drama.

Have you noticed how prone we are in childhood, or in the beginnings of social life, to fashion a model for ourselves with our own hands, often without our own volition? For instance, a clerk in a banking-house, as he enters his employer's salon, dreams of possessing a similar salon himself. If he prospers, the magnificence that will sit enthroned under his roof twenty years later will not conform to the fashions then in vogue, but to the old-fashioned magnificence which caught his fancy years before. Nobody knows all the absurd performances attributable to this retrospective jealousy, just as nobody knows how many idiotic acts are due to the unacknowledged rivalry which impels men to copy the pattern they have set themselves, to expend their strength to attain the emptiness of moonshine. Crevel was deputy-mayor because his employer had been deputy-mayor; he was a major because he had envied César Birotteau's epaulettes. In like manner, impressed as he had been, by the marvellous creations of the architect Grindot at the time when fortune had carried his employer to the top of the wheel, Crevel, as he expressed it, *didn't think twice about it,* when he came to furnish his own apartments; he applied, with eyes closed and purse open, to Grindot, then altogether forgotten. We cannot tell how long extinct celebrities may live on, when upheld by belated admirers.

Grindot thereupon started in for the thousandth time on one of his white and gold salons hung with red damask. The violet-wood furniture, carved without delicacy, as are the carvings of to-day, had aroused in the province a just pride in Parisian handicraft at the time of the Exposition of industrial products. The candelabra, the sconces, the fender, the chandelier, the clock, were all in the *rocaille* style. The round table, immovably fixed in the centre of the salon, had a marble top inlaid with all varieties of Italian and antique marbles brought from Rome, arranged in a sort of mineralogical map, strongly resembling a tailor's samples, and which periodically excited the admiration of all the good bourgeois whom Crevel invited to his house. The portraits of the late Madame Crevel, of Crevel, of his daughter and his son-in-law, products of the pencil of Pierre Grassou, the favorite painter with the bourgeoisie, to whom Crevel owed his absurd Byronic attitude, were hung in couples upon the walls. The frames, which cost a thousand francs each, were quite in harmony with all this restaurant-like splendor, which would surely have made a true artist shrug his shoulders in disdain.

Never did wealth lose the slightest occasion to exhibit its stupidity. We might reckon up ten Venices in Paris to-day if our retired merchants had the instinctive appreciation of great things which distinguishes the Italians. Even in our days a Milanese merchant bequeaths five hundred thousand francs to the *Duomo* to gild the colossal Virgin which crowns its cupola. Canova, in his testament, enjoins upon his brother to build a church worth four millions, and the brother adds something of his own.

Would a citizen of Paris—and they all have, like Rivet, love for their Paris at the bottom of their hearts—ever think of building the spires which are lacking on the towers of Notre-Dame? Just reckon up the sums that revert to the State for lack of heirs. All the much-needed embellishment of Paris might have been completed for the money expended upon absurdities in cardboard statuary, gilded pasteboard, miscalled sculptures, during the past fifteen years by individuals of the genus Crevel.

At the end of the salon was a smaller room

magnificently furnished with tables and cabinets in imitation of Boulle.

The bed-room, with chintz hangings and chintz-covered furniture, also opened into the salon. Mahogany, in all its glory, held sway in the dining-room, where the walls were adorned with Swiss landscapes, handsomely framed. Père Crevel, who dreamed of a trip to Switzerland, was determined to own that country in the form of paintings until such time as he should visit the reality. Crevel, a former deputy-mayor, decorated, and an officer in the National Guard, had, as we see, faithfully reproduced all the grandeur, even in the way of furniture, of his unfortunate predecessor. Where the one had fallen, under the Restoration, the other, altogether forgotten, had risen, not by any mere freak of fortune, but by the force of events. In revolutions, as in tempests at sea, the solidly built vessels go to the bottom, while objects of little weight float on the surface of the water. César Birotteau, a royalist, in high favor, envied, became the target for the bourgeois opposition, while the triumphant bourgeoisie was typified in Crevel.

This suite, rented at a thousand crowns, and which overflowed with all the vulgarities that money can buy, occupied the first floor of an old mansion, standing between courtyard and garden. Everything there was kept as carefully as beetles at an entomologist's, for Crevel lived there very little.

This luxurious "abode" constituted the legal

domicile of the ambitious bourgeois. His establishment consisted of a cook and a valet de chambre; he hired two additional servants, and ordered his state dinner at Chevet, when he feasted his political friends, people to be dazzled, or when he received his family. The seat of Crevel's real existence, formerly at Mademoiselle Héloïse Brisetout's on Rue Notre-Dame de Lorette, had been transferred, as we have seen, to Rue Chauchat. Every morning the *former merchant*—all retired tradesmen style themselves *former merchants*—passed two hours on Rue des Saussayes, looking after matters of business, and gave the rest of his time to Zaïre, to Zaïre's extreme annoyance. Orosmane-Crevel had a hard and fast bargain with Mademoiselle Héloïse; she owed him five hundred francs worth of pleasure every month, without arrearages. Crevel also paid for his dinner and all the *extras*. This contract, with options, for he made her many presents, seemed a thrifty one to the ex-lover of the famous songstress. Talking on this subject with merchants who had lost their wives and were too much attached to their daughters, he would say that it was much better to use hired horses than to have a stable of one's own. Nevertheless, if we remember the confidential information given the baron by the concierge on Rue Chauchat, it will be evident that Crevel did not get along without a coachman and a groom.

Crevel had, as we see, turned his excessive affection for his daughter to the advantage of his pleasures. The immorality of his situation was justified by considerations of the highest morality. Furthermore, the former perfumer acquired from this mode of life—necessary perhaps, but dissolute, reminiscent of the Regency, Pompadour, Maréchal de Richelieu, etc.—a certain gloss of superiority. Crevel posed as a man of broad views, as a great lord on a small scale, as a generous-minded man, without narrowness in his ideas, and all by virtue of some twelve or fifteen hundred francs a month. This was not the effect of politic hypocrisy, but of bourgeois vanity, which, however, led to the same result. On the Bourse Crevel was looked upon as a person superior to his time, and above all things as a high liver. In this respect Crevel believed that he had gone beyond the worthy Birotteau by a hundred cubits.

"Well, well," cried Crevel, flying into a rage at the sight of Cousin Bette, "so it's you who are marrying Mademoiselle Hulot to a young count you have raised for her at your apron-strings?"

"Anyone would think that that annoys you?" replied Lisbeth with a searching glance at Crevel. "What interest have you, pray, in preventing my cousin's marriage? for you put a stop to the match with Monsieur Lebas's son, so they tell me?—"

"You are a good girl and know when to hold your tongue," rejoined Père Crevel. "Very good, do you suppose I will ever forgive *Monsieur* Hulot for the crime of stealing Josépha from me,—especially when he makes of a virtuous girl, whom I would have ended by marrying in my old-age, a good-for-naught, a female mountebank, an opera singer?—No, no, never!"

"He's a good fellow, though, is Monsieur Hulot," said Cousin Bette.

"Agreeable, very agreeable, too agreeable!" replied Crevel; "I wish him no ill; but I want my revenge, and I'll have it. That's my one idea!"

"Is it because of your desire for revenge that you have ceased to visit Madame Hulot?"

"Perhaps—"

"Aha! so you paid court to my cousin, did you?" said Lisbeth with a smile. "I suspected as much."

"And she treated me like a dog; worse than a dog, like a lackey; I would say rather like a political prisoner! But I shall succeed," he added, striking his forehead with his clenched fist.

"Poor man, it would be a terrible thing to find his wife false after being cast off by his mistress!—"

"Josépha!" cried Crevel; "has Josépha left him, cast him off, turned him out of doors?—Bravo, Josépha! Josépha, you have avenged me! I will send you a pair of pearls to wear in your ears, my ex-hussy!—I know nothing about this, for, after I saw you the day after the fair Adeline once more begged me to get out of her house, I went to see the Lebas, at Corbeil, and have just returned. Héloïse moved heaven and earth to get me into the country, and I knew what she was up to: she wanted to have a house-warming without me on Rue Chauchat, with a lot of artists, strolling players and literary fellows—I have been fooled! I will forgive Héloïse, though, for she amuses me. She's a sort of unpublished Déjazet. What a rascal she is, the hussy! here's the note I found last night:

"'My dear old man: I have pitched my tent on Rue Chauchat. I took the precaution to have the plaster dried by friends. All goes well. Come when you choose, monsieur. Hagar awaits her Abraham.'"

"Héloïse will tell me the news, for she knows her Bohemia inside and out."

"But my cousin took this set-back very well," said Cousin Bette.

"Impossible!" cried Crevel, pausing in his pendulum-like stride.

"Monsieur Hulot is well along in years," suggested Lisbeth maliciously.

"I know it," returned Crevel; "but we resemble each other in one respect: Hulot cannot get along without an attachment to somebody. He says to himself that he is capable of returning to his wife. That would be a novelty to him, but farewell to my revenge. You smile, Mademoiselle Fischer—aha! you know something?—"

"I am laughing at your ideas," Lisbeth replied. "Yes, my cousin is still lovely enough to inspire passion. I would fall in love with her if I were a man."

"Who has drunk, will drink!" cried Crevel; "you are laughing at me! The baron has found somebody to console him."

Lisbeth bent her head in token of assent.

"Ah! he's very lucky to replace Josépha between one day and the next!" continued Crevel. "But I am not surprised, for he told me one evening at supper that, in his younger days, in order not to be left in the lurch, he always had three mistresses, the one he was about to drop, the reigning one, and the one he was paying court to for future use. He must have had some grisette in reserve in his fish-pond! in his *Parc-aux-cerfs!* He's a regular Louis XV., the scamp! Oh! how lucky he is to be a handsome man! Nevertheless, he's growing old, he's *marked*—he must have taken on some little work-girl."

"Oh! no," said Lisbeth.

"Ah!" exclaimed Crevel, "what wouldn't I give to prevent him from being able to put on his hat! It was impossible for me to take Josépha from him; women of that sort never return to their first love. And then, love never comes back, they say. But, Cousin Bette, I would give, that is to say, I would willingly spend fifty thousand francs, to take that tall, handsome fellow's mistress away from him, and show him that a fat old boy with the paunch of a major and the skull of a future mayor of Paris, doesn't allow his fair one to be whistled away without giving tit for tat—"

"My position," rejoined Bette, compels me to hear everything and know nothing. You can talk with me without fear, for I never repeat a word of what anyone chooses to confide to me. Why should

I break the law that governs my conduct in that respect? no one would ever trust me again."

"I know it," returned Crevel; "you are the pearl of old maids.—Look you! *Sapristi,* there are exceptions. Tell me, have they ever made you any allowance in the family?—"

"Why, I have some pride of any own, and I don't choose to cost anybody anything," said Bette.

"Ah! if you would assist me to avenge myself," rejoined the former tradesman, "I would settle an annuity of ten thousand francs on your head. Tell me, dear cousin, who it is that has taken Josêpha's place, and you shall have the wherewithal to pay your rent, your little breakfast in the morning, the nice coffee you're so fond of, you can indulge in pure mocha—eh? Oh! how delicious pure mocha is!"

"I don't care so much for the annuity of ten thousand francs, which would give me an income of about five hundred, as I do for keeping my own counsel absolutely; for, you see, my dear Monsieur Crevel, the baron is very kind to me, he is going to pay my rent—"

"Oh! yes for a long while! rely on him for that!" cried Crevel. "Where would the baron get the money?"

"Ah! that I don't know. However, he is spending more than thirty thousand francs on the apartments he is fitting up for this lady—"

"A lady! What, can it be some woman in society? The villain, what a lucky dog! nobody has such luck as he!"

"A married woman, *comme il faut*," replied Cousin Bette.

"Really?" cried Crevel with wide-open eyes, inflamed no less by desire than by the magic phrase: *Comme il faut*.

"Yes," replied Bette, "talented, a musician, twenty-three years old, a pretty, innocent face, skin of dazzling whiteness, teeth like a young dog's, eyes like stars, a superb forehead—and tiny little feet,—I never saw the like,—they're no wider than her corset busk."

"And her ears?" queried Crevel, his pulses quickened by this lover's description.

"Ears to be modeled," she replied.

"Little hands?—"

"I tell you, in a word, she's a jewel of a woman, and so virtuous, so modest, so refined!—a lovely creature, an angel, distinguished in every way, for her father's a marshal of France—"

"A marshal of France!" cried Crevel, with a violent start. "*Mon Dieu! saperlotte!* bless my soul!—Ah! the blackguard!—Forgive me, cousin, I am going mad!—I would give a hundred thousand francs, I think—"

"Oh yes! I tell you she's an honest woman, a virtuous woman. So the baron has done things handsomely."

"He hasn't a sou—I tell you."

"There's a husband whom he has pushed forward—"

"In what way?" asked Crevel with a bitter smile.

"He's already appointed deputy-chief of department, is this husband, who will be complaisant no doubt; he's in a fair way to get the cross."

"The government should be careful and show respect to those it has decorated by not being too lavish with the cross," said Crevel with an expression of political pique. "But what has this great cur of an old baron in his favor after all?" he continued. "So far as I can see I'm quite as good as he is," he added, surveying himself in a mirror, and striking his attitude. "Héloïse has often told me, at a time when women don't lie, that I was a wonder."

"Oh!" rejoined Bette, "women like fat men, for they are almost always good-natured; and between you and the baron, I would choose you. Monsieur Hulot is clever and a handsome man, he has a distinguished bearing; but you are substantial, and then you know—you seem to be a wickeder wretch than he!"

"It's incredible how all women, even the most pious, take to men who have that appearance!" cried Crevel, putting his arm around Bette's waist, so exhilarated was he.

"That's not where the difficulty is," pursued Bette. "You understand that a woman who has so much done for her, won't be unfaithful to her protector for trifles, and *that* would cost more than a hundred and some odd thousand francs, for the little lady in question imagines her husband chief of a department two years hence.—

It's poverty that drives the poor little angel into the abyss."

Crevel strode up and down his salon like a madman.

"He must think a great deal of this woman?" he asked after a moment's silence, during which his desire, thus whetted by Lisbeth, became a sort of frenzy.

"Judge for yourself!" replied Lisbeth. "I don't think he has obtained that as yet!" said she, snapping her thumb-nail against one of her huge white incisors, "and he has already spent ten thousand francs in presents."

"Oh! what a good farce!" cried Crevel, "if I should get in ahead of him!"

"Good heavens, it is very wrong in me to tell you all this stuff," said Lisbeth, as if stricken with remorse.

"No. I want to put your family to the blush. To-morrow, I will settle a sum of money on you that will bring you an income of six hundred francs at five per cent., but you must tell me all: Dulcinea's name, and where she lives. I may as well own to you that I have never had a woman in society for my mistress, and it is the height of my ambition to know such a one. The houris of Mahomet are nothing in comparison with my idea of women of the world. In short this is my ideal, my mania, and to such an extent, look you, that Baroness Hulot will never be fifty years old in my eyes," said he, unconsciously adopting the thought of one of the finest minds of the last century. "Come, my good Lisbeth, I have decided to sacrifice one hundred, two hundred,—Hush! here are my children, I see them crossing the courtyard. I will never say that I learned anything from you, I give you my word of honor, for I don't want you to lose the baron's confidence, quite the contrary.—He must be amazingly fond of this woman, must my old chum!"

"Oh! he's mad over her!" said Bette. "He didn't know where to find forty thousand francs for his daughter's *dot*, but he has raised them for this new passion."

"And you think that he is loved?" queried Crevel.

"At his age!—" was the old maid's reply.

"Oh! what a fool I am!" cried Crevel. "I who shut my eyes to Héloïse's artist, exactly as Henri IV. did with regard to Gabrielle and Bellegarde. Oh! old age! old age!—Good afternoon, Célestine, good afternoon, my jewel; and your little brat? Ah! there he is! Upon my word he begins to look like me.—How are you, Hulot, my friend, is everything all right?—We shall soon have another marriage in the family."

Célestine and her husband shook their heads as they pointed to Lisbeth, and the daughter boldly asked her father:

"Whose, pray?"

Crevel assumed a cunning expression, implying that his indiscretion would be easily repaired.

"Hortense's," he replied; "but it's not altogether decided. I have just come from Lebas', and they are talking of Mademoiselle Popinot for our young councilor at the royal court of Paris, who would not object to becoming a president in the provinces.—Come to dinner."

*

At seven o'clock Lisbeth was already on her way home in an omnibus, for she was in haste to see Wenceslas, whose dupe she had been for some three weeks, and to whom she was carrying her satchel filled with fruit selected by Crevel himself, whose affection for *his* Cousin Bette had redoubled. She ran up to the attic so quickly that she lost her breath, and found the artist at work finishing the decoration of a box that he proposed to present to his dear Hortense. The border of the lid was carved to represent hortensias, amid which Loves were frolicking. The poor lover, to pay for the box which was of malachite, had made two candle-holders for Florent and Chanor, two masterpieces, which he sold to them outright.

"You have been working too hard these last few days, my dear fellow," said Lisbeth, wiping the perspiration from his brow and kissing him. "Such activity in the month of August seems to me dangerous. Really your health may suffer by it.—See, here are some peaches and plums from M. Crevel's.—Don't worry so; I have borrowed two thousand francs, and unless something happens, we can return them if you sell your clock!—And yet I have some suspicion of the man who loaned them to me, for he has just sent me this stamped paper."

She placed the notice of the application for arrest under the sketch of Maréchal Montcornet.

"For whom are you making these lovely things?" she asked, taking up the branches of hortensias in red wax, which Wenceslas had laid aside in order to eat the fruit.

"For a jeweler."

"What jeweler?"

"I don't know; Stidmann begged me to *twist* them for him, he is so hurried."

"Why, these are hortensias," said she in a hollow voice. "How is it that you have never modeled any wax for me? Was it so hard, pray, to invent a dagger, a casket, no matter what, for a souvenir?" she added, casting a withering glance at the artist, whose eyes, luckily, were cast down. "And you say that you love me!"

"Do you doubt it—mademoiselle?"

"Oh! what a very warm *mademoiselle!*—Look you, you have been my only thought since I saw you dying, over yonder.—When I saved you, you gave yourself to me; I have never spoken to you of this engagement, but I bound myself to you in my own mind! I said to myself: 'Since this poor fellow gives himself to me, I mean to make him rich and happy!' Very good; I have succeeded in making your fortune!"

"How, pray?" asked the poor artist, happy beyond words, and too innocent to suspect a trap.

"This is how," replied the Lorrainer.

Lisbeth could not deny herself the savage pleasure

of watching Wenceslas, who was gazing at her with a filial affection, into which his love for Hortense overflowed, and thus deceived the old maid. When she saw for the first time in her life, the fire of passion alight in the eyes of a man, she thought that she herself had lighted it.

"Monsieur Crevel will furnish us with a hundred thousand francs to set up in business, if, he says, you choose to marry me; he has strange ideas, the vulgar old fellow.—What do you think about it?" she asked.

The artist, who had turned pale as a dead man, looked at his benefactress with eyes in which no light shone and which did not conceal his thoughts. He remained open-mouthed and stupefied.

"I was never told so plainly before," she went on with a bitter smile, "that I was frightfully ugly!"

"Mademoiselle," replied Steinbock, "my benefactress will never be ugly in my eyes; I have a very warm affection for you, but I am not yet thirty, and—"

"And I am forty-three!" said Bette. "My cousin Hulot, who is forty-eight, still drives men mad; but she is beautiful, she is!"

"Fifteen years difference between us, mademoiselle! what sort of a household would ours be? For our own sakes I think we should do well to reflect. My gratitude will certainly be equal to your benefactions. Besides, your money will be repaid in a few days."

"My money!" she cried. "Oh! you treat me as if I were a heartless money-lender."

"Forgive me," rejoined Wenceslas, "but you speak of it so often.—In short, you made me,—do not destroy me."

"You want to leave me, I see," said she, shaking her head. "Who has given you the strength to be ungrateful, you who are like a man made of *papier mâché?* Do you lack confidence in me, your good genius?—in me, who have so often passed the night working for you! who have given you the savings of my whole life! who, for four years, have shared my bread, the bread of a poor work-girl, with you, and who have loaned you everything, even my courage!"

"Enough! Enough! Mademoiselle," said he, throwing himself on his knees and holding out his hands to her. "Don't say another word! In three days I will speak, I will tell you everything; let me be happy," he said, kissing her hands, "I love, and I am loved."

"Well, then, be happy, my child," said she, raising him—

Thereupon she kissed him on the brow and hair with the frenzy of a man condemned to death breathing the air of his last morning.

"Ah! you are the noblest and best of creatures, you are the equal of my beloved," said the poor artist.

"I love you dearly enough to tremble for your future," she rejoined gloomily. "Judas hanged himself!—all ingrates come to a bad end! You leave me and you will do nothing more of any account! Consider that, even if we don't marry—for I am an old maid, I know,—I have no wish to smother the flower of your youth, your poetic talent, as you call it, in my arms which are like branches of a vine; but can't we remain together without marrying? Listen to me; I have the business instinct, and I can get together a fortune by ten years' work, for my name is Economy; while with a young woman, who will be all for spending, you will squander everything and work only to make her happy. Happiness creates nothing but memories. When I think of you I sit for whole hours with my arms hanging at my sides.—Come, Wenceslas, stay with me.—You see I understand all about it; you shall have mistresses, pretty women like little Marneffe, who is anxious to see you, and who will afford you the pleasure you cannot find with me. Then, when I have got together an income of thirty thousand francs for you, you shall marry."

"You are an angel, mademoiselle, and I shall never forget this moment," replied Wenceslas, wiping away his tears.

"That's the way I like to have you, my child," said she, gazing at him wildly.

Vanity is so strong in us all that Lisbeth believed she had triumphed. She had made such a great concession in suggesting Madame Marneffe! She experienced the keenest emotion of her whole life, for the first time she felt joy pouring in a flood into her heart. She would have sold her soul to the devil for another such hour.

"I am betrothed," he replied, "and I love a woman with whom no other can successfully contend. But you are, and will always be, the mother I have lost."

These words fell like an avalanche of snow upon a flaming crater. Lisbeth sat down and gazed with a sombre expression at the distinguished beauty, the glowing youth, the artist's brow, the beautiful hair, everything which aroused in her the suppressed instincts of her sex, and tiny tears, instantly dried, moistened her eyes for a moment. She resembled one of those slender statues which the sculptors of images of the Middle Ages were accustomed to place in a sitting posture upon tombs.

"I do not curse you," said she, rising abruptly, "you are only a child. May God protect you!"

She went down stairs and locked herself into her apartments.

"She loves me," said Wenceslas to himself, "poor creature. How eloquent she was in her excitement! She is mad."

This last effort of this unimaginative, matter-of-fact nature, to keep with her the image of beauty and poesy, was so violent that it can be fitly-compared only to the savage energy of the shipwrecked sailor in his last supreme struggle to reach the shore.

Two days later, at half-past four in the morning, just when Count Steinbock was sleeping most profoundly, he heard a knock at the door of his attic;

he left his bed to open the door, whereupon two shabbily dressed men entered, accompanied by a third, whose garb indicated a bailiff in adverse circumstances.

"You are Monsieur Wenceslas, Comte Steinbock?" said this last-mentioned personage.

"Yes, monsieur."

"My name is Grasset, monsieur, successor to Monsieur Louchard, constable—"

"What then?"

"You are under arrest, monsieur, and must go with us to the prison at Clichy.—Be good enough to dress.—We have had consideration for you, as you see; I didn't bring any police officer, and there is a fiacre below."

"You are well looked out for,—" said one of the understrappers; "so we count on your generosity."

Steinbock dressed and went down stairs, each arm in the grasp of one of the followers; when he was inside the fiacre the driver started off without orders, like a man who knows where to go; within half an hour the hapless foreigner found himself well and duly registered on the prison books, without having uttered a word of remonstrance, so great was his surprise.

At ten o'clock he was sent for to the office of the prison, and found Lisbeth there, dissolved in tears; she gave him money with which to live comfortably, and to procure a room large enough to work in.

"My child," said she, "don't mention your arrest

to anybody, don't write to a living soul, for it would ruin your future; we must hide this stigma, and soon I shall have set you free; I am going to get the money together—never fear. Write me what I must bring you for your work. I will die, or you shall soon be free."

"Oh! I shall owe you my life twice over!" he cried, "for I should lose more than life, if people believed me to be a worthless fellow."

Lisbeth left him with joy at her heart; she hoped to be able, by keeping her artist under lock and key, to put an end to his marriage with Hortense by saying that he was married, that he was pardoned through the efforts of his wife, and had started for Russia. In execution of this plan she called at the baroness's about three o'clock, although it was not her regular day for dining there; but she longed to enjoy the torture which her younger cousin would suffer as the time approached for Wenceslas to appear.

"Have you come to dinner, Bette?" asked the baroness, concealing her disappointment.

"Why yes."

"Good!" said Hortense, "I will go and give orders to have it served promptly, for you don't like to wait."

Hortense made a gesture intended to reassure her mother; for she proposed to tell the footman to send Monsieur Steinbock away when he called; but as the footman had gone out Hortense was compelled to give the order to the maid, and the maid went to her room to get her work, preparatory to taking up her station in the anteroom.

"What about my lover?" said Cousin Bette to Hortense, when she returned; "you don't mention him any more."

"By the way, what has become of him?" said Hortense, "for he is famous now. You ought to be very happy," she added in her cousin's ear, "for everybody is talking about Monsieur Wenceslas Steinbock."

"A great deal too much," she replied aloud. "Monsieur is taking to bad courses. If it were only a question of keeping his mind occupied to the point of carrying the day over the dissipations of Paris, I know my power; but they say that in order to attract an artist of his calibre to his court, the Emperor Nicholas has pardoned him—"

"Oh! nonsense!" exclaimed the baroness.

"How do you know that?" asked Hortense, seized with something like cramp at her heart.

"Why," replied the fiendish Bette, "a person to whom he is bound by the most sacred of bonds, his wife, wrote him to that effect yesterday. He is anxious to go; ah! he would be a fool to leave France for Russia—"

Hortense glanced at her mother as her head fell forward; the baroness had just time to catch her fainting daughter, who was as white as the lace of her neckerchief.

"Lisbeth! you have killed my child!—" cried

the baroness. "You were born to bring misfortune upon us."

"Well, well! how am I at fault in this, Adeline?" demanded the Lorrainer, rising and assuming a threatening attitude, to which in her dismay, the baroness paid no heed.

"I was wrong," replied Adeline, holding Hortense in her arms. "Ring!"

At that moment the door opened, the two women turned their heads simultaneously and beheld Wenceslas Steinbock, whom the cook had admitted in the maid's absence.

"Hortense!" ejaculated the artist, rushing forward to the group formed by the three women. And he kissed his affianced bride before her mother's eyes, but with such pious veneration that the baroness was not angry. It was a more efficacious salt for the swoon than all the English salts in the world. Hortense opened her eyes, saw Wenceslas, and the color returned to her cheeks. A moment more and she was herself again.

"So this is what you've been hiding from me?" said Cousin Bette, smiling at Wenceslas, and making a pretence of guessing the truth by virtue of the confusion of her two cousins.—"How did you steal my lover from me?" she said to Hortense, leading her into the garden.

Hortense naively narrated to her cousin the romance of her love. Her mother and father, convinced that Bette would never marry, had, she said, authorized the Comte Steinbock's visits. But

Hortense, like Agnes of old, attributed to chance the purchase of the group and the author's visit, due, so she said, to his desire to know the name of his first customer. Steinbock almost immediately joined the cousins to thank the old maid effusively for his speedy deliverance. Lisbeth jesuitically replied that, as the creditor would make only the vaguest promises, she did not expect to procure his release until the next day, and that he must have been ashamed of such trivial persecution and taken the initiative himself. The old maid seemed well-pleased, however, and congratulated Wenceslas on his good fortune.

"Bad boy!" she said to him before Hortense and her mother, "if you had confessed to me night before last that you loved my Cousin Hortense, and that she loved you, you would have spared me many tears. I thought that you meant to abandon your old friend, your schoolmistress, while on the contrary you are going to be my cousin; henceforth you will belong to me, the bond between us rather feeble, to be sure, but strong enough for the sentiment I entertain for you—"

And she kissed Wenceslas on the forehead. Hortense threw herself into her cousin's arms and burst into tears.

"I owe my happiness to you," said she; "I shall never forget it—"

"Cousin Bette," added the baroness, embracing Lisbeth in her intense excitement at seeing things fall out so happily, "the baron and I owe you a debt, and we will pay it; come and let us talk a little business in the garden," said she leading her away.

Thus Lisbeth to all appearance was playing the role of the good angel of the family; she was adored by Crevel, by Hulot, by Adeline and Hortense.

"We don't want you to work any more," said the baroness. "Supposing that you can earn forty sous a day, Sundays excepted, that makes six hundred francs a year. Now, what do your savings amount to?"

"Forty-five hundred francs."

"Poor cousin!" said the baroness.

She raised her eyes heavenward, so touched was she as she thought of all the hardships and privations implied by the mention of that sum, laid by in thirty years. Lisbeth, who misunderstood the meaning of the exclamation, saw therein the pitying disdain of the parvenu, and her hatred was increased by a formidable dose of gall, at the very moment that her cousin was laying aside all her suspicions of the tyrant of her childhood.

"We will increase that sum by ten thousand five hundred francs," said Adeline, "we will place the whole in your name as entitled to the income, and in Hortense's name as trustee; thus you will have an income of six hundred francs.—"

Lisbeth seemed to be as happy as a woman can be. When she returned, with her handkerchief at her eyes, wiping away the tears of joy, Hortense told her of all the favors which were raining upon Wenceslas, the well-beloved of the whole family.

Thus when the baron returned home he found his family complete, for the baroness had officially saluted Count Steinbock by the name of son, and appointed the wedding for the fifteenth, subject to her husband's approbation. And so, as soon as he appeared in the salon, the councilor of state was assailed by his wife and daughter, who ran to meet him, one to whisper in his ear, the other to kiss him.

"You have gone too far in binding me thus, madame," said the baron sternly. "This marriage isn't a fact yet," he added, glancing at Steinbock, who turned pale.

"He knows of my arrest," said the unlucky artist to himself.

"Come, children," continued the father, leading his daughter and her lover into the garden. And he sat down with them on one of the moss-covered benches in the summer-house.

"Monsieur le Comte, do you love my daughter as dearly as I loved her mother?" he demanded of Wenceslas.

"More dearly, monsieur," said the artist.

"The mother was a peasant's daughter and hadn't a sou."

"Give me Mademoiselle Hortense as she sits there, without even a trousseau—"

"I should think so!" said the baron with a smile; "Hortense is the daughter of Baron Hulot d'Ervy, Councilor of State, director at the War Department, grand officer of the Legión of Honor, brother of Comte Hulot, whose glory is undying, and who will soon be a marshal of France. And—she has a dowry!—"

"It is very true," said the love-lorn artist, "that I may seem to be ambitious; but if my dear Hortense were a workman's daughter I would marry her—"

"That's what I wanted to know," rejoined the baron. "Off with you, Hortense, and let me talk with the count; you see that he loves you sincerely."

"O father! I knew that you were joking," replied the happy girl.

"My dear Steinbock," said the baron, with infinite grace of diction and great charm of manner, when he was alone with the artist, "I allotted to my son two hundred thousand francs for his marriage portion, of which the poor boy has never received two liards; he will never have any of it. My daughter's *dot* will be two hundred thousand francs of which you will acknowledge the receipt—"

"Yes, Monsieur le Baron—"

"How fast you go," said the Councilor of State. "Be good enough to listen to me. One can not ask from a son-in-law the self-sacrificing devotion one is entitled to expect from a son. My son was aware of all that I could do and what I will do for his future; he will be a minister, he will easily find his two hundred thousand francs. In your case, young man, it's a very different matter! You will receive sixty thousand francs in a five per cent government bond in your wife's name. This fund will be charged with a small annuity to be paid to Lisbeth, but she will not live long, she is consumptive, I know. Don't mention that secret to anybody; let the poor girl die in peace. My daughter will have a trousseau costing twenty thousand francs; her mother contributes her diamonds to the amount of six thousand francs,—"

"Monsieur, you overwhelm me!" said Steinbock, dumfounded.

"As for the remaining hundred and twenty thousand francs—"

"Pray cease, monsieur," said the artist, "I do not wish that my dear Hortense—"

"Will you kindly hear me out, O hot-headed young man? As for the hundred and twenty thousand francs, I have them not; but you will receive them—"

"Monsieur!—"

"You will receive them in orders which I will obtain for you from the government, I give you my word of honor. You see you are to have a studio at the marble-warehouse. Exhibit a few fine statues and I will procure your admission to the Institute. My brother and I are looked upon with favor in high places, so I hope to succeed in procuring commissions for you for sculptures at Versailles to a fourth of the amount. Furthermore, you will receive orders from the city of Paris and some from the Chamber of Peers; you shall have them, my dear fellow, in such numbers that you will be obliged to have assistants. That's the way I will perform my obligation. Consider whether the *dot* paid in this way will meet your wishes,—take counsel of your strength—"

"I feel that I have the strength to make a fortune for my wife single-handed, if everything else should fail!" exclaimed the noble artist.

"That's what I like!" cried the baron, "ardent youth oppressed by no doubts! I would have overthrown whole armies for a wife! Very good," said he, taking the young sculptor's hand and shaking it warmly, "you have my consent. Next Sunday the contract, and the following Saturday at the altar; it's my wife's birthday!"

"All goes well," said the baroness to her daughter with her face glued to the window, "your father and your intended are embracing."

When he returned home that evening Wenceslas found the explanation of the enigma of his release; the concierge handed him a bulky, sealed package which contained the papers relating to his debt with a release in due form indorsed at the foot of the judgment, and accompanied by the following letter:

"My dear Wenceslas:

"I went to see you this morning at ten o'clock to present you to a royal highness who wishes to make your acquaintance. There I learned that the English had taken you off to one of their little islands, the capital of which is called *Clichy's Castle*.

"I at once called on Léon de Lora, to whom I said jokingly that you couldn't leave the country-house where you were for lack of four thousand francs, and that your future would be compromised unless you exhibited yourself to your royal patron. Bridau, that man of genius, who has known what poverty is, and who knows your story, was there by good luck. My son, between them they made up the sum, and I went off to pay the Tartar who committed the crime of *lèse génie* by bottling you up. As I had to be at the Tuileries at noon, I could not take a look at you inhaling the air of liberty. I know you are a gentleman, and I answered for you to my two friends: but go and see them to-morrow.

"Léon and Bridau won't touch your money: each of them will ask you for a group, and they will do well. That is what I think, who would like to be able to call myself your rival, but am only your comrade.

"STIDMANN."

"P. S.—I told the prince that you would not return from your journey until to-morrow, and he said: 'Very well, to-morrow!' "

Comte Wenceslas slept free from all disturbing care between the purple sheets, with which we are provided by Favor, that limping divinity, who, where men of genius are concerned, moves even more slowly than Justice and Fortune, because Jupiter ordained that she should wear no bandage over her eyes. Easily led astray by the display of charlatans, attracted by their gaudy costumes and their trumpets, she wastes, in watching and paying for their empty shows, the time she ought to spend searching out men of merit in the corners where they are hiding.

*

It remains to be explained now how Monsieur le Baron Hulot had succeeded in collecting the component parts of Hortense's *dot*, and in meeting the appalling expense of the delightful suite in which Madame Marneffe was to be installed. His financial conception bore the stamp of the talent which guides the steps of spendthrifts and hotheads, in the quagmires where mishaps of so many sorts bring about their destruction. Nothing will more clearly demonstrate the strange power imparted by vice, to which are to be attributed the masterstrokes achieved now and then by ambitious individuals, by voluptuaries, in short, by all the subjects of the devil.

On the morning of the preceding day, the aged Johann Fischer, because of his inability to pay thirty thousand francs collected by his nephew, found himself confronted by the necessity of stopping payment unless the baron should repay them to him.

This venerable, white-haired old man of seventy had such blind confidence in Hulot, who, in the eyes of the old Bonapartist, was a beam from the Napoleonic sun, that he walked calmly to and fro with the clerk from the Bank in the reception-room of the little ground-floor apartment, hired at eight hundred francs a year, in which he superintended his various enterprises in the way of grain and forage.

"Marguerite has gone to get the money not two steps away," he said.

The man in the gray coat trimmed with silver lace was so well aware of the old Alsatian's uprightness, that he would have left the notes of hand for thirty thousand francs with him; but the old fellow compelled him to wait, as eight o'clock had not struck. A cabriolet stopped at the door, the old man darted into the street and held out his hand with sublime confidence to the baron, who gave him thirty thousand francs in bank-notes.

"Go three doors farther on, I will tell you why," said old Fischer.—"Here you are, young man," he said, returning and counting out the paper to the Bank's representative, whom he thereupon escorted to the door.

When the clerk was out of sight, Fischer ordered the driver of the cabriolet, in which his august nephew, Napoleon's right arm, was waiting, to turn about, and said as he led him into the house:

"Do you want them to know at the Bank of France that you turned over to me the thirty thousand francs on which you were endorser?—Indeed it was too much in the first place to have placed the signature of a man like you on them!—"

"Let us go to the end of your little garden," said the high official. "You are solid," he resumed, taking his seat under a vine-clad trellis and eyeing the old man as the mistress of a bagnio sizes up a substitute.

"Solid enough to invest in an annuity," jocosely replied the thin, wrinkled, nervous, keen-eyed old man.

"Does the heat make you ill?—"

"On the contrary."

"What do you say to Africa?"

"A fine country!—The French went there with the Little Corporal."

"It's necessary to save us all, for you to go to Algeria," said the baron.

"And what about my business?—"

"A clerk in the War Department, about to retire, with no means of earning his living, will buy your establishment."

"What am I to do in Algeria?"

"Furnish the provisions of war—grain and forage; I have your commission already signed. You will procure your supplies in the country at prices seventy per cent below what we shall allow you for them."

"Where shall I get them?—"

"From the *razzias*, the *achour*, the caliphates. There is in Algeria—a country even now but little known although we have been there eight years—an enormous quantity of grain and forage. Now, when these crops belong to the Arabs, we take them from them under innumerable pretexts; and, when they are ours, the Arabs do their best to take them from us. There is a deal of fighting over the grain;

but no one ever knows the exact quantities that have been stolen on one side and the other. There's no time, in a level country, to measure out wheat by the hectolitre as at the market, or hay as on Rue d'Enfer. The Arab chiefs, as well as our Spahis, prefer money, and sell the crops at a very low price. The army administration has fixed needs; it can purchase in the markets only at exorbitant prices, based upon the difficulty of procuring supplies and the danger the transports run. Such is Algeria from the commissary's standpoint. It is a foul puddle, blackened by the ink bottle of every new administration. We officials shall not be able to see clearly there for ten years to come, but private individuals have sharp eyes. So I send you thither to make your fortune; I place you there, as Napoleon placed a poor marshal at the head of a kingdom where he could secretly countenance contraband trade. I am ruined, my dear Fischer. I must have a hundred thousand francs within a year from now—"

"I see no harm in taking them from the Arabs," calmly rejoined the Alsatian. "That sort of thing was done under the Empire—"

"The purchaser of your establishment will come to see you this morning, and will pay you ten thousand francs," continued Baron Hulot. "Isn't that all you need to go to Algeria?"

The old man made a sign of assent.

"As for funds over there, you need have no fear," said the baron. "I will take the balance of the price of your establishment here; I need it."

"Everything is yours, even my blood," said the old man.

"Oh! don't you be alarmed," replied the baron, crediting his uncle with more perspicacity than he possessed; "as to matters of impost your probity shall not suffer; everything depends on the persons in authority; now, it was I who appointed the persons in authority and I am sure of them. This, Papa Fischer, is a secret of life and death; I know you, and I have spoken to you without disguise or circumlocution."

"I will go," said the old man. "And this will last?—"

"Two years! you will have a hundred thousand francs of your own to live happily in the Vosges."

"It shall be as you wish, my honor is yours," said the old man calmly.

"That's the way I like to hear a man talk. However, you mustn't go until you have seen your grand-niece happily married; she will be a countess."

The *achour*, the *razzia* of *razzias*, and the price paid by the retired clerk for the Fischer establishment could not produce at once sixty thousand francs for Hortense's *dot*, including the trousseau, which would cost about five thousand francs, and the forty thousand francs expended or to be expended for Madame Marneffe. For that matter, how had the baron raised the thirty thousand francs he had just brought to Père Fischer? In this way. Some days before, Hulot had insured his life for a hundred and fifty thousand francs, for three years, in two companies. Armed with the policies, on which the premiums were paid, he thus addressed Monsieur le Baron de Nucingen, peer of France, as he took a seat in his carriage to go to dinner with him after a session of the Chamber of Peers.

"Baron, I am in need of seventy thousand francs, and I ask you to let me have them. You will accept a guarantor to whom I will assign for three years the assignable portion of my salary, amounting to twenty-five thousand francs a year, that is to say, seventy-five thousand francs. You will say: 'you may die.'"

The baron bent his head assentingly.

"Here is an insurance policy for a hundred and fifty thousand francs, which will be made over to you to the extent of eighty thousand francs," continued the baron, taking a paper from his pocket.

"And subbose you were dizmisd?—" queried the millionaire baron, with a laugh.

The other baron, anti-millionaire, became thoughtful.

"Don'd pe alarmed. I vould not haf made the opjection egzept to zhow you dat I am endidled to zome gredit vor gifing you der money. You moost pe fery hart bressed, for der Pank has your zignadure."

"I am marrying my daughter," said Baron Hulot, "and I am without means, like all those who continue to hold offices in the departments in an ungrateful age, when the five hundred bourgeois who sit on the benches in the Chamber will never think of paying faithful servants handsomely, as the Emperor did."

"Ah! bud you haf hat Zhosépha!" rejoined the peer of France, "and that egsplains everyding! Bedween us the Duc d'Hérufille did you a gread zervice by taking that bloot-zucker away from your burse.

"I have known that trial, and know how to combat it,"

he added, fancying that he was quoting a line of poetry. "Listen to a friend's advice: Glose your zhop or you will be undone."

This disreputable affair was arranged through the medium of a petty usurer named Vauvinet, one of those reptiles who hang about in front of great banking-houses like the little fish which seems to act as servant to the shark. This lynx was so anxious to secure the patronage of so illustrious a personage as Monsieur le Baron Hulot, that he promised to discount his notes for thirty thousand francs, at ninety days, agreeing to renew them four times, and not to put them in circulation.

Fischer's successor was to give forty thousand francs for his establishment, but with the promise of a contract to furnish forage in some department near Paris.

Such was the ghastly labyrinth in which his passions involved one who had been one of the most upright men on earth hitherto, one of the most skilful constructors of the Napoleonic administration;

extortion to pay usury, usury to indulge his passions and arrange his daughter's marriage. This science of prodigality, all these expedients were resorted to in order to appear great in the eyes of Madame Marneffe, to be the Jupiter of that middle-class Danaë. A man does not display more energy, more intelligence, more audacity, in making his fortune honestly, than the baron displayed in plunging head-first into a wasp's nest; he did not neglect the affairs of his division, he hurried up the upholsterers, overlooked the workmen, and scrutinized minutely the most trifling details of the establishment on Rue Vanneau. Although he was entirely at Madame Marneffe's service, he still attended the sittings of the Chamber, he was everywhere at once, and neither his family nor anyone else observed his preoccupation.

Adeline, surprised beyond measure to learn that her uncle was saved, and to see a marriage-portion set down in the contract, felt somewhat ill at ease amid the happiness afforded her by Hortense's marriage brought about upon such honorable conditions; but, on the eve of her daughter's marriage, so arranged by the baron as to coincide with the day when Madame Marneffe took possession of her suite on Rue Vanneau, Hector put an end to his wife's astonishment by this ministerial communication:

"Adeline, our daughter will soon be married, so all our agony on that subject is at an end. The time has come for us to withdraw from the world, for I have hardly three years now, to remain in my place, before I shall complete the term of service which permits me to retire. Why should we continue to incur expenses that are no longer necessary? Our apartments cost us six thousand francs a year, we have four servants, and we run through thirty thousand francs a year. If you wish me to carry out my agreements, for I have assigned my salary for three years to obtain the necessary sums for Hortense's settlement and to take up your uncle's notes—"

"Ah! you did well, my dear," she said, interrupting her husband and kissing his hands.

This avowal put an end to Adeline's fears.

"I have some trifling sacrifices to ask of you," he resumed, withdrawing his hands, and depositing a kiss on his wife's brow. "I have found, on Rue Plumet, a lovely apartment on the first floor, suitable in every way, with magnificent wainscotings, the rent of which is only fifteen hundred francs, where you will need but one maid, and I shall get along very well with one servant."

"Yes, my dear."

"By living simply, while keeping up appearances, you will hardly spend more than six thousand francs a year, exclusive of my private expenses which I will take care of—"

The noble-hearted woman threw her arms joyfully about her husband's neck.

"What bliss to be able to show you once more how dearly I love you!" she cried, "and what a man of resources you are!—"

"We will receive our family once a week, and I, as you know, dine at home but rarely.—You can, without causing remark, dine twice a week with Victorin and twice with Hortense; and as I think that I can bring about a thorough reconciliation between Crevel and ourselves, we will dine once a week with him, and those five dinners, with our own, will fill out the week, assuming that we have an invitation outside the family now and then."

"I will be economical," said Adeline.

"Ah!" he cried, "you are the pearl of women."

"My dear, divine Hector, I will bless you with my last breath," she replied, "for you have arranged our dear Hortense's marriage so handsomely."

Thus began the diminution of lovely Madame Hulot's household, and, if we must say it, the desertion solemnly promised to Madame Marneffe.

Pursy little Père Crevel, being naturally invited to the signing of the contract, bore himself on that occasion as if the scene with which this story opened had never taken place, as if he had no grievance against Baron Hulot. Célestin Crevel was most amiable in fact; he was always a little too much the former dealer in perfumery, but he was beginning to rise to the majestic, by virtue of his major's commission. He talked about dancing at the wedding.

"My dear madame," said he graciously to the baroness, "people like us know how to forget; don't banish me from your house, and condescend to adorn my apartments now and then by coming there with your children. Have no fear, I will never mention what I have at the bottom of my heart. I acted like an idiot, for I should lose too much if I am never to see you any more—"

"Monsieur, a virtuous woman has no ears for such speeches as those to which you allude; and, if you keep your word, you can have no doubt of the pleasure with which I shall see the end of a rupture which is always most painful in families—"

"Well, old sulker," said Baron Hulot forcibly carrying Crevel away into the garden, "you avoid me everywhere, even in my own house. Ought two old admirers of the fair sex to quarrel over a petticoat? Upon my word, that shows the grocer."

"Monsieur, I am not so handsome a man as you, and my limited powers of fascination prevent me from making good my losses as easily as you do—"

"Sarcasm!" rejoined the baron.

"Sarcasm is allowable against the victor, when one is whipped."

Begun in this strain the conversation ended in a complete reconciliation; but Crevel was firm in maintaining his right to be revenged.

Madame Marneffe insisted upon an invitation to Mademoiselle Hulot's wedding. In order to enjoy the pleasure of seeing his future mistress in his salon, the Councilor of State was compelled to invite the employés of his division, down to and including deputy-chiefs. Thereupon a large ball became a necessity. Like a careful housewife, the baroness calculated that an evening party would be less expensive than a dinner, and would make it possible to receive a larger company. Thus Hortense's wedding caused a great commotion.

The Maréchal Prince de Wissembourg, and the Baron de Nucingen, on behalf of the bride, Comtes de Rastignac and Popinot on behalf of Steinbock, were the witnesses. Inasmuch as the celebrity of Count Steinbock had led the most illustrious of the Polish refugees to seek him out, he thought that he ought to invite them. The Council of State, the government departments, in which the baron held office, the army, which wished to do honor to the Comte de Forzheim, were to be represented by high functionaries. The invitations thus made necessary numbered two hundred. Who will fail now to comprehend little Madame Marneffe's ambition to appear in all her glory in such an assemblage?

A month before, the baroness had contributed the value of her diamonds toward putting in order her daughter's future home, after setting aside the finest for the trousseau. The sale realized fifteen thousand francs, five thousand of which were absorbed by Hortense's trousseau. But what were ten thousand francs to furnish the apartments of the young couple, when we reflect upon the exigencies of modern luxury? But Monsieur and Madame Hulot the younger, Père Crevel and the Comte de Forzheim made valuable presents, for the old uncle kept a certain sum in reserve for a service of plate. Thanks to all this outside assistance, the most exacting Parisian woman would have been content with the surroundings of the young couple in the apartments they had chosen on Rue Saint-Dominique, near the Esplanade des Invalides. Everything there was in harmony with their love, pure, outspoken and sincere, on both sides.

At last the great day arrived, and a great day it was to be for the father as well as for Hortense and Wenceslas; Madame Marneffe had decided to have her house-warming on the day following her fall and the wedding of the lovers.

Who has not, at least once in his life, been present at a wedding ball? Every reader can search his memory, and will surely smile as he recalls all those guests arrayed in their Sunday best, by the expression of their faces, no less than by their stiff, conventional garb. If there was ever a social fact that proved the influence of surroundings is it not that? Indeed the festal array of this class so reacts upon their fellow-guests that even those who are most accustomed to wear clothes suited to the occasion seem to belong to the same category with those for whom the wedding marks an epoch in their lives. And then, do you remember those sober-faced individuals, those old men who are so indifferent to everything that they have retained the black coats they wear every day; and the old married folks, whose faces betray their mournful experience of the life the youthful bride and groom are just beginning; and the lusts of the flesh, which are present like the carbonic acid gas in champagne; and the envious maidens, the women thinking of naught but the success of their costumes, and the poor relations, whose seedy appearance contrasts so strongly with the gorgeously arrayed, and the gourmands, who think only of the supper, and the gamblers, of their game? All classes are there, rich and poor, envious and envied, philosophers and visionaries, all grouped like the flowers in a bouquet around one rare blossom, the bride. A wedding ball is the world in miniature.

At the moment when the scene was most animated, Crevel took the baron by the arm and said in his ear, in the most natural way imaginable:

"*Tudieu!* what a pretty little creature that is in pink, bombarding you with her glances!—"

"Whom do you mean?"

"The wife of that deputy-chief you are pushing ahead, God knows how! Madame Marneffe."

"How do you know that?"

"Look here, Hulot, I will try to forgive you for the wrong you have done me if you will take me to her house, and I will receive you at Héloïse's. Everybody's asking who that charming creature is. Are you sure that no one in your department will explain how her husband's appointment happened to be made?—Oh! you lucky rascal! she's worth more than a whole department.—Ah! I would be glad to visit her department.—Come, Cinna, let us be friends!—"

"Better friends than ever," said the baron to the dealer in perfumery, "and I promise to be a good fellow. Within a month I'll take you to dinner with the little angel.—For we're dealing with angels now, old comrade. I advise you to do as I have done and give up the devils—''

Cousin Bette, safely installed on Rue Vanneau, in a pretty little suite on the third floor, left the ball at ten o'clock, in order to go home and look at the title to her twelve hundred francs of income, in two certificates; the reversion of one was vested in Countess Steinbock, of the other in Madame Hulot the younger. It will be understood now how Monsieur Crevel was enabled to speak to his friend Hulot of Madame Marneffe, and to have knowledge of a mystery of which everybody was ignorant; for, Monsieur Marneffe being absent, Cousin Bette, the baron and Valérie were the only ones in the secret.

The baron had committed the imprudence of presenting Madame Marneffe with a toilette much too splendid for the wife of a deputy-chief; the other women were jealous both of Valérie's costume and her beauty. There was a deal of whispering behind fans, for Marneffe's lack of funds had been the talk of the department; the clerk was begging for assistance just when the baron fell in love with madame. Moreover, Hector could not conceal his ecstasy at the success achieved by Valérie, who, with modest reserve but great dignity, envied by all, underwent the critical scrutiny which women dread so keenly, when they make their first appearance upon a new social level.

Having bestowed his wife, his daughter and his son-in-law in a carriage, the baron found a way to escape unobserved, leaving his son and daughter-in-law to play the part of master and mistress of the house.

He entered Madame Marneffe's carriage and escorted her home; but he found her silent and thoughtful, almost melancholy.

"My happiness makes you very sad, Valérie," said he, drawing her to his side on the back seat of the carriage.

"Why, my friend, don't you think that a poor woman should always be pensive when committing her first sin, even though her husband's infamous conduct gives her her freedom?—Do you think I have no soul, no faith, no religion? You exhibited your joy this evening in the most indiscreet way, and placarded me outrageously. Upon my word a college student wouldn't have been so silly as you were. And so all those fine ladies tore me to pieces with their haughty glances and biting words! What woman doesn't cling to her reputation? You have ruined me. Ah! I am yours, you know, and I have no other way to obtain forgiveness for the sin than to be faithful to you.—Monster!" said she, with a laugh, and allowing him to kiss her, "you knew very well what you were doing. Madame Coquet, the wife of our department chief, came and sat down by me to admire my lace. 'It's English,' said she. 'Is it very expensive, madame?'—'I have no idea,' I replied. 'The lace came to me from my mother, I'm not rich enough to buy anything of the sort!'"

Madame Marneffe, as we see, had ended by fascinating the old beau of the Empire so completely, that he thought that he was the first to lead her astray, and that he had aroused in her heart a passion so great as to make her forget her duty. She said that she was abandoned by the infamous Marneffe after they had been married three days, and for unspeakable reasons. Since then she had remained the most pure of maidens, and very happy, for marriage seemed to her a horrible thing. Hence her present sadness.

"If it should be with love as with marriage!—" said she weeping.

These artful falsehoods, which almost all women resort to in the position in which Valérie then was, gave the baron a glimpse of the roses of the seventh heaven.

Thus did Valérie play her cards, while the amorous artist and Hortense were, it may be, impatiently awaiting the baroness's final blessing, and her last kiss for her daughter. At seven o'clock in the morning the baron, inexpressibly happy, for he had found in his Valérie a combination of the most innocent of maidens and consummate demons, returned home to relieve Monsieur and Madame Hulot the younger from their ungrateful task.

The dancers, male and female, almost strangers to the family, who eventually take possession of the ground at all weddings, were in the midst of those interminable contradances called *cotillons*, the *bouillotte* players were intent upon their game, and Père Crevel had won six thousand francs.

The newspapers, distributed by carriers, contained this little notice among the happenings in Paris:

"The celebration of the marriage of M. le Comte Steinbock and Mademoiselle Hortense Hulot, daughter of Baron Hulot d'Ervy, Councilor of State, and Director at the War Department, niece of the illustrious Comte de Forzheim, took place this morning at the church of Saint-Thomas d'Aquin. This ceremony attracted a large assemblage. We noticed among the guests several of our artistic celebrities: Léon de Lora, Joseph Bridau, Stidmann, Bixiou; officials of the War Department and Council of State, and several members of the two Chambers; also the most eminent of the Polish *émigrés,* Comte Paz, Comte Laginski, etc.

"M. le Comte Wenceslas Steinbock is the grand-nephew of the celebrated general of King Charles XII. of Sweden. The young count, having taken part in the Polish insurrection, fled for refuge to France, where the just renown of his talent has procured for him letters of limited naturalization."

Thus, notwithstanding the distressing financial condition of Baron Hulot d'Ervy, nothing of all that public opinion demands, not even newspaper notoriety, was lacking to the success of his daughter's marriage, the celebration of which was in every detail similar to that of the younger Hulot with Mademoiselle Crevel. This festive occasion caused a marked decrease in the current gossip concerning the director's financial condition, just as the marriage-portion bestowed upon his daughter explained the necessity he was under, of having recourse to borrowing.

Here ends, in a certain sense, the introduction to this story. This narrative is to the drama which completes it, what the premises are to a syllogism, what the preliminary explanation is to every classical tragedy.

*

When, in Paris, a woman has determined to offer her beauty for sale, it does not by any means follow that her fortune is made. One meets there many adorable creatures, very clever too, in distressingly slender circumstances, ending very miserably a life begun in dissipation. This is the reason. It is not enough for a woman to adopt the trade of a courtesan, with the purpose of enjoying all its advantages, while still retaining unsullied the robe of a virtuous wife. Vice does not easily achieve its triumphs; it bears this resemblance to genius that they both require a combination of fortunate circumstances to bring about the conjunction of fortune and talent. But for the extraordinary phases of the Revolution, there would have been no Emperor; he would have been simply a second edition of Fabert. Venal beauty without admirers, without celebrity, without the cross of dishonor which squandered wealth bestows, is a Correggio in a garret, genius expiring in its attic. A Laïs at Paris must therefore, first of all, find a rich man who will fall so deeply in love with her as to give her her price. She ought, above all things, to maintain an air of great refinement, which is a sort of advertisement for her, to have sufficiently-good manners to flatter a man's self-esteem, to possess the Sophie Arnould variety of wit which arouses the rich from their apathy; she ought, lastly, to make herself attractive to libertines, by seeming to be faithful to some one man, whose good fortune thereupon becomes a subject of envy.

These conditions, which women of this sort call *luck*, are not readily satisfied in Paris, although it is a city filled with millionaires, idlers, and *blasé*, capricious old men. Providence has most assuredly protected, in this way, the households of clerks and small tradesmen, for whom these obstacles are, to say the least, doubled by the surroundings amid which they perform their evolutions. Nevertheless, there are still enough Madame Marneffes in Paris for Valérie to stand as a type, in this history of morals. Some of these women act in obedience to real passion and necessity at the same time, like Madame Colleville, who was for so long attached to one of the most famous orators of the Left, the banker Keller; others are impelled by vanity, like Madame de la Baudraye, who almost retained her virtue despite her flight with Lousteau; these are drawn on by the exigencies of the toilette, those by the impossibility of supporting a family upon salaries that are evidently too small. The niggardliness of the State, or of the Chambers if you will, is the cause of many a downfall, it engenders much corruption. It is fashionable just now to express much compassion for the fate of the working-classes, who are represented as ground down by the manufacturers; but the State is a hundred times harder in its dealing than the most grasping of manufacturers; it carries economy in the matter of salaries to the point of absurdity. Work hard, and your trade pays you something in reason for your work; but what does the State give to its multitude of obscure and faithful toilers?

To swerve from the path of honor is, for a married woman, an unpardonable sin; but there are degrees therein. Some women, far from being depraved, hide their missteps and remain virtuous women so far as appearance goes, like the two whose adventures were adverted to but now; while some of them add to their faults the ignominy of speculating upon them. Madame Marneffe may be considered the type of those ambitious married courtesans who, in the first place, enter upon a career of depravity willing to accept all its consequences, and who are determined to make their fortune and enjoy themselves at the same time, with little scruple as to the means; but such women, like Madame Marneffe, almost always have their husbands for decoys and accomplices. These Macchiavellis in petticoats are the most dangerous of women; and of all the unsavory varieties of the female Parisian, they are the worst. A true courtesan, like the Josépha, the Schontzes, a Malaga or Jenny Cadine, carries with her, in the absolute independence of her condition, an advertisement as unmistakable as the red lantern of the house of prostitution or the Quinquet lamps of the gambling-den. A man knows then that he is going to his ruin. But the mawkish pretensions to chastity and virtue, the hypocritical manœuvres of a married woman, who never allows anything to be seen but the vulgar needs of a household, and who makes a pretence of shunning all frivolities, lead him on without éclat to ruin,—ruin which is the more extraordinary in that we excuse it although we do not seek to explain it. It is the ignoble book of expenditures, and not the joyous caprice of the moment, which devours fortunes. A father of a family ruins himself ingloriously, and the great consolation of satisfied vanity fails him in his poverty.

This tirade will pierce like an arrow to the heart of many families. We find Madame Marneffes on all the floors of the social structure, and even amid courts; for Valérie is a sad reality, modeled from life even to the smallest details. Unhappily this portrait will cure no one of the mania for loving angels with a sweet smile, a pensive air, and an innocent face, whose hearts are strong-boxes.

About three years after Hortense's marriage, in 1841, Baron Hulot d'Ervy was generally supposed to have reformed, to have unharnessed, to adopt the expression of the first surgeon of Louis XV., and yet Madame Marneffe was then costing him twice as much as Josépha had ever done. But Valérie, although she was always well-dressed, affected the simplicity of a deputy-chief's wife; she reserved her splendor for her *robes de chambre*, for her house costumes. Thus she sacrificed the vanity of a true Parisian to her beloved Hector. And yet, when she went to the play, she always appeared in a stylish hat and a costume of the greatest elegance; the baron escorted her thither in a carriage, to a choice box.

The suite on Rue Vanneau, which occupied the whole second floor of a modern mansion with a courtyard in front and a garden behind, was redolent of virtue. Its splendor consisted in chintz hangings, in handsome and comfortable furniture. The only exception was the bed-room, in which was displayed the profusion of a Jenny Cadine or a Schontz. There were lace-curtains, cashmeres, brocade portières, mantel ornaments, of which the models were made by Stidmann, and a little cabinet filled with marvels of art. Hulot did not choose that his Valérie should dwell in a nest inferior in magnificence to the gold and pearl-bedizened den of a Josépha. The two principal rooms, the salon and the dining-room, were furnished, one in red damask, the other in carved oak.—But, impelled by the desire to secure perfect harmony, the baron, at the end of six months, reinforced this ephemeral magnificence with something more enduring, by presenting her with sundry articles of great value, as for example, a service of silver-plate which cost more than twenty-four thousand francs.

Madame Marneffe's establishment, in two years gained the reputation of being very attractive. There was card-playing there. Valérie herself was speedily discovered to be an amiable and intellectual person. To justify the change in her circumstances the report was spread that her *natural father*, Marēchal Montcornet, had left her a handsome legacy in the care of a trustee. With one eye to the future Valērie had added religious hypocrisy to her social hypocrisy. Regular in her attendance at service on Sunday, she received all the honors of piety. She collected alms, became interested in charitable work, passed the consecrated bread, and did some good in the quarter, all at Hector's expense. Thus everything about her establishment was conducted with perfect propriety; so that many people maintained the purity of her relations with the baron, dwelling upon the age of the Councilor of State, to whom they attributed a platonic liking for Madame Marneffe's refined wit, charm of manner and entertaining conversation, almost equal to the late Louis the Eighteenth's fondness for well-turned notes.

The baron left the house with all the other guests, about midnight, and returned a quarter of an hour later. Herein lies the secret of this profound secret:

The concierges of the house were Monsieur and Madame Olivier, who, through the influence of the baron, a friend of the landlord, who was in quest of a concierge, had removed from their obscure and unproductive quarters on Rue du Doyenné to these lucrative and magnificent quarters on Rue Vanneau. Now Madame Olivier, who was formerly a laundress in the household of Charles X., and was deprived of that *position* with the fall of the legitimate monarchy, had three children. The eldest, already a notary's clerk, was the especial object of the adoration of the Oliviers. This Benjamin, over whose head hung the threat of being forced to become a soldier for six years, was about to see his brilliant career rudely interrupted, when Madame Marneffe procured his exemption from military service for one of those defects in physical conformation, which the councils of revision had no difficulty in discovering, when a request to that effect was whispered in their ears by some ministerial power. Olivier, once a whipper-in in the employ of Charles X., and his wife, would therefore have nailed Jesus to the cross again for Baron Hulot and Madame Marneffe.

What could the world say, to whom the earlier episode of the Brazilian, Monsieur Montès de Montejanos, was unknown? Nothing. Moreover, the world is full of indulgence for the mistress of a salon where people enjoy themselves. Madame Marneffe in addition to all her charms possessed the advantage, highly-valued, of being an occult power. For instance, Claude Vignon, recently appointed secretary to the Maréchal Prince de Wissembourg, and who dreamed of being admitted to the Council of State in the capacity of master of requests, was a frequenter of her salon, whither came, also, several deputies, who were good fellows and gamblers. Madame Marneffe's circle was formed with judicious moderation; it consisted only of people whose opinions and morals were in accord, who were interested in upholding each other and in proclaiming the infinite merit of the mistress of the house.

Complicity in vice—remember this axiom—is the true Holy-Alliance, in Paris. Worldly interests always end by breaking asunder; vicious people always understand each other.

In the third month of her residence on Rue Vanneau, Madame Marneffe had received Monsieur Crevel, who had forthwith become mayor of his arrondissement, and officer of the Legion of Honor. He hesitated long; it was a question of laying aside the famous uniform of the National Guard in which he was accustomed to strut about at the Tuileries, imagining himself as great a soldier as the Emperor; but ambition, counseled by Madame Marneffe, was stronger than vanity. Monsieur le Maire deemed his liaison with Mademoiselle Héloïse Brisetout altogether incompatible with his political elevation. Long before his accession to the civic throne of the mayoralty his amours were wrapped in profound mystery. But Crevel, as may be imagined, had purchased the right to take his revenge for the abduction of Josépha, as often as he could, by a certificate for a yearly revenue of six thousand francs, in the name of Valérie Fortin, wife of Monsieur Marneffe, from whom she was living apart. Valérie, who was endowed, by her mother perhaps, with the species of genius peculiar to the kept-mistress, divined at a glance the character of this grotesque adorer. The remark: "I have never known a woman in good position!" made by Crevel to Lisbeth, and by Lisbeth repeated to her dear Valérie, entered largely into her calculations in the transaction to which she owed her income of six thousand francs in the five per cents. Since then she had never allowed her prestige to suffer any diminution in the eyes of César Birotteau's former traveling salesman.

Crevel had married, for money, the daughter of a miller of La Brie, an only child, whose inheritance made up three-fourths of his fortune, for retail shopkeepers, in the majority of cases, acquire wealth not so much in their business, as by an alliance between the shop and the results of rural thrift. A great number of farmers, millers, milk-dealers, and husbandmen in the outskirts of Paris dream of the glories of the counting-room for their daughters, and see in a retail shopkeeper, a jeweler, or a money-changer, a son-in-law much more after their heart than a notary or an attorney, whose social elevation gives them a feeling of uneasiness; they are afraid of being looked down upon later, by these more eminent members of the middle-class. Madame Crevel, a very vulgar and foolish person, and far from beautiful, died seasonably, having afforded her husband no other enjoyment than that of being a father. At the outset of his commercial career this rake, held in check by the demands of his business, and restrained by lack of means, played the rôle of Tantalus. Having relations, as he expressed it, with the most fashionable ladies in Paris, he would bow them out of his shop with the effusive courtesy of the shopkeeper, filled with admiration of their grace, their manner of wearing the latest styles, and all the unnameable effects of what is called *race*. To raise himself to the level of one of these salon fairies, was a longing formed in his youth, and held in subjection in his heart. *To obtain favors* from Madame Marneffe therefore was not only to endow his chimera with life, but it was with him a matter of pride, of vanity, of self-esteem, as we have seen. His ambition was intensified by success. His head was enormously exalted, and when the head is captivated, the heart feels the effect, and the enjoyment is increased tenfold. Moreover Madame Marneffe led Crevel into paths of investigation of which he had no suspicion, for neither Josépha nor Héloïse had ever loved him, while Madame Marneffe deemed it necessary to thoroughly deceive this man, in whom she saw an inexhaustible treasure-chest. The cajoleries of purchased love are more charming than the real thing. True love is quite consistent with bitter quarrels, wherein one or other is wounded to the quick; but the quarrel in jest is, on the other hand, a caress bestowed upon the self-esteem of the dupe. The infrequency of his interviews served to maintain Crevel's desire at the level of ardent passion. He was forever jostling against the virtuous sternness of Valérie, who would feign remorse, and talk about what her father must think of her in the paradise of heroes. There was a sort of coldness to overcome, and the sly creature would make him believe that he had triumphed over it, by making a show of yielding to his mad passion; but the next moment, as if ashamed, she would reassert the pride of a respectable woman, resume her virtuous airs, for all the world like an Englishwoman, and would crush her Crevel beneath the weight of her dignity, for Crevel had at first willingly believed her virtuous.

In short, Valérie possessed certain specialties in the matter of gallantry, which rendered her indispensable to Crevel as well as to the baron. In presence of the world she displayed the fascinating combination of modest and dreamy innocence, irreproachable respectability, and wit heightened by refinement and the charming manners of the Creole; but, in a tête-à-tête, she excelled the courtesans themselves; she was mischievous, amusing, fertile in inventions. This contrast is vastly agreeable to a man of the Crevel stamp; he is flattered at the thought that he is the sole author of the comedy, he believes that it is played for his sole benefit, and he laughs at the charming hypocrisy, while he admires the clever actress.

Valérie had taken possession of Baron Hulot in a wondrous way; she had compelled him to grow old by a bit of sly flattery, which will perhaps serve to depict the diabolical cunning of women of her type. In generously endowed organizations there comes a time when, as in a besieged city which long makes a brave resistance, the real condition of affairs declares itself. As she foresaw the approaching dissolution of the old beau of the Empire, Valérie deemed it advisable to hasten it.

"Why do you put yourself to so much trouble,

my old grumbler?'' said she, some six months after their clandestine and doubly-adulterous union. "Can it be that you have pretensions elsewhere? would you like to be unfaithful to me? For my own part, I should like you much better if you didn't paint. Sacrifice these borrowed charms of yours to my wish. Do you think that the two sous' worth of varnish on your boots, your rubber belt, your corsets and your false forelock are what I love in you? And then, too, the older you are the less fear I shall have of my Hulot being stolen from me by a rival!''

Believing, therefore, as implicitly in the divine friendship as in the love of Madame Marneffe, with whom he expected to pass the rest of his life, the Councilor of State followed the advice of his privy councilor by ceasing to dye his whiskers and hair. After he had received from Valérie this touching declaration, the tall and handsome Hector made his appearance one fine morning as white as snow. Madame Marneffe easily satisfied her dear Hector that she had seen, a hundred times, the white line at the roots of his hair.

"White hair suits your face admirably,'' said she, as she looked him over; "it tones it down; you are infinitely handsome, you are lovely.''

Once started in this direction the baron finally discarded his leather waistcoat and his corsets, and got rid of all his paraphernalia. His paunch fell into place, and obesity declared itself. The oak became a tower, and the heaviness of his movements was the more appalling in that the baron had really aged prodigiously in playing the rôle of Louis XII. The eyebrows remained black, and vaguely reminded one of the once handsome Hulot, as in the ruins of certain old feudal walls, some trifling detail of carving remains to show what the castle was in its prime. This incongruity rendered the still keen and youthful glance all the more extraordinary in that sallow face, where flesh-tints à la Rubens had flourished so long; because one could detect there, by dint of sundry livid marks, and in the depth of the wrinkles, the struggles of a passion in rebellion against nature. Hulot at this time was one of those grand human ruins where virility still gives token of its presence by the tufts of hair in the ears and nose, and on the fingers, producing the effect of the moss that grows upon the almost immortal monuments of the Roman Empire.

How had Valérie succeeded in keeping Crevel and Hulot under her roof side by side, when the vindictive major was determined to achieve a notorious triumph over Hulot? Without answering this question at once, for it will be solved as the drama proceeds, we may remark that Lisbeth and Valérie, between them, had invented a prodigious machine, whose powerful agency assisted in bringing about that result. Marneffe, when he saw how his wife shone in the surroundings amid which she was enthroned, like the sun of a stellar system, appeared, in the eyes of the world, to have experienced a renewal of his passion for her, he had gone mad over her. If this jealousy made Monsieur Marneffe a kill-joy, it imparted an extraordinary value to Valérie's favors. Marneffe nevertheless exhibited a confidence in his chief, which degenerated into a meekness of demeanor that was almost laughable. The only person who aroused his resentment was no other than Crevel.

Marneffe, ruined by those varieties of debauchery peculiar to great capitals, described by the Roman poets, and for which our modern sense of decency has no name, had become as hideous as an anatomical wax-figure. But this walking pestilence, dressed in the finest of broadcloth, crawled along upon shriveled legs encased in trowsers of the latest style. The wrinkled breast was swathed in the whitest of perfumed linen, and the fetid odors of human decay were smothered with musk. This ghastly spectacle of expiring vice, with red heels to his shoes,—for Valérie had dressed Marneffe in conformity with her means, with his decoration and his office,—terrified Crevel, who found it difficult to meet the deputy-chief's white eyes. Marneffe was the mayor's nightmare. When he became conscious of the extraordinary power Lisbeth and his wife had conferred upon him, the miserable villain derived keen enjoyment from it, and played upon it as upon a musical instrument; and as the gambling tables in the salon were the last resource of his mind, which was as worn out as the body that contained it, he plucked Crevel, who thought it best to *deal gently* with the respectable official, *whom he was deceiving!*

When he saw that Crevel cut so poor a figure with this hideous and despicable mummy, whose corruption was a secret to the worthy mayor, and more especially when he saw how utterly Valérie despised him, for she laughed at Crevel as one laughs at a clown, the baron probably deemed himself so secure from all rivalry that he constanly invited him to dinner.

Valérie, under the protection of these two passions on sentry duty at her sides, and of a jealous husband, attracted every eye, and kindled a flame in every breast, in the circle in which she shone. Thus, while keeping up appearances, she had succeeded, in about three years, in fulfilling the most difficult conditions of the success to which courtesans aspire, and which they so rarely attain, with the assistance of scandal, their own audacity, and the public notoriety of their lives. Like a well-cut diamond superbly set by Chanor, Valérie's beauty, once buried in the mine of Rue du Doyenné, was worth more than its real value; it made people unhappy!—Claude Vignon loved her secretly.

This retrospective explanation, a necessary evil when we meet people again after an interval of three years, is Valérie's balance-sheet, as it were. Now let us glance at that of her partner Lisbeth.

In the Marneffe household Cousin Bette occupied the position of a relation who performed the dual functions of companion and housekeeper; but she knew nothing of the twofold humiliation to which, in most cases, the poor creatures are subjected who are so unfortunate as to accept such equivocal positions. Lisbeth and Valérie presented the touching spectacle of one of those friendships, which are so strong and so little likely to be formed by women, that the Parisians, who always know too much, immediately make scandalous remarks about them. The contrast between the cold, masculine nature of the Lorrainer, and Valérie's sprightly Creole temperament helped to give color to the calumny. Moreover, Madame Marneffe had unwittingly furnished material to the gossips, by the care she took of her friend, in the interest of a certain matrimonial project, which was destined, as we shall see, to complete Lisbeth's vengeance. A tremendous revolution had taken place in Cousin Bette; Valérie, who insisted upon dressing her, had derived the greatest benefit from it. The eccentric old maid, now in the clutches of the corset, displayed a slender figure; she consummated her submission by wearing *bandoline* upon her glossy hair, she accepted her dresses as they were sent to her from the dressmaker, and wore stylish boots and gray silk stockings, all of which, by the way, were included by the dealers in Valérie's account and paid for by whom it may concern. Thus restored, although still dressed in yellow cashmere, Bette would have been unrecognizable to one who had met her after these three years. A black diamond, rarest of all diamonds, cut by a skilful hand, and mounted in an appropriate setting, she was appreciated at her full value by certain aspiring clerks.

One who saw Bette for the first time would shudder involuntarily at sight of the wild poetic beauty which Valérie had cleverly brought into strong relief by humanizing this savage nun through the agency of the toilette, by artfully framing, with broad bands of ribbon, the sharp, olive-skinned face, in which shone a pair of eyes that matched the hair in blackness, and by making the most of the rigid form. Like one of Cranach's or Van Eyck's *Virgins*, or like a Byzantine *Virgin*, that had left its frame, Bette retained the rigidity, the symmetry of those mysterious figures, cousins-german to Isis and other divinities reared upon pedestals by the Egyptian sculptors. She was a walking mass of granite, basalt, porphyry. Free from want for the rest of her days, Bette was always in charming humor, and carried joviality with her, wherever she went to dine. The baron moreover paid the rent of her little suite, furnished, as we have seen, with the cast-off goods and chattels of Valérie's boudoir and bed-room.

"Having begun life," said she, "like a famished goat, I am ending it like a lioness."

She continued to do the most difficult bits of lace-work for Monsieur Rivet, simply, as she said, to avoid wasting her time. And yet her life was, as we shall see, very fully occupied; but it is in the nature of those who come from the country never to abandon their means of livelihood, in which respect they resemble the Jews.

Every morning at daybreak, Cousin Bette went

herself to the great market, with the cook. In Bette's scheme, the account-book, which ruined Baron Hulot, was to enrich her dear Valérie, and so it did in fact.

What mistress of a household has not, since 1838, felt the disastrous effects of the antisocial doctrines spread among the lower classes by incendiary writers? In every household the servant evil is the most painful of all pecuniary evils. With very few exceptions, and they deserve the Montyon prize, a cook, male or female, is a domestic thief, an insolent, paid thief, to whom the government obligingly holds itself out as a receiver of the booty, thus smoothing the path to theft, which is almost authorized in respect of cooks by the old jest *faire danser l'anse du panier*,—"to make the handle of the basket dance"—said of cooks who receive commission on the provisions they buy.

Where these women formerly asked for forty sous to buy a lottery-ticket, they take to-day fifty francs for the savings-bank. And the cold-blooded Puritans, who amuse themselves by making philanthropic experiments in France, believe that they have made us a moral people! Between the table of the householder and the market these people have established a secret tariff of their own, and the city of Paris is not so skilful in collecting its entry dues, as they are in collecting their duties upon everything. In addition to the fifty per cent which they add to the cost of the supplies for the kitchen, they exact handsome presents from the dealers. The most eminent tradesmen tremble before this occult power; they pay what it demands, without a word; everybody, carriage-makers, jewelers, tailors, etc. If anyone undertakes to watch them, the servants retort with insolence, or with the no less costly inanities of pretended confusion; to-day they seek information concerning the masters, as the masters used to do concerning them. The evil, which has in very truth reached its height, and against which the courts are beginning to take stern measures, but to no purpose, will not disappear until a law be passed which will require hired domestic servants to have a workman's certificate. Then the evil will cease as by enchantment. Every servant being compelled to produce his certificate, and the masters being compelled to indorse thereon the cause of dismissal, the present demoralization would certainly meet with a vigorous check. Those people who are occupied with the important political questions of the moment, have no idea to what lengths the depravity of the lower classes at Paris has gone; it is on a par with the jealousy by which they are consumed. Statistics are silent as to the appalling number of young workmen of twenty who marry cooks of forty or fifty, made rich by theft. One shudders to think of the result of such unions from the three-fold point of view of criminality, degeneration of the race, and unhappy households. As for the purely financial evil resulting from these thefts by servants, it is enormous from a political standpoint. The two-fold increase in the cost of living debars many households from all luxuries. Luxuries!—they make the half of international commerce, even as they are the refining element of life. Books and flowers are as necessary as bread, to many people.

Lisbeth, who was well aware of this terrible ulcer of Parisian households, was thinking of undertaking the management of Valérie's establishment, when she promised her her support, in the terrible scene when they swore to be as sisters to each other. She sent for a relation on her mother's side, from the heart of the Vosges, once cook for the Bishop of Nancy, a pious old maid and honest to the last degree. Fearing, however, her lack of experience of Paris, and especially the evil counsels which make a wreck of so much weak-kneed loyalty, Lisbeth always went with Mathurine to the great market, and tried to teach her how to buy. To know the actual price of articles in order to secure the dealer's respect, to live on unsubstantial dishes, such as fish, for example, when they are cheap, to be posted as to the market value of articles of food, and to foresee a rise in price so as to purchase cheaply, this housekeeper's instinct is most essential to domestic economy in Paris. As Mathurine received good wages, as she was overwhelmed with presents, she liked the place well enough to exult over good bargains. So it was that for some time past she had rivaled Lisbeth herself, who considered her sufficiently-well instructed and reliable to go alone to the market except on days when

Valérie was to have company, which, by the way, happened quite frequently. This is the reason. The baron began by maintaining the strictest decorum; but his passion for Madame Marneffe became in a short time so ardent and so exacting, that he wished to be separated from her as little as possible. After dining there at first four times a week, he thought it would be delightful to take his dinner there every day. Six months after his daughter's marriage, he began to pay two thousand francs a month under the name of board. Madame Marneffe invited those persons whom her dear baron desired to entertain. The dinner-table was always laid for six, as the baron might bring three friends unexpectedly. Lisbeth, by her thrifty ways, solved the difficult problem of keeping up the table handsomely for a thousand francs a month and giving a thousand francs to Madame Marneffe. As Valérie's toilette was paid for, in great measure, by Crevel and the baron, the two friends found it possible to lay aside a thousand-franc note each month on account of that item. Thus this pure, innocent creature possessed at this time about a hundred and fifty thousand francs that she had saved. She had capitalized her income and her monthly perquisites, and had added enormously to them, thanks to the generosity with which Crevel admitted the capital of *his little duchess* to a share in his successful financial operations. Crevel had initiated Valérie into all the slang of the Bourse and the methods of speculation; and like all Parisian women she speedily became more skilful than her master. Lisbeth, who did not spend a sou of her twelve hundred francs, whose rent and dresses were paid for, who never took a sou from her pocket, also possessed a little capital of five to six thousand francs which Crevel, with fatherly interest, invested for her.

*

Nevertheless, the baron's love and Crevel's were a heavy burden for Valérie. On the day when the story of this drama recommences, excited by one of those events which perform in life the function of the bell, at the stroke of which the bees begin to swarm, Valérie had gone up to Lisbeth's room to indulge in one of those lengthy plaints, emitted languidly, as women smoke cigarettes, to soothe their petty miseries.

"Lisbeth, my love, this morning two hours of Crevel to endure; it's murderous! Oh! how I wish I could send you in my place!"

"Unfortunately that cannot be," said Lisbeth with a smile. "I shall die a virgin."

"To think of belonging to these two old men! there are times when I am ashamed of myself! Ah! if my poor mother could see me!"

"You mistake me for Crevel," said Lisbeth.

"Tell me, dear little Bette, that you do not despise me?"

"Aha! if I had been pretty I would have had—adventures!" cried Lisbeth. "There's your justification."

"But you would have listened to your heart only," said Madame Marneffe, with a sigh.

"Bah!" replied Lisbeth; "Marneffe is a dead

man they've forgotten to bury, the baron is like a husband to you, Crevel is your adorer; I look upon you, like all women, as being perfectly unexceptionable."

"No, my dear, adorable girl, it isn't that that causes my sorrow; you don't choose to understand me—"

"Oh! indeed I do!" cried the Lorrainer; "for what's understood is part of my vengeance. What would you have?—I am at work at it."

"To love Wenceslas till I fairly lose flesh over it, and not to be able to succeed in seeing him!" said Valérie stretching out her arms. "Hulot suggests to him to dine here and my artist refuses! The monster of a man doesn't know how I idolize him! What's his wife? a pretty piece of flesh! yes, she is lovely but I,—I know what I am; I am worse!"

"Never fear, my little girl, he will come," said Lisbeth, in the tone a nurse might use to an impatient child, "I wish him to—"

"But when?"

"This week perhaps."

"Let me kiss you."

As will be seen, the two women were but one; all Valérie's acts, even the most giddy, her pleasures, her fits of pouting, were decided upon after mature deliberation between them.

Lisbeth, strangely moved by this courtesan's life, advised Valérie in everything, and followed the course of her vengeance with a pitiless logic. She adored Valérie too, she had taken her for her daughter, her friend, her love; she found in her the obedience of the Creole, the pliability of the voluptuary; she chatted with her every morning with more pleasure than with Wenceslas; they could laugh at their mutual mischievousness, at the folly of men, and reckon up together the growing interest of their respective treasures. Furthermore Lisbeth had found in her undertaking and in her new friendship a much more extensive field for activity than in her absurd love for Wenceslas. The pleasures of satisfied hate are the keenest, the dearest to the heart. Love is, as it were, the gold, and hate the iron of the mine of sentiments which exists within us. Lastly Valérie offered to Lisbeth, in all its glory, the beauty she adored as one adores whatever one does not possess; beauty much more manageable than that of Wenceslas, who had always been cold and insensible to her.

After nearly three years Lisbeth was able to mark the progress of the subterranean mine upon which she was expending her life, and to which she was devoting all her intelligence. Lisbeth did the thinking, Madame Marneffe the acting. Madame Marneffe was the axe, Lisbeth the hand that guided it, and that hand was hewing down, with oft-repeated blows, the family that became more hateful to it from day to day, for one's hate increases just as one loves more and more every day, when one is in love. Love and hate are sentiments which feed upon themselves; but of the two hate is the longer-lived. Love is circumscribed by its limited forces, it derives its power from life and prodigality; hate resembles death, or avarice—it is in a certain sense an active abstraction, above beings and things. Lisbeth, having entered upon an existence which was congenial to her, unfolded all her faculties; she reigned after the manner of the Jesuits, an unseen power. The regeneration of her person was complete. Her face was radiant. Lisbeth dreamed of becoming Madame la Maréchale Hulot.

This scene, in which the two friends bluntly spoke out their every thought without mincing matters, took place just after Lisbeth's return from the market, where she had been to procure the materials for a dainty dinner. Marneffe, who coveted the office of Monsieur Coquet, was entertaining him with the virtuous Madame Coquet, and Valérie hoped to negotiate through Hulot for the resignation of the chief of the bureau that very evening. Lisbeth dressed to go to the baroness's, where she was to dine.

"You will come back to pour the tea for us, my Bette?" said Valérie.

"I hope so—"

"What! you hope so? Have you got to the point of sleeping with Adeline so as to drink her tears while she's asleep?"

"If I only could!" replied Lisbeth with a laugh, "I wouldn't say no. She is paying for her good luck, and I am happy, for I remember my childhood.

Everyone in her turn. She will be in the gutter, and I shall be Comtesse de Forzheim!—"

Lisbeth bent her steps toward Rue Plumet, whither she had been in the habit of going for some time, as one goes to the theatre, to feast upon emotion.

The apartments selected by Hulot for his wife consisted of a large and high antechamber, a salon and a bed-room with dressing-room. The dining-room adjoined the salon at the side. Two servant's chambers and a kitchen, on the third floor, completed the suite, which was not unworthy of a Councilor of State and director in the War Department. The house itself, the courtyard and the staircase were majestic. The baroness, being obliged to furnish her salon, bed-room and dining-room, with the remnants of her former splendor, had selected the best from among the ruins at the mansion on Rue de l'Université. Indeed the poor woman loved these dumb witnesses of her past happiness; in their very silence there was an eloquence that helped to comfort her. In her memory she caught glimpses of bright flowers, just as she could distinguish in the faded carpets, the roses that were hardly visible to others.

Upon entering the immense reception-room, where a dozen chairs, a barometer, a tall stove and long white calico curtains trimmed with red, recalled the dreary antechambers of the government departments, one's heart was fairly wrung; one instinctively felt the loneliness of the life this woman was living. Grief, like pleasure, creates an atmosphere of its own. The first glance at the interior of a house is enough to tell us whether love or despair rules therein. We should find Adeline in an enormous bed-room, furnished with handsome pieces manufactured by Jacob Desmalters, in spotted mahogany embellished with ornaments dating from the Empire, those bronzes which succeeded in being colder than Louis the Sixteenth's brasses! And we should shudder to see her sitting in a Roman armchair, in front of the sphinxes that adorned a work-table, her color all gone, feigning a deceitful air of cheerfulness, and retaining her imperial bearing, as she had retained the blue velvet dress she wore at home. Her proud heart sustained her body and kept her beauty from fading. At the end of her first year in this abode, the baroness had drunk the cup of unhappiness to the dregs.

"In bestowing me here, my Hector has made life even more pleasant for me than it should be for a simple peasant-girl," she said to herself. "He wishes me to live thus: his will be done! I am Baroness Hulot, sister-in-law to a marshal of France; I have never done the slightest wrong, my two children are settled in life, and I can await death, wrapped in the spotless veil of my wifely purity, in the crêpe of my vanished happiness."

The portrait of Hulot in the uniform of commissary-general of the Imperial Guard, painted by Robert Lefebvre in 1810, hung above the work-table, where on the announcement of a visitor,

Adeline would close the *Imitation of Christ*, which was her ordinary reading. This irreproachable Madeleine heard also the voice of the Holy Spirit in her desert.

"Mariette, my girl," said Lisbeth to the cook who opened the door for her, "how's my dear Adeline?"

"Oh! very well, so far as appearances go, mademoiselle; but, between you and me, if she goes on as she's going now she'll kill herself," said Mariette in Lisbeth's ear. "Really you ought to persuade her to live better. Yesterday madame made me give her in the morning two sous' worth of milk and a little one-sou loaf; for dinner a herring or a little cold veal, and told me to cook a pound of it for the week, when she dines alone here, of course. She won't spend but ten sous a day on her food. That isn't reasonable. If I should tell monsieur le maréchal of this fine scheme of hers, he might have a row with monsieur le baron and disinherit him; but you, you're so good and clever, you can arrange things—"

"Well, why don't you speak to my cousin the baron?" said Lisbeth.

"Ah! my dear young lady, it's about twenty or twenty-five days since he was here,—indeed he hasn't been here since we saw you last! And then madame told me never to ask monsieur for money or she'd send me away. But when you talk about suffering—ah! poor madame has suffered! It's the first time monsieur has forgotten her so long.—

Every time anyone rang she'd run to the window, but for the last five days she doesn't leave her chair. She reads! Whenever she goes to see madame la comtesse she says to me; 'Mariette,' says she, 'if monsieur comes tell him I'm at home and send the concierge for me; he shall be well paid for his run.' "

"Poor cousin!" said Bette, "it breaks my heart. I speak of her to my cousin every day. What can I do? He says: 'You're right, Bette, I'm a miserable wretch; my wife's an angel, and I'm a monster! I'll go to-morrow.'—And he stays at Madame Marneffe's. That woman is ruining him and he adores her; he fairly lives by her side. For my part, I do what I can! If I weren't there, if I hadn't Mathurine with me, the baron would have spent twice what he has; and, as he has almost nothing, perhaps he would have blown his brains out before this. And mark my words, Mariette, Adeline would die if her husband died, I'm sure. At all events I try to make both ends meet and to keep my cousin from wasting too much money.—"

"Ah! that's what poor madame says; she knows how much she owes you," said Mariette; "she said that she misjudged you for a long time—"

"Aha!" said Lisbeth. "She didn't say anything else?"

"No, mademoiselle. If you want to please her, talk to her about monsieur; she thinks you're very lucky to see him every day."

"Is she alone?"

"No, the marshal's here. Oh! he comes every day and she always tells him that she saw monsieur in the morning and that he comes home very late at night."

"Is there a good dinner to-day?" queried Bette.

Mariette was hesitating how to answer, and seeking to avoid the Lorrainer's eye, when the door of the salon opened and Maréchal Hulot rushed out in such haste that he bowed to Bette without looking at her, and dropped a piece of paper. Bette picked up the paper and ran out to the stairs, for it was useless to cry out to a deaf man; however, she took good care not to overtake the marshal, but soon returned and furtively read what follows, written in pencil:

"MY DEAR BROTHER: My husband gave me money for the quarter's expenses; but my daughter Hortense needed it so sadly that I loaned her the whole amount, which was hardly enough to relieve her embarrassment. Can you loan me a few hundred francs? for I don't want to ask Hector again for the money; a reproach from him would cut too deep."

"Aha!" thought Lisbeth, "what extremity can she be in now that she has subdued her pride to this point?"

She entered the salon, surprised Adeline weeping and threw herself upon her neck.

"Adeline, my dear child, I know all!" said Cousin Bette. "See, the marshal dropped this paper, he was so excited; he was running like a greyhound.—That wretched Hector hasn't given you any money since—?"

"He gives it to me very promptly," replied the baroness, "but Hortense needed it, and—"

"And you hadn't the means of buying dinner for us," interrupted Bette. "Now I understand Mariette's embarrassment, when I spoke about the soup. You are acting like a child, Adeline! Come, let me give you my savings."

"Thanks, dear Bette," Adeline replied, wiping away a tear. "This little pinch is only temporary, and I have provided for the future. My expenses after this will be twenty-four hundred francs a year, including rent, and I shall have them. Above all things, Bette, not a word to Hector. Is he well?"

"Oh! as the Pont Neuf! he's as gay as a lark, and thinks of nothing but his little witch of a Valérie."

Madame Hulot was gazing at a tall silver pine which she could see from her window, and Lisbeth was unable to read anything of what her cousin's eyes might express.

"Did you remind him that it was the day when we were all to dine together here?"

"Yes; but, pshaw! Madame Marneffe gives a large dinner, and hopes to arrange for Monsieur Coquet's resignation! and that takes precedence of everything. Adeline, listen to me: you know my disposition, how fierce I am in the matter of being independent. Your husband, my dear, will certainly ruin you. I thought I might possibly be of service to all of you under that woman's roof, but she is a creature whose depravity goes beyond all bounds, and she will obtain things from your husband that will put him in a fair way to disgrace you all."

Adeline started like one who receives a dagger-thrust in the heart.

"But I tell you I am sure of it, my dear Adeline. I must try to enlighten you. Let us think of the future! The marshal is old, but he will live a long while, and he has a handsome salary; his widow, if he should die, would have a pension of six thousand francs. With that sum I would undertake to provide for you all. Use your influence with the good old man to make a match between us. It isn't for the sake of being Madame la Maréchale; I care as little for such trifles as for Madame Marneffe's conscience; but you will all have bread. I see that Hortense must be in want of it, as you give her yours."

The marshal made his appearance at this juncture; the old soldier had run so fast that he was wiping his forehead with his silk handkerchief.

"I handed two thousand francs to Mariette," he said in his sister-in-law's ear.

Adeline blushed to the roots of her hair. Two tears trembled on her still long eye-lashes, and she silently pressed the hand of the old man, whose face shone with the joy of a happy lover.

"I intended to make you a present of that money, Adeline," he continued; "instead of returning it to me, do you select whatever you would like best."

He took the hand Lisbeth held out to him and kissed it, so distraught was he by his delight.

"That is promising," said Adeline to Lisbeth, with something as near a smile as she could command.

At that moment the younger Hulot and his wife arrived.

"Does my brother dine with us?" asked the marshal sharply.

Adeline took a pencil and wrote these words upon a little square of paper:

"I expect him; he promised me this morning to dine here; but if he doesn't come the marshal must have detained him, for he is overburdened with business."

Then she handed him the paper. She had invented this method of conversing with the marshal, and a supply of small square pieces of paper and a pencil were placed upon her work-table.

"I know," rejoined the marshal, "that he is overburdened with work on Algerian affairs."

Hortense and Wenceslas entered at this moment, and when she saw all her family about her, the baroness cast a glance at the marshal, the meaning of which was understood by Lisbeth alone.

Good fortune had considerably improved the artist, who was adored by his wife, and petted by the world. His face had become almost full, his graceful figure brought out in relief the advantages that blood confers on all true noblemen. His premature renown, his eminent position, the deceitful praise which the world tosses to artists, as carelessly as we say "good morning," or talk about the weather, gave him that consciousness of his own importance, which degenerates into fatuity, when the talent disappears. The cross of the Legion of Honor put the finishing touch, in his own eyes, to the great man he believed he had become.

After three years of married life Hortense and her husband were like a dog and its master; she followed his every movement with a look which resembled a question, she kept her eyes constantly fixed upon him, like a miser on his hoard, she touched one's heart by her admirable self-abnegation. In her behavior could be seen the spirit and the counsel of her mother. Her beauty, still as great as ever, was for the moment clouded, poetically clouded, by the soft shadows of hidden melancholy.

As she watched her cousin's entrance Lisbeth thought that the lamentation, long held in check, was about to break through the fragile envelope of discretion. Since the early days of the honeymoon it had seemed to her that the revenues of the young couple were too slender to support so great a passion.

As she kissed her mother, Hortense exchanged with her from lip to ear and from heart to heart a few words, whose secret was betrayed to Bette by sundry shakings of their heads.

"Adeline is going to work for her living like me," thought Cousin Bette. "I propose that she shall let me know what she does.—So at last those pretty fingers will know, as mine do, what enforced work means."

At six o'clock the family went to the dining-room. A cover was laid for Hector.

"Let it stay!" said the baroness to Mariette; "monsieur sometimes comes late."

"Oh! father will come," said the younger Hulot to his mother; "he promised me when he left us at the Chamber."

Lisbeth, like a spider in the centre of its web, kept an eye on all the faces about her. Having known Hortense and Victorin from their birth, their faces were to her like glass through which she could read what was taking place in their young hearts. By certain covert glances that Victorin cast in his mother's direction, she was convinced that some disaster was likely to befall Adeline, and that Victorin hesitated to make it known. The eminent young advocate was sad at heart. His deep veneration for his mother was manifest in the sorrowful expression with which he glanced at her. Hortense was evidently absorbed in her own troubles; for a fortnight Lisbeth had known that she was suffering from the first anxiety that lack of money brings to honest people, to young wives on whom life has always smiled, and who conceal their suffering. And so Cousin Bette instantly divined that the mother had given nothing to her daughter. So the fastidious Adeline had descended to the falsehoods which want suggests to borrowers. Hortense's preoccupation and her brother's, and the profound sadness of the baroness made the dinner a melancholy affair, especially if we consider the inevitable constraint caused by the old marshal's deafness. Three persons contributed to the animation of the occasion, Lisbeth, Célestine and Wenceslas. Hortense's affection had developed in the artist the natural animation of the Pole, the Gascon quickness of wit, the good-natured boisterousness characteristic of those Frenchmen of the North. His state of mind and the expression of his face were enough to make it plain that he believed in himself, and that poor Hortense, faithfully following her mother's advice, concealed all her domestic afflictions.

"You ought to be very happy," said Lisbeth to her younger cousin as they left the table; "your mamma helped you out of your difficulty by giving you her money."

"Mamma!" replied Hortense in amazement. "Oh! poor mamma; money, to me who would gladly make some for her! You don't know, Lisbeth, but I have a dreadful suspicion that she is working in secret."

They were then walking across the immense dark, unlighted salon, following Mariette, who carried the lamp, from the dining-room to Adeline's bed-room. At that moment Victorin touched Lisbeth's arm and Hortense's; both of them, understanding the meaning of the touch, left Wenceslas, Célestine, the marshal and the baroness to go to the bed-room, and remained standing together in a window-recess.

"What is it, Victorin?" said Lisbeth. "I'll bet it's some trouble caused by your father."

"Alas! yes," Victorin replied. "A money-lender named Vauvinet holds father's notes of hand for sixty thousand francs, and means to proceed against him! I tried to talk to father about the wretched affair at the Chamber, but he pretended not to understand me, and almost avoided me. Shall we tell mother?"

"No, no," said Lisbeth, "she has too much trouble now, you would give her her death-blow; we must be very careful what we say to her. You don't know what a plight she's in; but for your uncle you would have had no dinner here to-day."

"Oh! my God, Victorin, we are monsters," said Hortense; "Lisbeth has to tell us what we ought to have guessed. My dinner chokes me!"

Hortense did not finish; she put her handkerchief over her mouth to stifle a sob and wept.

"I told this Vauvinet to come and see me to-morrow," continued Victorin, "but will he be content to accept me as a guarantor? I don't think it. Those people want cash in order to sweat people with their usurious rates of discount."

"Let us sell our property," said Lisbeth to Hortense.

"What would that amount to? fifteen or sixteen thousand francs," rejoined Victorin, "and we must have sixty thousand!"

"Dear cousin!" cried Hortense, embracing Lisbeth with the enthusiasm of a pure heart.

"No, Lisbeth, keep your little fortune," said Victorin, after pressing the Lorrainer's hand. "I shall see to-morrow what the fellow has in his bag. If my wife consents, I will find a way to prevent, or delay his proceedings; for to see father's reputation assailed!—why, it would be frightful. What would the Minister of War say? Father's salary, which was assigned for three years, won't be free until December; so we can't offer that as security. This Vauvinet has renewed the notes eleven times, so you can judge of the sum father has paid in interest! We must close up that hole."

"If Madame Marneffe would only leave him,—" said Hortense bitterly.

"God forbid!" said Victorin. "Father might then go elsewhere, and there the most considerable expenses have already been incurred."

What a change in children formerly so respectful, and whom their mother had so long maintained in absolute admiration of their father! they had already passed judgment upon him.

"If it weren't for me," said Lisbeth, "your father would be more nearly ruined than he is."

"Let us go back to the others," said Hortense; "mamma is very sharp, she will suspect something, and, as dear Lisbeth says, we must keep it all from her—let's seem to be in good spirits!"

"Victorin, you have no idea where your father is carrying you all with his passion for women," said Lisbeth. "Think about making sure of sufficient means for yourselves by making a match between the marshal and me. You must all speak to him about it this evening; I will go early on purpose."

Victorin entered the bed-room.

"Well, my poor little dear," whispered Lisbeth to her second cousin, "how will you get along?"

"Come and dine with us to-morrow, and we will talk it over," replied Hortense. "I don't know which way to turn; you are acquainted with the difficulties of life, you will advise me."

*

While the whole family were endeavoring to preach marriage to the marshal, and while Lisbeth was returning to Rue Vanneau, there occurred there one of those catastrophes which stimulate the energy of vice in women like Madame Marneffe, by forcing them to bring into play every resource of perversity. Let us bear in mind, however, this constant fact: life is too fully occupied in Paris for vicious people to do evil by instinct; they defend themselves, with the aid of vice, against aggression, that's all.

Madame Marneffe, whose salon was filled with her faithful subjects, had just started the whist tables, when the footman, a retired soldier lured into her service by the baron, announced:

"Monsieur le Baron Montès de Montejanos."

Valérie's heart gave a violent bound, but she darted quickly to the door, crying:

"My cousin!—"

And when she reached the Brazilian's side she whispered in his ear:

"Be my cousin, or everything is at an end between us!—Well, well, Henri," she continued aloud, leading the Brazilian to the fireplace, "so you weren't shipwrecked as they told me you were? I have wept for you three years."

"How are you, my dear fellow," said Marneffe

extending his hand to the Brazilian, whose costume was that of a genuine Brazilian millionaire.

Monsieur le Baron Henri Montès de Montejanos, to whom the equatorial climate had imparted the physique and coloring which we attribute to the Othello of the play, was rather a forbidding personage, on account of his sombre expression, but the effect was purely plastic; his disposition was in reality excessively gentle and affectionate and made him the predestined victim of the arts weak women practice upon strong men. The disdainful expression of his face, the muscular development to which his well-knit figure bore witness, all his physical strength was exhibited only toward men, a bit of flattery aimed at the ladies, and which they relish so keenly, that men with their mistresses on their arms assume all the swaggering airs of the Matamoras of the old Spanish comedies. With his superb figure, set off to perfection by a blue coat with buttons of solid gold, and black trowsers, his feet encased in shoes of the finest leather immaculately polished, gloved in the latest fashion, the baron had nothing of the Brazilian about him save a huge diamond worth about a hundred thousand francs, which shone like a planet on a rich cravat of blue silk, framed by a white waist-coat, cut so as to afford a glimpse of a shirt of fabulously fine linen. His forehead, bulging like a satyr's, a sign of persistence in passion, was surmounted by an abundance of jet black hair as thick as a primeval forest, beneath which gleamed two bright eyes, so wild in expression as to lead one to think that the baron's mother must have been frightened by a jaguar while she was enceinte.

This magnificent example of the Portuguese-Brazilian race stood with his back to the fireplace, in an attitude which disclosed his familiarity with Parisian ways; and, hat in hand, his arm resting on the velvet-covered sofa, he stooped over Madame Marneffe in order to talk with her in an undertone, paying very little heed to the dreadful bourgeois, who, according to his idea, were very much in the way in the salon.

The Brazilian's appearance on the scene, his attitude and expression caused two exactly similar spasms of curiosity mingled with distrust, in the breasts of Crevel and the baron. Both of them had the same foreboding and expressed it in the same way, and the antics inspired by these two real passions became so comical, because of their absolute coincidence in time, that they caused those persons to smile who were intelligent enough to understand the revelation contained therein. Crevel, always and under all circumstances the narrowed-minded shopkeeper, although he was a Mayor of Paris, unluckily remained in position longer than his colleague, so that the baron was enabled to seize, as it were in passing, upon his involuntary revelation. This was one more shaft in the heart of the amorous old fellow, who determined to have an explanation with Valérie.

"This evening," Crevel also was saying to

himself, while arranging his cards, "we must make an end of this—"

"*You have a heart!*—" Marneffe cried, "and you have just renounced hearts."

"Ah! I beg your pardon," said Crevel, trying to take back his card.—"This baron seems to me very much in the way," he continued to himself. "Let Valérie live with *my* baron, that's part of my revenge, and I know how to get rid of him; but this cousin! he's one baron too many; I don't choose to be gulled, and I propose to find out how he's related to her!"

That evening, by one of those lucky chances which fall to the lot of none but pretty women, Valérie was ravishingly arrayed. Her white breast glistened beneath guipure lace of a russet shade which showed off to the best advantage the satin whiteness of the lovely shoulders, characteristic of the fair Parisians, who succeed—by what process no one knows!—in retaining a beautiful skin and at the same time remain slender. She was dressed in a black velvet gown, which seemed ready to slip from her shoulders at any moment, and her head-dress was of lace interspersed with grape blossoms. Her arms, which were dainty and plump at the same time, emerged from elbow sleeves ruffled with lace. She resembled luscious fruit, attractively arranged on a plate, and which makes the knife blade fairly itch.

"Valérie," said the Brázilian in her ear, "I have come back faithful to you; my uncle is dead, and I

Georges Cain

am twice as rich as I was when I went away. I mean to live and die in Paris, with you and for you."

"Speak lower, Henri! for pity's sake!"

"Bah! if I have to throw all these people through the window, I propose to talk with you to-night, especially after I have wasted two days hunting for you. I shall be the last to go, shall I not?"

Valérie smiled at her pretended cousin.

"Remember," said she, "that you are the son of my mother's sister, who married your father during Junot's campaign in Portugal."

"I, Montès de Montejanos, great-grandson of one of the conquerors of Brazil, lie!"

"Lower, or we shall never meet again—"

"Why not, pray?"

"Marneffe, like all dying men, who always take it into their heads to long for something, has conceived a passion for me—"

"That cur?—" said the Brazilian who knew his Marneffe of old; "I'll buy him off—"

"How violent you are!"

"Aha! where did you get all these fine things?—" said the Brazilian, noticing at last the sumptuous furnishings of the salon.

She began to laugh.

"What wretched form, Henri!" said she.

She had received two glances inflamed with jealousy, which penetrated so far as to compel her to look at the two souls in torment. Crevel was playing against the baron and Monsieur Coquet, with Marneffe for his partner. The sides were evenly matched because of the distracted state of mind of Crevel and the baron, who piled error upon error. The two amorous old men confessed, in a twinkling, the passions Valérie had succeeded in making them hide for three years; but she was utterly unable to extinguish in her eyes the reflection of her happiness at seeing once more the man who first made her heart beat, the object of her first love. The rights of such fortunate mortals are as long-lived as the women over whom they have acquired them.

Between these three despotic passions, one relying upon the insolence of wealth, another upon the right of possession, the third upon youth, strength, fortune and priority, Madame Marneffe remained as calm and self-possessed as General Bonaparte, when at the siege of Mantua he had to make head against two armies seeking to continue the blockade of the place. Jealousy, playing over Hulot's features, made them as terrible to look upon as the late Maréchal Montcornet leading a cavalry charge upon a Russian square. In his capacity of squire of dames the Councilor of State had never known jealousy, just as Murat never knew fear. He had always deemed himself certain of triumph. His setback in the case of Josépha, the first in his life, he attributed to greed of gold; he said to himself that he was beaten by a million of money, and not by an abortion, speaking of the Duc d'Hérouville. The poison and the frenzy, which that unreasoning sentiment produces in torrents, went surging through his heart in an instant. He turned from the whist-table to the fire-place by dint of contortions à la Mirabeau, and when he laid down his cards to cast an aggressive glance at Valérie and the Brazilian, the habitués of the house felt that thrill of fear mingled with curiosity, naturally caused by the consciousness that an ebullition of violence is momentarily threatened. The pretended cousin looked at the Councilor of State as he might have examined a bulky Chinese vase. This state of things could not last; it must end in a terrible explosion. Marneffe feared Baron Hulot as much as Crevel feared Marneffe, for he had no desire to die a deputy-chief. The moribund believes in life as galley-slaves believe in liberty. This man was determined to be chief of his bureau at any price. Justly alarmed by the pantomime indulged in by Crevel and the Councilor of State, he rose and said a word in his wife's ear; to the vast astonishment of the assemblage, Valérie walked into her bed-room with the Brazilian and her husband.

"Did Madame Marneffe ever mention that cousin to you?" Crevel asked Baron Hulot.

"Never!" replied the baron as he rose from the table. "Enough for this evening," he added; "I have lost two louis and there they are."

He tossed two gold pieces on the table, and took his seat upon the divan with an expression which everybody interpreted as notice to quit. Monsieur and Madame Coquet, having exchanged a word or two, left the salon, and Claude Vignon, in despair, followed their example. Their departure gave the signal to the less intelligent guests, who saw that they were in the way. The baron and Crevel alone remained behind, without speaking a word. Hulot, who was so excited that he did not see Crevel, walked on tiptoe to the door of the bed-room to listen, and gave a tremendous leap backward when Monsieur Marneffe opened the door and appeared with serene countenance, apparently amazed to find only two persons.

"What about the tea?" said he.

"Where is Valérie?" rejoined the baron furiously.

"My wife," replied Marneffe; "why she has gone up to mademoiselle your cousin, who has just returned."

"Why has she left us planted here, for the sake of that stupid goat?"

"Why," said Marneffe, "Mademoiselle Lisbeth came home from the baroness's, your wife's, with an attack of indigestion, and Mathurine came and asked Valérie for tea, so she went up to see what was the matter with mademoiselle, your cousin."

"And *her* cousin?"

"He's gone!"

"Do you believe that?" queried the baron.

"I put him in his carriage," said Marneffe, with a hideous smile.

The rumbling of a carriage was heard on Rue Vanneau. The baron, looking upon Marneffe as a cipher, left the room and went up to Lisbeth's apartments. There passed through his brain one of those thoughts which the heart sends thither when it is on fire with jealousy. Marneffe's despicable character was so well known to him that he imagined the most scandalous connivance between the husband and wife.

"What has become of all the ladies and gentlemen?" asked Marneffe, finding himself alone with Crevel.

"When the sun goes to rest, the barn-yard does likewise," was the reply; "Madame Marneffe disappeared, her adorers took their leave. Suppose we play a game of piquet," added Crevel, who was determined to remain.

He also believed the Brazilian to be in the house. Monsieur Marneffe accepted. The mayor was as shrewd as the baron; he could stay on indefinitely playing with the husband, who, since the suppression of public gaming-houses, had to content himself with the petty, insignificant game played in society.

Baron Hulot ran rapidly up to his cousin Bette's room; but he found the door locked and the customary questions and answers through the door consumed enough time to allow two active and tricky women to arrange the spectacle of indigestion killed by tea. Lisbeth was in such pain, that she inspired in Valérie the keenest anxiety; and so Valérie hardly noticed the baron's tempestuous entrance. Illness is one of the screens which women most frequently interpose between themselves and the stormy gusts of a quarrel. Hulot furtively looked all about, and failed to detect in Cousin Bette's bed-room any suitable place to conceal a Brazilian.

"Your indigestion, Bette, is very complimentary to my wife's dinner," he said, as he scrutinized the old maid, who played her part marvelously well, and tried to imitate the convulsive gurgling of the stomach as she swallowed her tea.

"See how lucky it is that dear Bette is living with me! If it weren't for me the poor girl would die—" said Madame Marneffe.

"You look as if you believe that I am perfectly well," said Lisbeth to the baron, "and that would be an outrage."

"Why?" asked the baron; "so you know the cause of my visit?"

And he peeped at the door of a dressing-room from which the key had been taken.

"Are you talking Greek?—" rejoined Madame Marneffe with a heartrending expression of unappreciated affection and fidelity.

"Why it's on your account, my dear cousin; yes, it's your fault that I'm in the state you see me in," said Lisbeth vehemently.

This exclamation changed the current of the baron's thoughts, and he stared at the old maid in profound amazement.

"You know whether I am fond of you," continued Lisbeth; "I am here, that tells the whole story. I am wearing my life out looking after your interests in caring for those of our dear Valérie. It doesn't cost one-tenth as much to run her house as it does to run any other house that is kept up like hers. If it weren't for me, cousin, you would have to turn in three or four thousand francs a month instead of two thousand.

"I know all that," retorted the baron testily; "you protect our interests in many ways," he added, returning to Madame Marneffe and putting his arm about her neck, "doesn't she, my dear little love?"

"Upon my word," cried Valérie, "I believe you're mad!—"

"Very well, you don't doubt my attachment to you," said Lisbeth; "but I love my cousin Adeline too, and I found her in tears. She hasn't seen you for a month! No, that isn't to be allowed. You leave poor Adeline without money. Your daughter Hortense nearly died when she learned that it was due to your brother that we had any dinner to eat! There wasn't a crust in your house to-day! Adeline has made the heroic resolve to be sufficient unto herself. 'I will do as you do!' she said to me. Those words made my heart ache so, that, after dinner, as I sat thinking of what my cousin was in 1811 and what she is in 1841, thirty years after! my digestion stopped.—I tried to fight down the pain, but when I reached home I thought I was dying—"

"You see, Valérie, how far my adoration for you carries me!—to commit crimes against my own family—"

"Oh! I did well to remain an old maid!" cried Lisbeth with savage delight. "You are a kind-hearted good man, Adeline's an angel, and this is the reward of blind devotion."

"An old angel!" said Madame Marneffe, casting a glance, half tender, half mocking, at her Hector, who was eyeing her as a magistrate eyes a suspected criminal.

"Poor woman!" said the baron. "Here it is more than nine months since I gave her any money, but I find some for you Valérie, and at what a price! No one else will ever love you as I do, and what unhappiness you cause me in return!"

"Unhappiness!" she repeated. "Pray, what do you call happiness then?"

"I don't know yet what your relations may have been with this pretended cousin, whom you have never mentioned to me," continued the baron, without noticing the words let fall by Valérie. "But when he came in I felt something like a knife-thrust in my heart. However blinded I may be I am not blind. I read what was said by your eyes and his. In short that monkey's eyes shot sparks which fell in a shower upon you, and your look—Oh! you never looked at me so, never! But this mystery will be cleared up, Valérie.—You are the only woman who ever taught me what jealousy means, so don't be surprised at what I say to you.—But another mystery which has burst its shell, and which seems to me infamous—"

"Go on! go on!" said Valérie.

"Is that Crevel, that mass of flesh and idiocy, loves you, and that you receive his attentions kindly enough for the donkey to have exhibited his passion to everybody—"

"And number three? Did you notice no others?" queried Madame Marneffe.

"There may be others!" said the baron.

"If Monsieur Crevel loves me, he's within his rights as a man; if I should look favorably on his passion it would be the act of a coquette or else of a woman to whom you leave many things to be desired.—Well, love me with my faults, or leave me. If you give me back my liberty, neither you nor Monsieur Crevel will come here again. I will take my cousin in order not to lay aside the charming habits you give me credit for. Adieu, Monsieur le Baron Hulot."

She rose, but the Councilor of State seized her arm and forced her to sit down again. The old man could not replace Valérie now, she had become a necessity to him, more imperious than the necessaries of life, and he preferred to remain in uncertainty than to obtain the slightest proof of Valérie's infidelity.

"My dear Valérie," said he, "don't you see what I suffer? I only ask you to justify yourself.—Give me good reasons—"

"Very well, go and wait for me below, for I presume you don't care to be present at the various ceremonies your cousin's condition necessitates."

Hulot slowly withdrew.

"You old rake," cried Cousin Bette, "so you don't even ask for news of your children?—What will you do for Adeline? In the first place, I shall carry her my savings to-morrow."

"One ought at least to supply his wife with wheaten bread," said Madame Marneffe with a smile.

The baron, without taking offense at the tone assumed by Lisbeth, who bullied him as roughly as Josépha, left the room like a man overjoyed to avoid an embarrassing question.

The key was no sooner turned in the lock than the Brazilian left the dressing-room, where he was waiting, and appeared with his eyes filled with tears, in a pitiable state. He had evidently heard all.

"You no longer love me, Henri! I see that," said Madame Marneffe, hiding her face in her handkerchief and bursting into tears.

It was the cry of true love. A woman's noisy despair is so persuasive that it extorts the forgiveness which lies waiting in the hearts of all lovers, when the woman is young, pretty, and so *décolletée* that she could readily emerge from her dress, at the top, in the costume of Eve.

"But why don't you leave everything for me, if you love me?" demanded the Brazilian.

The American, after the manner of all men born where nature still reigns, as he put his arm around Valérie's waist, at once took up the conversation at the point where he had dropped it.

"Why?—" said she, raising her head and subjugating Henri with a love-saturated glance. "Why, my pet, I am married; we are in Paris, and not among the savannas, the pampas, the solitudes of America. My dear Henri, my first and only love, pray listen to me. This husband of mine, a simple deputy-chief in the War Department, is ambitious to be chief of bureau and officer of the Legion of Honor; can I prevent him from having that ambition? Now, for the same reason that he left us two entirely alone—it was nearly four years ago, do you remember, bad boy?—Marneffe to-day forces Monsieur Hulot upon me. I cannot rid myself of this horrible functionary who breathes like a seal and has whiskers in his nostrils, who is sixty-three years old, and has aged ten years in three by trying to be young, who is so hateful to me that on the day after Marneffe becomes chief of bureau and officer of the Legion of Honor—"

"How much will that be worth to your husband?"

"A thousand crowns."

"I'll pay him that sum for life," said Baron Montès; "let us leave Paris and go—"

"Where?" said Valérie with one of those bewitching pouts with which women defy men of whom they are sure. "Paris is the only city where we can live happily. I depend too much upon your love to care to see it grow less when we are living alone in some desert; Henri, you are the only man I love in the universe; write that on your tiger's skull."

Women invariably convince men of whom they have made sheep that they are lions and have an iron will.

"Now, listen to what I say! Monsieur Marneffe hasn't five years to live; he is tainted to the very marrow of his bones; he spends seven months out of the twelve drinking drugs and potions, and he lives in flannel; in a word, he is liable to be mowed down at any moment, so the doctor says; a sickness that would amount to nothing for a sound man would be fatal to him, for his blood is corrupt, the vital principle is undermined. For five years I have refused to let him kiss me once, for the man is the plague in person! Some day, and that day is not far distant, I shall be a widow; when that day comes, I, who have already been sought by a man with an income of sixty thousand francs, and who have him under my control as completely as I have this piece of sugar, I swear to you that if you were a pauper like Hulot, a leper like Marneffe, and if you should beat me, I would have you for my husband, for you are the only man I love and whose name I choose to bear, and I am ready to give you all the pledges of love you wish—"

"Well, then, this evening—"

"But, child of Rio, my superb jaguar, who has left the primeval forests of Brazil for my sake," said she, taking his hand and kissing and caressing it, "pray have a little respect for a creature you would make your wife.—Shall I be your wife, Henri?"

"Yes," said the Brazilian, vanquished by the unbridled volubility of her passion.

And he knelt at her feet.

"Look you, Henri," said Valérie taking both his hands and gazing earnestly into his eyes, "will you swear to me here, in the presence of Lisbeth, my best and only friend, my sister, that you will take me for your wife at the end of my year of widowhood?"

"I swear it."

"That's not enough! swear by your mother's ashes and her everlasting salvation, swear by the Virgin Mary and your hopes as a good Catholic!"

Valérie knew that the Brazilian would keep that oath even if she should have fallen to the bottom of the foulest social pest-hole. He took the solemn oath, with his nose almost touching Valérie's white breast, and with fascinated eyes; he was drunk with passion, as one is drunk upon meeting again the woman one loves, especially after a voyage of a hundred and twenty days!

"Very good; now have no fear. Respect in Madame Marneffe the Baronne de Montejanos that is to be. Don't spend a sou upon me, I forbid it. Stay here, in the next room, and lie down on the little couch; I will come myself and tell you when you can leave your post.—To-morrow morning we will breakfast together, and you will leave us about one o'clock, as if you had come to call on me at noon. You need have no fear, for the concierges belong to me as if they were my father and mother.—I am going down to my own rooms now to serve the tea."

She made a sign to Lisbeth who went out to the head of the stairs with her. There Valérie whispered in the old maid's ear:

"That black-a-moor came back a little too soon! for I shall die if I don't revenge you on Hortense!"

"Never fear, my dear pretty little demon," said the old maid kissing her on the forehead, "love and vengeance, hunting in couples, will never have the underhand. Hortense expects me to-morrow; she is in want. To get a thousand francs Wenceslas will kiss you a thousand times."

*

On leaving Valérie, Hulot had gone down to the office and appeared suddenly before Madame Olivier.

"Madame Olivier?—"

When she heard this imperious question and saw the gesture with which the baron emphasized it, Madame Olivier left her room and followed him into the court-yard, to the spot to which he led the way.

"You know that if anyone can smooth the way for your son to set up an office for himself, some day, I am the man; you can thank me that he is now third clerk to a notary and is finishing his law studies."

"Yes, Monsieur le Baron; and Monsieur le Baron may count on our gratitude. There isn't a day that I don't pray God for Monsieur le Baron's happiness."

"Not so many words, my good woman," said Hulot, "but proofs—"

"What must I do?" asked Madame Olivier.

"A man came here to-night in a carriage; do you know him?"

Madame Olivier had not failed to recognize Montès; how could she have forgotten him? Montès used to slip a hundred sous into her hand every time he left the house on Rue du Doyenné a little too early in the morning. If the baron had applied to Monsieur Olivier perhaps he would have learned all. But Olivier was asleep. Among the lower classes not only are the women superior in intellect to the men, but they almost always rule them. Madame Olivier had long since made up her mind what course to adopt in case of a collision between her two benefactors; she looked upon Madame Marneffe as the stronger of the two powers.

"Do I know him?" she replied; "no, faith, I never saw him before!—"

"What! Madame Marneffe's cousin never came to see her when she lived on Rue du Doyenné?"

"Oh! he's her cousin!—" cried Madame Olivier. "He may have come there, but I didn't recognize him. The first time I see him, monsieur, I will look at him carefully—"

"He's coming down now," said Hulot hastily, cutting her short.

"Why he's gone," rejoined Madame Olivier, who understood the whole affair. "The carriage isn't here."

"Did you see him go?"

"As plainly as I see you. 'To the Embassy!' he said to his servant."

Her tone and her words extorted a sigh of joy from the baron; he took Madame Olivier's hand and pressed it.

"Thanks, dear Madame Olivier; but that's not all!—What about Monsieur Crevel?"

"Monsieur Crevel? What do you mean? I don't understand," said Madame Olivier.

"Hear what I say! he's in love with Madame Marneffe—"

"Impossible, Monsieur le Baron! impossible!" said she, clasping her hands.

"He's in love with Madame Marneffe!" repeated the baron imperatively. "What do they do? I don't know, but I propose to know, and you must find out. If you can put me on the track of this intrigue your son shall be a notary."

"Monsieur le Baron, *don't feed on your blood* like this," said Madame Olivier. "Madame loves you and she loves no one else; her maid knows it, and we tell each other that you are the luckiest man on earth, for you know what a treasure madame is.—Ah! she's perfection.—She gets up at ten o'clock every day, then she breakfasts; so far so good. Well, then she takes an hour or two for her toilette and that brings us to two o'clock; after that she goes out to walk at the Tuileries in the sight and hearing of all the world, and is always at home again at four o'clock, when it's time for you to come. Oh! she's as regular as a clock. She has no secrets from her maid and Reine has none from me! No, Reine can't have any, on account of my son, for she thinks a great deal of him.—So you see that, if Madame had anything to do with Monsieur Crevel, we should *know* it."

The baron, with beaming face, reascended the stairs to Madame Marneffe's, fully convinced that he was the only man loved by that pernicious courtesan, as deceitful, but as beautiful and alluring, as a siren.

Crevel and Marneffe were just beginning a new game of piquet. Crevel was losing, as everybody is sure to lose who doesn't pay attention to his game. Marneffe, who knew the cause of the mayor's distraction, profited by it without scruple; he looked at the cards to be taken, and discarded accordingly; then, after looking into his adversary's hand, he played a sure game. The value of the chip being twenty sous he had already robbed the mayor of thirty francs when the baron returned.

"Well, well," said the Councilor of State, amazed to find the salon empty, "you are alone! Where are they all?"

"Your good humor frightened everybody away," replied Crevel.

"No, it was the arrival of my wife's cousin," said Marneffe. "The ladies and gentlemen thought Valérie and Henri must have something to say to each other after a separation of three years, and so they discreetly took their leave.—If I had been here I'd have kept them; but perhaps I should have made a mistake, for Lisbeth's sickness has put everything in confusion as she always pours the tea at half past ten—"

"Lisbeth is really sick then?" demanded Crevel in a rage.

"So I understood," replied Marneffe with the disgusting indifference of a man for whom women no longer exist.

The mayor had kept watch on the clock; and by that reckoning the baron had apparently passed forty minutes in Lisbeth's room. Hulot's joyous bearing seriously incriminated Hector, Valérie and Lisbeth.

"I have just seen her, she is suffering terribly, poor girl," said the baron.

"Does it please you so much to see somebody else suffer, my dear friend," retorted Crevel sourly, "for you return to us with a most jubilant face? Is Lisbeth in danger of dying? Your daughter will be her heir, they say. You don't look like yourself, for you went away with the face of the Moor of Venice, and you come back with that of Saint-Preux!—I'd like well to see Madame Marneffe's face—"

"What do you mean by those words?" demanded Monsieur Marneffe, gathering up his cards and laying them in front of him.

The lack-lustre eyes of the man, infirm at forty-seven, brightened perceptibly, a slight color overspread his cold, flabby cheeks, he half opened his toothless mouth, while to his black lips came a sort of thick, white foam like chalk. This exhibition of rage on the part of an impotent man, whose life hung by a thread, and who, in a duel, would have risked nothing, whereas Crevel would have had everything to lose, terrified the good mayor.

"I say," he replied, "that I would like to see Madame Marneffe's face, and I have the more reason for saying it, because yours at this moment is extremely disagreeable. 'Pon honor, you are frightfully ugly, my dear Marneffe—"

"Do you know that you're not civil?"

"A man who wins thirty francs from me in forty-five minutes never looks handsome to me."

"Ah! if you'd seen me seventeen years ago,—" said the deputy-chief."

"You were good-looking then?" queried Crevel.

"That's what ruined me; if I had been like you I should have been a peer, and mayor."

"Yes," rejoined Crevel with a smile, "you have done too much fighting, and, of the two metals a man acquires by worshipping the god of commerce, you chose the wrong one, the drug!"

With that Crevel burst out laughing. Though Marneffe might lose his temper anent his imperiled honor, he always took such low, vulgar jests very pleasantly; they were the small-change of conversation between Crevel and him.

"Eve costs me very dear; but faith, my motto's 'short and sweet.'"

"I prefer 'long and happy,'" retorted Crevel.

Madame Marneffe entered the room, saw her husband playing with Crevel, and that they, with the baron, were its only occupants; she understood, simply by the municipal functionary's expression, all the thoughts that had excited him, and she immediately determined upon the course to pursue.

"Marneffe, my dear!" said she, leaning over her husband's shoulder, and running her taper fingers through his ugly gray hair, which was too scanty to cover his head, "it's very late for you, and you must go to bed. You know you must take a purgative to-morrow, the doctor told you so, and Reine will bring you some herb soup at seven o'clock.—If you want to live, stop your game—"

"Shall we make it five points?" Marneffe asked Crevel.

"Very well, I have two already," Crevel replied.

"How long will that last?" asked Valérie.

"Ten minutes," said Marneffe.

"It's eleven o'clock now," Valérie rejoined. "Really, Monsieur Crevel, anyone would say you wanted to kill my husband. Hurry up, at all events."

This equivocal remark caused Crevel, Hulot and Marneffe himself to smile. Valérie went and talked with her Hector.

"Go out, my love," she said in his ear, "and walk up and down Rue Vanneau; you can come back when you see Crevel leave the house."

"I prefer to go out and then come back to your bed-room by way of the dressing-room; you can tell Reine to open the door for me."

"Reine is upstairs looking after Lisbeth."

"Very well, suppose I go up to Lisbeth's room?"

There was danger on all sides for Valérie, who, as she anticipated an explanation with Crevel, did not want Hulot in her bed-room where he could overhear all that was said.—And the Brazilian was waiting in Lisbeth's room.

"Upon my word," she said to Hector, "when you men take a fancy into your head, you'd burn a house down to get into it. Lisbeth is in a condition that makes it impossible for her to receive you.

Are you afraid of taking cold in the street?—Go out—or else good-night!"

"Adieu, messieurs," said the baron aloud.

Once he was attacked in his self-esteem as an old man, Hulot was determined to prove that he could play the young man by awaiting the happy moment in the street, and he left the house.

Marneffe bade his wife good-night, and, as he did so, took her hands with a great show of affection. Valérie gave his hand a significant pressure, which meant:

"Pray rid me of Crevel."

"Good-night, Crevel," thereupon said Marneffe; "I hope you won't stay long with Valérie. I'm jealous, you see—it's taken me late in life, but it's got me,—and I'll come back and see if you've gone."

"We have some business to talk over, but I shall not stay long," said Crevel.

"Speak low! What do you want of me?" said Valérie in two different tones, looking at Crevel with an expression in which pride was mingled with contempt.

As his eyes met this haughty stare, Crevel, who was immensely useful to Valérie, and was inclined to presume upon that fact, became humble and submissive once more.

"This Brazilian,—"

Dismayed by Valérie's disdainful glance, he stopped short.

"Well?" said she.

"This cousin—"

"He isn't my cousin," she replied. "He is my cousin in the eyes of the world and of Monsieur Marneffe. If he were my lover you would have no right to say a word. A shop-keeper who buys a woman to be revenged on some man is, in my estimation, far below him who buys her with love. You weren't in love with me, but you saw in me Monsieur Hulot's mistress, and you bought me as one buys a pistol to shoot his enemy. I was hungry, so I agreed!"

"But you haven't carried out your bargain," retorted Crevel, once more the tradesman.

"Ah! you want Baron Hulot to know that you have taken his mistress in order to have your revenge for the abduction of Josépha, do you?—Nothing shows your meanness more clearly. You say you love a woman, you treat her like a duchess, and you seek to disgrace her! After all, my dear, you're right; the woman I speak of isn't to be compared to Josépha. That damsel has the courage of her infamy, while I am a hypocrite, and ought to be scourged in public. Alas! Josépha protects herself by her talent and her fortune. My only defence is my honor; I am still a virtuous and worthy bourgeoise; but if you make a scandal, what will become of me? If I were rich, well and good! But I have an income now of fifteen thousand francs at most, haven't I?"

"Much more," said Crevel; "I have doubled your capital within two months in the Orleans."

"Very good; one doesn't begin to be esteemed in

Paris at less than fifty thousand francs income, and you haven't the money to pay me for the position I shall lose. What is it that I want? to have Marneffe appointed chief of bureau; he would then have a salary of six thousand francs; he has been in the service twenty-seven years, and after three years I should be entitled to a pension of fifteen hundred if he died. And you whom I have loaded with favors, you who are fairly surfeited with good fortune, cannot wait!—And that's what he calls love!" she cried.

"Although I began as a matter of business," said Crevel, "I have since become your little dog. You trample on my heart, you crush me, you humiliate me, and I love you as I never loved before. Valérie, I love you as dearly as I love Célestine! For you I am capable of anything.—Look you! instead of coming to Rue du Dauphin twice a week, come three times."

"Nothing but that! You are growing young, my dear—"

"Let me send Hulot away, humble him, rid you of him," continued Crevel, without noticing this bit of insolence; "don't receive this Brazilian again, but be all mine, and you shall not be sorry. In the first place, I will give you a certificate for eight thousand francs a year, but for your life only; I won't give you the funds that produce it until you have been true to me five years—"

"Still bargaining! a bourgeois can never learn how to give! You want to arrange relays of love throughout your life, by certificates for annuities, eh?—Ah! you shop-keeper, you dealer in pomade! you put a label on everything! Hector told me that the Duc d'Hérouville carried Josépha money enough to give her thirty thousand francs a year in a horn of sugar-plums! I am worth six Joséphas! Ah! to be loved!" she said, re-arranging her curls and going to take a look at herself in the mirror. "Henri loves me and would kill you like a fly at a wink from me! Hulot loves me, and he leaves his wife in want! Go, and be a good paterfamilias, my dear. Oh! you have for your little follies, three hundred thousand francs outside your fortune,—a pretty little hoard, and you think of nothing but increasing it—"

"For you, Valérie, for I offer you half of it!" he exclaimed, falling on his knees.

"What, you still here!" cried Marneffe the hideous, appearing in his dressing-gown. "What are you doing?"

"He is asking my pardon, my love, for an insulting proposal he has just made me. As he couldn't obtain anything from me, it occurred to monsieur to try and buy me—"

Crevel would have liked to go down into the cellar through a trap-door, as they do on the stage.

"Rise, my dear Crevel," said Marneffe with a smile, "you are making a fool of yourself. I can see by the way Valérie acts that I'm in no danger."

"Go to bed and sleep peacefully," said Madame Marneffe.

"How clever she is!" thought Crevel; "she's adorable! she has saved my life!"

When Marneffe had returned to his room the mayor took Valérie's hands and kissed them, leaving the marks of tears upon them.

"All in your name!" he said.

"That sounds like love," she whispered in his ear. "Well, love for love. Hulot is down in the street. The poor old fellow is waiting for me to put a candle in one of my bed-room windows as a signal to him to return; I give you leave to go and tell him that you are the only man I love; he will never believe you, so do you take him to Rue du Dauphin, give him the proofs, overwhelm him; I give you leave, yes, I order you to do it. The old porpoise bores me, he wears me out. Keep your man at Rue du Dauphin all night, roast him over a slow fire, take your revenge on him for stealing Josépha! Hulot will die of it perhaps; but we will save his wife and children from awful suffering. Madame Hulot is working for her living!—"

"Oh! the poor woman! on my word it's atrocious!" cried Crevel, his natural kindliness resuming its sway.

"If you love me, Célestin," she whispered low in his ear, which she touched with her lips, "keep him with you or I am lost. Marneffe is suspicious, Hector has the key of the hall-door and expects to return!"

Crevel pressed Madamé Marneffe in his arms, and left her, in a transport of joy; Valérie affectionately accompanied him as far as the head of the stairs; then, as if drawn by a magnet, she went down to the first floor, and kept on to the foot of the last flight.

"My Valérie! go back, don't compromise yourself in the eyes of the concierge.—Go; my life and my fortune, everything is yours!—Go, my duchess!"

"Madame Olivier!" cried Valérie softly, when the door was closed.

"What! you here, madame?" exclaimed Madame Olivier in blank amazement.

"Throw the bolts above and below on the front door, and don't open it again."

"Very well, madame."

As soon as the bolts were thrown Madame Olivier described the attempt at corruption to which the high official had descended in her regard.

"You acted like an angel, my dear Olivier; but we will talk of this to-morrow."

Valérie flew up to the third floor with the swiftness of an arrow, knocked three light knocks on Lisbeth's door, then returned to her own apartments, where she gave her orders to Mademoiselle Reine; for a woman never misses the opportunity offered by a Montès arriving from Brazil.

*

"No! saperlotte, only women in good society know how to love like that!" said Crevel to himself. "How she came down stairs, lighting the way with her glances, and it was I drew her on! No more Josépha!—Josépha, she's trash!" cried the quondam traveling salesman. "What's that I said? *a jade!*—Great God! I'm quite capable of letting that out some day at the Tuileries.—No, unless Valérie educates me, I can never amount to anything—And I am so anxious to appear like a great lord.—Ah! what a woman! she gives me as bad a pain as the colic when she looks coldly at me.—What grace! what wit! Josépha never moved me so. And then her unseen perfections!—Aha! there's my man!"

He saw, in the darkness of Rue de Babylone, the tall form of Hulot, slightly bent, skulking along by the hoarding of a house in process of construction, and he walked straight up to him.

"Good-morning, baron, for it's past midnight, my friend! What the devil are you doing here?—you are still walking about and there's a nice little mist. At our age it's a bad thing. Do you want me to give you some good advice? let's both go home; for, between ourselves, you won't see any light in the window—"

At this last phrase, the baron began to realize

that he was sixty-three years old and that his cloak was damp.

"Who could have told you that?—" he cried.

"*Parbleu,* Valérie! *our* Valérie who chooses to be *my* Valérie alone. We have won a game each, and we'll play the rubber for the lady whenever you choose. You can't lose your temper over it, for you know that I stipulated for the right to take my revenge; it took you three months to steal Josépha from me; I have taken Valérie away from you in—But let's not talk of that," he continued. "Now I propose that she shall be all mine. But we will continue to be good friends none the less."

"None of your pleasantry," replied the baron in a voice choked with rage; "this is a matter of life or death."

"Hoity-toity, how you take it!—Baron, don't you remember what you said to me the day Hortense was married: 'Ought two old gray-beards like us to quarrel over a petticoat? That's like a grocer, that's like people of no account.—' We are, I agree, thoroughbred aristocrats, Regency, Pompadour, eighteenth century, Maréchal de Richelieu to the core, *rocaille,* and, if I may venture to say so, true heroes of *Les Liaisons Dangereuses!*—"

Crevel might have gone on heaping up his epithets for a long while, for the baron listened as deaf men listen when their deafness first comes upon them. But when he saw, by the light of the street-lamp, his enemy's face turned white, the victor paused. It was a crushing blow to the baron after Madame Olivier's statements and after Valérie's last glance.

"My God! there were so many other women in Paris!—" he cried at last.

"That's what I told you when you took Josépha away from me," retorted Crevel.

"Look here, Crevel, it's impossible.—Give me your proofs!—Have you a pass-key, as I have?"

And the baron, as they were now in front of the house, inserted a key in the lock; but he found the door immovable, and tried in vain to shake it.

"Don't make a row here in the middle of the night," said Crevel calmly. "Come, baron, I have better keys than yours."

"Proofs! proofs!" repeated the baron nearly mad with rage and grief.

"Come, and I will give you them," Crevel replied.

Following Valérie's instructions he dragged the baron away toward the quay by Rue Hillerin-Bertin. The unfortunate Councilor of State walked along like a merchant on the eve of stopping payment; he was lost in conjectures as to the explanation of the depravity that lay hidden at the bottom of Valérie's heart, and he believed that he was the dupe of some trickery. As they crossed the Pont Royal, his life seeemd to him so empty, so completely lived out, and in such confusion on account of his financial difficulties, that he was on the point of yielding to the evil thought that came to him of throwing Crevel into the river and jumping in after him.

When they reached Rue du Dauphin, which, at that time, had not been widened, Crevel halted in front of a door. This door opened upon a long corridor paved with black and white flagstones, forming a peristyle, at the end of which were a staircase and a porter's lodge lighted by a small interior courtyard, like so many others in Paris. This courtyard, which was shared in common with the adjoining property, was remarkable in this respect that it was unequally divided. Crevel's little house, for he was the owner, had a glass-roofed addition, built upon the adjoining lot and laboring under the disadvantage of having been built under protest, it was entirely hidden from sight by the lodge and the projections of the stairway.

This structure had long been used as a storehouse, back-shop and kitchen for one of the two shops on the street. Crevel detached these three ground-floor rooms from the property as rented, and Grindot transformed them into a snug little establishment. There were two ways of reaching it, one through the shop of a dealer in furniture, to whom Crevel let it at a low price and by the month, so that he might be able to punish him in case of indiscretion; and the other by a door concealed in the wall of the corridor so skilfully that it was almost invisible. This little suite, composed of a dining-room, a salon and a bedroom, lighted from above, partly on the neighbor's land and partly on Crevel's, was thus almost impossible to discover. With the exception of the dealer in second-hand furniture, the tenants were ignorant of the existence of this little paradise. The female concierge, liberally paid for being Crevel's accomplice, was an excellent cook. The mayor therefore could go in and out of his little establishment at any hour of the day or night without fear of being spied upon. Even in the daytime, a woman dressed as Parisian women dress when they go out shopping, and provided with a key, incurred no risk in visiting Crevel; she might notice the second-hand furniture, haggle a little over prices, enter the shop and leave it, without arousing the least suspicion if anyone chanced to meet her.

When Crevel had lighted the candelabra in the boudoir, the baron was greatly amazed at the tasteful and coquettish display of luxury. The quondam perfumer had given Grindot carte blanche, and the old architect had distinguished himself by a performance after the Pompadour style, which cost, by the way, sixty thousand francs.

"I want it to be so that a duchess on entering the rooms would be surprised," said Crevel to Grindot.

He wished to have the most beautiful of Parisian Edens, in which to enjoy his Eve, his woman of the world, his Valérie, his duchess.

"There are two beds," said Crevel, as he pointed to a divan from which he drew out a bed as one takes a drawer from a desk. "Here's one, and the other's in the bed-room. So we can both pass the night here."

"The proofs!" said the baron.

Crevel took a candle and led his friend into the bed-chamber, where Hulot saw upon a sofa a magnificent dressing-gown belonging to Valérie, which she wore on Rue Vanneau in his honor, before making use of it at Crevel's little establishment. The mayor pressed the spring of the secret drawer in a pretty little piece of inlaid furniture called a *bonheur-du-jour*, felt in the drawer, seized a letter, and handed it to the baron:

"Take this and read it."

The Councilor of State read this little penciled note:

"I have waited for you for nothing, old stingy! A woman like myself never waits for a man who has sold perfumery. There was no dinner ordered nor cigarettes. You shall pay me for all this."

"Is that her writing?"

"My God!" said Hulot, falling upon a chair completely crushed. "I recognize all her things; there are her caps and her slippers. Damnation! tell me, since when—?"

Crevel made a sign that he understood, and took a package of bills from the little inlaid cabinet.

"Look, my old friend! I paid the contractors in December, 1838. In October, two months before, this charming little house was used for the first time."

The Councilor of State hung his head.

"How the devil do you manage it? for I know how her time is occupied, hour by hour."

"And what about the walk at the Tuileries?" queried Crevel, rubbing his hands gleefully.

"Well, what about it?—" rejoined Hulot in a dazed sort of way.

"Your soi-disant mistress goes to the Tuileries and is supposed to walk about there from one o'clock to four; but presto! in a twinkling she's here. Are you familiar with Molière? Well, baron, there's nothing imaginary in your title."

Hulot, having no further pretext for doubting, maintained a gloomy silence. Disaster drives all strong, intelligent men to philosophy. The baron, morally speaking, was like a man trying to find his way in a dense forest at night. His dejected silence, the change which took place upon his woebegone face, aroused Crevel's anxiety, for he did not desire his colleague's death.

"As I was saying, my old friend, we have each won a game, let's play the rubber. Come, will you play the rubber? and may the best man win!"

"Why is it," said Hulot to himself, "that out of every ten women at least seven are utterly bad?"

The baron's distress was too great to allow him to solve the problem. Beauty is the greatest of all human powers. Every form of power without counterpoise, without some autocratic curb, leads to abuse, to acts of madness. Arbitrariness is the insanity of power. In a woman caprice is arbitrariness.

"You have no reason to complain, my dear fellow; you have the loveliest of wives, and she is virtuous."

"I deserve my fate," said Hulot, "I have never appreciated my wife, I have made her suffer terribly, and she is an angel! O, my poor Adeline, you are well avenged! She suffers alone, in silence, she is worthy of adoration, she deserves my love, and I ought—for she is lovely still, fair as a lily, and like a young girl again.—But was there ever a more despicable, infamous, wicked creature than this Valérie?"

"She's a good-for-naught," said Crevel, "she ought to be whipped on the Place du Châtelet; but, my dear Canillac, if we are aristocrats, Maréchal de Richelieu,—old fool,—Pompadour, Du Barry, downright eighteenth century rakes, in short, still we have no lieutenant of police to-day."

"How can one make a woman love one?—" Hulot asked himself, paying no heed to Crevel.

"It's absurd for such old fellows as we are to want to be loved, my dear boy," said Crevel; "at best we can only expect to be endured, for Madame Marneffe is a hundred times more depraved than Josépha—"

"And avaricious! she has cost me a hundred and ninety-two thousand francs!" cried Hulot.

"And how many centimes?" asked Crevel with the insolence of the man of wealth, deeming the sum a paltry one.

"It's easy to see that you don't love her," said the baron sadly.

"I have had enough of her," replied Crevel, "for she has had more than three hundred thousand francs from me!—"

"Where is it? where does it all go?" said the baron burying his face in his hands.

"If we had had an understanding, like the young fellows who club together to keep a grisette of the two sous kind, she would have cost us less—"

"There's something in that!" the baron assented; "but she would deceive us still, for what do you think of this Brazilian, old fellow?"

"Ah! old fox, you're right; we are cheated like—like shareholders!" said Crevel. "All these women are regular limited-liability companies!"

"So it was she who told you about the light in the window?" said the baron.

"My good man," replied Crevel, striking his favorite attitude, "we are gulled! Valérie's a—She told me to keep you here—I understand now—She has her Brazilian—Ah! I give her up, for if you held her hands she'd find a way to deceive you with her feet! Damme, she's an infamous wretch! she's a strumpet!"

"She's lower than the common prostitutes," said the baron. "Josépha and Jenny Cadine were within their rights in deceiving us, for they trade on their charms!"

"But she, who plays the saint, the prude!" said Crevel. "Come, Hulot, go back to your wife, for your affairs are in a bad way, and people are beginning to talk about certain notes of hand discounted by a petty money-lender, whose specialty consists in lending to lorettes—one Vauvinet. As for myself I've had enough of society women. And then, at our age, what need have we of the hussies, who, I honestly believe, can't help deceiving us? You have white hair and false teeth, baron. I look like Silenus. I propose to begin to save money. Money never deceives. If the treasury is thrown open every six months to everybody, at least it pays interest, and with that woman it's all outgo.—With you, my dear colleague, Gubetta, my old partner in sin, I might accept a situation *chocnoso*—no, philosophically; but a Brazilian, who, it may be, has brought suspicious colonial wares from his home—"

"The woman," said Hulot, "is an inexplicable creature!"

"I can explain her," said Crevel; "we are old, the Brazilian is young and handsome—"

"Yes, that's true," said Hulot; "we are growing old, I admit. But, my friend, how are we to give up watching the lovely creatures undressing themselves, doing up their hair, looking at us with a sly smile through their fingers when they are putting on their curl-papers, playing all their tricks, telling their fibs, and swearing that we don't love them, when they see that we are annoyed by matters of business, and distracting our minds in spite of everything?"

"Yes, on my word! it's the only pleasant thing in life,—" cried Crevel. "Ah! when a pretty face smiles on you, and says: 'My dear love, do you know what a dear fellow you are? I must be made differently from other women, who go mad over little dandies with goatees, idiots who smoke and are as vulgar as footmen! for their youth makes them impertinent!—However, they come, say good-morning, and go.—I, whom you suspect of flirting, prefer men of fifty to such little whipper-snappers, for one can keep them a long while; they are devoted, for they know how hard it is to find the right woman, and they appreciate us.—That's why I love you, you great rascal!—' And they accompany these—confessions, you might call them, with their little airs and graces, and—Ah! they're as false as the programmes at the Hotel de Ville—"

"A lie is often better than the truth," said Hulot, to whose mind Crevel's pantomime in imitation of Valérie recalled some charming scenes. "They have to elaborate the lie, to sew the spangles on to their stage clothes—"

"And then, after all, we have the liars!" said Crevel brutally.

"Valérie's a fairy," cried the baron; "she transforms an old man into a youth—"

"Aye," rejoined Crevel, "she's an eel that slips through your fingers; but she's the loveliest of eels—white and sweet as sugar!—mischievous as Arnal; and as for her tricks! ah!"

"Ah! she's very clever!" cried the baron, thinking no more of his wife.

The two associates went to bed the best friends in the world, reminding each other of Valérie's charms one by one,—the tones of her voice, her coquettish ways, her gestures, her mischievous antics, her flashes of wit, her moments of tenderness; for this artist in love was remarkable for her impulsive outbursts, like some tenors who sing better one day than another. And they were both lulled to sleep by these alluring, diabolic reminiscences, lighted by the fires of hell.

The next morning at nine o'clock Hulot spoke of going to the department, and Crevel had business in the country. They left the house together, and Crevel gave the baron his hand, saying:

"We part friends, don't we? for neither of us thinks any more about Madame Marneffe."

"Oh! that's all done with!" Hulot replied with a horrified gesture.

At half-past ten Crevel mounted Madame Marneffe's staircase four stairs at a time. He found the vile creature, the adorable enchantress, in the most bewitching déshabille imaginable, eating a dainty little breakfast with Baron Henri Montès de Montejanos and Lisbeth. Notwithstanding the shock he felt at the sight of the Brazilian, Crevel begged Madame Marneffe to grant him a moment's interview. Valérie went into the salon with him.

"Valérie, my angel," said the amorous old fellow, "Monsieur Marneffe hasn't long to live; if you will be true to me, at his death we will be married. Think it over. I have got rid of Hulot for you.—So do you consider whether this Brazilian will bear comparison with a mayor of Paris, a man who, for your sake, would seek to attain the highest of dignities, and who already has an income of eighty and some odd thousand francs."

"I'll think about it," said she. "I will be at Rue du Dauphin at two o'clock, and we'll talk it over; but be prudent! and don't forget the transfer of funds you promised me yesterday."

She returned to the dining-room, followed by Crevel, who flattered himself that he had discovered a way of having Valérie all to himself; but he there found Baron Hulot, who had come in during their short conference, intent upon a similar design. The Councilor of State requested a moment's audience, as Crevel had done. Madame Marneffe rose to return to the salon, smiling at the Brazilian, as if to say: "They are mad! for heaven's sake don't they see you?"

"Valérie, my child," began the Councilor of State, "this cousin of yours is an American cousin—"

"Oh! enough of that!" she cried, interrupting him. "Marneffe never has been, never will be, never can be my husband. The first, the only man I ever loved has returned, unexpectedly.—It isn't my fault! But do you look well at Henri and at yourself. Then ask yourself if a woman, especially when she loves, can hesitate. My dear, I am nobody's kept mistress. From this day out I do not propose to stand like Suzanne between two old men. If you still care for me, you shall be, you and Crevel, our good friends; but all this nonsense is at an end, for I am twenty-six years old, and I propose hereafter to be a saint, an exemplary, dignified wife —like your own."

"Indeed?" said Hulot. "Ah! this is the way you receive me when I come, like the Pope, with my hands full of indulgences!—Very well, your husband will never be chief of bureau or officer of the Legion of Honor—"

"We'll see about that!" said Madame Marneffe, with a meaning glance at Hulot.

"Let's not part in anger," said he in despair, "I will come this evening, and we will have an understanding."

"To Lisbeth's room, yes!"

"Very well," said the lovesick old fellow, "to Lisbeth's room!"

Hulot and Crevel went down stairs together, without exchanging a word until they reached the street; but when they stood upon the sidewalk they looked at each other with a joyless laugh.

"We are two old fools!—" said Crevel.

"I have sent them away," said Madame Marneffe to Lisbeth as she resumed her seat at the table. "I have never loved, I do not love, and I never shall love anybody but my jaguar," she added, smiling at Henri Montès. "Lisbeth, my girl, I haven't told you, have I?—Henri has forgiven me for the despicable things to which poverty reduced me."

"It's my own fault," said the Brazilian, "I ought to have sent you a hundred thousand francs—"

"Poor boy!" cried Valérie; "I ought to have

worked for my living, but my fingers weren't made for that—ask Lisbeth."

The Brazilian went away the happiest man in Paris.

About noon Valérie and Lisbeth were talking together in the sumptuously furnished bed-room while the formidable Parisian put those last touches to her toilette which a woman is always particular to attend to herself. With bolted doors and curtains drawn Valérie described all the occurrences of the evening, the night and the morning, not omitting the most trifling details.

"Are you satisfied, my jewel?" she asked Lisbeth when her tale was at an end. "Which should I be some day, Madame Crevel or Madame Montès? What's your opinion?"

"Crevel hasn't more than ten years to live, old rake that he is," was Lisbeth's reply, "and Montès is young. Crevel will leave you thirty thousand francs a year or thereabout. Let Montès wait; he'll be happy enough as long as he continues to be the Benjamin. And so, when you're about thirty-three, my dear child, by taking care to retain your beauty, you can marry your Brazilian, and cut a great swath with sixty thousand francs a year of your own, especially under the patronage of a marshal's wife—"

"Yes, but Montès is a Brazilian, he'll never amount to anything," observed Valérie.

"We are living in railroad times," said Lisbeth, "and foreigners in France, end by occupying important positions."

"We'll see," said Valérie, "when Marneffe is dead, and he hasn't long to suffer."

"These attacks which keep returning," said Lisbeth, "seem like remorse on the part of his constitution.—Well, I'm going to see Hortense."

"All right, go, my angel," Valerie replied, "and bring me my artist! To think that in three years I haven't gained an inch of ground! We ought both to be ashamed! Wenceslas and Henri, they are my only passions. One is love, the other caprice."

"Aren't you lovely this morning!" said Lisbeth putting her arm around Valérie's waist and kissing her on the brow. "I enjoy all your enjoyment, your fortune, your lovely costumes.—I never lived until the day we became sisters—"

"Wait a minute, my tigress," laughed Valérie, "your shawl is all awry.—You don't know yet how to wear a shawl, in spite of all my lessons for three years, and you want to be Madame la Maréchale Hulot—"

Shod in plum-colored boots, with gray silk stockings, and arrayed in a magnificent silk dress, with her hair *en bandeau* beneath a pretty little black velvet capote lined with yellow satin, Lisbeth betook herself to Rue Saint-Dominique by the Boulevard des Invalides, wondering whether Hortense's discouragement would finally put that steadfast heart in her power, and if the innate Sarmatian inconstancy, taken by storm at a moment when anything is possible to such natures, would cause Wenceslas to waver in his love for her.

*

Hortense and Wenceslas occupied the ground floor of a house that stood just at the spot where Rue Saint-Dominique meets the Esplanade des Invalides. Their apartments, once fully in harmony with the spirit of the honeymoon, now presented a half-fresh, half-faded aspect which we may call their autumn. Newly-married people are bunglers; without knowing or intending it they ruin everything about them just as they abuse their love. Being absorbed in themselves they care little for the future, which, at a later period, fills the thoughts of the wife and mother.

Lisbeth found that her cousin Hortense had just finished dressing a little Wenceslas who had been sent out to the garden.

"Good-morning, Bette," said she, as she herself opened the door for her cousin.

The cook had gone to market; the maid, who was also the children's nurse, was washing.

"Good-morning, my dear child," replied Lisbeth as she kissed her. "Is Wenceslas in his studio?" she asked in her ear.

"No, he is talking with Stidmann and Chanor in the salon."

"Can we be alone!" asked Lisbeth.

"Come to my room."

This room, hung in chintz with pink flowers

and green leaves on a white ground, on which, as on the carpet, the sun shone all day long, was no longer pretty. The curtains had not been washed for a long while. The smell of Wenceslas' cigar was very perceptible; as he had become a past-master of his art and was of noble birth, he deposited his ashes on the arms of chairs, on the prettiest pieces of furniture, after the manner of a beloved husband at whose hands anything will be endured, or like a rich man, who does not bother his head about vulgar trifles.

"Come, let us talk of your affairs," said Lisbeth, seeing that her cousin sat silent in the armchair into which she had thrown herself. "Why, what's the matter? You're quite pale, my dear."

"Two new articles have appeared in which my poor Wenceslas is shamefully abused; I read them, but I am keeping them from him, for he would be discouraged altogether. The marble statue of Maréchal Montcornet is considered absolutely bad. They have mercy on the bas-reliefs, so that they may, with atrocious bad faith, glorify Wenceslas' talent as a mere maker of ornaments, and thus add more weight to the opinion that *art*, strictly speaking, is a closed book to us! Stidmann, when I implored him to tell me the truth, drove me to despair by confessing that his own opinion agreed with that of all the artists and critics and the public generally. 'If,' he said to me out in the garden before lunch, 'Wenceslas doesn't produce a masterpiece next year, he must abandon the highest form of sculpture, and confine himself to idyllic subjects, small figures, jeweiry and goldsmith's work!' This judgment caused me the keenest grief, for Wenceslas would never agree to it, he is so conscious of his own power, and has so many lovely ideas—"

"You can't pay tradespeople with ideas," observed Lisbeth; "I used to wear myself out telling him so.—You need money for that. Money is paid only for things that are finished and which catch the bourgeois fancy sufficiently to be purchased. When it's a question of living, it's much better that the sculptor should have on his board the model of a candlestick, a fender or a table, than a group or a statue; for everybody needs those things, while you may have to wait long months for the lover of groups and his money—"

"You are right, dear Lisbeth! pray tell him that; I haven't the courage.—But, as he said to Stidmann, if he goes back to ornaments and petty sculpture, he must give up the Institute, and all thought of any great artistic creations, and we shall lose the three hundred thousand francs' worth of commissions that Versailles, the city of Paris, and the ministry were holding in reserve for us. That's what we lose by these frightful articles, dictated by rivals who would like to inherit our commissions."

"And that's not what you have been dreaming, of my poor little kitten!" said Bette, kissing Hortense on the forehead; "you wanted to have a nobleman for your husband, a ruling power in the world of art, at the head of all sculptors.—But that's all poetry, you see.—That dream requires fifty thousand francs a year, and you have only twenty-four hundred while I live; three thousand after my death.''

The tears gathered in Hortense's eyes, and Bette lapped them up with her glance as a cat drinks milk.

The story of the honeymoon is here given in a few words; perhaps it may contain something of a lesson for artists.

Moral labor, the hunt in the lofty regions of the intelligence, is one of the greatest efforts demanded of man. The one quality which above all others deserves to be rewarded with renown in art—and by that word we must understand all the creations of the thought—is courage; a form of courage of which the common herd has no idea, and which is here described, it may be for the first time. Driven by the terrible pressure of poverty, maintained by Bette in a situation similar to that of a horse who is made to wear blinders to prevent his looking to right or to left, goaded by the stern old maid, the personification of Necessity, a sort of secondary Destiny, Wenceslas, a born poet and dreamer, had proceeded from conception to execution, crossing, without measuring, the chasms which separate those two hemispheres of art. To think, to dream, to conceive lovely works of art is a delightful occupation. It is as if one were smoking enchanted cigars, it is the life of the courtesan intent upon the gratification of her caprice. The work then appears in all the charm of infancy, in the mad joy of generation, with the bright colors and sweet perfume of the flower, and the fast-flowing juice of the fruit, tasted in anticipation. Such is conception and its delights. He who can sketch his plan in words is at once deemed an extraordinary man. This faculty all artists and writers possess. But to produce! to bring forth! to rear the child with infinite toil, to put it to bed every night gorged with milk, to embrace it every morning with a mother's inexhaustible love, to lick away the dirt, to clothe it a hundred times over in the loveliest jackets, which it constantly tears to bits; to refuse to be discouraged by the vagaries of this wild creature, and to make of it the living masterpiece, which appeals to every eye in sculpture, to every mind in literature, to every memory in painting, to every heart in music,—such is execution and its attendant labors. The hand should be constantly put forward, ready at any moment to obey the head. Now, it is no more true that the head has at command the creative faculty, than that love always flows smoothly.

This habit of creation, this indefatigable passion for maternity, which makes the mother,—that chef-d'œuvre of nature so thoroughly understood by Raphaël!—in a word, this maternity of the brain, so difficult of attainment, may be lost with marvelous ease. Inspiration is genius's opportunity. It runs away, not keeping low; it is in the air and flies off, as quick to take alarm as a crow; it wears no scarf by which the poet can lay hold of it; its hair is aflame; it takes to its wings, like the gorgeous red and white flamingoes, the despair of hunters. Thus the labor is a fatiguing struggle, dreaded and yet loved by the noble and powerful natures, which are so often shattered by it. A great poet of the present day once said in speaking of this appalling toil: "I began it in despair, and I leave it with chagrin." Let those who are uninformed take heed! If the artist does not rush headlong into his work, as Curtius plunged into the gulf, as the soldier rushes upon the redoubt, without reflection; and if, in that crater, he does not work like a miner buried under a landslip; if, in short, he stands gazing at the difficulties in his path instead of overcoming them one by one, after the manner of the lovers in fairy tales, who, to obtain their princesses, fight with monsters who come to life as often as they are slain, the work remains unfinished, it breathes its last in a corner of the studio, where production becomes impossible, and the artist assists at the suicide of his talent. Rossini, Raphaël's brother in genius, affords a striking example, by virtue of his poverty-stricken youth contrasted with his opulent old age. Thus do we account for the fact that a like reward, a like triumph, the same wreath of laurel is accorded to great poets and generals.

Wenceslas, by nature a dreamer, had expended so much energy in giving form to his conceptions, in learning, and in working under the despotic guidance of Lisbeth, that love and good fortune brought about a reaction. His true character reappeared. The slothful indifference, the effeminacy characteristic of the Sarmatian, returned and took up their abode in his heart, in the willing furrows whence the school-master's rod had expelled them. The artist, during the first months of their union, loved his wife. Hortense and Wenceslas gave themselves over to the fascinating follies of a legitimate, happy, unreasoning passion. Hortense was therefore the first to excuse Wenceslas from all labor, being overjoyed to achieve this triumph over her rival, sculpture. A woman's caresses put the muse to flight, and softened the fierce, the brutal steadfastness of the laborer. Six or seven months passed, and the sculptor's fingers had forgotten how to hold the boasting-tool. When the necessity of beginning to work once more became apparent, when the Prince de Wissembourg, president of the subscription committee, desired to see the statue, Wenceslas made the reply to which all idlers resort: "I am just going to work on it!" And he soothed his dear Hortense with deceitful words, with the magnificent schemes of the artist who is a smoker. Hortense's love for her poet redoubled, she saw in her mind's eye a sublime statue of Maréchal Montcornet. Montcornet was to be the idealized type of intrepidity, the model cavalry officer, the personification of courage à la Murat. Why, by a mere glance at the statue, one could imagine all the Emperor's victories. And then the execution! The pencil responded promptly to the thought.

In place of a statue there came a fascinating little Wenceslas.

Whenever the subject was broached, of going to the workshop at Gros-Caillou to mould the clay, and cast the model either the prince's clock demanded Wenceslas' presence at Florent and Chanor's workshop, where the figures were being carved; or else it was a gray, gloomy day; to-day a press of business; to-morrow a family dinner; without counting the infirmities of talent and of the body; and lastly, the days when he remained at home to romp with an adored wife. The Maréchal Prince de Wissembourg was forced to lose his temper, and to say that he would reconsider his decision, in order to obtain the model. It was only after a thousand reproofs and innumerable harsh words that the committee of subscribers at last succeeded in obtaining a sight of the plaster cast. Every day that he worked Steinbock returned home visibly tired out, complaining of this sort of mason's work, and of his physical weakness. During this first year the young couple were in comparatively easy circumstances. Countess Steinbock, doting upon her husband, absorbed in the joy of satisfied love, cursed the Minister of War; she went to see him, and told him that great works of art were not made like so many pieces of cannon, and that the State should be content to await the pleasure of genius, as Louis XIV. was, and François I. and Leo X. Poor Hortense, believing that she had a Phidias in her arms, treated Wencelas with the weak motherly indulgence of a wife who carries love to the verge of idolatry.

"Don't be in a hurry," she said to her husband, "our whole future depends upon this statue; take your time and produce a chef-d'œuvre."

She would go to the studio. Steinbock, still in love, would waste five hours out of seven, describing his statue to his wife instead of working at it. In this way it took him eighteen months to complete this work, which was to him of the highest importance.

When the clay was run through the mould, and the model actually existed, poor Hortense, having been an eye-witness of the superhuman exertions put forth by her husband, whose health suffered from the fatigue which attacks the sculptor's body, arms and hand,—Hortense considered it a wonderful piece of work. Her father, who knew nothing of sculpture, and the baroness, who was no less ignorant, were loud in their admiration of the chef-d'œuvre; the Minister of War came to look at it, at their request, and under the influence of their enthusiasm, expressed his satisfaction with the model, as it stood all by itself, in a good light, and cunningly placed in front of a green curtain. But alas! at the Exhibition of 1841 the unanimous censure found expression in hootings and mockery, in the mouths of a public incensed with the idol they had been in such haste to place upon a pedestal. Stidmann sought to enlighten Wenceslas, as a friend,—he was accused of jealousy. In Hortense's eyes the articles in the newspapers were the shrieks of envy. Stidmann, like the good fellow he was, procured the insertion of articles wherein the animadversions of the critics were combated, wherein it was pointed out that sculptors so modified their works between the plaster and the marble, that the marble was exhibited. "Between the original conception in plaster and the completed statue in marble," said Claude Vignon, "a chef-d'œuvre may be ruined, or a wretched failure transformed into a great success. The plaster is the manuscript, the marble is the book."

In two years and a half Steinbock produced a statue and a child. The child was sublimely beautiful, the statue was detestable.

The prince's clock and the statue paid the debts of the young couple. Thereupon Steinbock contracted the habit of going into society, to the play, to the Italiens; he talked wonderfully well upon art, and in the eyes of society maintained his position as a great artist by his conversation, by his critical explanations. There are men of genius in Paris who pass their lives in listening to their own conversation, and who are content with a sort of salon celebrity. Steinbock, copying these entertaining hybrids, contracted an aversion to labor that waxed greater day by day. He detected all the difficulties of the task as soon as he set about it, and the consequent discouragement weakened his resolution. Inspiration, the frenzy of intellectual generation, fled at once at the sight of this sick lover.

Sculpture is like dramatic art, at once the most difficult and the simplest of all forms of art. Copy a model, and the task is done; but to impart a soul, to produce the type of a whole class in the figure of a man or a woman, is like the sin of Prometheus. Successful achievement in this line is recorded in the annals of sculpture, as the names of poets are recorded in the annals of humanity. Michael Angelo, Michael Colombo, Jean Goujon, Phidias, Praxiteles, Polycletus, Puget, Canova, Albert Dürer are brothers to Milton, Virgil, Dante, Shakespeare, Tasso, Homer and Molière. The work these men did was of such noble proportions that one statue was enough to immortalize a man, as Figaro, Lovelace and Manon Lescaut were enough to immortalize Beaumarchais, Richardson and Abbé Prévost. Superficial persons—and artists count many such in their ranks—have said that real sculpture existed only in the nude, that it died with Greek art, and that our modern raiment made it impossible. In the first place, the ancients produced sublime statues draped from head to foot, as for example, the *Polhymnia*, *Julia*, etc., and we have never found the tenth part of their works. In the second place, let all true lovers of art go to Florence and see Michael Angelo's *Penseur*, or to the cathedral at Mayence and see the *Virgin* by Albert Dürer, an ebony statue of a living woman beneath her triple robes, with the silkiest, loveliest hair that ever lady's maid dressed. Let the ignoramuses hasten thither, and all will agree that genius can embody a thought in coat, dress or armor, and place a body therein, even as man impresses his character and his habits upon his outer covering.

Sculpture is the constant realization of that fact which, for the first and only time, is called in painting, Raphaël! The solution of this arduous problem is to be found only in constant, unremitting toil, for the material obstacles must be so thoroughly overcome, the hand so chastened, so willing and obedient, that the sculptor may contend soul to soul with that intangible moral nature which must be transfigured in the process of materialization. If Paganini, whose soul found utterance through the strings of his violin, had passed three days without studying, he would have lost, with his power of expression, the *register* of his instrument; he so designated the union that existed between the violin, the bow, the strings and himself; that union once dissolved, he would suddenly have become a commonplace violinist. Constant labor is the law of art as of life; for art is creation idealized. And so great artists and full-grown poets do not await orders or customers; they produce to-day, to-morrow, all the time. Hence the habit of constant labor, the unerring appreciation of the obstacles to be overcome, which keeps them in touch with the muse and her creative forces. Canova lived in his studio, as Voltaire lived in his study. Homer and Phidias must have done likewise.

Wenceslas Steinbock was upon the dreary path

trodden by these great men, and which leads to the Alpine heights of fame, when Lisbeth chained him down in his attic. Happiness, in the guise of Hortense, made the poet a sloth once more, the normal condition of all artists, for with them slothfulness is activity. It is like the enjoyment of a pacha in his seraglio; they welcome ideas caressingly, they drink to excess of the springs which supply the mind. Great artists like Steinbock, consumed by the habit of dreaming, have been justly called *dreamers.* These opium-eaters all come to want; whereas, if they had been kept to their work by inflexible circumstances, they would have been great men. Such demi-artists are charming fellows, men like them, and make them drunk with praise; they seem superior to the veritable artists, who are taxed with self-conceit, boorishness, and rebellion against the laws of society. For this reason: Great men belong to their works. Their dissociation from all other interests, their devotion to their work stamps them as egotists in the eyes of fools, who would like to see them dressed in the same clothes as the fashionable dandy, going through the evolutions called social duties. They would like to see the lions of Atlas curled and scented like a marchioness's lap-dog. Such men, who have few equals and seldom encounter them, fall into the habit of exclusiveness, born of a solitary life; they become inexplicable enigmas to the majority of mankind, made up, as we know, of fools and of envious, ignorant, superficial people.

Do you understand now the part a woman has to play living beside one of these magnificent hybrids? A woman must not only be what Lisbeth was for five years, but must also offer him love, submissive and discreet, always ready and always smiling.

Hortense, enlightened by her mother's suffering, discovered too late, under the pressure of dire poverty, the errors her excessive love had led her involuntarily to commit; but, like her mother's own daughter, her heart was torn at the idea of worrying Wenceslas; she loved her dear poet too well to be his executioner, and she watched the approach of the moment when she, her son and her husband would be in absolute want.

"Come, come, my little one," said Bette, as she saw the tears gathering in her cousin's lovely eyes, "you mustn't despair. A tumblerful of your tears won't pay for a plate of soup! How much do you need?"

"Only five or six thousand francs."

"I have only three thousand at the outside," said Lisbeth. "What is Wenceslas at work on now?"

"They propose that he shall undertake, with Stidmann, a dessert service for the Duc d'Hérouville for six thousand francs. In that case Chanor agrees to pay four thousand francs due Messieurs Léon de Lora and Bridau, a debt of honor."

"What! you have had the money for the statue and bas-reliefs of the monument to Maréchal Montcornet, and you haven't paid that!"

"Why, for three years," said Hortense, "we

have spent twelve thousand francs a year, and my income is two thousand. The marshal's monument, after all expenses were paid, brought us no more than sixteen thousand. Really, if Wenceslas doesn't work, I don't know what will become of us. Ah! if I could only learn to make statues, how I'd make the clay fly!" said she, extending her beautiful arms.

It will be seen that the woman fulfilled the promise of the girl. Hortense's eye sparkled; the blood flowed swift and strong through her veins; she deplored having to waste her energy in holding her child.

"Ah! my dear little pet, a wise girl should only marry an artist when his fortune is made,—not when he has it to make."

At that moment they heard the steps and voices of Stidmann and Wenceslas, escorting Chanor to the door, and the two former soon made their appearance. Stidmann, an artist prominent in the social circle of journalists, illustrious actresses and celebrated lorettes, was a young man of fashion whom Valérie wished to add to her circle, and whom Claude Vignon had already introduced to her. Stidmann had recently ceased his connection with Madame Schontz, who had been married a few months before this time, and had gone to live in the provinces. Valérie and Lisbeth, being informed of the rupture by Claude Vignon, deemed it advisable to attract this friend of Wenceslas to Rue Vanneau. As Stidmann, as a matter of prudence, was an infrequent visitor at the Steinbocks', and as Lisbeth was not present at the time of his recent introduction by Claude Vignon, this was her first meeting with him. As she scrutinized the famous artist, she surprised several glances directed by him at Hortense, which opened to her mind the possibility that he might be given to Countess Steinbock as a consolation, if Wenceslas should betray her. It had, in fact, occurred to Stidmann that if Wenceslas were not his good friend, Hortense, his youthful and superbly beautiful countess, would make an adorable mistress; but that desire, restrained by the sentiment of honor, kept him away from the house. Lisbeth noticed the significant embarrassment which attacks a man in the presence of a woman with whom he is forbidden to flirt.

"He's a very good-looking young fellow," she whispered to Hortense.

"Ah! do you think so? I never noticed it,—" she replied.

"Stidmann, my boy," said Wenceslas in his comrade's ear, "we don't stand on ceremony with each other, and we have some business to talk over with this old maid."

Stidmann bowed to the cousins and took his leave.

"It's settled," said Wenceslas, returning after he had shown Stidmann out; "but the work will take six months, and we must have something to live on all that time."

"I have my diamonds," cried the young Countess

Steinbock, with the sublime impulsiveness of women who love.

The tears came to Wenceslas' eyes.

"Oh! I am going to work," said he, sitting down beside his wife, and taking her on his knee. "I am going to make gewgaws at odd times, wedding presents and bronze groups—"

"But, my dear children," said Lisbeth,—"for you are my heirs, you know, and I'll leave you a pretty little pile, my word for it, especially if you help me to marry the marshal,—if we should succeed soon, I'd take you to board with me, you and Adeline. Ah! we could live very happily together. Just for this time, take the advice of my experience. Don't resort to the Mont-de-Piété, it means ruin to the borrower. I have always found that those who are in want haven't the necessary money to pay the interest when the time for renewal comes around, and it's all lost. I can arrange for a loan for you at five per cent on your own note."

"Ah! that would save us!" said Hortense.

"Very well, little one, let Wenceslas call on the person who will accommodate him at my request. It's Madame Marneffe; by a little judicious flattery, for she's as vain as all parvenus, you can induce her to help you out of your embarrassment in the most obliging way. Come to her house, my dear Hortense."

Hortense looked at Wenceslas with such an expression as men condemned to death must wear when they mount the scaffold.

"Claude Vignon has presented Stidmann there," replied Wenceslas. "It's a very pleasant house."

Hortense hung her head. A single word will serve to describe the sensation that came over her: it was not grief, it was a deathly pang.

"Why, my dear Hortense, pray learn what life is!" cried Lisbeth, comprehending the full meaning of Hortense's eloquent movement. "If you don't, you will be like your mother, banished to a deserted chamber, where you will weep like Calypso after the departure of Ulysses, in an age when there are no Telemachuses!—" she added, repeating one of Madame Marneffe's jocose remarks. "We must look upon the people in the world as tools to be made use of, to be taken up or laid aside, according to their usefulness. Make use of Madame Marneffe, my dears, and drop her later on. Are you afraid that Wenceslas, who adores you, will conceive a passion for a woman four or five years older than you, faded as a truss of hay and—"

"I much prefer to pledge my diamonds," said Hortense. "Oh! never go there, Wenceslas!—it's a perfect hell!"

"Hortense is right!" said Wenceslas, embracing his wife.

"Thanks, my dear," replied the young woman, happy beyond expression.—"Oh! Lisbeth, my husband's an angel; he doesn't gamble, we go everywhere together, and if he could go to work in earnest—no, I should be too happy. Why should we show ourselves at the house of our father's mistress, a woman who is ruining him, and who is the cause of the sorrow which is killing dear, heroic mamma?"

"My child, that isn't the source of his ruin; it was his songstress who ruined him, and then your marriage!" rejoined Cousin Bette. "Great heavens! Madame Marneffe is very useful to him!—but I ought to say nothing—"

"You stand up for everybody, dear Bette—"

Here Hortense was summoned to the garden by the shrieks of her child, and Lisbeth remained alone with Wenceslas.

"You have an angel for a wife, Wenceslas!" said she; "love her dearly, never make her unhappy."

"Yes, I love her so dearly that I conceal our situation from her," Wenceslas replied; "but I can speak to you, Lisbeth—Well then, if we should pawn my wife's diamonds at the Mont-de-Piété, we should be no better off."

"Then borrow from Madame Marneffe,—" said Lisbeth. "Induce Hortense to let you come there, or else,—why, come without her suspecting it!"

"That's what occurred to me," replied Wenceslas, "just as I refused to go so as not to grieve Hortense."

"Listen to me, Wenceslas; I love you both too dearly not to warn you of the danger. If you come there, hold your heart with both hands, for the woman's a demon; every one who sees her worships her; she's so depraved, so alluring!—She's as fascinating as a masterpiece of art. Borrow her money, but don't leave your heart in pawn. I should never forgive myself if my cousin were to be wronged.—Here she is!" cried Lisbeth; "say no more, I'll arrange the matter for you."

"Kiss Lisbeth, my angel," said Wenceslas to his wife, "she will help us out of our trouble by loaning us her savings."

He made a sign to Lisbeth which she understood.

"Then I hope you will go to work, my cherub?" said Hortense.

"Oh yes!" replied the artist, "to-morrow."

"It's this 'to-morrow' that ruins us," said Hortense with a smile.

"Ah! my dear child, I leave it to you if something hasn't turned up every day, obstacles of one sort or another, or business?"

"Yes, you are right, my love."

"I have ideas here!" continued Steinbock striking his brow.—"oh! but I mean to surprise all my enemies. I mean to make a table service in the German style of the Sixteenth Century, the dreamy style! I will fashion leaves filled with insects; I will have children lying upon them, and I will mingle with them chimeras never seen before, real chimeras, the substance of our dreams!—I have them here! It will be intricate in execution, airy and at the same time substantial. Chanor went away filled with wondering admiration.—I needed encouragement, for the last article on the Montcornet monument was too much for me to bear."

When Lisbeth and Wenceslas were left alone for a moment during the day, the artist agreed to call upon Madame Marneffe the next day, when he would either have obtained his wife's permission, or would go on the sly.

*

Valérie, being made acquainted with this triumph the same evening, required Baron Hulot to promise that he would invite Stidmann, Claude Vignon and Steinbock to dinner; for she was beginning to tyrannize over him as women of her stamp can tyrannize over old men, who trot all over the city and carry invitations to anyone whose presence is essential to the interests or vanity of their pitiless mistresses.

The next day Valérie put herself under arms, by making one of those toilettes to which fair Parisians resort when they wish to make the most of all their advantages. She made a careful study of the task, as a man who is about to fight a duel rehearses his *feints* and his *parries*. Not a fold, not a wrinkle. Valérie's skin was never so soft and white and fine. Her patches, too, insensibly attracted the eye. It is commonly believed that the patches of the Eighteenth Century have been forgotten or suppressed; this is an error. To-day the ladies, more clever than their predecessors, resort to audacious stratagems to attract the fire of the opera-glass. Such an one was the first to invent the cockade of ribbons, in the centre of which a diamond is placed, and she monopolizes the public gaze for a whole evening; such another rehabilitates the net, or plants a dagger in her hair to turn the mind to thoughts of her garter; this one wears black-velvet wrist-bands; that one reappears with lace in the coiffure These sublime efforts, the Austerlitzes of coquetry or of love, thereupon become the fashion for those in less exalted spheres, just when their lucky inventors are inventing others. For the evening in question, on which Valérie wished to achieve a notable success, she arranged three patches. She had her hair dressed with a water which changed her blonde locks for a few days to gray. Madame Steinbock was a brilliant blonde, and she was determined not to resemble her in any respect. This unfamiliar color imparted a something piquant and strange to Valérie's appearance, and engrossed the attention of her faithful servitors to such a degree that Montès said to her: "What's the matter with you this evening, pray?"—Then she wore a black velvet ribbon around her neck, of sufficient width to bring out the dazzling whiteness of her breast. The third patch might be compared to the *assassines* our grand-mothers used to wear. Valérie planted the sweetest little rose-bud in the middle of her corsage just where the dress meets the flesh, in the prettiest of furrows. It was enough to make every man under thirty lower his eyes.

"I am pretty enough to eat!" said she, practising all her poses before the mirror exactly as a ballet-dancer practises her bends.

Lisbeth had gone to market, and the dinner was to be one of those extra dainty repasts which Mathurine used to cook for the bishop when he entertained his brother of the next diocese.

Stidmann, Claude Vignon and Count Steinbock arrived almost at the same time, toward six o'clock. An ordinary, or, if you choose, a natural woman on hearing his name, would have run to meet the being she so ardently desired; but Valérie, who had been waiting in her bed-room since five o'clock, left her three guests together, well assured that she would be the subject of their conversation, or at least of their secret thoughts. In ordering the arrangement of her salon she had put in evidence the pretty trifles which Paris alone of all cities can produce, which reveal the woman, and announce her presence, so to speak; keepsakes bound with enamel, and embroidered with pearls, cups filled with lovely rings, chefs-d'œuvre of Sevres or Saxony porcelain mounted with exquisite taste by Florent and Chanor, statuettes, too, and albums, and all the other knick-knacks which command fabulous prices, and are ordered from the manufacturers by passion in its first frenzy, or for a final reconciliation. Valérie was under the spell of the intoxication caused by success. She had promised Crevel to be his wife, if Marneffe should die; whereupon the amorous Crevel had caused the ten thousand francs of revenue to be transferred to the name of Valérie Fortin, that being the interest upon his gains in railroad speculation during the past three years,—the net profits of the capital of a hundred thousand crowns he had offered Baroness Hulot.

Thus Valérie was possessed of thirty-two thousand francs a year. Crevel had just let slip a promise of vastly greater importance than this gift of his profits. In the paroxysm of passion in which he had passed the time from two o'clock to four with his *duchess*—he bestowed that title upon Madame *de* Marneffe in order to complete his illusion—for Valérie had outdone herself at Rue du Dauphin, he thought it wise to encourage her to persevére in her promised fidelity, by offering her the prospect of a pretty little house on Rue Barbette built by an imprudent contractor, and about to be sold. Valérie imagined herself living in that charming house with courtyard and garden, and with her own carriage!

"Where's the virtuous life that will bring one all this in so short a time, and so easily?" she said to Lisbeth as she was putting the finishing touches to her toilette.

Lisbeth dined with Valérie that day, so that she might say to Steinbock what no woman can say concerning herself. Madame Marneffe, her face beaming with happiness, made her entrée with modest grace, followed by Bette, who, being dressed in black and yellow, served as a set-off, in studio parlance.

"Good-evening, Claude," said she, giving her hand to the former famous critic.

Claude Vignon, like many another, had become a politician, a new word invented to designate an ambitious man at the first stage of his journey. The *politician* of 1840 resembles in some respects the *abbé* of the Eighteenth Century. No salon would be complete without its politician.

"My dear, this is my second-cousin Comte Steinbock," said Lisbeth, presenting Wenceslas, whom Valérie did not appear to have noticed.

"I recognized Monsieur le Comte," said Valérie with a graceful inclination of her head. "I saw you frequently on Rue du Doyenné, and I had the pleasure of being present at your wedding.—My dear," said she to Lisbeth, "it's difficult to forget your former child even though one had seen him but once.—Monsieur Stidmann is very good," she continued, bowing to the sculptor, "to accept my invitation on such short notice; but necessity knows no law! I knew you to be the friend of both these gentlemen. Nothing is colder or more disagreeable than a dinner where the guests are not known to each other and I drafted you on their account; but you will come another time on mine, won't you?—do say yes!"

And she walked to and fro a few seconds with Stidmann, apparently entirely engrossed with him. One after another was announced, Crevel, Baron Hulot, and a deputy named Beauvisage. This personage, a provincial Crevel, one of those men who were sent into the world to swell the crowd, voted under the banner of Giraud, Councilor of State, and Victorin Hulot. These two statesmen aimed at forming a knot of progressists in the great phalanx of conservatives. Giraud sometimes came in the evening to Madame Marneffe's, who flattered herself that she could hook Victorin Hulot also; but the Puritanical advocate had thus far succeeded in finding excuses for resisting his father and father-in-law. To visit the woman who caused his mother's tears to flow, seemed to him a crime. Victorin Hulot was to the Puritans in politics what a piously-inclined woman is to the devotees. Beauvisage, formerly a hosier at Arcis, wished to follow the fashion at Paris. This man, one of the pillars of the Chamber, formed his manners under the roof of the delightful, the captivating Madame Marneffe, where, being charmed with Crevel, he accepted him from Valérie as his model and his master; he consulted him in everything, he asked him for his tailor's address, he copied him, he tried to strike an attitude like his; in short Crevel was his great man. Valérie, surrounded by these functionaries and the three artists, and accompanied by Lisbeth, appeared to Wenceslas a woman superior to other women, especially as Claude Vignon praised her with the enthusiasm of a man in love.

"'She's Madame de Maintenon in Ninon's skirts!" said the former critic. "To please her is a matter of a single evening, if one has wit, but to win her love is a triumph which may well satisfy a man's pride and fill out his life."

Valérie, apparently cold and indifferent to her former neighbor, touched his vanity; she did it unconsciously, however, for she knew nothing of the Polish character. There is a childish side to the Slav, as there is to all peoples originally in a state of barbarism, and which have rather made an irruption among civilized nations than really become civilized. This race has overspread the globe like a flood, and has occupied a vast space thereon. It dwells in deserts where in the boundless space it can live in comfort; men do not elbow one another there as in Europe, and civilization is impossible without the continual friction of minds and interests. The Ukraine, Russia, the plains of the Danube, the whole Slavic race in short, are the link between Europe and Asia, between civilization and barbarism. So it is that the Poles, the richest fraction of the Slavic race, have in their character the childish traits and the inconstancy of beardless nations. They possess courage, intellect and strength; but they are so inconsistent, that this courage possesses neither method nor intelligence, for the Pole is as fickle as the wind that sweeps over his vast, swampy plains; if he is as impetuous as the whirlwinds which tear up and carry away houses, he also resembles those awful atmospheric avalanches in that he disappears in the nearest pond, dissolved in water. Man always assimilates something of the surroundings in which he lives. Being constantly at war with the Turks, the Poles have acquired the taste for oriental magnificence; they frequently sacrifice the necessaries of life in order to make a brilliant show, they adorn themselves like women, and yet the climate has endowed them with the rugged constitution of the Arab. So the Pole, sublime in his suffering, has tired out the arms of his oppressors, by his indifference to death, thus renewing, in the Nineteenth Century, the spectacle offered by the early Christian martyrs. Introduce ten per cent of English cunning into the frank, outspoken Polish character, and the noble-hearted white eagle would reign to-day wherever the two-headed eagle has crept in. A little Machiavellism would have prevented Poland from saving Austria, the author of the partition of Poland; from borrowing from Prussia, her usurer, who preyed upon her vitals; and from being rent by factions at the time of the first partition. At the baptism of Poland, doubtless some fairy Carabosse, who had been overlooked by the genii who endowed that attractive nation with its most brilliant qualities, appeared and said: "Keep all the gifts my sisters have poured out upon you, but you shall never know what you desire!" If, in her heroic duel with Russia, Poland had triumphed, the Poles would to-day be fighting among themselves in their Diets, as in former days, to prevent one another from being king. On the day when this nation, composed entirely of brave, sanguine men, has the good sense to seek out a Louis XI. of its own flesh and blood and to accept from him tyranny and a new dynasty, it will be saved. What Poland was in politics, most Poles are in their private lives, especially when disaster overtakes them. Thus, Wenceslas Steinbock, who had adored his wife for three years, and who knew that he was a god in her eyes, was so piqued to find that Madame Marneffe hardly noticed him, that he made it a point of honor to obtain some attention from her. As he compared Valérie with his wife the former carried off the palm.

Hortense was a lovely piece of flesh, as Valérie said to Lisbeth; but Madame Marneffe was bright and witty, and her wit was clothed in the alluring guise of vice. Hortense's devotion was a sentiment, which, in a husband's eyes, seems no more than his due; one's appreciation of the immeasurable value of a woman's undivided love soon passes away, just as a debtor fancies, after awhile, that the money loaned him is his own. This sublime loyalty becomes in a certain sense the daily bread of the heart, and infidelity is as seductive as a sweetmeat. The disdainful woman, an especially dangerous type, stimulates one's interest, as spices give zest to food. Moreover, contempt, so well feigned by Valérie, was a novelty to Wenceslas, after three years of pleasure freely bestowed. Hortense was the wife, Valérie the mistress.

Many men desire these two editions of the same work, although it is a most eloquent proof of a man's inferiority that he does not know how to make his wife his mistress. Fickleness in this regard is a sign of weakness. Constancy will always be the genius of love, the symbol of a vast force, the force which makes the poet! A man should have all wives in his own, as the filthy poets of the Seventeenth Century made Irises and Chloes of their Manons.

"Well," said Lisbeth to her cousin, as soon as she saw that he was fairly fascinated, "what do you think of Valérie?"

"She's too charming!" Wenceslas replied.

"You wouldn't listen to me," retorted Cousin Bette. "Ah! Wenceslas, if we had stayed together, you might have been this siren's lover, you could have married her as soon as she was left a widow, and you would have had her forty thousand francs a year!"

"Really?—"

"Why, yes," said Lisbeth. "But, beware now; I warned you of the danger, so don't burn your fingers at the candle! Give me your arm, dinner's served."

No speech could have been more demoralizing than that, for, show a Pole a precipice and he will instantly jump over the edge. That race has above all the true cavalry instinct, that leads them to think that they can beat down all obstacles and come out victorious. The blow of the spur by which Lisbeth goaded her cousin's vanity, was supported by the spectacle of the dining-room, where a magnificent service of silver plate shone resplendent, and where Steinbock observed all the refinement and elegancies of Parisian luxury.

"I should have done better," said he to himself, "to marry Cilimène."

During the dinner, Hulot, well pleased to see his son-in-law there, and even more delighted over the certainty of a reconciliation with Valérie, of whose fidelity he flattered himself that he had made sure by the promise of the succession to Coquet, was in a charming mood. Stidmann responded to the baron's affability with flashes of Parisian wit, and the entertaining conceits of an artist. Steinbock did not choose to be eclipsed by his comrade; he exerted his powers, he distinguished himself by his sallies of wit, he made an impression, and was well content with himself; Madame Marneffe smiled upon him several times, showing that she understood him. The good cheer, the excellent wines, completed Wenceslas' immersion in what we must call the pest-hole of pleasure. Slightly elevated by the wine he had taken, he stretched himself out after dinner upon a divan, under the spell of a sense of physical and moral well-being which Madame Marneffe heightened beyond measure by sitting down beside him, a graceful, perfumed creature, lovely enough to damn the angels. She leaned over Wenceslas, and almost touched his ear in order to whisper:

"This evening is no time for us to talk business, unless you choose to stay till the last. You and Lisbeth and I, between us, can arrange matters to accommodate you—"

"Oh! madame, you are an angel!" said Wenceslas, replying in the same way. "I did an awfully foolish thing in not listening to Lisbeth—"

"What did she say to you?"

"On Rue du Doyenné she declared that you loved me!—"

Madame Marneffe glanced at Wenceslas, pretended to be confused, and rose abruptly. A young and pretty woman never with impunity aroused in a man the idea of instantaneous success. This impulsive movement of a virtuous woman, repressing a passion stored away in the depths of her heart, was a thousand times more eloquent than the most impassioned declaration.

Thus was the flame of desire kindled in the breast of Wenceslas, and he redoubled his attentions to Valérie. A woman in sight, a woman desired! Hence the appalling power of actresses. Madame Marneffe, realizing that she was being studied, bore herself like a successful actress. She was fascinating, and achieved a complete triumph.

"My father-in-law's passion no longer surprises me," said Wenceslas to Lisbeth.

"If you talk so, Wenceslas," was her reply, "I shall repent all my life that I procured you this loan of ten thousand francs. Shall you be like all the rest of them," she said, pointing to the guests, "mad with love for this creature? Consider that you will be your father-in-law's rival. But most of all think of all the sorrow you will cause Hortense."

"True," said Wenceslas, "Hortense is an angel, and I should be a monster!"

"It's quite enough to have one in the family," rejoined Lisbeth.

"Artists ought never to marry!" cried Steinbock.

"Aha! that's what I told you on Rue du Doyenné. Your children are your groups, your statues, your masterpieces."

"What are you talking about over there?" demanded Valérie, joining Lisbeth.—"Pour the tea, cousin."

Steinbock, with true Polish swagger, chose to appear on intimate terms with this fairy of the salon. Having insulted Stidmann, Claude Vignon and Crevel with a glance, he took Valérie's hand and forced her to sit beside him on the divan.

"You are much too great a nobleman, Comte Steinbock!" said she, resisting a little.

And she began to laugh as she sank into a seat beside him, not without showing him the little rosebud which adorned her corsage.

"Alas! if I were a great nobleman," said he, "I should not come here as a borrower."

"Poor child! I remember your nights of toil on Rue du Doyenné. You have been a little bit stupid. You got married, as a starving man pounces on a bit of bread. You don't know Paris! See what you've come to! But you turned a deaf ear to Bette's devotion, as well as to the love of the Parisian, who knows her Paris by heart."

"Say no more!" cried Steinbock, "I am beaten."

"You shall have your ten thousand francs, my dear Wenceslas; but only on one condition," said she, playing with his beautiful thick locks.

"What is it?"

"Well, I want no interest—"

"Madame!—"

"Oh! don't be angry; you must give me a bronze group instead. You began the story of Samson—finish it.—Make a Delilah cutting off the locks of her Jewish Hercules!—But I hope that you—you will be a great artist, if you take my advice—I hope that you will grasp the subject. The idea is to bring out the power of the woman. Samson counts for nothing in that scene. He is the dead body of strength. Delilah is the passion that destroys everything. Just as that *replica*—is that what you call it?—" she added, cunningly, as she saw Claude Vignon and Stidmann approaching them when they heard them talking about sculpture; "just as that replica of Hercules at Omphale's feet is much more beautiful than the Grecian myth! Did Greece copy from Judea? or did Judea derive that symbol from Greece?"

"Ah! there you touch upon a serious question, madame! that of the periods at which the various books of the Bible were composed. The great and immortal Spinoza, who is so absurdly ranked among atheists, although he has mathematically demonstrated the existence of God, claimed that Genesis and the political portion of the Bible, so to speak, date from the time of Moses, and he pointed out the interpolated passages by philological proofs. For that reason he was stabbed three times at the door of the synagogue."

"I didn't know I was so learned," said Valérie, disgusted at the interruption of her tête-à-tête.

"Women know everything by instinct," rejoined Claude Vignon.

"Well, will you promise me?" she asked Steinbock, taking his hand with the shrinking gesture of a love-lorn maiden.

"You are very lucky, my dear fellow," cried Stidmann, "to have madame ask you for anything—"

"What is it?" said Claude Vignon.

"A little bronze group," replied Steinbock; *Delilah cutting off Samson's hair.*

"That will be difficult," observed Claude Vignon, "on account of the bed—"

"On the contrary it's extremely easy," retorted Valérie with a smile.

"Ah! give us some sculpture of your own!"—said Stidmann.

"Madame's the thing to be sculptured!" exclaimed Claude Vignon with a meaning glance at Valérie.

"Now," she continued, "this is my idea of the composition. Samson has awakened without his hair, like many a dandy with a false forelock. The hero is sitting on the edge of the bed, so you have only to imagine the base, hidden by the bedclothes, draperies, etc. He sits there like Marius on the ruins of Carthage, with arms folded and shaven head—Napoléon at St. Helena, how's that? Delilah is on her knees, almost like Canova's *Magdalen.* When a woman has ruined her man, she adores him. According to my idea the Jewess was afraid of Samson when he was powerful and awe-inspiring, but she must have loved him when he was a child again. So Delilah bewails her sin, she would like to restore his locks to her lover, she dares not look at him, yet she does look at him with a smile on her face, for she sees her pardon in Samson's weakness. This group and the group of the barbarian Judith would together expound the nature of woman. Virtue cuts off your head, Vice only cuts off your hair. Look out for your forelocks, messieurs!"

And she left the two bewildered artists, singing a chorus of praise in her honor with the critic.

"No one could be more fascinating!" cried Stidmann.

"Oh! she's the brightest, the most desirable woman I ever saw," said Claude Vignon. "It is so rare to see wit and beauty united!"

"If you, who have had the honor of an intimate acquaintance with Camille Maupin, pronounce such a judgment," said Stidmann, "what are we to think?"

"If you will make your Delilah a portrait of Valérie, my dear count," said Crevel, who had left the card-table for a moment and had heard the whole conversation, "I will give you a thousand crowns for a copy of the group. Oh! yes, sapristi! I'll fritter away a thousand crowns!"

"*I'll fritter away!* what does that mean?" Beauvisage asked Claude Vignon.

"In that case Madame must condescend to pose

for me,"—said Steinbock to Crevel, with a wave of his hand towards Valérie. "Go and ask her."

At that moment Valérie herself brought Steinbock a cup of tea. This was more than a distinction, it was a marked favor. There is an entire language in the way a woman acquits herself of that duty; but they know it well, and so it is a curious study to watch their movements, gestures, glances or looks, tones, accents, when they perform this act of courtesy, apparently so simple. Between the question: "Do you take tea?—Will you have some tea?—A cup of tea?" asked in an indifferent tone, and followed by the order to the nymph who tends the urn to bring it, to the inspiring poem of the odalisk coming from the tea-table, cup in hand, to the pacha of her heart, and presenting it to him with a submissive air, a caressing voice, and a glance overflowing with voluptuous promises—between the two a physiologist may discover every feminine sentiment, from aversion or indifference, to Phædra's declaration to Hippolyte. At such times a woman can, at will, make herself disdainful to the point of insult, or as humble as the slave in an Eastern harem. Valérie was more than a woman, she was the serpent in the guise of woman, and she completed her devilish work by walking up to Steinbock, a cup of tea in her hand.

"I will take," said the artist in Valérie's ear, as he rose and touched her fingers with his own, "as many cups of tea as you choose to offer me, for the sake of seeing you come and give them to me like this!—"

"What are you saying about posing?" she asked, giving no sign that she had received, full in the heart, the explosion so passionately awaited.

"Père Crevel offers to buy a copy of your group for a thousand crowns."

"A thousand crowns for a group?"

"Yes, if you will pose for Delilah," said Steinbock.

"He won't be there, I trust," she replied; "in that case the group would be worth more than his whole fortune, for Delilah should be slightly *décolletée.*"

Just as Crevel had his favorite attitude, so all women have a triumphant, carefully studied pose, in which they are irresistible. Some there are who pass all their time, when in a salon, looking at the lace of their chemisettes, and adjusting the shoulder-straps of their dresses, or displaying the brilliancy of their eyes by looking up at the cornice. Madame Marneffe did not display her triumph facing her victim, as all other women do. She turned about abruptly as if to join Lisbeth at the tea-table. This dancer's movement, in fluttering her dress, which had conquered Hulot, now fascinated Steinbock.

"Your vengeance is complete," Valérie whispered to Lisbeth. "Hortense will cry her eyes out and curse the day she stole Wenceslas from you."

"So long as I am not Madame la Maréchale, I

shall have accomplished nothing," replied the Lorrainer; "but *they* are all beginning to desire it.—This morning I went to Victorin's, I forgot to tell you that. The young Hulots have taken up the baron's notes of hand held by Vauvinet, and tomorrow they will sign a bond for seventy-two thousand francs at five per cent, payable in three years, secured by a mortgage on their house. So they are safe to be in straitened circumstances for three years to come; it would be impossible for them to raise money on the property now. Victorin is in a terribly depressed state, for he has found his father out. Crevel is quite capable of disowning his children, he'll be so enraged at this devotion."

"The baron must be without means now?" said Valérie in Lisbeth's ear, with a smile at Hulot.

"I don't see what he can have; but his salary will be unencumbered again in September."

"And he has his insurance policy, he's renewed that! It's high time he made Marneffe chief of bureau; I must play the deuce with him this evening."

"Go now, my cousin, I beg you," said Lisbeth, going over to Wenceslas. "You are making yourself ridiculous, staring at Valérie in a way to compromise her, and her husband's jealousy goes beyond all bounds. Don't imitate your father-in-law, but return home; I am sure Hortense expects you."

"Madame Marneffe bade me stay till the last, to arrange our little affair between us three," said Wenceslas.

"No," said Lisbeth, "I'll hand you the ten thousand francs, for her husband has his eye on you, and it would be imprudent for you to remain. Bring the note of hand to-morrow at eleven; at that hour that old ass Marneffe will be at his office, and Valérie will be left in peace.—So you've asked her to pose for a group, have you?—Come to my room first.—Ah! I knew," said Lisbeth, catching Steinbock's glance as he saluted Valérie, "that you were a libertine in germ. Valérie is very lovely, but try not to make Hortense unhappy."

Nothing annoys a married man so much as to have his wife at every turn stand between him and any whim, however ephemeral.

*

Wenceslas returned home about one o'clock in the morning; Hortense had been expecting him since half-past nine. From half-past nine until ten she listened to the carriages, saying to herself that Wenceslas never returned so late when he, without her, dined with Chanor and Florent. She sat sewing by her son's crib, for she was beginning to save a seamstress's wages by doing some mending with her own hands. Between ten and half-past ten she had a moment of suspicion and asked herself: "Has he really gone to dine with Chanor and Florent, as he said? He wanted his best scarf and his prettiest pin. He took more time to dress than a woman who wants to look even prettier than she is.—But I am mad! he loves me. Here he is, too."

But the carriage she heard passed on, instead of stopping. From eleven o'clock till midnight, Hortense was in an unheard of terror, caused by the solitude of the neighborhood.

"If he were walking home," she said to herself, "something might have happened to him. People are killed sometimes by stumbling over a curbstone, or by not looking out for holes in the ground. Artists are so absent-minded!—Suppose he was waylaid by robbers!—This is the first time he has left me all alone here six hours and a half.—Why do I torment myself so? he loves me only."

Men ought to be faithful to the wives who love them, were it only for the sake of the never-ending miracles produced by true love in that sublime world called the *spiritual world.* A loving woman is, in respect to the man she loves, in the position of a somnambulist, to whom the mesmerist should give the sad power—in ceasing to be the mirror of the world—of being conscious, as a woman, of what she sees as a somnambulist. Passion exalts a woman's nervous force to that ecstatic state wherein presentiment is equivalent to the second-sight of seers. A woman knows that she is betrayed, but she will not listen, she doubts, so dearly does she love! and she gives the lie to the cry of her pythoness' power. Men should fall down and worship this paroxysm of love. In noble minds admiration of this divine phenomenon will always be a barrier between them and infidelity. How can one fail to adore a lovely, intelligent creature whose heart leads her to such manifestations?—At one in the morning Hortense's agony had reached such a point that she rushed frantically to the door when she recognized Wenceslas by his manner of ringing the bell; she took him in her arms and pressed him to her heart like a mother.

"Here you are at last!—" she said, recovering the use of her tongue. "After this, my dear, I shall go wherever you go, for I don't want to endure the torture of such suspense again. I fancied you stumbling over a curbstone and breaking your neck! killed by robbers!—No, I know I should go mad another time.—So you've had a good time, have you—without me? bad boy!"

"What would you have, my dear little angel! There was Bixiou, who gave us some fresh orders; Léon de Lora, whose wit is as keen as ever; Claude Vignon, to whom I owe the only encouraging article that has been written on Maréchal Montcornet's monument. There was—"

"There were no women?—" inquired Hortense eagerly.

"The respectable Madame Florent—"

"You said it was to be at the *Rocher de Cancale*—it was at their house, was it?

"Yes, at their house; I made a mistake—"

"You didn't come home in a carriage?"

"No."

"You walked from Rue des Tournelles?"

"Stidmann and Bixiou came with me along the boulevards to the Madeleine; we were busy talking."

"It must be very dry then on the boulevards and the Place de la Concorde and Rue de Bourgogne, for you're not muddy," said Hortense, scrutinizing her husband's varnished boots.

It had been raining; but between Rue Vanneau and Rue Saint-Dominique, Wenceslas had had no chance to soil his boots.

"See, here are five thousand francs Chanor was generous enough to loan me," said Wenceslas to cut short this quasi-judicial examination.

He had made two packages of his ten one-thousand franc notes, one for Hortense, and one for himself, for he had five thousand francs' worth of debts of which Hortense knew nothing. He owed his rough-hewer and his workmen.

"At last your mind can be at rest, my dear," he said, as he embraced his wife. "I am going to work to-morrow! Oh! to-morrow I must be off at half-past eight, and I am going to the studio. So I'll go to bed at once in order to be up bright and early; you are willing, my pet?"

The suspicion that had crept into Hortense's heart disappeared; she was a thousand miles from the truth. Madame Marneffe! she did not give her a thought. She dreaded the society of lorettes for her Wenceslas. The names of Bixiou and Léon de Lora, two artists notorious for their licentious lives, had aroused her anxiety.

The next day, when Wenceslas left the house at nine o'clock, she was entirely free from distrust.

"Now he's really at work," she said to herself as she dressed her child. "Oh! I can see that now he's in the mood for it! Ah well, if we don't attain the renown of Michael Angelo, we shall be as famous as Benvenuto Cellini!"

Lulled thus by her own hopes, Hortense dreamed of a happy future; and she was talking to her son, then twenty months old, in the onomatopoetic language that makes children smile, when, about eleven o'clock, the cook, who had not seen Wenceslas go out, ushered in Stidmann.

"Excuse me, madame," said the artist. "How's this; Wenceslas gone already?"

"He's at his workshop."

"I came to have an understanding with him about our work."

"I will go and send for him," said Hortense, motioning to Stidmann to be seated.

The young woman, thanking heaven mentally for the opportunity, wished to detain Stidmann in order to gather from him some details as to the party of the night before. Stidmann bowed in acknowledgment of the favor. Madame Steinbock rang, and bade the cook go to the workshop for monsieur.

"You must have had a fine time last night?" Hortense began, "for Wenceslas didn't come home until one o'clock in the morning."

"A fine time?—Well, not exactly," replied the artist, who had hoped to *do* Madame Marneffe on that occasion. "One doesn't have a fine time in society, unless there is something to interest one. That little Madame Marneffe is very clever, but she's a flirt."

"And what did Wenceslas think of her?—" asked poor Hortense, trying to remain calm. "He didn't tell me anything about her."

"I'll only tell you one thing," rejoined Stidmann, "and that is that I think she's a very dangerous woman."

Hortense turned as pale as a woman in child-bed.

"So it was really—at Madame Marneffe's—and not—at Chanor's—that you and Wenceslas—dined —yesterday?" she faltered,—"and he—"

Stidmann, without a clear idea as to what the

catastrophe was that he had caused, saw that there was something. The countess did not finish her sentence, but fainted outright. The artist rang, and the maid answered the bell. When Louise attempted to carry the countess to her room, she was seized with an hysterical attack of the greatest gravity, with horrible convulsions. Stidmann, like all those who by unwitting indiscretion destroy the scaffolding of falsehood built by a husband in his domestic circle, could not believe that his words could have produced such an effect; he thought that the countess must be in that delicate condition in which the slightest annoyance may be attended with danger. Unfortunately the cook announced in a loud voice that monsieur was not at his studio. The countess heard this statement in the midst of her paroxysm, and the convulsions began again with renewed violence.

"Go and fetch madame's mother!" said Louise to the cook; "run!"

"If I knew where Wenceslas is, I would go and tell him," said Stidmann, at his wits' end.

"He's at that woman's!—" cried poor Hortense. "He dressed very differently than if he were going to the studio."

Stidmann hurried off to Madame Marneffe's, realizing the probable accuracy of this suggestion, attributable to the *second sight* of passion. At that moment Valérie was posing for Delilah. Stidmann, much too clever to ask for Madame Marneffe, passed the concierge's quarters, looking neither to right nor left, and ran hastily up to the second floor, reasoning thus with himself: "If I ask for Madame Marneffe, she won't be at home. If, like a fool, I ask for Steinbock, they'll laugh in my face. So I'll just take the bull by the horns!"

Reine answered the bell.

"Tell Monsieur le Comte Steinbock to go home, his wife is dying!—"

Reine, being quite as cunning as Stidmann, gazed at him with a decidedly stupid expression.

"But, monsieur, I don't know—what you—"

"I tell you that my friend Steinbock is here, and his wife is dying; it's a matter of sufficient importance for you to disturb your mistress."

With that Stidmann went away.

"Oh! he's there," he said to himself.

Indeed, Stidmann, loitering a few seconds on Rue Vanneau, saw Wenceslas leave the house, and motioned to him to make haste. Having described the tragedy being enacted in Rue Saint-Dominique, Stidmann scolded Steinbock for not warning him to say nothing concerning the dinner-party of the night before.

"I am lost," Wenceslas replied, "but I forgive you. I entirely forgot our appointment for this morning, and I made the fatal mistake of not telling you that we were supposed to have dined at Florent's. But what can I do? that Valérie has driven me mad; but, my dear fellow, renown or misfortune—she's worth all.—Ah! she's —My God! but I'm in a terrible pickle! Advise me. What shall I say? how shall I excuse myself?"

"Advise you? I don't know how," rejoined Stidmann. "But your wife loves you, doesn't she? Very well, then she'll believe anything. Above all things tell her that you were on your way to my house while I was coming to yours; in that way you will save your *pose* of this morning. Adieu!"

At the corner of Rue Hillerin-Bertin, Lisbeth, who had been informed by Reine, and at once ran after Steinbock, overtook him; for she dreaded his Polish naïveté. Not wishing to be compromised herself, she said a few words to Wenceslas, who, in his delight, kissed her right in the street. Doubtless she had thrown the artist a plank on which to cross this conjugal torrent.

At the sight of her mother, who arrived in breathless haste, Hortense shed floods of tears. By this fortunate turn of affairs the nervous hysteria assumed a very different aspect.

"Betrayed, dear mamma!" she cried. "Wenceslas, after giving me his word of honor not to go there, dined at Madame Marneffe's yesterday, and didn't come home till one o'clock this morning!—If you only knew—the night before we had, not a quarrel but an understanding. I said such touching things to him: that I was jealous, that any infidelity would kill me; that I was suspicious, but he ought to respect my weaknesses because they all came from my love for him; that I had as much of my father's blood in my veins as of yours; that in the first moment after learning of his treachery, I should be insane enough to do insane things, to avenge myself, to dishonor us all, him and his son and myself; that I should be capable of killing him and then myself! etc. And he went there, he's there now! That woman has undertaken to drive us all to despair! Yesterday Victorin and Célestine bound themselves to take up notes of hand for seventy-two thousand francs, all given for that vile creature.—Yes, mamma, they were going to prosecute father and put him in prison. Hasn't the frightful woman enough, with father and your tears? Why take Wenceslas from me? I'll go to her house, and I'll plunge a dagger in her heart!"

Madame Hulot, wounded to the heart's core by the ghastly secret Hortense in her frenzy had unwittingly confided to her, conquered her own grief by one of those heroic efforts of which noble mothers are capable, and laid her daughter's head against her breast to cover it with kisses.

"Wait till Wenceslas comes, my child, and everything will be explained. The harm done can't be so great as you think! I, too, have been betrayed, dear Hortense. You think I am beautiful, and I am virtuous, and yet I have been deserted for twenty-three years, for the Jenny Cadines and Josépha and Marneffes!—did you know it?"

"You, mamma, you!—you have been suffering like this for twenty?—"

She paused, horrified at her own thoughts.

"Follow my example, my child," continued the

mother. "Be gentle and kind, and your conscience will be at rest. On his death-bed a man says to himself: 'My wife has never caused me the slightest unhappiness!'—And God, who listens to these last words, counts them in our favor. If I had abandoned myself to frenzies of rage, as you are doing, what would have happened?—Your father would have felt bitterly toward me, perhaps he would have left me altogether, and he wouldn't have been deterred by the fear of wounding me; our ruin, which is now complete, would have come ten years sooner, we should have afforded the spectacle of a husband and wife living apart, a hideous and heart-breaking scandal, for scandal means death to the family. Neither your brother nor yourself could have been married.—I sacrificed myself, and I did it with such a cheerful face that, except for this last liaison of your father the world would still believe me happy. My courageous and pardonable falsehoods have protected Hector thus far; he is still highly considered; but I can see that this old man's passion is carrying him too far. His mad behavior will, I fear, break down the screen I have placed between the world and ourselves.—But for twenty-three years I have held this curtain behind which I have been weeping, with no mother, no confidant, no resource save religion, and for twenty-three years I have kept the family honor intact—"

Hortense listened to her mother with her eyes fixed upon vacancy. The calm voice and the resignation of this supreme sorrow soothed the irritation of the younger woman's first wound; her tears flowed in torrents. In a burst of filial devotion, abashed by her mother's sublimity, she knelt before her, seized the hem of her dress and kissed it, as devout Catholics kiss the blessed remains of a martyr.

"Rise, my Hortense," said the baroness; "such a proof of my daughter's love effaces many unpleasant memories! Come to my heart, which is now oppressed by your sorrow only. My poor little girl's despair, for her joy was my only joy, has broken the tomb-like seal which nothing should have removed from my lips. Yes, I intended to carry my sorrows to the tomb; 'twould have been but one shroud more. In order to allay your excitement, I spoke—God will forgive me! Oh! if my life were to be yours, what would I not do?—Men, society, chance, nature, and even God, I think, sell love to us at the cost of the most cruel tortures. I have paid with twenty-four years of despair, of bitterness, of incessant pain, for ten happy years—"

"You had ten years, dear mamma, and I have had but three!—" said the selfish lover.

"Nothing is lost yet, my love; wait for Wenceslas."

"Mother," said she, "he lied! he deceived me!—He said: 'I will not go there,' and he went. And that, too, standing by his child's cradle!"—

"For their pleasure, my angel, men commit the most dastardly acts, the greatest infamies and crimes; it seems to be in their nature. We women are offered up as a sacrifice. I believed that my woes were at an end, and they are just beginning, for I did not expect to suffer twice by suffering in my daughter. Courage and silence!—My own Hortense, swear that you will not mention your troubles to anyone but me, that you won't let them appear before others.—Oh! be as proud as your mother!"

At that moment Hortense started, for she heard her husband's step.

"It seems," said Wenceslas as he entered the room, "that Stidmann came here while I was on the way to see him."

"Really?—" cried poor Hortense with the savage irony of a woman wounded to the heart, who uses words as a dagger.

"Why, yes, we just met," replied Wenceslas, feigning astonishment.

"But last night?—" continued Hortense.

"Well, I deceived you, my dear love, and your mother shall decide between us—"

This frank confession relieved the oppression at Hortense's heart. All truly noble women prefer truth to falsehood. They do not want to see their idol degraded, but to be proud of the domination to which they submit.

There is something of this sentiment in the Russians regarding their Czar.

"Listen, dear mother,—" said Wenceslas; "I love my good, sweet Hortense so dearly, that I concealed the extent of our distress from her. What would you have! she was still nursing the boy, and worry would have done her much harm. You know all that a woman risks at such a time. Her beauty, her bloom, her health are all in danger. Did I do wrong?—She believes that we owe only five thousand francs, but I owe five thousand more.—Day before yesterday we were in despair!—No one on earth will ever loan to artists. They distrust our talents as much as they do our vagaries. I knocked in vain at every door. Lisbeth offered us her savings."

"Poor girl!" said Hortense.

"Poor girl!" echoed the baroness.

"But what did Lisbeth's two thousand francs amount to?—Much to her, nothing to us. Then, you know, our cousin spoke to us of Madame Marneffe, whose self-respect wouldn't allow her to accept any interest whatever, she owes so much to the baron.—Hortense wanted to send her diamonds to the Mont-de-Piété. We might have got two or three thousand francs on them, and we needed ten thousand. The ten thousand francs were to be had there for a year, without interest!—I said to myself: 'Hortense won't know anything about it, so I'll go and take them.' The woman sent my father-in-law to me to ask me to dine yesterday, giving me to understand that Lisbeth had told her that I should have the money. Between Hortense's despair and that dinner, I did not hesitate. That's the whole story. How can Hortense, at twenty-four years, a fresh, pure, virtuous creature, who is my whole happiness and my glory, whom I have not left since we were married,—how can she imagine that I could prefer to her—what?—a sallow, faded and seedy creature," said he, resorting to an atrocious bit of studio slang to induce belief in his contempt, by one of those exaggerated flights which women delight in.

"Ah! if your father had only spoken to me like that!" cried the baroness.

Hortense threw herself gracefully upon her husband's neck.

"Yes, that's what I would have done," said Adeline. "Wenceslas, my dear, your wife was near dying," she continued gravely. "You see how she loves you. She is yours, alas!" And she sighed heavily.

"He may make her a martyr or a happy woman," she said to herself, thinking what all mothers think at the time of their daughters' marriages.—"It seems to me," she added aloud, "that I suffer enough to be permitted to see my children happy."

"Never fear, dear mamma," said Wenceslas, overjoyed at the happy termination of this tempest. "In two months I shall have returned that horrible woman's money.—What would you have!" he continued, repeating that essentially Polish expression with the Polish charm of manner; "there are times when one would borrow from the devil. After all, it's family money. And, after I was once invited, should I have obtained this money, which costs us so dear, if I had met courtesy with discourtesy?"

"Oh! mamma, how papa has wronged us all!" cried Hortense.

The baroness placed her finger on her lips, and Hortense regretted that wail, the first word of reproach she had ever allowed her lips to utter concerning the father so heroically sheltered by a sublime silence.

"Adieu, my children," said Madame Hulot, "pleasant weather has returned. But don't fall out again."

When Wenceslas and his wife had returned to their room after going with the baroness to the door, Hortense said:—

"Tell me about your evening!"

She watched Wenceslas' face as he told his story, interrupted as it was by the questions which flock to a woman's lips under such circumstances. What she heard made Hortense thoughtful, for she guessed at the diabolical entertainment artists were likely to find in that vicious circle.

"Be frank, my Wenceslas!—Stidmann was there, Claude Vignon, Vernisset, and who else?—At all events you enjoyed yourself!"

"Enjoyed myself?—I thought of nothing but our ten thousand francs, and I kept saying to myself: 'My Hortense need have no more anxiety!'"

This cross-examination was vastly fatiguing to the Livonian, and he seized upon a moment of gaiety to say to Hortense:

"Tell me, my angel, what would you have done if your artist had been guilty?—"

"I would have taken Stidmann," said she with a little determined nod, "but without loving him, of course!"

"Hortense!" cried Steinbock, rising abruptly, and with a theatrical gesture, "you wouldn't have had time, I would have killed you."

Hortense threw herself upon her husband, embraced him almost to the point of suffocation, covered him with kisses, and said:

"Ah! you do love me, Wenceslas! come, I have no fear now! But no more Marneffe. Don't again plunge into such mud-holes—"

"I swear, my dear Hortense, that I will not go there again except to take up my note—"

She pouted, but as loving women pout, who seek the reward of their pouting. Wenceslas, tired out by such a morning, left his wife pouting, and started for his studio to make the clay model of the *Samson and Delilah* group, the sketch of which he had in his pocket. Hortense, disturbed at the result of her pouting, and thinking that Wenceslas was angry, went to the studio after him, and walked in just as he was retouching the clay with the intense eagerness which artists exhibit when under the sway of a fresh fancy. At the sight of his wife, he hastily threw a damp cloth over the rough draught of the group, and took Hortense in his arms.

"Ah! my pet, we are not angry, are we?" he said.

Hortense had seen the group and the cloth thrown over it; she said nothing then, but before leaving the studio she turned, snatched off the rag, looked at the sketch, and asked:

"What's that?"

"A group that came into my head."

"Why did you hide it from me?"

"Because I didn't want to show it to you till it was done."

"The woman's very pretty!" said Hortense.

And a myriad suspicions sprang up in her heart, as the tall, luxuriant plants of the Indies spring up between night and morning.

*

After about three weeks Madame Marneffe became deeply irritated with Hortense. Women of her stamp have a species of self-esteem, they would have their victims kiss the devil's hoof, they never forgive the virtue that does not fear their power or that contends with them. Now, Wenceslas had not paid a single visit to Rue Vanneau, not even the visit simple politeness demanded after a lady had posed as Delilah for him. Every time that Lisbeth had called at the Steinbocks' she had found nobody at home. Monsieur and madame were living at the studio. Lisbeth, who hunted down the turtle-doves even to their nest at Gros-Caillou, saw Wenceslas working with great ardor, and learned from the cook that madame never left monsieur. Wenceslas was undergoing the despotism of love. Thereupon Valérie espoused Lisbeth's hatred for Hortense on her own account. Women cling as persistently to the lovers whose possession is disputed with them, as men cling to the women who are sought by several dandies. And so the reflections we have indulged in concerning Madame Marneffe apply equally well to libertines, who are, so to speak, man-courtesans. Valérie's whim was a passion, and she was particularly bent upon having her group; she was contemplating going to call on Wenceslas at his studio, when there occurred one of those events of grave importance, which may be called, in the case of such women, *fructus belli.* This is the way in which Valérie made known this event, which was entirely personal. She was breakfasting with Lisbeth and Monsieur Marneffe.

"Tell me, Marneffe, do you suspect yourself of being a father for the second time?"

"Are you really enceinte?—Oh! let me kiss you—"

He rose and walked around the table, and his wife held up her forehead to him in such a way that the kiss was imprinted on her hair.

"By this stroke," said he, "I am chief of bureau, and officer of the Legion of Honor! Look you, my dear, I don't want Stanislas to be ruined! Poor little fellow!—"

"Poor little fellow?—" cried Lisbeth. "It's seven months since you saw him; at the boarding-school I am supposed to be his mother, for I'm the only one in this house who ever thinks of him!—"

"A child that costs us a hundred crowns every three months!—" said Valérie. "However, he's your child, that one, Marneffe! you certainly ought to pay his board out of your salary.—The newcomer, instead of calling forth bills from soup-dealers, will save us from want—"

"Valérie," retorted Marneffe, imitating Crevel's attitude, "I hope Monsieur le Baron Hulot will take care of his son and won't burden a poor clerk with him; I propose to be very exacting with him. So, collect your evidence, madame! try to get some letters from him in which he speaks of his good fortune, for he seems very long-winded about securing my appointment."

With that Marneffe set out for the department, where the invaluable friendship of his director permitted him to remain away from his office until eleven o'clock; moreover, he did but little work there, because of his notorious incapacity and his distaste for work.

When they were left alone Lisbeth and Valérie looked at each other for a moment like soothsayers, and simultaneously broke forth in a great roar of laughter.

"Tell me, Valérie, is it true?" said Lisbeth, "or is it only a comedy?"

"It's a physical truth!" Valérie replied. "Hortense wears out my patience! And last night it occurred to me to toss this child like a bomb into Wenceslas' household."

She went into her bedroom, followed by Lisbeth, and showed her the following letter all written:

"Wenceslas, my dear, I still believe in your love, although I have not seen you for nearly three weeks. Is it disdain? Delilah cannot think so. Is it not rather the tyranny of a woman, whom you told me you could never love again? Wenceslas, you are too great an artist to allow yourself to be domineered over in this way. The family is the tomb of glory!—Think whether you resemble the Wenceslas of the Rue de Doyenné? You missed fire with my father's monument; but in you the lover is much more powerful than the artist, and you are more fortunate with the daughter. My adored Wenceslas, you are a father. If you should not come to see me in my present condition you would be esteemed a wretched creature by your friends; but I love you so madly that I feel I should never have the strength to curse you. May I call myself ever

"THY VALÉRIE?"

"What do you say to my plan of sending this letter to the studio when our dear Hortense is alone there?" Valérie asked Lisbeth. "Last night I learned from Stidmann that Wenceslas was to call for him at eleven o'clock to go to Chanor's on business; so that hussy of a Hortense will be alone."

"After such a trick," Lisbeth replied, "I could no longer remain your friend openly; it would be necessary for me to leave you, and let it be supposed that I had ceased to see you or even speak to you."

"Evidently," said Valérie; "but—"

"Oh! don't you worry," Lisbeth interrupted. "We will meet again when I am Madame la Maréchale; *they* all wish it now; the baron alone knows nothing of the project, but you must bring him around to it."

"But," said Valérie, "it's possible that I may soon be on rather delicate terms with the baron."

"Madame Olivier's the only one who can be trusted to ensure that Hortense shall intercept that letter," said Lisbeth; "we must send her first to Rue Saint-Dominique before she goes to the studio."

"Oh! our pretty little one will be at home," Madame Marneffe replied, ringing for Reine to summon Madame Olivier.

G. Cain del.   Gery Bichard sc.

Ten minutes after the fatal letter was despatched, Baron Hulot arrived. Madame Marneffe sprang upon the old man's neck with the movement of a cat.

"Hector, you are a father!" she whispered in his ear. "That's what comes of falling out and making up again."

Noticing the start of surprise which the baron could not repress quickly enough, Valérie assumed a cold demeanor which drove the Councilor of State to despair. She made him extort the most decisive proofs from her one by one. When conviction, taken gently by the hand by vanity, had made its way into the old man's mind, she spoke to him of Monsieur Marneffe's rage.

"My old grumbler," said she, "it's very cruel of you not to appoint your responsible publisher,—our agent if you choose,—chief of bureau and officer of the Legion of Honor, for you have ruined the man; he adores his Stanislas, the little *monstrico* who takes after him, and whom I can't endure. Unless you prefer to give Stanislas twelve hundred francs a year,—the principal I mean, of course,—the income to be in my name."

"But if I provide funds I prefer they should stand in my son's name, and not in the *monstrico's!*" said the baron.

This imprudent remark, wherein the words *my son* were uttered with the brutal impetuosity of a river overflowing its banks, was metamorphosed, after an hour's conversation, into a formal promise to settle twelve hundred francs a year on the unborn child. This promise was, upon Valérie's tongue and in her face, what a drum is in the hands of a small boy; she had it to play with for three weeks.

Just as Baron Hulot, as happy as the man a year married, who longs for an heir, left the house on Rue Vanneau, Madame Olivier had driven Hortense to extort from her the letter she was to hand to the count in person. The young woman gave her a twenty-franc piece for the letter. The suicide pays for his opium, his pistol, his charcoal. Hortense read the letter and re-read it; she saw nothing but the white paper striped with black lines; there was nothing but that piece of paper in the world, everything was black about her. The glare of the conflagration which was consuming the edifice of her happiness lighted up the paper, for the most profound darkness reigned about her. The cries of her little Wenceslas, who was playing near by, sounded to her ear as if he were in the depths of a valley, and she on the summit of a mountain. Outraged thus at twenty-four, in all the splendor of her beauty, enveloped in a pure, devoted love, the blow was not a mere dagger-thrust, it was death itself. The earlier attack was purely nervous, her body writhed in the embrace of jealousy; but this certainly attacked the heart, and the body was as nothing. For about ten minutes Hortense remained in this dazed condition. Then her mother's image appeared before her, and created a revolution. She became calm and cold and recovered her reason. She rang for her maid.

"Let Louise help you, my dear," she said to the cook. "You must pack up, as soon as possible, everything here that belongs to me, and all that has to do with my son. I give you an hour. When everything is ready, call a carriage from the square and let me know. No remarks! I am going to leave the house and take Louise. You will stay here with monsieur! take good care of him."

She went to her room, sat down at her desk, and wrote the following letter:

"MONSIEUR LE COMTE:

"The letter attached to mine will explain the resolution I have taken.

"When you read these lines I shall have left your house, and taken shelter with my mother, with our child.

"Do not imagine that I shall ever reverse this decision. Do not believe that it is due to the impulsiveness and inconsiderate haste of youth, or to the sharp sting of young love wounded; you would be sadly mistaken.

"I have thought very deeply for two weeks past concerning life and love, union and duty to each other. I have heard the whole story of my mother's devotion, and she has told me of her sorrows! Every day for twenty-three years she has shown herself a heroine; but I do not feel that I am strong enough to follow her example, not that I have loved you less than she loves my father, but for reasons based upon my temperament. Our home would become a hell on earth, and I might lose my head so completely as to bring dishonor upon you, upon myself, upon my child. I do not choose to be a Madame Marneffe; and, in such a career, a woman of my disposition would perhaps never stop. Unluckily for myself, I am a Hulot, not a Fischer.

"Living alone, and at a distance from the sight of your evil courses, I can answer for myself, especially as I have our child to care for, near my sublimely strong-hearted mother, whose life will soothe the tumultuous impulses of my heart. There, I can be a good mother, bring up our son carefully, and live. With you, the wife would kill the mother, and incessant quarreling would embitter my disposition.

"I would welcome instant death; but I do not choose to be ill for twenty-five years, as my mother has been. If you have been false to me for my father's mistress, after three years of absolute, uninterrupted love, what rivals should I not have to contend with later? Ah! monsieur, you are beginning much earlier than my father the career of libertinage and extravagance, which dishonors the father of a family, which lessens his children's respect for him, and at the end of which disgrace and despair await him.

"I am not implacable. Unchangeable sentiments are not becoming in feeble creatures who live under the eye of God. If you win renown and fortune by persistent work, if you abandon courtesans, and turn aside from these unsavory, miry paths, you will again find a wife who is worthy of you.

"I believe you to be too much of a gentleman to have recourse to the law. You will respect my wishes, Monsieur le Comte, by leaving me with my mother; and, above all things, never go there. I have left you all the money that hateful woman loaned you. Adieu!

"HORTENSE HULOT."

The writing of this letter was a painful task; Hortense abandoned herself again and again to paroxysms of weeping, and to the cries of strangled passion. She laid aside her pen and took it up again in the effort to express in simple language what love ordinarily declares rhapsodically in these quasi-testamentary letters. Her heart overflowed in exclamations, in lamentations and tears; but her reason dictated the words.

When informed by Louise that everything was in readiness she walked slowly through the little garden, the bed-room, the salon, and gazed at everything for the last time. Then she urged the cook most earnestly to look to monsieur's welfare, promising to reward her if she should be honest. At last she entered the carriage to go to her mother's, heart-broken, weeping so bitterly as to move her maid to tears, and covering little Wenceslas with kisses in a delirious joy, which betrayed still a world of love for his father.

The baroness already knew from Lisbeth that the father-in-law was much to blame for her son-in-law's sin; she was not surprised at her daughter's arrival, but approved the step she had taken and consented to keep her beneath her roof. Adeline, upon reflecting that meekness and devotion had never checked her Hector, for whom her esteem was beginning to grow less, concluded that her daughter did well to adopt a different course. Within three weeks the poor mother had received two wounds, which caused her suffering, keener than all the agony she had hitherto undergone. The baron had brought Victorin and his wife to financial straits, and, according to Lisbeth, he was the cause of Wenceslas' going astray,—he had debauched his son-in-law. The majesty of this father of a family, so long upheld by foolish sacrifices, was sadly fallen. Without regretting their money, the younger Hulots became distrustful of the baron, and at the same time anxious concerning him.

These sentiments, which were quite perceptible, deeply afflicted Adeline, who foresaw the break-up of the family. Thanks to the marshal's money, she speedily transformed the dining room into a bedroom for her daughter, and the reception-room became, as in so many houses, the dining-room.

When Wenceslas returned home, and had finished reading the two letters, he was conscious of a feeling of satisfaction mingled with sadness. Having been kept in sight, so to speak, by his wife, he had inwardly rebelled against this sort of confinement à la Lisbeth. Cloyed with love for three years, he also had reflected during the past two weeks; and his conclusion was that the family was a heavy burden to bear. He had just been congratulated by Stidmann on the passion with which he had inspired Valérie; for Stidmann, with a hidden motive not difficult to imagine, deemed it advisable to flatter Hortense's husband's self-love, hoping to console the victim. So Wenceslas was happy to be able to return to Madame Marneffe. But he remembered the perfect, innocent happiness he had enjoyed, he recalled Hortense's charms, her virtue, her outspoken, innocent love, and he regretted her keenly. He longed to rush to his mother-in-law's to obtain forgiveness, but he did as Hulot and Crevel did, he went to see Madame Marneffe, to whom he carried his wife's letter, in order to show her what a catastrophe she had caused, and so to speak to discount his misfortune by demanding, in return, pleasures from his mistress. He found Crevel with Valérie. The mayor, swollen with pride, was pacing up and down the salon, like a man in intense excitement. He kept striking his attitude as if he were about to speak, but he dared not. His face was beaming, and he ran to the window to drum on the glass with his fingers. He gazed at Valérie with a deeply moved expression. Luckily for Crevel, Lisbeth appeared.

"Do you know the news, cousin?" he whispered in her ear. "I am a father! It seems to me that I care less for poor Célestine. Oh! that's what it is to have a child by a woman one idolizes! To combine paternity of the heart with paternity of blood! Oh! I pray you tell Valérie this: I will work for the child, I mean he shall be rich! She tells me that from certain indications she thinks it will be a boy! If it's a boy, I want him to take the name of Crevel; I'll consult my notary."

"I know how much she loves you," said Lisbeth; "but, in the name of your future and hers, contain yourself; don't rub your hands so all the time."

While Lisbeth was carrying on this aside with Crevel, Valérie had demanded her letter from Wenceslas, and was whispering in his ear words which dissipated his gloom.

"So you're free, my dear," said she. "Ought great artists ever to marry? You have no existence except in the play of your imagination and in perfect freedom! Ah! I will love you so dearly, my dear poet, that you will never regret your wife.

However, if you prefer, like many men, to maintain an appearance of propriety, I will undertake to bring Hortense back to your house in a very short time."

"Oh! if it were possible!"

"I am sure of it," said Valérie, slightly piqued. "Your poor father-in-law is done for in every respect, but through self-esteem he wants to have the appearance of being loved, and to make people think he has a mistress; and he is so vain on that point that I rule him absolutely. The baroness is still so fond of her Hector—it always seems to me as if I were talking about the *Iliad*—that the two old people will bring about a reconciliation with Hortense. But if you prefer not to have storms at home, don't let three weeks go by without coming to see your mistress.—I should die. My darling, a gentleman owes some consideration to a woman whom he has placed in such a compromising position as mine, especially when that woman has to take many precautions touching her reputation.—Stay to dinner, my angel,—and remember that I must seem colder to you because you are the author of this too visible sin."

Baron Montès was announced; Valérie rose, ran to meet him, whispered to him for a few seconds, and warned him concerning her demeanor toward him, as she had just warned Wenceslas; for the Brazilian had a diplomatic countenance, most appropriate for the reception of the great news, which overwhelmed him with joy; he was certain of his claim to the title of father.

By dint of this strategy, based upon the self-love of man as lover, Valérie had at her table, all of them joyous, lively and happy, four men who believed themselves to be adored by her, and whom Marneffe, understanding the whole plot, jocosely dubbed to Lisbeth the "Five Fathers of the Church."

Baron Hulot alone wore an anxious expression at first; just as he left his office he met the Superintendent of Employés of the department, a general, and his intimate friend for thirty years, and he spoke to him of appointing Marneffe to Coquet's place, the latter consenting to resign.

"My dear friend," said he, "I prefer not to ask this favor of the maréchal unless we are in accord, and I have your approval of the appointment."

"My dear fellow," replied the Superintendent of Employés, "permit me to say to you that, for your own sake, you ought not to insist upon this appointment. I have already told you my opinion. It would cause a scandal in the department, where there is already far too much talk of yourself and Madame Marneffe. This between ourselves. I have no wish to touch you on a sensitive spot, nor to disoblige you in anything under heaven, and I will give you a proof of it. If you really insist upon it, if you are determined to ask for Monsieur Coquet's place, who would truly be a great loss to the War Department,—he has been there since 1809,—I will go into the country for a fortnight, in order to leave you a clear field with the maréchal, who loves you like a son. Thus I shall be neither for nor against, and I shall have done nothing to offend my conscience as a government official."

"I thank you," the baron replied, "and I will think over what you have said."

"If I allow myself to say so much, my dear friend, it is because your personal interest is much more deeply concerned than my interest or my self-esteem. In the first place the maréchal is the master. In the second place, my friend, we are blamed for so many things that what is one more or less! we are not virgins so far as criticism is concerned. Under the Restoration people were appointed to office to give them the salary, and without considering the good of the service.—We are old comrades—"

"True," rejoined the baron, "and it was because I did not want to interrupt our long-standing, precious friendship, that I—"

"All right," said the superintendent, observing the embarrassment depicted upon Hulot's face, "I'll take a little trip, old fellow.—But take care! you have enemies, that is to say, men who covet your handsome salary, and you have but one anchor out. Ah! if you were a deputy as I am, you would have nothing to fear; so look well to yourself.—"

This most friendly language made a deep impression on the Councilor of State.

"But what is it, Roger? Don't play the mysterious with me!"

The functionary whom Hulot called Roger looked him in the face, took his hand and pressed it.

"We have been friends too long for me to shrink from giving you a piece of advice. If you wish to retain your position, you must make your own bed. And so, if I were in your position, instead of asking the maréchal for Monsieur Coquet's place for Monsieur Marneffe, I would beg him to use his influence to keep me in regular service at the Council of State, where I would die in peace; and like the beaver I would give over my general directorship to the hunters."

"What! could the maréchal forget?—"

"My old friend, the maréchal has defended you so vigorously in the Council of Ministers that there is no longer any thought of turning you out; but it has been talked of!—So don't give them any pretext—I won't say anything further. At this moment you can make your own terms, being a Councilor of State and peer of France. If you wait too long, if you give them a hold on you, I'll answer for nothing.—Shall I go into the country?"

"Wait until I see the maréchal," replied Hulot, "and I will send my brother to feel the ground about the master."

We can understand in what frame of mind the baron returned to Madame Marneffe's; he had almost forgotten that he was a father, for Roger had acted the part of a kind and true comrade in enlightening him as to his position. Nevertheless, so great was Valérie's influence over him that, before the dinner was half over the baron entered into the spirit of the occasion, and was all the more jovial because he had additional cares to drown; but the wretched man did not suspect that before the evening was over, he should himself be compelled to choose between his own happiness and the danger pointed out by the superintendent, that is to say between Madame Marneffe and his office. About eleven o'clock, just when the scene was most animated, for the salon was filled with guests, Valérie took Hector with her to a corner of her divan.

"My dear old friend," she whispered, "your daughter is so deeply irritated because Wenceslas comes here, that she has made a stand upon that point. A bad-tempered creature, that Hortense. Ask Wenceslas to show you the letter the little fool wrote him. This separation of two lovers, of which I am said to be the cause, may do me immeasurable harm, for that's the way virtuous women attack each other. It's scandalous to play at being victimized, so as to throw the blame upon a woman who has done no other wrong than having a pleasant house. If you love me, you will exculpate me by reconciling the two turtle-doves. Besides I'm not at all set upon receiving your son-in-law; you brought him to me, take him away again! If you have any authority in the family it seems to me that you might very properly require your wife to bring about a reconciliation. Tell her from me, dear old lady, that if I am unjustly charged with having caused trouble between a young couple, with having disturbed the harmony of a family and taken both the father and the son-in-law, I'll earn my reputation by raising the deuce with them, in my own way! Why, here is Lisbeth talking of leaving me! She prefers her family to me, and I can't blame her for it. She won't stay here, she says, unless the young people are reconciled. Left to ourselves the expense here will be tripled!—"

"Oh! as to that," said the baron, upon being informed of his daughter's escapade, "I'll arrange matters all right."

"Very well," replied Valérie, "there's another thing. What about Coquet's place?"

"That," replied Hector lowering his eyes, "is more difficult, not to say impossible!—"

"Impossible, my dear Hector," said Madame Marneffe in the baron's ear; "why you don't know to what extremes Marneffe will go. I am in his power; like most men, he is immoral in his own interest, but he is exceedingly vindictive after the manner of all small-minded, impotent men. In the situation in which you have placed me, I am at his discretion. I am obliged to go back with him for a few days, and he is quite capable of never leaving my room again."

Hulot gave a prodigious start.

"He would leave me in peace on condition that he is made chief of bureau. It's infamous, but logical."

"Valérie, do you love me?"

"That question, my dear, in my present condition, is an insult worthy of a lackey—"

"Very well, if I make up my mind to try, simply to try to ask the maréchal for a place for Marneffe, I am no longer anybody and Marneffe is dismissed."

"I thought that you and the prince were intimate friends!"

"Surely, he has given me substantial proofs of his friendship; but, my child, there is someone above the maréchal,—for instance, the whole council of ministers.—With a little time, by standing off and on, we shall get there. To be sure of success we must wait for the moment when they ask for some service at my hands. Then I can say: 'I pass you the cassia, pass me the senna.—' "

"If I tell Marneffe that, my poor Hector, he'll play us some vile trick. Do you tell him yourself that he must wait; I won't undertake it. Oh! I know my fate; he knows how to punish me and he won't leave my room.—Don't forget the twelve hundred francs a year for the little one."

Hulot took Marneffe aside, feeling that his enjoyment was threatened; and for the first time he dropped the lofty tone he had thus far adopted toward him, so dismayed was he by the idea of that moribund creature in his pretty wife's bed-room.

" Marneffe, my dear fellow," said he, "we've been talking about you to-day! But you won't be chief of the bureau at the first stroke.—We must take time."

"I will be, monsieur le baron," retorted Marneffe bluntly.

"But, my dear—"

"I will be, monsieur le baron," repeated Marneffe coldly, glancing from the baron to Valérie. "You have made it necessary for me to be reconciled with my wife, and I'll keep her; for, *my dear friend*, she is fascinating," he added with terrible sarcasm. "I am master here,—rather more so than you are at the department."

The baron was conscious of one of those eternal pangs, which produce in the heart, the effect of a raging tooth-ache and he was very near allowing tears to be seen in his eyes. During the short scene Valérie was whispering to Henri Montès the fable concerning Marneffe's purpose, and thus making sure that she would be rid of him for some time.

Of the faithful four, Crevel alone, possessor of the thrifty little house on Rue du Dauphin, was excepted from this measure; so that his countenance wore an expression of the most insolent beatitude, notwithstanding the tacit reproofs Valérie addressed to him by frowns and significant gestures; but his paternity beamed joyously in his every feature. At a word of reproof Valérie whispered in his ear, he seized her hand, and replied:

"To-morrow, my duchess, you shall have your little house!—to-morrow the sale will be definitely concluded."

"And the furniture?" she replied with a smile.

"I have a thousand shares of Versailles, Left Bank, which I bought at a hundred and twenty-five francs, and they'll go to three hundred on account of a fusion of the two roads, that I was let into the secret of. You shall be furnished like a queen!—But you will be all mine after this, won't you?—"

"Yes, my fat mayor," said this middle-class Madame de Merteuil with a smile; "but my housekeeping! respect the future Madame Crevel."

"My dear cousin," Lisbeth said to the baron, "I shall be at Adeline's early to-morrow, for you understand that I can't decently remain here. I shall go and keep house for your brother the marshal."

"I shall go home this evening," said the baron.

"Very good, and I'll come to lunch to-morrow," Lisbeth replied with a smile.

She realized how necessary her presence was at the family party to take place the next day. And so in the morning she went to Victorin's and told him of the separation of Hortense and Wenceslas.

*

When the baron returned home, about half-past ten at night, Mariette and Louise, after a hard day's work, were just closing the outer door of the suite, so that he was not obliged to ring. The husband, sorely annoyed at the necessity of being virtuous, went straight to his wife's bed-room; and through the half-open door he saw her prostrated before her crucifix, absorbed in prayer, in one of those significant attitudes, which bring renown to painters or sculptors who are fortunate enough to produce them faithfully after they have seen them. Adeline, in the fervor of her exaltation, was saying aloud:

"O God, vouchsafe to give him light!"

She was praying for her Hector. At this sight, so different from the one he had just left, and with these words, called forth by the occurrence of the day, in his ears, the baron was deeply moved, and a deep sigh escaped him. Adeline turned, her face covered with tears. She so thoroughly believed that her prayer was granted, that she sprang to her feet and seized her Hector with the strength born of happy passion. She had cast aside all her own interests as a wife, grief had blotted out everything even to memory; there was naught left but motherly love, solicitude for the honor of the family, and a Christian wife's pure affection for a husband who has gone astray; the saint-like affection that survives all else in a woman's heart. All this was apparent at a glance.

"Hector!" she said at last, "have you come back to us? Has God had pity on our family?"

"Dear Adeline!" replied the baron, entering the room and seating his wife by his side upon a couch, "you are the most saintly creature I have ever known, and for a long while I have felt that I am not worthy of you."

"You would have but little to do, my dear," she said, holding Hulot's hand and trembling so violently that she seemed on the verge of hysteria, "very little to put things to rights—"

She dared not go on, for she felt that every word would be a reproach, and she did not choose to banish the happiness that this interview was pouring in torrents into her soul.

"Hortense brings me here," Hulot resumed. "Our little girl may do us more harm by her precipitate step, than my absurd passion for Valérie has done. But we will talk of this to-morrow morning. Hortense is asleep, Mariette tells me, and we will leave her in peace."

"Yes," said Madame Hulot, suddenly overwhelmed by a feeling of profound melancholy. She saw that the baron had been led to return to her, not so much by the desire of seeing his family as by some outside interest.

"Let us leave her in peace to-morrow too, for the

poor child is in a deplorable condition; she has been weeping all day," said the baroness.

The next morning at nine o'clock, the baron was walking up and down the vast, unused salon, awaiting his daughter, to whom he had sent word to come to him, and inventing arguments with which to overcome the most difficult of all forms of obstinacy to be overcome,—that of a wounded, implacable young wife, to whom the shameful shifts of society are unknown, because she knows nothing of its passions and interests.

"Here I am, papa!" said Hortense in a trembling voice; her suffering had driven all the color from her cheeks.

Hulot sat down on a chair, took his daughter by the waist and forced her to sit upon his knees.

"Well, my child," said he, kissing her on the forehead, "so there's a little trouble in the household, and we went off at a tangent?—That's not the way a well-bred young woman should act. My Hortense ought not, on her own responsibility, to take such a decisive step as leaving her house and abandoning her husband without consulting her parents. If my dear Hortense had come first to see her dear, kind mother, she would not have caused me the deep annoyance that I feel!—You don't know the world; it's very cruel. People may say that your husband sent you back to your parents. Children brought up as you have been in their mother's lap remain children longer than others, and know nothing of life! An innocent, outspoken passion, like yours for Wenceslas, unfortunately takes no heedof consequences, but acts on the first impulse. Our little heart starts off and the head follows. We would burn Paris for revenge, without a thought of the Assizes! When your old father comes to you and tells you that you haven't observed the proprieties, you can safely believe him; I say nothing of the profound grief I have felt, but it is very keen, for you throw the blame upon a woman of whose heart you know nothing, and whose enmity may be a terrible thing.—Alas! you are so sincere and innocent and pure, that you suspect nothing; you may be besmirched and slandered. Moreover, my dear little angel, you are making a serious matter of a mere jest, and I can answer to you for your husband's innocence. Madame Marneffe—"

Thus far the baron, like an artist in diplomacy, had managed his remonstrances with great skill. He had, as we see, with no ordinary cleverness, led up to the introduction of that name; but Hortense, when she heard it, started as if she were cut to the quick.

"Listen to me; I have experience and I have watched everything that has been going on," continued the father, preventing his daughter from speaking. "The lady in question treats her husband very coldly. Yes, you have been made the victim of a practical joke, and I'll prove it to you. See, yesterday Wenceslas dined—"

"He dined there?—" demanded the young woman, springing to her feet and gazing at her father with horror depicted on every feature. "Yesterday! after reading my letter?—O my God!—Why didn't I go into a convent instead of marrying? My life is no longer my own, I have a child!" she sobbed.

Her tears cut Madame Hulot to the heart; she rushed out of her bed-room, ran to her daughter, took her in her arms, and plied her with such unmeaning questions as come first to the lips of a sorrowing mother.

"Tears!—" said the baron to himself, "and everything was going so well! What's to be done with a parcel of weeping women?"

"My child," said the baroness to Hortense, "listen to your father! he loves us, you know—"

"Come Hortense, my darling little girl, don't cry, or you'll spoil your beauty," said the baron. "Come, listen to reason. Be wise and return to your house, and I promise you that Wenceslas shall never set foot in that other place. I ask this sacrifice of you, if it is a sacrifice to forgive the most trifling of sins to a husband who loves you! I ask it of you by my white hairs, by your love for your mother.—You don't want to fill my declining years with bitterness and chagrin?—"

Hortense threw herself like a madwoman at her father's feet, with such desperate violence that her loosely secured hair fell about her shoulders, and she held out her hands to him with a gesture expressive of her despair.

"Father, you ask me for my life!" said she; "take it if you will, but take it at least pure and undefiled; I will give it up to you with pleasure, most assuredly. But do not ask me to die dishonored, stained with crime! I am not like my mother! I will not swallow insults! If I return to my husband's roof, I may strangle him in a paroxysm of jealousy, or do something even worse than that. Do not require me to attempt a task beyond my strength. Do not weep for me while I live! for the least evil that can befall me is to go mad. I feel that madness is not more than two steps away. Yesterday! yesterday! he dined with that woman after he had read my letter!—Are other men made like that?—I give you my life, but do not let me die in ignominy!—His sin?—trifling!—To have a child by that woman!"

"A child?" exclaimed Hulot, recoiling. "Nonsense! that is certainly a joke."

At that juncture Victorin and Cousin Bette appeared, and stood aghast at the spectacle. The daughter was crouching at her father's feet. The baroness, torn by the conflict between her maternal and her conjugal affections, was looking on in silence, her grief-stricken face wet with tears.

"Lisbeth," said the baron, seizing the old maid's hand and pointing to Hortense; "you can assist me here. My poor Hortense's head is turned; she believes that Madame Marneffe loves her Wenceslas, while Valérie simply desired to have him make a group for her."

"Delilah!" cried the young woman; "the only thing he has done quickly since we were married.

This gentleman couldn't work for me or for his son, but he bestirred himself for that strumpet, with an ardor—Oh! make an end of me, father, for every word you say is like the stroke of a dagger."

Lisbeth shrugged her shoulders, and with a compassionate gesture called the attention of the baroness and Victorin to the baron, who could not see her.

"You may be sure, cousin," said she, "that I had no idea what Madame Marneffe was when you urged me to take up my quarters on the floor above her and keep house for her; but in three years one learns many things. That creature is a *harlot!* and a harlot whose depravity can be compared only to that of her despicable, hideous husband. You are the dupe, the *Milord Pot-au-feu* of those people, and they will carry you farther than you think! I must speak to you plainly, for you are at the bottom of a gulf—"

As Lisbeth uttered these words, the baroness and her daughter cast upon her such glances as those with which pious persons might return thanks to the Madonna for having saved their lives.

"The horrible creature has determined to break up your son-in-law's household; for what motive? I have no idea, for my intellect is too limited for me to see my way through such dark, wicked, infamous, disgraceful intriguing. Your Madame Marneffe doesn't love your son-in-law, but she wants him at her knees for revenge. I have just treated the miserable creature as she deserves. She's a shameless prostitute, and I told her that I should leave her house, that I proposed to extricate my honor from that sink of infamy.—I belong to my family before everything. I heard that my second-cousin had left Wenceslas, and so I came here. Your Valérie, whom you take for a saint, is the cause of this cruel separation; can I stay on with such a woman? It may be that our dear little Hortense," she said, touching the baron's arm significantly, "is the dupe of a longing such as women of her stamp feel—women who would sacrifice a whole family to obtain a jewel. I don't think Wenceslas is guilty, but I do think he's weak, and I don't say he won't yield at last to such refinement of coquetry. My mind is made up. That woman is your evil genius, she'll bring you to the gutter. I don't choose to have the appearance of being concerned in the ruin of my family, when I have been there three years for the express purpose of preventing it. The wool is pulled over your eyes, cousin. Just say firmly that you won't have anything to do with the appointment of that contemptible Monsieur Marneffe, and you'll see what will happen. There's a famous rod in pickle for you in that event."

Lisbeth raised her second-cousin from the floor and kissed her passionately.

"My dear Hortense, stand to your guns," she whispered.

The baroness embraced Cousin Bette with the enthusiasm of a woman who feels that she is avenged. The whole family remained in profound silence about this father, who was clever enough to know what this silence meant. That he was in a towering rage, was evident from the cloud that passed over his face; every vein was swollen, his eyes were suffused with blood, and his face became livid. Adeline impulsively threw herself on her knees at his feet, and took his hands:

"My dear, my dear, in pity's name!"

"I am hateful to you!" said the baron, giving utterance to the cry of his conscience.

We are all in the secret of our own wrong-doing. We almost always credit our victims with the sentiment of hatred which thirst for vengeance might well arouse in them; and despite the struggles of hypocrisy, our tongue or our face confesses under the goad of unanticipated torture, as in old times the criminal confessed when he was in the hands of the executioner.

"Our children," he said, as if to retract his confession, "are becoming our enemies."

"Father,—" said Victorin.

"You dare interrupt your father!—" thundered the baron, glaring at his son.

"Listen, father," said Victorin in a firm, distinct voice, the voice of a Puritan deputy. "I am too well aware of the respect I owe you, ever to fail in it, and you will certainly always have in me a most submissive and obedient son."

All who have been present at sittings of the Chambers will recognize the peculiarities of parliamentary strife in these long-drawn out phrases, to which orators resort to allay irritation and gain time.

"We are far from being your enemies," said Victorin; "I have quarreled with my father-in-law, Monsieur Crevel, because I took up the Vauvinet notes for seventy-two thousand francs, and that money is unquestionably in Madame Marneffe's hands. Oh! I don't reproach you, father," he added, at a gesture from the baron; "but I simply wish to add my voice to Cousin Lisbeth's, and to remind you that, although my devotion for you is blind, father, and unlimited, unluckily my dear father, our pecuniary resources are very limited."

"Money!" said the enraged old man, falling back upon his chair, crushed by this reasoning. "And this is my son!—Your money shall be repaid, monsieur," he exclaimed, rising.

He strode toward the door.

"Hector!"

This cry made the baron turn about, and he suddenly exhibited to his wife a face inundated with tears, and she threw her arms about him with the strength of despair.

"Don't go away so—don't leave us in anger. I didn't say anything!"

At this sublime outcry the children threw themselves at their father's feet.

"We all love you," said Hortense.

Lisbeth stood like a statue, watching the group, with a superb smile upon her lips. At that moment Maréchal Hulot's voice was heard in the reception room. The family realized the importance of secrecy, and the scene suddenly changed. The two children rose, and they all struggled to conceal their emotion.

Meanwhile a wrangle was in progress at the door between Mariette and a soldier, who was so persistent that the cook at last came to the salon.

"Monsieur, the quartermaster of a regiment just returned from Algiers insists upon speaking to you."

"Let him wait."

"Monsieur," said Mariette in her master's ear, "he told me to tell you quietly that it's on business connected with monsieur your uncle."

The baron started; he thought of the remittance he had secretly requested two months since to take up his notes, so he left his family and hurried to the reception-room. He saw there a man with the features of an Alsatian.

"Is dis Mennesir la Paron Hilotte?—"

"Yes—"

"Himself?"

"Himself."

The quartermaster, who was fumbling in the lining of his képi during this brief colloquy, took therefrom a letter, which the baron hurriedly unsealed, and he read what follows:

"MY DEAR NEPHEW:

"Instead of being able to send you the hundred thousand francs you request, I have to tell you that my position is not tenable unless you take prompt measures to save me. We have on our backs a king's attorney, who talks morality, and indulges in idle chatter concerning the administration. It's impossible to keep the pettifogger's mouth shut. If the War Department allows these black-coats to eat from its hand, I am done for. The bearer is a sure man; try to give him a lift, for he has done us good service. Don't leave me to the crows!"

This letter was like a thunderbolt; the baron saw therein the beginning of the implacable internal warfare between the civil and the military factions, which is tearing at the vitals of the government of Algiers to this day, and he felt the necessity of immediately applying palliatives to this fresh sore. He bade the soldier return on the following day, and, having dismissed him, not without alluring promises of promotion, he returned to the salon.

"Good-morning and good-bye, brother!" he said to the maréchal.—"Farewell, my children; farewell, dear Adeline.—What's going to become of you, Lisbeth?" said he.

"I am going to keep house for the maréchal, for I must round out my career by always making myself useful to one or another of you."

"Don't leave Valérie until I have seen you," said Hulot in his cousin's ear.—"Adieu, Hortense, my little rebel; try to be more reasonable; I have important business to attend to, we will discuss the question of your reconciliation again. Think it over, my good little pet," he said as he kissed her.

He took leave of his wife and his children, so manifestly disturbed in mind, that they were the prey of the liveliest apprehensions.

"Lisbeth," said the baroness, "we must find out what can be the matter with Hector, for I never saw him in such a state; stay two or three days more with that woman; he tells her everything, and in that way we shall learn what has changed him so suddenly. Have no fear but that we will bring about your marriage with the maréchal, for it's most essential that it should come off."

"I shall never forget the courage you showed this morning," said Hortense, embracing Lisbeth.

"You avenged our poor mother," said Victorin.

The maréchal watched with interest the demonstrations of affection showered upon Lisbeth, who returned and described the scene to Valérie.

This little sketch will make clear to innocent-minded readers the different varieties of family disruption caused by the Madame Marneffes, and by what means they attack poor virtuous women, apparently so far beyond their sphere. But, if we take the trouble to imagine these same disorders as existing in the higher social circles, about the throne; if we consider what kings' mistresses must have cost the nation, we can appreciate the magnitude of the nation's obligation to its rulers, when they set the example of good morals and happy domestic life.

*

In Paris, each department is a little city whence women are banished; but there is as much gossiping and underhand scheming going on as if the whole feminine population were admitted there. After three years Monsieur Marneffe's position had been made clear, exposed to the sunlight, so to speak, and the clerks in the bureaus were wondering: "Will Monsieur Marneffe be Monsieur Coquet's successor or will he not?" just exactly as deputies formerly used to wonder in the Chamber: "Will the estimates pass, or not?" The slightest sign of life in the office of the Superintendent of Employés was noted, and everything that took place in Baron Hulot's division was closely watched. The shrewd Councilor of State had enlisted on his side the victim of Marneffe's promotion, a capable official, by telling him that if he chose to do Marneffe's work he would infallibly succeed him, and he pointed to Marneffe as a man on the brink of the grave. This clerk, therefore, was scheming in Marneffe's interest.

When Hulot passed through his audience-room,

which was filled with visitors, he saw Marneffe's pallid face there in a corner, and Marneffe was the first one summoned.

"What have you to ask me, my dear fellow?" said the baron, concealing his uneasiness.

"Monsieur le Directeur, they are making sport of me in the bureaus, for they have just learned that the Superintendent of Employés went away on leave this morning for his health, to be gone a month. Everybody knows what it means to wait a month. You make me the laughing-stock of my enemies, and it's quite enough to be drummed on on one side; with two at work at once, Monsieur le Directeur, the drum may burst."

"My dear Marneffe, we must be patient in order to attain our object. You cannot be chief of bureau, if at all, in less than two months. I can't request a scandalous promotion, just when I am going to be obliged to strengthen my own position."

"If you are kicked out, I shall never be chief of bureau," said Marneffe coolly; "have me appointed, it won't make any difference."

"So I must sacrifice myself to you?" demanded the baron.

"If it were otherwise I should lose many of my illusions concerning you."

"There's too much Marneffe about you, Monsieur Marneffe!—" said the baron, rising and showing the deputy-chief the door.

"I have the honor to salute you, Monsieur le Baron," rejoined Marneffe humbly.

"What an infernal rascal!" said the baron to himself. "This is much like a summons to pay in twenty-four hours on pain of expropriation."

Two hours later, just as the baron had finished schooling Claude Vignon, whom he proposed to send to the Department of Justice in search of information concerning the judicial functionaries in whose jurisdiction Johann Fischer was, Reine opened the door of his office and handed him a note, requesting an answer.

"To send Reine!" said the baron to himself. "Valérie's mad; she'll compromise us all and endanger that hideous Marneffe's appointment."

He dismissed the minister's private secretary, and read what follows:

"Ah! my dear, what a scene I have just gone through; if you have made me happy for three years, I have paid dearly for it! He returned from his office in a furious rage, that was enough to make one shudder. I knew that he was ugly, but he was positively revolting. His four natural teeth fairly shook, and he threatened me with his hateful company if I continued to receive you. My poor pet, alas! our door will be closed to you henceforth. You can see my tears, they are falling upon my paper, and drenching it! can you read my heart, dear Hector? Ah! to see you no more, to give you up, when I have within me a little of your life as I believed that I had your heart, is enough to kill me. Think of our little Hector! don't abandon me; but do not discredit yourself for Marneffe or give way to his threats! Ah! I love you as I have never loved! I remember all the sacrifices you have made for your Valérie; she is not, and never will be ungrateful; you are, you shall be my only husband. Think no more of the twelve hundred francs a year I asked you to give the dear little Hector who will come in a few months;—I don't propose to be any further expense to you. But my fortune will always be at your disposal.

"Ah! if you loved me as I love you, my Hector, you would retire on a pension, we would both leave our families, our worries, our surroundings, where hatred is the prevailing sentiment, and go, with Lisbeth, to some pleasant spot in the provinces to live,—Bretagne or wherever you choose. There we should see no one, and should be happy together, away from all this crowd. Your retiring pension, and the little property I have in my own name, will be enough for us. You are jealous; very well, your Valérie's whole time shall be given to her Hector, and you will never have to shout at me as you did the other day. I shall have but one child, and that will be ours, rest assured of that, my darling old grumbler. No, you can't imagine my frenzy, for to do that you must know how he treated me, and the vile things he vomited out upon your Valérie! such words would soil the paper, and a woman like myself, Montcornet's daughter, ought never to have been compelled to listen to a single one of them in her whole life. Oh! I would have liked you to be there to punish him by the spectacle of the insane passion for you that seized upon me. My father would have cut down the miserable wretch; I can do only what lies in a woman's power: love you to distraction! And so, my love, in my present state of exasperation it is impossible for me to give up seeing you. Yes! I propose to see you secretly, every day! We are like that, we women; I espouse your anger. For heaven's sake if you love me don't make him chief of bureau, but let him die deputy-chief!—At this moment, I haven't any head left; I can hear his insults still. Bette, who was determined to leave me, has taken pity on me and will remain a few days longer.

"My dearest love, I do not yet know what to do. I can think of nothing but flight. I always adored the country—Bretagne, Languedoc, wherever you choose, provided I can love you without hindrance. Poor dear, how I pity you! you are forced to return to your old Adeline, that urn of tears, for he probably told you, the monster, that he should watch me night and day; he talked about the commissioner of police! Don't come here! I know that he is capable of anything, ever since he made me the victim of a most degrading speculation. For that reason I would that I could return you all that I owe to your generosity. Ah! my dear Hector, I may have flirted, and have seemed fickle to you, but you don't know your Valérie; she loved to torment you, but she prefers you to all the world. No one can prevent you from coming to see your cousin, and I can invent with her some way by which we can talk together. My dear one, for pity's sake write me a line to comfort me, as I can not have your dear presence—oh! I would give my hand to have you in my arms on our divan. A letter will work upon me like a talisman; write me something in which I can read your dear heart; I will send back your letter, for we must be prudent; I shouldn't know where to conceal it, for he ferrets everywhere. Comfort your Valérie, your wife, the mother of your child. That I, who have seen you every day, should be obliged to write you! 'I did not appreciate my good fortune,' I say to Lisbeth. A thousand kisses, my pet. Always love

"YOUR VALÉRIE."

"Tears!"—said Hulot to himself, when he had finished the letter; "tears that make her name undecipherable.—How is she?" he asked Reine.

"Madame is in bed with hysterics," was the reply. "The nervous attack twisted madame up like a stick; it took her after she wrote. Oh! how she cried!—She heard monsieur's voice on the stairs."

The baron, in his excitement, wrote the following letter on his official paper with a printed head:

"Never fear, my angel, *he* shall die a deputy-chief! Your idea is an excellent one; we will go and live far away from

Paris, and be happy with our little Hector; I will go on the retired list, and I can find a good position on some railroad. Ah! my sweet love, I feel that your letter has made me young again! I will begin life anew, and make a fortune for our dear little one, as you shall see. As I read your letter, a thousand times more glowing than those in the Nouvelle Héloïse, it worked a miracle! I did not believe that my love for you could grow greater. This evening at Lisbeth's you will see

"Yours for life,

"HECTOR."

Reine took this letter, the only one the baron had ever written to his *sweet love.* Such keen emotion formed a counterpoise to the storms that were rumbling on the horizon; but, at that moment, the baron, feeling sure that he could ward off the blows aimed at his uncle Johann Fischer, thought only of the deficit.

One of the peculiarities of the Bonapartist character is faith in the power of the sword, the certainty of the continued pre-eminence of the military over the civil administration. Hulot laughed at the idea of the king's attorney in Algeria, where the War Department reigned supreme. Man remains what he has been. How could the officers of the Imperial Guard forget that they had seen the mayors of the good cities of the Empire, the Emperor's prefects, emperors themselves on a small scale, coming to receive the Imperial Guard and to compliment them at the confines of the departments they passed through, and in short rendering them sovereign honors?

At half-past four the baron went straight to Madame Marneffe's; his heart was beating like a young man's as he ascended the stairs, for he was asking himself this question: "Shall I see her, or not?" How could he remember the scene of the morning, when his whole family in tears was at his feet? Did not Valérie's letter, folded away forever in a little pocket-book over his heart, prove that she loved him more dearly than the most lovable of young men?

After he had rung, the wretched baron heard the dragging feet and disgusting cough of the invalid Marneffe. Marneffe opened the door, but immediately struck an attitude and pointed to the staircase with a gesture precisely like that with which Hulot had pointed to the door of his office.

"There's too much Hulot about you, Monsieur Hulot!—" said he.

The baron tried to pass, but Marneffe took a pistol from his pocket and cocked it.

"Monsieur le Conseiller d'État, when a man is so vile as I am,—for you think me a vile creature, don't you?—he would be the worst of criminals, if he did not collect all the profits of his bartered honor. You choose war, and it will be a hot one and without quarter. Don't come again and don't try to pass; I have informed the commissioner of police of my relations with you."

Taking advantage of the baron's stupefaction, he pushed him out and locked the door.

"What a deep rascal!" Hulot said to himself as

he went on upstairs to Lisbeth's. "Ah! now I understand the letter. Valérie and I will leave Paris. Valérie is mine for the rest of my life; she will close my eyes."

Lisbeth was not at home. Madame Olivier informed Hulot that she had gone to the baroness's, expecting to find the baron there.

"Poor girl! I wouldn't have believed she could be so cunning as she was this morning," said the baron to himself, recalling Lisbeth's performance as he walked from Rue Vanneau to Rue Plumet.

At the corner of Rue Vanneau and Rue de Babylone, he looked back at the Eden whence Hymen, with the sword of the law in his hands, had driven him forth. Valérie was at her window looking after him; when he raised his head she waved her handkerchief, but the villainous Marneffe struck his wife on the head and roughly pulled her away from the window. A tear came to the Councilor's eyes.

"To be so dearly loved! to see a woman abused, and to be almost seventy years old!" he muttered.

Lisbeth had gone to announce the good news. Adeline and Hortense already knew that the baron, having refused to degrade himself in the eyes of the whole department by nominating Marneffe chief of bureau, would be turned out of door by that gentleman, the baron's enemy. Wherefore Adeline in her joy had ordered dinner on such a scale that her Hector should find it superior to Valérie's, and the devoted Lisbeth was assisting Mariette to achieve that difficult result. Cousin Bette was a sort of idol; the mother and daughter kept kissing her hands, and had told her with a delight that was touching to see, that the maréchal consented to take her for his housekeeper.

"And from that, my dear, to becoming his wife is but a step," said Adeline.

"Indeed he didn't say no when Victorin mentioned it to him," said Countess Steinbock.

The baron was welcomed by his family with such warm and touching demonstrations of affection, which told of such boundless depths of love, that he was obliged to conceal his chagrin. The maréchal came to dinner. After dinner Hulot did not go away. Victorin and his wife came in, and they made up a whist table.

"It's a long while, Hector," said the maréchal gravely, "since you gave *us* such an evening!—"

This remark, coming from the old soldier, who was accustomed to spoil his brother, and yet reproved him thus implicitly, made a deep impression. It disclosed the long, deep wounds of a heart, in which all the others' sorrow, which he had divined, had echoed loudly.

At eight o'clock the baron himself volunteered to escort Lisbeth home, promising to return.

"Well, Lisbeth, *he* abuses her!" he said as soon as they were in the street. "Oh! I never loved her so dearly!"

"And I wouldn't have believed that Valérie was so fond of you!" replied Lisbeth. "She is free and easy, she likes to flirt and to be courted, to have the comedy of love played for her, as she says; but you are the only one to whom she is really attached."

"What did she say for me?"

"This," said Lisbeth. "She has, as you know, shown some favors to Crevel; you mustn't bear her ill-will for that, for it was he who put her out of reach of want for the rest of her days; but she detests him, and it's almost over. Well, she has kept the key of a suite—"

"On Rue du Dauphin!" cried Hulot in ecstasy. "For that alone, I would forgive her for Crevel.—I have been there, and I know—"

"Here's the key," said Lisbeth; "have one made like it to-morrow, two if you can."

"What then?—" said Hulot eagerly.

"Well, I will come and dine with you again to-morrow, and you must return Valérie's key to me, for Père Crevel may ask her for the one he gave her. Day after to-morrow you will meet there, and agree upon your plans. You will be quite safe, for there are two ways out. If by any chance Crevel, who has the morals of the Regency no doubt, as he says, should come in by the back street you can go out through the shop, and vice versa. Well, you old rascal, you owe this to me. What will you do for me?"

"Whatever you wish!"

"Well, then, don't oppose my marriage to your brother."

"You, Maréchale Hulot! you, Comtesse de Forzheim!" cried Hector in blank amazement.

"Adeline's a baroness!—" retorted Bette in a bitter and threatening tone. "Listen, you old rake; you know what a mess your affairs are in! Your family may find themselves without bread and in the gutter.—"

"That's my constant fear!" said Hector in dismay.

"If your brother dies, who will support your wife and daughter? The widow of a maréchal of France can obtain a pension of at least six thousand francs, can't she? Very good, I propose to marry simply to make sure that your wife and daughter will have bread to eat, you old fool!"

"I did not think of that result!" said the baron. "I will preach it into my brother, for we're sure of you. Tell my angel that my life is *hers!*"

And, having seen Lisbeth safely within doors on Rue Vanneau, the baron returned to his whist, and remained at home. The baroness was happy beyond words; her husband seemed to have become one of the family once more; for about two weeks he went to the department every morning at nine, returned home for dinner at six, and passed the evening in the bosom of his family. Twice he took Adeline and Hortense to the theatre. The mother and daughter paid for three masses of thanksgiving, and prayed God to preserve the husband and father He had restored to them. One night, Victorin Hulot said to his mother, when the baron had gone to his bed-room:

"We are very happy, for father has come back

to us; my wife and I don't regret the loss of our money, if this keeps on.—''

"Your father will soon be seventy years old,'' the baroness replied; "he still thinks of Madame Marneffe, I have discovered that; but soon he will think no more of her. The passion for women is not like gambling, speculation, or avarice; we can imagine its coming to an end.''

The lovely Adeline, for she was still lovely despite her fifty years and her sorrows, was mistaken in this respect. Libertines, men whom nature has endowed with the highly-prized faculty of loving beyond the limits it has fixed for loving, almost always seem younger than they are. During this relapse into virtuous ways the baron went three times to Rue du Dauphin, and there he was never seventy years old. Rekindled passion renewed his youth, and he would have placed his honor, his family, everything, in Valérie's hands without a regret. But Valérie had changed her tactics entirely; she never mentioned money to him, nor the twelve hundred francs a year for their son; on the other hand, she offered him money; she loved Hulot as a woman of thirty-six loves a handsome law-student, very poor, very poetic, and very much in love. And poor Adeline thought she had made a new conquest of her dear Hector! The fourth meeting of the lovers was agreed upon, at the last moment of the third, precisely as in old days at the Comédie-Italienne the next day's bill used to be announced at the close of the performance. The hour appointed was nine o'clock in the morning. On the day when this good fortune fell due, the anticipation of which reconciled the passionate old man to life with his family, Reine enquired for the baron about eight o'clock. Hulot, fearing some disaster, went out to speak to her, as she refused to come in. The faithful maid handed him the following letter:

"Don't go to Rue du Dauphin, my old grumbler; our nightmare is ill and I have to nurse him; but be there this evening at nine. Crevel is at Monsieur Lebas's, at Corbeil, so I am sure that he'll bring no princess to his little house. I have made arrangements here to have the night for my own, and I can return before Marneffe is awake. Send me an answer; for perhaps your stately poem of a wife won't give you any more liberty than she used. They say she is so lovely still that you are quite capable of being false to me, you're such a terrible rake! Burn my letter, I distrust everybody."

Hulot wrote these few lines in reply:

"My love, my wife has not interfered with my pleasure for twenty-five years, as I told you before. I would sacrifice a hundred Adelines to you! I will be at the temple Crevel at nine this evening, awaiting my divinity. May the deputy-chief settle his accounts soon! then we shall be separated no more; such is the dearest wish of

"YOUR HECTOR."

That evening the baron told his wife that he was going to attend to some business with the minister at Saint-Cloud, and would return at four or five o'clock in the morning; and he went to Rue du Dauphin. It was late in the month of June.

Few men have really experienced in their lives the fearful sensation of going to meet their death; those who have returned alive from the scaffold are among the number; but some dreamers have felt that agony in a most vivid form in their dreams; they have gone through the whole performance, and have even felt the knife against their necks just as the awakening came, with daybreak, to rescue them.—But the sensation which the Councilor of State felt at five o'clock in the morning, in Crevel's dainty and luxurious bed, far surpassed in horror that of feeling one's neck resting on the fatal block, in the presence of ten thousand spectators glaring at you with twenty thousand rays of flame. Valérie was sleeping in a bewitching pose. She was beautiful as all women are who are sufficiently so to be lovely in their sleep. It was art invading the province of nature, it was the realization of the painter's conception. In his horizontal position the baron's eyes were about three feet from the floor; as they wandered about at random, as every man's eyes do just as he awakes and collects his thoughts, they rested upon the door, covered with flowers painted by Jan, an artist who snapped his fingers at fame. The baron did not see, like the condemned man, twenty thousand visual rays; he saw but a single person, whose glance was in very truth more piercing than the ten thousand of the public square. It is unquestionably true that a great number of splenetic Englishmen would pay a high price for such a sensation in the midst of their

G. Cain del. Gery Bichard sc.

pleasure,—a sensation much rarer than that felt by a condemned man. The baron remained in his horizontal position, literally bathed in cold perspiration. He would have liked to doubt the evidence of his senses, but that murderous eye had a tongue. He heard voices whispering behind the door.

"What if it were only Crevel trying to play a joke on me!" said the baron to himself, no longer able to doubt the presence of a stranger in the temple.

The door was thrown open. French law, which comes next to royalty on the placards, appeared in all its majesty, in the guise of a nice little commissioner of police, accompanied by a long-legged justice of the peace, both under the escort of Monsieur Marneffe. The commissioner, whose feet were encased in shoes tied with ribbons which were covered with mud, terminated above in a yellow cranium, poorly supplied with hair, the man's whole aspect denoting a crafty, good-natured, mettlesome blade, who knew all the secrets of life in Paris. The expression of his eyes, as seen through the glasses he wore, was shrewd and bantering. The magistrate, a former lawyer, and a worshipper of the fair sex, of long standing, envied the man who had made himself amenable to the law.

"Pray pardon the harshness of our errand, Monsieur le Baron!" said the officer, "we are requisitioned by a complainant. Monsieur le Juge de Paix was a witness of my entry into the house. I know who you are, and who your companion is."

Valérie opened her eyes wide, in amazement,

uttered the piercing shriek invented by actresses to announce an attack of insanity on the stage, and writhed in convulsions on the bed, like a demoniac of the Middle Ages in her chemise of sulphur on a bed of burning fagots.

"Death!—dear Hector, the police? Oh! never!"

She leaped out of bed, flitted like a white cloud between the three spectators, and crouched under the *bonheur-du-jour*, hiding her face in her hands.

"Lost! dead!—" she shrieked.

"Monsieur," said Marneffe to Hulot, "if Madame Marneffe should go mad, you would be worse than a libertine, you'd be a murderer—"

What can a man do or say, when he is taken by surprise in a bed that does not belong to him, even as a tenant, and with a woman who also does not belong to him? This.

"Monsieur le Juge de Paix, Monsieur le Commissaire de Police," said the baron with dignity, "be good enough to look to the welfare of the unfortunate woman whose reason seems to me in danger, —and then you can make your report. Of course the doors are secured and you have no reason to anticipate flight on her part or my own, considering the condition we are in."

The two functionaries complied with the Councilor's suggestion.

"Come and speak with me, you vile wretch!"—said Hulot in an undertone to Marneffe, taking him by the arm and pulling him to his side. "I should not be the assassin, but you! You want to be chief of bureau and officer of the Legion of Honor?"

"Above all things, director," Marneffe replied, with an inclination of his head.

"You shall be both; go and reassure your wife and send these men away."

"Nay, nay," Marneffe shrewdly retorted. "These gentlemen must draw up their report that you were caught in the act, for, without that document, which is the foundation of my complaint, what would become of me? They know no end of tricks at headquarters. You stole my wife and didn't make me chief of bureau, Monsieur le Baron, and I give you only two days to redeem yourself. Here are the letters—"

"Letters!" cried the baron, interrupting him.

"Yes, the letters proving that the child my wife is carrying at this moment is yours.—Do you understand? you must give my son an income equal to the portion this bastard takes from him. But I will be moderate, for it's none of my business, and I am not drunk with the joys of paternity, myself! A hundred louis a year will do. I shall be Monsieur Coquet's successor to-morrow morning, and my name placed on the list of those who are to be made officers of the Legion at the July fêtes or—the report will be deposited with my complaint at police headquarters. I'm a generous fellow, am I not?"

"Great God! what a pretty woman!" said the magistrate to the officer. "What a loss to society if she should go mad!"

"She's not mad," the commissioner sententiously replied.

A police officer is always the incarnation of suspicion.

"Monsieur le Baron Hulot has stepped into a trap," he added loud enough to be overheard by Valérie.

She shot a glance at the commissioner which would have struck him dead if glances could transmit the fury they express. The commissioner smiled, for he too had set a trap, and the lady fell into it. Marneffe bade his wife return to the bed-room and dress herself decently, for he had come to an understanding on every point with the baron. The latter took a dressing-gown and withdrew to the adjoining room.

"Gentlemen," said he to the two functionaries, "I need not urge secrecy upon you."

The magistrate and the officer bowed. The latter tapped lightly twice on the door, whereupon his secretary entered, sat down at the *bonheur-du-jour*, and began to write what the commissioner dictated to him in a low voice. Valérie continued to weep bitterly. When she had finished her toilette, Hulot went into the bed-room and dressed. Meanwhile the report was drawn up. Thereupon Marneffe started to take his wife away; but Hulot, believing that it was the last time he should see her, implored by a gesture the favor of speaking with her.

"Monsieur, madame has cost me enough for you to allow me to bid adieu to her,—in the presence of you all, of course."

Valérie came to his side, and Hulot whispered in her ear:

"There is nothing left for us now but flight; but how shall we correspond? We have been betrayed—"

"By Reine!" she replied. "But, my dear friend, after this scandal, we ought to meet no more. I am dishonored. Besides they will tell you infamous things about me, and you will believe them—"

The baron made a gesture of denial.

"You will believe them, and I thank heaven for it, for perhaps you will not regret me."

"*He won't die a deputy-chief!*" said Marneffe in the Councilor's ear, as he returned to get his wife, to whom he said roughly: "Enough of this, madame; if I am weak toward you, I don't propose to be made a fool of by others."

Valérie left the Crevel establishment with such a wicked parting glance at the baron, that he believed she still adored him. The magistrate gallantly offered his hand to escort her to the carriage. The crestfallen baron, who was required to sign the report, was left alone with the commissioner of police. When the Councilor of State had written his name, the official cast a shrewd glance at him over his spectacles.

"You are very fond of that little lady, Monsieur le Baron?"

"To my discomfiture, as you see—"

"Suppose she didn't love you?" continued the official; "suppose she was playing you false?"

"I have seen her before in this place, monsieur.—Monsieur Crevel and I have an understanding.—"

"Aha! you are aware that you are on Monsieur le Maire's premises?"

"Perfectly."

The commissioner raised his hat slightly to salute the old fellow.

"You are very much in love, so I will hold my tongue," said he, "I have as much respect for inveterate passions as physicians have for inve—I have seen Monsieur de Nucingen the banker suffering from a passion of that sort—"

"He's a friend of mine," rejoined the baron. "I have often supped with the fair Esther; she was well worth the two millions she cost him."

"More," said the commissioner. "The old financier's fancy cost four persons their lives. Oh! these passions are like the cholera."

"What were you going to say to me?" demanded the Councilor of State, who took this indirect advice decidedly ill.

"Why should I deprive you of your illusions?" replied the commissioner; "a man so seldom retains them at your age."

"Rid me of them!" cried the Councilor.

"You may curse the physician afterward," the commissioner answered with a smile.

"I appeal to you, Monsieur le Commissaire.—"

"Well, that woman was in league with her husband."

"Oh!—"

"That happens, monsieur, about twice in ten times. Oh! I know what I'm talking about."

"What proof have you of her complicity?"

"First of all, the husband!" said the clever official with the tranquillity of a surgeon accustomed to probe wounds. "Speculation is written upon that ghastly, hideous face. But do you not value highly a certain letter written by this woman in which something is said about a child?"

"I value that letter so highly that I always carry it about me," replied the baron, feeling in his breast pocket for the little pocket-book that never left him.

"Leave the pocket-book where it is," said the commissioner, in the thundering tones of a public prosecutor; "here's the letter. I know now all I wanted to know. Madame Marneffe must be in the secret of the pocket-book's contents?"

"She and nobody else in the world."

"So I thought.—Now, here's the proof you desire of the little woman's complicity."

"Let's have it!" said the baron, still incredulous.

"When we arrived here, Monsieur le Baron, that villain Marneffe came in first and got this letter, which his wife had, without doubt, placed on that piece of furniture," said the commissioner, indicating the *bonheur-du-jour*. "Evidently that place had been agreed upon between the husband and wife, always supposing that she succeeded in filching the letter while you were asleep; for the letter the lady wrote you, with those you have written her, would be decisive in criminal proceedings.''

The commissioner showed Hulot the letter he received through Reine in his office at the department.

''It's a part of the papers in the case,'' said he; ''give it back to me, monsieur.''

"Well, monsieur,'' said Hulot, with discomposed countenance, "that woman is libertinage reduced to a science; I am certain now that she has three lovers!''

"That's not uncommon,'' said the commissioner. "Ah! they're not all on the street. When they practice that profession, Monsieur le Baron, in carriages or in salons or in their own houses, it's no longer a matter of francs and centimes. Mademoiselle Esther, whom you have just mentioned and who poisoned herself, devoured millions.—If you take my advice, you'll cut loose, Monsieur le Baron. This last trick will cost you dear. That beast of a husband has the law on his side. Indeed, but for me the little woman would have hooked you again!''

"Thanks, monsieur,'' said the Councilor of State, trying to maintain a dignified countenance.

"Monsieur, we will close the rooms now, the farce is played out, and you can hand the key to Monsieur le Maire.''

*

Hulot returned home in a depressed condition very near to prostration, and absorbed by the most gloomy thoughts. He awoke his noble-hearted, pure and saint-like wife, and hurled the story of the last three years into her heart, sobbing like a child deprived of a favorite toy. This confession of an old man still young at heart, this distressing, heart-rending epic, while it moved Adeline deeply, inwardly caused her the keenest joy, and she thanked Heaven for this latest stroke, for she imagined her husband restored for ever to the bosom of his family.

"Lisbeth was right!" said Madame Hulot in a soft voice, and without indulging in useless reproaches, "she told us this beforehand."

"True! Ah! if I had listened to her, instead of losing my temper, the day I urged poor Hortense to return home in order not to endanger the reputation of that—Oh! dear Adeline, we must save Wenceslas! he's in the mire up to his chin!"

"My poor dear, the little bourgeoise succeeded no better with you than the actresses," said Adeline with a smile.

The baroness was terrified at the manifest change in her Hector; when she saw that he was unhappy, suffering keenly, bent beneath the weight of his misfortunes, she was all heart, all compassion, all love, and she would have shed her blood to make him happy.

"Stay with us, my dear Hector. Tell me what these women do to attach you to them so; I will try to do the same.—Why did you not form me according to your needs? Was it because I lack intelligence? I am still considered beautiful enough for men to pay their court to me."

Many married women, devoted to their duties and their husbands, may here ask themselves the question why these strong, kindly men, who are so compassionate to the Madame Marneffes, do not take their wives for the objects of their fancy and their passion, especially when they resemble Baroness Adeline Hulot. This is one of the most insoluble mysteries of the human organization. Love, that inordinate carousal of the reason, that manly, serious enjoyment of noble hearts; and sensual pleasure, that vulgar commodity offered for sale upon the streets, are two different phases of a single fact. The woman who satisfies these two boundless appetites of the dual nature is as rare in the sex as is the great general, the great writer, the great artist, the great inventor, in a nation. The man of superior mind as well as the imbecile, a Hulot as well as a Crevel, feels the need of the ideal and the need of the sensual; all alike go about in search of this mysterious hermaphrodite, this *rara avis* which, in a majority of cases, is found to be a work in two volumes. This search is a form of depravity for which society is to blame. Certainly, marriage should be looked upon as a task to be accomplished; it is life, with its toil and its bitter sacrifices, to be made on both sides. The libertines, the seekers after treasure, are as guilty as malefactors who are much more severely punished than they. These reflections are not mere moral patchwork; they furnish the explanation of many incomprehensible disasters. Moreover this Scene inculcates its own moral lessons of more than one variety.

The baron paid an early visit to the Maréchal Prince de Wissembourg, whose exalted patronage was his last resource. Having been for thirty-five years a protégé of the old war-horse, he had the *grande* and *petite entrée*, and was privileged to enter his apartments at his hour for rising.

"Ah! good morning, my dear Hector," said that great and warm-hearted officer. "What's the matter? You seem thoughtful. The session's at an end, however. Still another one gone! I speak of them now, as we used to speak of our campaigns. Faith I believe the newspapers call the sessions parliamentary campaigns."

"Indeed, maréchal, we did have some trouble; but it was due to the prevailing want!" said Hulot. "What can you expect? it's the way of the world. Every period has its drawbacks. The greatest misfortune of the year 1841 is that neither the King nor his ministers are untrammeled in their action as the Emperor was."

The maréchal darted at Hulot an eagle-like glance, proud, piercing, acute, which showed that, despite his years, his great heart was still strong and unflinching.

"You have a favor to ask of me?" he said, affecting a playful air.

"I find myself compelled to ask of you as a personal favor, the promotion of one of my deputy-chiefs to the rank of chief of bureau, and his nomination as an officer of the Legion of Honor."

"What's his name?" said the maréchal, with a glance like a flash of lightning.

"Marneffe!"

"He has a pretty wife, I saw her at your daughter's wedding.—If Roger—but Roger is no longer here. Hector, my boy, this is a matter connected with your amours. What! are you still at the old game? Ah! you do credit to the Imperial Guard! that's what it is to have been in the administration; you have forces in reserve!—Drop this matter right here, my dear boy, there's too much gallantry about it for it to become a department matter."

"No, maréchal, it's a very bad business, for the police court is mixed up in it; do you want to see me there?"

"Oh! the devil!" cried the maréchal, becoming serious. "Go on."

"You see me in the plight of a fox caught in a trap.—You have always been so kind to me, that you will consent to extricate me from my present disgraceful situation."

Hulot thereupon described his misadventure as wittily and cheerfully as possible.

"Do you want my brother, to whom you are so attached, prince, to die of shame," he said, as he concluded, "and to allow one of your directors, a Councilor of State, to be disgraced? My Marneffe is a miserable rascal, we'll put him on the retired list in two or three years."

"How coolly you talk of two or three years, my dear fellow!—" said the maréchal.

"But the Imperial Guard is immortal, prince."

"I am now the only maréchal left of the first promotion," said the minister. "Hark ye, Hector, you don't know how great my attachment to you is, but you shall see! On the day when I leave the ministry, we will leave it together. Ah! my friend, you are not a deputy. Many men have an eye on your place, and, except for me, you would no longer hold it. Yes, I have broken many a lance to keep you there.—Well, I grant your two requests, for it would be much too hard to see you sitting in the dock, at your age, and holding the position that you do. But you are making too many breaches in your credit. If this nomination raises any row, we shall be taken to account for it. I can afford to laugh at it, but it will be one thorn more in your foot. At the next session you will lose your place. Your office has been held out as a bait to five or six influential men, and you have been retained in it only by the subtlety of my arguments. I have urged that, on the day when you were retired and your place was given to some one else, we should have five malcontents and one content; while by leaving you *shaking in your shoes* for two or three years, we could hold our six votes. They began to laugh in the Council, and concluded that the *vieux de la vieille*, as they say, was coming out strong in parliamentary tactics.—I tell you all this frankly. Besides, you are growing gray.—What a lucky dog you are to be able still to get yourself into such a fix! Where are the days when Sub-lieutenant Cottin had mistresses!"

The maréchal rang.

"We must have that report destroyed!" he said.

"You are like a father to me, monseigneur! I didn't dare speak of my anxiety."

"I still wish that Roger was here," cried the maréchal, as Mitouflet, his orderly, entered the room, "and I was just going to send for him.—You may go, Mitouflet.—And do you, old comrade, go and draw up the nomination, and I'll sign it. But that infernal schemer sha'n't long enjoy the fruit of his crimes; he will be watched, and broken at the head of his company, at the slightest shortcoming. Now that you are saved, Hector, take heed to yourself. Don't tire out your friends. The appointment will be sent you this morning, and your man shall be an officer of the Legion!—How old are you now?"

"I shall be seventy in three months."

"What a buck you are!" said the maréchal with a smile. "You're the one who deserves promotion; but, a thousand cannon-balls! we're not living under Louis XV!"

Such is the effect of the good fellowship which unites the glorious relics of the Napoleonic phalanx; they think they are still around the camp-fire, and compelled to protect one another against the whole world.

"Another favor like that," said Hulot to himself as he crossed the courtyard, "and I am ruined."

The unhappy official went to Baron de Nucingen's, to whom he now owed only a trifling sum; he succeeded in borrowing from him forty thousand francs by assigning his salary for two years more; but the baron stipulated that, in case Hulot should be retired, the attachable portion of his pension should be applied to the payment of the loan, principal and interest in full. This last loan, like the former one, was negotiated in the name of Vauvinet, to whom the baron gave his notes for twelve thousand francs. The next day, the fatal report, the husband's complaint, and the letters, all were destroyed. The scandalous promotions of Monsieur Marneffe, hardly noticed amid the excitement of the July fêtes, were not commented on in any newspaper.

Lisbeth, who had, so far as appearances went, broken with Madame Marneffe, was installed at Maréchal Hulot's. Ten days after these occurrences the banns of the old maid's intended marriage to the illustrious veteran were published for the first time. To obtain his consent Adeline told him of her Hector's pecuniary disasters, begging him never to mention it to the baron, who, she said, was in a very gloomy, dejected and feeble state.

"Alas! he shows his age!" she added.

So Lisbeth had triumphed! She was on the point of attaining the goal of her ambition; she was about to see her scheme successful, her hatred satisfied. She enjoyed in anticipation the bliss of reigning over the family which had so long despised her. She promised herself that she would be the protectress of her protectors, the guardian angel who would support the ruined family; she addressed herself in secret as *Madame la Comtesse* or *Madame la Maréchale*, courtesying to herself before the mirror. Adeline and Hortense would end their days in poverty, struggling to drive away want, while Cousin Bette, having the *entrée* at the Tuileries, would be enthroned in society.

A shocking catastrophe hurled the old maid from the social eminence whereon she had so proudly taken her stand.

On the very day on which the banns were first published the baron received another message from Africa. A second Alsatian made his appearance, and delivered a letter after making sure that the recipient was Baron Hulot himself; and, having given his address, he left that dignitary overwhelmed by the perusal of the first lines of the following letter:

"MY NEPHEW:

"You will receive this letter, by my reckoning, on the seventh of August. Assuming that it takes you three days to send us the assistance we require, and two weeks more for it to reach here, it will arrive September first.

"If you can arrange matters thus you will have saved the honor and the life of your devoted Johann Fischer.

"This is what the clerk demands, whom you gave me as a confederate; for I am, as it appears, liable to be summoned before the Assizes or before a court-martial. You understand that Johann Fischer will never be dragged before any tribunal, but will go of his own motion before that over which God presides.

"Your clerk seems to me to be a wicked rascal, quite capable of compromising you; but he's as shrewd as any swindler. He claims that you ought to make a louder outcry than anybody, and send us an inspector, a special commissioner with instructions to detect the culprits, unearth abuses, and, in short, put on the screws; but who will interpose in the first place between the tribunals and us, by raising the question of jurisdiction?

"If your commissioner arrives by September 1, and has the countersign from you, if you send us two hundred thousand francs to replace in the warehouses the supplies that we claim to have in distant localities, we shall be looked upon as honest agents with clean hands.

"You can entrust to the soldier who will hand you this letter a draft to my order on some house in Algiers. He is a reliable man, a relation of mine, and utterly incapable of trying to find out what he is the bearer of. I have taken measures to provide for the boy's return. If you can do nothing I shall gladly die for him to whom we owe our Adeline's happiness."

The agony and the bliss of passion, and the catastrophe which had put an end to his gallant career, had prevented Baron Hulot from giving a thought to poor Johann Fischer, whose first letter, however, definitely foreshadowed the danger which had now become so pressing. He left the dining-room in such distress of mind that he threw himself on the couch in the salon. He was completely crushed, overpowered by the deathly torpor caused by a violent fall. He stared vacantly at a rose in the carpet, heedless of the fact that he held Johann's fatal letter open in his hand. Adeline from her bed-room heard her husband fall upon the couch like a lifeless mass. The sound was so unusual that she thought he must have had an apoplectic stroke. She looked through the door into the mirror, trembling with the deadly terror which checks the respiration, and roots one to the spot where one stands, and she saw her Hector lying as if he had been thrown down. She stole into the room on tiptoe; Hector heard nothing, so that she was able to approach him; she saw the letter, took it, read it, and trembled in every limb. She passed through one of those violent nervous upheavals, of which the body always retains the marks. When the first shock had passed away, the necessity of acting promptly gave her the strength which is drawn from the very well-springs of vitality; but, a few days later, she became subject to constant attacks of nervous trembling.

"Hector, come to my room," said she in a voice which resembled a sigh. "Don't let your daughter see you thus! Come, my dear, come."

"Where can I obtain two hundred thousand francs? I can arrange to have Claude Vignon sent as commissioner. He's a bright, intelligent fellow. —That's a matter of a day or two only.—But two hundred thousand francs! My son hasn't them, his house is mortgaged for three hundred thousand. My brother has laid by thirty thousand francs at the outside. Nucingen would laugh at me!—Vauvinet?—he consented with very bad grace to loan me ten thousand francs to make up the amount for that infernal Marneffe's son. No, it's all over; I must go and throw myself at the maréchal's feet, confess to him how things stand, hear myself called a vile dog, and receive his broadside so that I can go under decently."

"But, Hector, this is not ruin simply, it's dishonor!" said Adeline. "My poor uncle will kill himself. Kill only us; you have the right to do that, but don't be a murderer. Take courage, there must be some way of escape."

"Not one!" said the baron. "Not a man in the government could put his hand on two hundred thousand francs, even if it were a question of saving a ministry!—O Napoleon, where art thou?"

"My uncle! poor man! Hector, we cannot let him commit suicide in disgrace!"

"There might be one resource," said he; "but—it's very uncertain.—Yes, Crevel is at daggers drawn with his daughter.—Ah! he has plenty of money, he alone could—"

"Well, Hector, it's far better that your wife should die, than that we should let our uncle, your brother and the honor of the family die together!" said the baroness, as an idea flashed suddenly through her mind. "Yes, I can save you all.—

O my God! what a degrading thought! how could it have come to me?"

She clasped her hands, fell on her knees, and prayed. When she arose she saw a look of such insane joy on her husband's face, that the diabolical idea returned, and Adeline thereupon fell into a sort of idiotic melancholy.

"Go, my dear, run to the ministry," she cried, rousing herself from her torpor, "try to arrange for sending a commissioner; you must do it. *Wheedle it out of the maréchal!* And when you return, at five o'clock, perhaps you will find,—yes! you shall find two hundred thousand francs. Your family, your honor as a man, as a Councilor of State, as a government official, your reputation for honesty, your son, all will be saved; but your Adeline will be lost, and you will never see her again. Hector, my love," said she, kneeling at his feet, taking his hand and kissing it, "give me your blessing and bid me adieu!"

His wife's words and manner were so heartrending that Hulot said, as he raised her from the floor and kissed her:

"I don't understand you!"

"If you did," she replied, "I should die of shame, or else I should not be strong enough to carry through this last sacrifice."

"Madame, breakfast is served," said Mariette.

Hortense came in to bid her father and mother good-morning. They were forced to conceal their emotions and go to breakfast.

"Sit down to breakfast without me; I will join you in a moment!" said the baroness.

She sat down at her table and wrote the following letter:

"MY DEAR MONSIEUR CREVEL:

"I have a favor to ask of you; I shall look for you this morning, and I rely upon your gallantry, which is well known to me, not to keep me waiting too long.

"Your devoted servant,

"ADELINE HULOT."

"Louise," said she to her daughter's maid, who was waiting at the table, "take this letter down to the concierge, and tell him to carry it immediately to its address and ask for an answer."

The baron, who was looking over the newspapers, handed a republican sheet to his wife, and pointed out an article in it.

"Will it be in time?" he said.

The article in question, one of those terrible political tirades with which the newspapers flavor their political bread and butter, was as follows:

"One of our correspondents writes us from Algiers that such abuses have been unearthed in the commissary service in the province of Oran, that a judicial investigation has been set on foot. The malversations are unquestionable, and the guilty parties are known. If severe repressive measures are not taken we shall continue to lose more men by extortions which cut down their rations, than by the swords of the Arabs or the heat of the climate. We shall await further information before pursuing this deplorable subject. We are no longer surprised at the dismay caused by the establishment of the press in Algeria, as provided by the Charter of 1830."

"I must dress and go to the department," said the baron, leaving the table; "time is too precious, there's a man's life in every minute."

"O mamma, I have no more hope!" exclaimed Hortense.

Unable to restrain her tears, she handed her mother a *Revue des Beaux-Arts.* Madame Hulot's eye fell upon an engraving of the *Delilah* group by Count Steinbock, beneath which was printed: *Belonging to Madame Marneffe.* The first few lines of the article, which was signed V, revealed the talent and the complaisance of Claude Vignon.

"Poor darling!" said the baroness.

Dismayed by the almost indifferent tone in which her mother spoke, Hortense looked up at her, and saw in her expression the evidence of a sorrow, beside which her own was as nothing. She went to her and kissed her.

"What's the matter, mamma? what has happened?" she said; "can we be more wretched than we are?"

"My child, it seems that my terrible sufferings in the past have been nothing compared to what I bear to-day. When shall I cease to suffer?"

"In heaven, mother!" said Hortense gravely.

"Come, my angel, you shall help me dress.—But no,—I prefer that you should have nothing to do with my toilette to-day. Send Louise to me."

*

When she returned to her bed-room Adeline went and scrutinized herself in the mirror. She gazed at herself sadly and curiously, asking herself the question:

"Am I still beautiful?—Can I still arouse desire? —Have I any wrinkles?"

She pushed back her lovely blond hair, and uncovered her temples—all was as fresh as in a young girl. Adeline went farther; she bared her shoulders and was content. She felt a momentary thrill of pride. The beauty of shoulders which are really beautiful, is the last to leave a woman, especially when she has led a virtuous life. Adeline selected with care the elements of her toilette; but the chaste, pious creature was chastely dressed, despite her little attempts at coquetry. Why wear new gray silk stockings and satin buskins, when she was entirely unversed in the art of putting out her little foot at the decisive moment, a few inches beyond the skirt half-raised so as to open a vast field to desire? She donned her prettiest flowered muslin, with low neck and short sleeves; but she was so dismayed at the sight of her bare flesh that she covered her lovely arms with gauze sleeves, and veiled her breast and shoulders with an embroidered fichu. The English fashion of arranging the hair seemed too suggestive, so she destroyed its alluring effect with a very pretty cap; but with or without a cap would she have known how to play with her golden curls, so as to exhibit her slender hand to be admired?—This was her paint; the certainty that she was about to commit a crime, the deliberate preparations therefor threw the saintly woman into a violent fever, which restored the bloom of youth for the moment. Her eyes shone, her skin fairly glowed. Instead of assuming a seductive expression she viewed with horror what seemed to her her dissolute appearance. At Adeline's request Lisbeth had told her the circumstances of Wenceslas' infidelity, and the baroness then learned to her unbounded amazement that Madame Marneffe had made herself the bewitched artist's mistress in a single evening, in a moment.

"How do these women do it?" she asked Lisbeth.

There is nothing to equal the curiosity of virtuous women on this subject, for they long to possess the fascinating powers of vice and remain pure.

"Why they seduce men, it's their business," Cousin Bette replied. "You see, my dear, Valérie was lovely enough that night to damn an angel."

"Pray tell me how she went about it?"

"There's no theory in that trade, it's all practice," said Lisbeth jocosely.

The baroness, as she recalled this conversation, would have liked to consult Cousin Bette; but time was lacking. Poor Adeline, incapable of inventing a *patch*, of placing a rose-bud in the middle of her corsage, of devising wiles of the toilette calculated to reawaken in men deadened passion, was dressed with great care, nothing more. Wishing doesn't make one a courtesan! "Woman is man's soup," as Molière jocosely remarks by the mouth of the sage Gros-René. This simile imagines a sort of culinary science in love. The virtuous, dignified wife would then be the Homeric repast, the flesh thrown upon burning coals. The courtesan on the other hand would be the repast Carême, with its condiments, its spices and its dainty appointments. The baroness could not, did not know how to *serve up* her white breast in a magnificent dish of guipure lace, after the style of Madame Marneffe. She did not know the secret of certain poses, the effect of certain glances. In short, she had not her secret thrust. The noble woman might have turned and turned a hundred times without learning how to attract the libertine's practised eye.

To be a virtuous *prude*, in the eyes of the world, and a courtesan to one's husband, is to be a woman of genius, and there are few such. Therein lies the secret of long attachments, inexplicable to women who are not endowed with these two-fold, sublime qualities. Imagine Madame Marneffe virtuous!—you have the Marquise de Pescara! These grand and noble women, these lovely and virtuous Dianes de Poitiers can be counted on one's fingers.

The scene with which this serious and painful Study of Parisian Morals begins was to be reproduced, with this singular difference that the distress predicted by the captain of the citizen militia played a different part therein. Madame Hulot was awaiting Crevel with the purpose in view which had brought him to her, smiling on the Parisians from his milord, three years before. And strange to say, the baroness was faithful to herself, and to her love, while abandoning herself to the basest of all acts of infidelity, an act which even the mad ardor of passion does not condone in the eyes of some judges.

"What must I do to be a Madame Marneffe?" she said to herself as she heard the bell ring.

She forced back her tears, the fever imparted animation to her features, and she promised herself, poor, noble-hearted creature, that she would act the courtesan to the life.

"What the devil can good Baroness Hulot want of me?" Crevel was wondering as he ascended the broad staircase. "Bah! she wants to talk with me about my quarrel with Célestine and Victorin; but I'll not yield an inch!—"

As he entered the salon in following Louise, he said to himself, taking note of the bareness of the surroundings—à la Crevel—:

"Poor woman!—here she is like a lovely picture stowed away in the garret by a man who knows nothing about painting."

Crevel, who had seen Comte Popinot, Minister of Commerce, buying pictures and statues, aimed to make himself illustrious among those Parisian Mæcenases, whose love for the arts consists in trying to change twenty-sou pieces for twenty-franc pieces. Adeline welcomed Crevel with a gracious smile, and pointed to a chair near her own.

"Here I am, fair lady, at your service," said he.

The mayor, having become a politician, had adopted black broadcloth. His face appeared above that garb like a full moon surmounting a curtain of dark clouds. His shirt, studded with three huge pearls worth five hundred francs each, gave an exalted idea of his—thoracic capacity, and he seemed to say: "You see in me the future athlete of the tribune!" His great plebeian hands were encased in yellow gloves from early morning. His spotless boots betrayed the little one-horse brown coupé in which he had come. Ambition had somewhat modified his attitude in three years. Like the great painters he had reached his second manner. In society, when he went to the Prince de Wissembourg's, to the prefecture, to Comte Popinot's, etc., he held his hat in his hand in a careless fashion taught him by Valérie, and inserted the thumb of the other hand in the armhole of his waistcoat with a jaunty air, coquetting with his head and eyes. This latest *attitude* was attributable to the mischievous Valérie, who, on the pretext of rejuvenating her mayor, had endowed him with one absurd habit more.

"I asked you to come, dear, kind Monsieur Crevel," said the baroness in a trembling voice, "on business of the utmost importance.—"

"I can guess what it is, madame," said Crevel with a knowing look; "but you ask what is impossible.—Oh! I am not a barbarous father, a man, as

Napoléon said, *of the same length, breadth and height* in his avarice. Listen to me, dear madame. If my children ruined themselves for themselves, I would go to their assistance; but to become surety for your husband, madame?—why, it's like trying to fill the cask of the Danaïdes! A house mortgaged for three hundred thousand francs for an incorrigible father! They have nothing now, poor creatures! and they don't seem to find it amusing! Now they'll have to live on what Victorin can earn at the Palais. How your precious son does jabber!—Ah! he ought to be a minister, the little wiseacre! the hope of us all. A pretty little tug-boat that is idiotically running aground; for, if he had borrowed money to help himself along, if he had run in debt for entertaining deputies, or to obtain votes and increase his influence, I would say to him: 'Here's my purse, draw on it freely, my boy!' But to pay for papa's foibles, foibles that I predicted to you! Ah! his father has thrown him where he'll never come into power.—I'm the one that's going to be a minister.—"

"Alas! *dear Crevel,* it's not a question of our children, poor, devoted creatures!—If your heart is closed to Victorin and Célestine, I will love them so dearly that perhaps I can allay the bitter sorrow your anger has caused them. You punish your children for a kind action!"

"Yes, for a kind action ill-done! It was a half-crime!" said Crevel, well pleased with the expression.

"To do well, my dear Crevel," rejoined the baroness, "is not to take money from an overflowing purse! but to endure privation because of one's generosity, to suffer for one's well-doing! to anticipate ingratitude! Heaven takes no account of the charity that costs nothing."

"Saints, madame, are permitted to go to the hospital; they know that it is for them the gate of heaven. I am a worldly creature, I fear God, but I am even more afraid of the hell of poverty. To be penniless is the last degree of misfortune in our present social order. I am of my own time, and I honor money!—"

"You are right," said Adeline, "from the worldly point of view."

She found herself a hundred leagues away from the real question, and when she thought of her uncle she felt like Saint Lawrence on the gridiron; for she fancied that she saw him aiming a pistol at himself. She lowered her eyes, then raised them to Crevel's face, filled with angelic gentleness, and not with the tantalizing lewdness, so seductive in Valérie. Three years before she would have fascinated Crevel with that adorable glance.

"I have known you to be more generous," said she.—"You used to speak of three hundred thousand francs as a great nobleman would.—"

Crevel looked at Madame Hulot, who appeared to him like a lily near the close of its blooming; a vague idea passed through his mind; but he honored the saintly creature so much that he crowded the suspicion back to the libertine side of his heart.

"Madame, I am still the same, but a former merchant is, and should be, a great nobleman with method and economy; he carries his idea of order into everything. He opens an account with his follies, gives them a certain amount of credit, and devotes the profits of certain speculations to that account; but encroach upon his capital!—that would be downright madness. My children will have all that belongs to them: their mother's and mine; but of course they don't want their father to be bored to death, to turn monk or mummy!—I lead a joyous life! I am sailing gayly down the river! I perform all the duties imposed upon me by the law, my heart and my family, just as exactly as I used to take up my notes at maturity. Let my children do as I do in my household and I shall be satisfied; and, so far as the present is concerned, so long as my frolics,—for I sometimes indulge in them, cost nobody anything except the *lambs*—I beg your pardon! you don't know that word; it's used on the Bourse—they will have no right to reproach me, and will still have a handsome fortune at my death. Your children can't say as much of their father, who gambols about, ruining his own son and my daughter.—"

The further she went, the further removed she was from her object.—

"You are very ill-disposed toward my husband, my dear Crevel, and yet you would be his best friend, if you had found his wife a weak woman.—"

She darted a burning glance at Crevel. But in that she was like Dubois, who under the table kicked the Regent too often,—she disguised her real character too much, and his former licentious thoughts returned with such force to the mind of the Regency-perfumer, that he said to himself:

"Would she like to revenge herself on Hulot?—Does she think better of me as mayor than as National Guardsman?—Women are so odd!—"

And he struck an attitude in his second manner, looking at the baroness with a Regency expression.

"One would say," she continued, "that you were revenging yourself upon him for a virtue which held out against you, for a woman whom you loved enough to—to buy her," she added in an undertone.

"For a divine creature," replied Crevel with a meaning smile at the baroness, who lowered her eyes, the lashes wet with tears; "for you have swallowed many a mortfication these last three years,—eh, my dear?"

"Don't speak of my suffering, *dear Crevel;* it has been too much for mere human strength. Ah! if you still loved me you might lift me out of the abyss I am in! Yes, I am in hell! The regicides whose flesh was torn with red-hot pincers, who were drawn and quartered, were on a bed of roses compared to me, for only their bodies were dismembered, and my heart has been torn apart by four horses!—"

Crevel's hand left the armhole of his waistcoat, he laid his hat on the work-table, he abandoned his attitude, he smiled! His smile was so idiotic that the baroness misinterpreted it and took it for an expression of kindliness.

"You see before you a woman, not in despair, but suffering the death agony of honor, and resolved to do anything, *my dear*, to prevent crimes.—"

Fearing lest Hortense should come, she bolted her door; then threw herself impulsively at Crevel's feet, took his hand and kissed it.

"Be my savior!" said she.

She imagined that there might be some generous fibres in his tradesman's heart, and had a sudden gleam of hope that she might obtain the two hundred thousand francs without dishonoring herself.

"You who sought to buy my virtue, buy my heart!—" she continued, gazing wildly into his face. "Trust to my woman's probity, to my honor, well-known to you to be unswerving! Be my friend! Save a whole family from ruin, from disgrace, from despair; save it from wallowing in a slough where the mire will be made of blood! Oh! do not ask me to explain!—" she exclaimed at a gesture from Crevel, who tried to speak. "Above all don't say to me: 'I told you so!' like the fortunate friends of misfortune. Come!—obey her whom you once loved, a woman whose groveling at your feet is perhaps the height of nobleness; ask nothing at her hands, but expect everything from her gratitude!—No, give me nothing; but lend to me, lend to her whom you called Adeline!—"

At this point the tears came in such abundance, and Adeline sobbed so bitterly, that they moistened Crevel's gloves. The words: "I must have two hundred thousand francs!" were hardly distinguishable in the torrent of tears, just as the stones, thrown into an Alpine torrent swollen by the melting snow, however large, make no sound.

Such is the inexperience of virtue. Vice asks for nothing, as we have seen in the case of Madame Marneffe, but leads one on to offer everything. Women of that stamp do not become exacting until the time comes when they have made themselves indispensable, or when it is a question with them of making all they can out of a man, as is done with a quarry where the stone is becoming scarce, *in ruins*, the quarrymen call it. When he heard the words: "two hundred thousand francs!" Crevel understood the whole thing. He gallantly raised the baroness from the floor with this insolent remark: "Come, let's be calm, *my little mother,*" which Adeline in her excitement did not hear. The scene changed. Crevel became, to use his own expression, master of the situation. The enormity of the amount made such a strong impression upon him, that his keen emotion on seeing this lovely woman in tears at his feet melted away. Moreover, however angelic and saintlike a woman may be, when she weeps hot tears, her beauty disappears. The Madame Marneffes snivel a little sometimes, as we have seen; they allow a tear or two to glide down their cheeks; but as for melting away in tears and making their eyes and nose red!—they never make such a mistake as that.

"Come, *my child*, be calm, *sapristi!*" said Crevel taking lovely Madame Hulot's hands in his and patting them. "Why do you ask me for two hundred thousand francs? What do you propose to do with them? who are they for?"

"Don't ask me for any explanation, but give them to me!—You will have saved the lives of three people, and our children's honor."

"And do you suppose, my little mother," said Crevel, "that you will find a man in Paris, who, on the word of a woman who is almost mad, will go, *hic et nunc*, here and now, and take from a drawer or from somewhere else, no matter where, two hundred thousand francs, which are simmering softly there, waiting for her to come and skim them? Is that all you know of life and business, my beauty? —Your people are very ill, send them the sacraments; for none in Paris, except Her Divine Highness Madame la Banque, the illustrious Nucingen, or some miser who loves gold as madly as we other men love a woman, can perform such a miracle! The Civil List, however civil it may be, the Civil List itself would request you to call again to-morrow. Every one puts his money out at interest and does his best to make a profit. You make a mistake, dear angel, if you think that Louis-Philippe reigns, and he makes no such mistake himself. He knows, as we all do, that above the Charter there is the holy, the venerated, the substantial, the lovable, the gracious, the lovely, the noble, the young, the omnipotent hundred-sou piece! Now, my lovely angel, money demands interest, and is always busy collecting it! 'God of the Jews, thou rulest!' said the great Racine. In short, it's the immortal allegory of the golden calf!—In the time of Moses, there was stock-jobbing in the desert! We have gone back to the biblical days! The golden calf was the first known register of public loans," he continued. "You live far too much on Rue Plumet, my Adeline! The Egyptians owed the Hebrews enormous sums for borrowed money, and they did not run after God's people but after their capital."

He looked at the baroness with an expression which said: "What a witty creature I am!"

"You don't realize the love of every citizen for his "little-all!" he resumed after this brief pause. "I beg your pardon. Mark well what I say! Try to grasp my argument. You want two hundred thousand francs?—No one can let you have them without changing investments. Reckon it up!—In order to get two hundred thousand francs *cash*, one must sell what brings in about seven thousand francs a year at three per cent. Well, you couldn't get your money in less than two days. That's the shortest possible time. To induce anyone to part with a fortune—for two hundred thousand francs is the whole fortune of many people!—

you ought surely to tell him where it's all going, for what purpose—"

"My dear, kind Crevel, the lives of two men are at stake, one of whom will die of grief, the other will kill himself! And it concerns me, too, for I shall go mad! Am I not partly so already?"

"Not so mad after all," said he taking Madame Hulot by the knees; "Père Crevel has his price, since you have deigned to think of him, my angel."

"It seems that one must allow herself to be taken by the knees!" thought the saintly, noble woman, hiding her face in her hands.—"You offered me a fortune before," she said with a blush.

"Ah! my little lady, that was three years ago!—" retorted Crevel. "Oh! you are lovelier than I have ever seen you!" he cried, seizing the baroness's arm and pressing it against his heart. "*Sapristi!* you have a good memory, dear child.—Oh! well, just see what a mistake you made in playing the prude! for the three hundred thousand francs you so nobly refused are in another woman's purse. I loved you and I love you still; but let us go back to three years ago. When I said to you: 'I shall have you!' what was my motive? I wanted to be revenged on that villain Hulot. Now, my beauty, your husband took for his mistress a jewel of a woman, a pearl, an artful little minx, twenty-three years old at that time, for she's twenty-six to-day. I concluded that it would be more amusing, more complete, more Louis XV., more Maréchal de Richelieu, more Corsican, to whisk that charming creature away from him; besides she never loved Hulot, and for three years she has been mad over your humble servant.—"

As he harangued thus, Crevel, from whose hands the baroness had withdrawn hers, struck his attitude once more. He clung to his armholes, and flapped his arms against his sides like a pair of wings, thinking that he was a desirable and charming object. He seemed to say: "This is the man you turned out of doors!"

"So there we are, my dear child; I had my revenge and your husband knew it. I proved to him categorically that he was duped, what we call *hoist with his own petard.*—Madame Marneffe is *my* mistress; if Monsieur Marneffe die, she will be my wife.—"

Madame Hulot stared at Crevel almost wild-eyed.

"Hector knew that?"

"And he went back to her!" replied Crevel, "and I put up with it, because Valérie wanted to be the wife of a chief of bureau; but she swore to me that she would so arrange matters that he should be so thoroughly *mauled* that he would not appear again. And my little duchess—for the woman was born a duchess, on my word of honor!—has kept her word. She has given your Hector back to you, madame, as she wittily said, *virtuous in perpetuity!*—It was a kindly lesson, after all, and the baron has had some harsh ones; he won't keep any more ballet-dancers nor women *comme il faut;* he is radically cured, for he's been rinsed out like a beer-glass. If you had listened to Crevel instead of humiliating him, instead of showing him the door, you would have four hundred thousand francs, for my revenge has cost me all that. But I shall get my money back, I trust, at Marneffe's death.—I have banked on my future. That's the secret of my prodigalities. I have solved the problem of how to be an aristocrat cheaply."

"You would give your daughter such a stepmother?—" cried Madame Hulot.

"You don't know Valérie, madame," replied Hulot gravely, striking an attitude in his earlier manner. "She is well-born, and at the same time a woman who enjoys the highest consideration. For instance the vicar of the parish dined with her yesterday. We have presented the church with a superb monstrance, for she is very devout. Oh! she's a clever, bright, delightful, well-informed woman, and she has everything on her side. As for myself, dear Adeline, I owe the charming creature everything: she has sharpened my wits, as you see, and refined my language; she corrects my flights of fancy and suggests words and ideas to me. I no longer offend propriety by my remarks. People see a great change in me; you must have noticed it. In short she has aroused my ambition. I might be a deputy and I wouldn't make a fool of myself, for I consult my Egeria in the most trivial matters. All the great politicians, including Numa, our present illustrious minister, have had their Cumean Sibyl. Valérie receives a score or so of deputies, she is becoming very influential, and now that she's going to take up her abode in a delightful house with a carriage of her own, she'll be one of the unseen sovereigns of Paris. Such a woman as she, is a great one to get ahead! Ah! I have often thanked you for your harsh treatment!—"

"This would make one doubt the virtue of God Himself," said Adeline, indignation having dried her tears. "But no, the divine justice must hover over that head!—"

"You don't know the world, fair lady," retorted Crevel the great politician, deeply hurt. "The world, my Adeline, loves success! Tell me, does it come in search of your sublime virtue, which you appraise at two hundred thousand francs?"

These words fairly made Madame Hulot shudder, and she was taken with another attack of nervous trembling. She realized that the retired perfumer was taking his revenge on her in a despicable way, as he had taken his revenge on Hulot; her heart rose in disgust, and she was so choked by that sentiment that she could not speak.

"Money!—always money!" she exclaimed at last.

"You touched me deeply," rejoined Crevel, reminded by that exclamation of the woman's abasement, "when I saw you weeping here at my feet!—You don't believe me perhaps, but if I had had my pocket-book it would have been at your service. Tell me, must you have that amount?—"

At this question, pregnant with two hundred thousand francs, Adeline forgot all the outrageous insults of this cheap aristocrat, in face of this enticing hint of possible success held out with such Machiavelian ingenuity by Crevel, who simply wished to get to the bottom of Adeline's secrets in order to laugh over them with Valérie.''

"Oh! I will do anything!" cried the wretched woman. "Monsieur, I will sell myself,—I will become, if need be, a Valérie."

"That would be a difficult thing for you to do," rejoined Crevel. "Valérie is perfection in her class. My little mother, twenty-five years of virtue always repel a man, like a disease not properly cared for. And your virtue has grown sadly musty here, my dear child. But I'll show you how much I love you. I am going to let you have your two hundred thousand francs."

Adeline seized Crevel's hand and pressed it against her heart, unable to utter a word, while tears of joy stood in her eyes.

"Oh! wait a bit! there'll be some work to do! I, for my part, am a high liver, a good sort of fellow, without prejudices, and I'm going to tell you frankly just how things stand. You want to be a Valérie—well and good. That isn't enough; you must have a *gogo*, a broker, a Hulot. I know an old fat retired grocer, no he's a hosier. He's a dull, thick-headed creature without an idea in his head; I am forming him and I don't know how soon he will be able to do me credit. My man's a deputy, vain as a peacock and an idiot; kept hitherto in the depths of the provinces by the tyranny of some sort of a creature in a turban, in absolute virginity so far as regards the pleasures and dissipations of Parisian life; but Beauvisage—his name is Beauvisage—is a millionaire, and he would give three hundred thousand francs for the love of a woman *comme il faut,* as I would have done three years ago, my dear little woman.—"Yes," he continued, thinking that he had accurately interpreted Adeline's gesture, "he's jealous of me, you see!—yes, jealous of my good fortune with Madame Marneffe, and he's just the boy to sell a good property to become the proprietor of a—"

"Enough, Monsieur Crevel!" said Madame Hulot, no longer disguising her disgust, and allowing her shame to appear upon her face. "I am punished now more severely than my sin required. My conscience, with such difficulty restrained by the iron hand of necessity, cries out to me at this last insult that such sacrifices are impossible. I have no pride left, I do not lose my temper as I used, and I will not say to you: 'Go!' after receiving this mortal blow. I have lost the right, for I have offered myself to you like a prostitute.—Yes," she continued, replying to a gesture of denial, "I have besmirched my life, hitherto pure, by a degrading purpose; and I have no excuse, I know!—I deserve all the insults with which you crush me! May God's will be done! If He desires the death of two beings who are worthy to go to Him, let them die; I will weep for them, I will pray for them! If He desires the humiliation of our family, let us bow our heads beneath His avenging sword, and kiss it, Christians that we are! I know how to expiate this momentary degradation, which will be the torment of my declining years. Monsieur, it is no longer Madame Hulot who speaks to you, but the poor, humble sinner, the Christian whose heart will contain henceforth but a single sentiment—repentance; and whose life will be given to charity and prayer. The power of my sin makes me the lowest of women and the first of penitents. You have been the means of my return to reason, and by the voice of God which now speaks within me, I thank you!—"

She was trembling with a nervous affection, which from that moment, never left her. Her sweet voice was in strong contrast to the feverish words of the woman who had resolved upon her own dishonor to save a family. The blood left her cheeks, she became pale as death, and her eyes were dry.

"Besides, I played my part very badly, did I not?" she resumed, looking at Crevel with an expression of such gentleness as the martyrs must have assumed when looking upon the proconsul. "True love, the holy and devoted love of a wife, has other pleasures than those which are sold in the market of prostitution!—But why these words?" said she, changing her tone and advancing one step further toward perfection; "they seem like sarcasm, and I have none in my heart! forgive me for them. Indeed, monsieur, it may have been only myself whom I wished to wound—"

The majesty of virtue, its celestial radiance, had swept away the momentary unchastity of the woman, and now, resplendent with the beauty which was all her own, she seemed vastly greater in Crevel's eyes. At that moment Adeline was as sublime as the figures of Religion, upheld by a cross, which the old Venetians painted; but she made manifest all the grandeur of her own misfortune and that of the Catholic Church, to which she turned for refuge like a wounded dove. Crevel was dazzled, abashed.

"Madame, I am at your service unconditionally!" said he in a burst of generosity. "We will look into the matter, and—What do you want?—is it the impossible?—I will do it. I will deposit consols at the Bank, and within two hours you shall have your money."

"My God, what a miracle!" exclaimed poor Adeline, falling on her knees.

She repeated a prayer with a fervor which affected Crevel so deeply that Madame Hulot saw tears in his eyes when she rose, having finished her prayer.

"Be my friend, monsieur!—" said she. "Your heart is kinder than your acts and your words. God gave you your heart, and you get your ideas from the world and your passions! Oh! I will love you dearly!" she cried with angelic warmth, in strange contrast with her wretched little coquetries.

"Don't tremble so," said Crevel.

"Am I trembling?" asked the baroness, who had

not noticed the infirmity that had come upon her so rapidly.

"Yes, look," said Crevel, taking her arm and pointing out to her how it was shaking. "Come, madame," he added respectfully, "calm yourself; I am off to the Bank.—"

"Return quickly! Consider, my friend," said she, disclosing her secrets, "that it's a question of preventing the suicide of my poor Uncle Fischer, whom my husband has got into trouble; for I have confidence in you now and tell you everything! Oh! if we do not act in time, I know the maréchal so well, he is so sensitive that he would die very soon."

"I go then," said Crevel, kissing the baroness's hand. "But what has poor Hulot done?"

"He has stolen from the State!—"

"Oh! my God!—I fly, madame; I understand you now and admire you."

Crevel bent his knee, kissed the hem of Madame Hulot's dress, and disappeared, saying:

"I will see you again soon!"

*

Unluckily, on his way from Rue Plumet to his own quarters to get his certificates, Crevel passed through Rue Vanneau, and he could not resist the temptation to call upon his little duchess. His face still bore traces of emotion when he arrived. He entered Valérie's bedroom and found her having her hair dressed. She looked at Crevel in the glass, and like all women of her class, was put out, without knowing why, to see him under the influence of a strong emotion of which she was not the cause.

"What's the matter, my buck?" said she. "Is this the way for a man to come into his little duchess's room? I wouldn't be a duchess for you, monsieur, unless I was still your *little louloute*, old monster!"

Crevel replied with a sad smile, and pointed to Reine.

"Reine, my girl, enough for to-day; I'll finish my hair myself. Give me my Chinese silk dressing-gown, for *my gentleman* acts amazingly like *a Chinaman.*—"

Reine, a maiden whose face was punctured like a sieve, with the small-pox, and who seemed to have been made expressly for Valérie, exchanged a smile with her mistress, and brought the dressing-gown. Valérie removed her *peignoir*, appeared in her chemise, and in a moment was as comfortable in her dressing-gown as an adder under its tuft of grass.

"Madame is at home to no one?"

"What a question!" said Valérie.—"Come, my fat old puss, tell me, has the Left Bank gone down?"

"No."

"Somebody's overbid you for the house?"

"No."

"You don't believe you're the father of your little Crevel?"

"What nonsense!" replied the man who was sure that she loved him.

"Faith, I'm done then!" said Madame Marneffe. "When I ought to draw my friend's troubles out of him, as one draws the cork from a bottle of Bordeaux, I have to leave them all there.—Go away, you pre—"

"It's nothing," said Crevel. "I must have two hundred thousand francs in two hours."

"Oh! you'll find them! By the way, I haven't used the fifty thousand francs for the Hulot report, and I can ask Henri for fifty thousand."

"Henri! always Henri!—" cried Crevel.

"Do you think, you great fat budding Machiavel, that I'll send Henri away? Does France disarm her fleet?—Henri,—why he's the dagger hanging in its sheath on a nail. The boy," she continued, "helps me to find out whether you love me.—And you don't love me this morning!"

"I don't love you, Valérie!" cried Crevel; "I love you like a million!"

"That's not enough!—" she retorted, jumping on his knees and throwing her arms about his neck, as she might have clung to a *patera.* "I want to be loved like ten millions, like all the gold in the world, and more too. Henri would never stay with me five minutes without telling me what he has in his heart. Come, what's the matter, my chubby dear? Let's unload our little cargo.—Let's tell our *little louloute* everything, and do it quickly!"

She brushed Crevel's face with her hair and twisted his nose.

"Can a man have a nose like that," she went on, "and keep a secret from his Vava-lélé-ririe!—"

At *Vava,* the nose went to the right; at *lélé* to the left; at *ririe* it resumed its normal position.

"Well, I have just seen—"

Crevel checked himself and looked at Madame Marneffe.

"Valérie, my bijou, you must promise me on your honor,—our honor, you know?—not to repeat a word of what I am going to tell you."

"Stop there, mayor! I hold up my hand, see!—and my foot!"

She struck an attitude well calculated to make Crevel, as Rabelais says, *barefoot from his head to his heels,* so mischievous was she, and so sublime the charms half visible through the mists of fine lawn.

"I have just seen virtue in despair!"

"Does virtue ever despair?" said she, shaking her head and folding her arms à la Napoléon.

"It was poor Madame Hulot; she must have two hundred thousand francs! otherwise the maréchal and Père Fischer will blow their brains out; and as you are in a measure the cause of it all, my little duchess, I propose to repair the evil. Oh! I know her well, she's a saint, and she'll return it all."

At the words "Hulot" and "two hundred thousand francs," Valérie darted a glance between her long lashes, that gleamed like the flash of a cannon through its smoke.

"For God's sake what did the old lady do to arouse your pity? She showed you what? her—her religion?"

"Don't make fun of her, dear heart, for she's a perfect saint, a noble, pious woman, worthy of respect!—"

"So I am not worthy of respect, eh?" said Valérie, with a threatening glance at Crevel.

"I said nothing of the kind," he replied, realizing how much any eulogium of virtue must wound Madame Marneffe.

"I am pious, too," said Valérie, sitting down in an easy-chair; "but I don't make a trade of my religion, I go to church secretly."

She said no more, and paid no more attention to Crevel. Becoming excessively uneasy he went and posed in front of the chair in which she had thrown herself, and found her absorbed by the thoughts he had so idiotically awakened.

"Valérie, my little angel!—"

Absolute silence. An enigmatical tear was furtively wiped away.

"One word, my *louloute.*—"

"Monsieur!"

"What are you thinking about, my love?"

"Ah! Monsieur Crevel, I am thinking of the day of my first communion! How lovely I was! how pure! how like a saint!—immaculate!—Oh! if anyone had come to my mother that day and had said to her: 'Your daughter will be *a harlot,* she will deceive her husband. Some day a police officer will find her in a *petite maison;* she will sell herself to a Crevel to be false to a Hulot, two villainous old men,—' God help me! she'd have died before the end of the sentence, she loved me so dearly, poor woman."

"Calm yourself!"

"You don't know how much one must love a man to silence the remorse that gnaws at the heart of an adulteress. I am sorry Reine has gone; she'd have told you that she found me this morning with tears in my eyes and praying. You see, Monsieur Crevel, I don't make sport of religion. Did you ever hear me say a word I should not have said on that subject?"

Crevel shook his head.

"'I forbid people to speak of it in my presence.—I'll chatter away on any subject you please: kings, politics, finance, everything that society holds sacred, judges, marriage, love, young girls, old men!—But the Church!—and God!—Oh! I draw the line at that. I am well aware that I am doing wrong, that I am sacrificing my future to you.—And you don't even suspect the extent of my love!"

Crevel clasped his hands.

"Ah! you must look into my heart, and measure the depth of my convictions, to realize all that I sacrifice to you!—I feel within me the stuff of which Magdalens are made. Why, see how respectfully I treat the priests! Count up the presents I have made to the church. My mother brought me up in the Catholic faith, and I understand the power of God. We wicked creatures are the ones to whom he speaks in the most awful tones."

Valérie wiped away two tears which were rolling down her cheeks. Crevel was in dismay. She rose to her feet in a state of intense excitement.

"Calm yourself, my *louloute!*" said he; "you frighten me!"

Madame Marneffe fell upon her knees.

"My God! I am not bad at heart!" she cried, clasping her hands. "Deign to gather thy wandering sheep into the fold, strike her and wound her to rescue her from the hands which make of her an infamous adulteress; with joy she will hide her face upon thy shoulder! she will return to the fold the happiest of women!"

She rose and gazed at Crevel, and Crevel was afraid of her white eyes.

"And do you know, Crevel, there are times when I am afraid,—God's laws are enforced in this world as strictly as in the other. What consideration can

I expect at God's hands? His vengeance is wreaked upon the guilty in all sorts of ways; it borrows all the characteristics of misfortune. All the misfortunes which fools can not explain are expiations. That is what my mother told me on her death-bed, speaking of her old age.—And if I should lose you!" she added, seizing Crevel and embracing him with savage energy,—"oh it would kill me!"

Soon she released him, knelt again in front of her chair, clasped her hands—and in what a ravishing attitude—and repeated with incredible fervor the following prayer:

"And you, Sainte Valérie, my kindly patron saint, why do you not more frequently visit her bedside who was entrusted to your care? Oh! come to-night, as you came this morning, to inspire me with righteous thoughts, and I will leave the crooked path; like Magdalen I will renounce the empty joys, the factitious splendor of the world, yes, even the man I love so well!"

"My *louloute!*" said Crevel.

"There is no *louloute* now, monsieur!"

She turned about with the haughty air of a virtuous wife; and confronted him with a cold, dignified, indifferent face, her eyes wet with tears.

"Leave me," she said, repelling him. "What is my duty?—to devote myself to my husband. The man is dying, and what am I doing? I am deceiving him as he stands on the brink of the grave! He believes that your son is his.—I am going to tell him the truth, to begin by purchasing his forgiveness, before seeking God's. Let us part!—Adieu, Monsieur Crevel!—" she continued standing before him and offering him an ice-cold hand. "Adieu, my friend, we shall meet again only in a better world.—You are indebted to me for some enjoyment, very criminal, it is true; but now I long for,—yes, I will have your esteem."

Crevel was weeping copiously.

"You great donkey!" she burst out, with a shriek of infernal laughter, "that's the way your pious women go to work to do you out of a paltry two hundred thousand francs! And you talk about the Maréchal de Richelieu, the prototype of Lovelace, and then allow yourself to be taken in by such trumpery balderdash! as Steinbock says. I would screw two hundred thousand francs out of you if I wanted them, you great gaby!—So keep your money! If you have any too much, the too much belongs to me! If you give two sous to that respectable dame, who plays at piety because she's fifty-seven years old, we shall see each other no more, and you can take her for your mistress; you'll come back to me the next day all sore from her angular fondlings; and surfeited with her tears, her *skimpy* little caps, and her whimpering, which must make her favors resemble a heavy shower!—"

"The fact is," said Crevel, "that two hundred thousand francs is a tidy sum."

"These pious women have a hearty appetite!—Ah! *microscope!* they sell their sermons at a better price than we get for the rarest and most reliable thing on earth,—pleasure. And they write novels! No?—ah! but I know them, I've seen some of them in my mother's house! They think they're at liberty to do anything for the Church, for—Why, you ought to be ashamed of yourself, my buck! you, who are so little inclined to give—for you haven't given me two hundred thousand francs in all!"

"Oh yes!" said Crevel, "the little house alone will cost that."

"So you have four hundred thousand francs, have you?" she asked pensively.

"No."

"Very well, monsieur! you proposed to lend that old horror the two hundred thousand francs that were to pay for my house, did you? That's *lèse-louloute!*"

"But just listen to me!"

"If you were giving the money to some absurd philanthropical fad, you would be looked upon as a man of the future," said she warming to her subject, "and I would be the first to advise you to do it; for you're too innocent to write thick volumes on politics, that would make your reputation; you haven't style enough to write pamphlets filled with nothing at all; you might pose as other men do who are in your position, and who cover their names with glory by putting themselves at the head of some social, moral, national or general undertaking. Benevolence you've been anticipated in; it's thought but little of now.—Ex-convicts who meet with a better fate than poor, honest devils, are played out. I would like to see you think up something harder, something really useful, for your two hundred thousand francs. You would be talked about as if you were a *little blue cloak*, as a Montyon, and I should be proud of you! But to throw two hundred thousand francs into a holy-water vase, to loan them to a devotee abandoned by her husband for some reason or other—there's always a reason, you know, for am I abandoned, pray?—would be a crazy idea which, in these days, could take root nowhere else than in the skull of an ex-perfumer! It smells of his counting-house. Two days after you wouldn't dare look at yourself in your mirror! Go and deposit your money in the sinking-fund; hurry, for I won't receive you again without a receipt for the amount. Go! go at once and quickly!"

She pushed Crevel out of the room by the shoulders, when she saw avarice blooming again upon his face. When the outer door of the suite was secured, she said to herself:

"Lisbeth's more than revenged now!—What a pity she's at the old maréchal's; how we would have laughed! Aha! so the old lady wants to take the bread out of my mouth!—I'll give her a good shaking for you!"

*

Being obliged to occupy apartments in keeping with the highest military dignity, Maréchal Hulot had taken up his quarters in a superb mansion on Rue du Mont-Parnasse, where the establishments of several princes were located. Although he had hired the whole house he occupied only the ground-floor. When Lisbeth came to keep house for him she at once wanted to sub-let the first-floor, which, she said, would pay the whole rent, so that the count could have his own quarters for almost nothing; but the old soldier refused. For several months the maréchal's mind had been much troubled. He had divined his sister-in-law's distress; he suspected that things were going wrong without detecting the cause. The old fellow, usually so cheerful in his deafness, became taciturn; he imagined that his house would some day become a place of refuge for Baroness Hulot and her daughter, and he was reserving the first floor for them. Comte de Forzheim's moderate circumstances were so well known, that the Prince de Wissembourg, Minister of War, had insisted upon it that his old comrade should accept an allowance to defray the expense of setting up his establishment. Hulot used this allowance to furnish the ground-floor, where everything was in harmony with his rank, for, as he himself expressed it, he did not want his maréchal's baton in order to carry it on foot. The mansion having been the property of a Senator under the Empire, the salons on the ground-floor were decorated with great magnificence, all white and gold, with much carved work, and were well preserved. The maréchal had furnished them with handsome old furniture in keeping with the decorations. He kept a carriage in the carriage-house, with the two crossed batons painted on the panels, and he hired horses when he had to go out in state, to the ministry or the château, for some ceremonial, or some holiday. For thirty years he had had as a servant an old soldier, now sixty years old, whose sister was his cook, so that he was able to save something like ten thousand francs a year, which he added to a little hoard intended for Hortense. Every day the old man went on foot from Rue du Mont-Parnasse to Rue Plumet by the boulevard; every veteran, when he saw him approaching, invariably drew up as if on parade and saluted him, and the maréchal as invariably rewarded him with a smile.

"Who is that man you drew yourself up so straight for?" a young mechanic one day asked an old captain of the Invalides.

"I'll tell you, boy," was the reply.

The young fellow assumed the pose of a man who resigns himself to listen to a garrulous old dotard.

"In 1809," said the veteran, "we were covering the flank of the *Grande Armée*, commanded by the Emperor, who was marching upon Vienna. We came to a bridge defended by a triple battery of cannons terraced on a sort of cliff, three redoubts one above the other, which raked the bridge. We were under Maréchal Massena. That man yonder was colonel of the grenadiers of the Guard, and I was marching with — Our columns were on one side of the river, the redoubts on the other. Three times they attacked the bridge and three times they were driven back. 'Send for Hulot!' said the maréchal; 'no one but he and his men can swallow that tid-bit.' We came up. The last general to be driven back from the bridge stopped Hulot under fire to tell him how to go to work, and he blocked up the road. 'I don't need advice, but room to pass,' said the general coolly, crossing the bridge at the head of his column—And then, hurrah! thirty guns opening fire on us—"

"Ah! bless my soul!" cried the workman, "that must have been where you got those crutches!"

"If you had heard him say that in the coolest way, as I did, my boy, you would salute that man till your hat touched the ground! That little affair isn't so well known as the Bridge of Arcola, but it was even finer perhaps. And in due course we were in among the batteries with Hulot. Honor to those who remained there!" exclaimed the officer removing his hat. "The *kaiserlicks* were taken by surprise. So the Emperor made the old man you see a count; he honored us all in our leader, and these new fellows have done very well to make him a maréchal."

"Vive le maréchal!" exclaimed the workman.

"'Oh! you can shout as loud as you please; the maréchal's deaf from listening to the cannon."

This anecdote will give an idea of the respect with which the veterans treated Maréchal Hulot, whose unchanging republican opinions won for him the popular regard throughout the quarter.

It was a heart-rending spectacle to see that pure and calm and noble heart suffering so intensely. The baroness could only lie and, with a woman's skill, conceal the whole terrible truth from her brother-in-law. During this disastrous morning, the maréchal, who like all men of his years slept but little, had obtained some information as to his brother's situation from Lisbeth, by promising to marry her as the reward of her indiscretion. Every one will understand the old maid's delight in allowing confidences to be extorted from her, which she had fully intended to make to her future spouse ever since she came beneath his roof; for in this way she would the better assure her marriage.

"Your brother is incurable!" Lisbeth shouted into the maréchal's good ear.

The Lorrainer's strong, distinct voice made it possible for her to talk with the old man. She tired out her lungs, so intent was she upon demonstrating to her future consort that he would never be deaf with her.

"'He has had three mistresses," said the old man," and he had an Adeline!—Poor Adeline!"

"If you take my advice," cried Lisbeth, "you

will use your influence with the Prince de Wissembourg to obtain an honorable position for my cousin; she will need it, for the baron's salary is assigned for three years."

"I will go to the department," he said, "see the maréchal, find out what he thinks about my brother, and ask his active protection for my sister. The idea of finding a place worthy of her!"

"The ladies who distribute alms in Paris have formed benevolent associations with the archbishop's concurrence; they need women to serve as inspectors, who are employed to find out those really in need, and are handsomely paid. Such duties would suit my dear Adeline, they would be after her own heart."

"Send for the horses," said the maréchal; "I am going to dress. I'll go to Neuilly if necessary!"

"How he loves her! So I am to find her in my way, always and everywhere!" muttered the Lorrainer.

Lisbeth was already queen of the household, but out of the maréchal's sight. She had inspired the three servants with dread. She had taken unto herself a maid, and exerted her old-maid energy in requiring a strict account of everything, peering into everything, and seeking to promote her dear maréchal's well-being in every respect. As strong a republican as her spouse that was to be, Lisbeth pleased him mightily with her democratic notions, and she flattered him too with amazing talent; so that within the last two weeks, the maréchal, finding that he lived better, and was as carefully looked after as a child by its mother, had at last concluded that Lisbeth was part of his dream.

"My dear maréchal," she screamed, accompanying him out to the steps, "put up the windows; don't sit in a draught, for my sake!—"

The maréchal, who had never been coddled, old bachelor that he was, smiled at Lisbeth as he drove away, although his heart was broken.

At that very moment Baron Hulot left the offices of the War Department, and bent his steps to the cabinet of the Maréchal Prince de Wissembourg, who had sent for him. Although there was nothing extraordinary in the mere fact of the minister's sending for one of his directors-general, Hulot's conscience was so ill at ease, that Mitouflet's face seemed strangely cold and forbidding.

"How's the Prince, Mitouflet?" he asked, closing his office, and overtaking the usher, who had gone on before.

"He must have a rod in pickle for you, Monsieur le Baron, for his voice and look and face are set for storms."

Hulot turned pale and said no more; he passed through the reception-room and the salons, and reached the door of the cabinet, with his heart beating tumultuously. The maréchal, at this time seventy years old, with snow-white hair, and the swarthy face common to men of his age, commanded respect by a brow of such amplitude that the imagination could see a whole battle-field thereon.

Beneath that snow-laden cupola, and shadowed by the very pronounced projection of two overhanging eyebrows, gleamed eyes of a Napoleonic blue, ordinarily sad, because of the bitter thoughts and regrets reflected therein. This rival of Bernadotte had hoped to find repose upon a throne. But those eyes became two awe-inspiring lightning flashes when any intense emotion called on them for expression. The voice, almost always cavernous, at such times came forth in sharp, strident tones. In his wrath the prince became a soldier once more, and spoke the language of Sub-lieutenant Cottin; he paid no heed to anything or anybody.

Hulot d'Ervy espied the old lion, whose hair was as scanty as a horse's mane, standing near the fire-place with his back against the mantel, his eyebrows drawn together, and his eyes apparently gazing into space.

"I am here at your command, my prince," said Hulot gracefully and with an unconcerned demeanor.

The maréchal gazed fixedly at the director without speaking a word while he walked from the door to within a few steps of him. This leaden glance was like the glance of God; Hulot could not meet it, but lowered his eyes in confusion.

"He knows all," he thought.

"Has your conscience nothing to say to you?" asked the maréchal in his deep, grave voice.

"It tells me, my prince, that I probably did wrong to make *razzias* in Algeria without mentioning it to you. After forty-five years of service I am without fortune, at my age and with my tastes. You know the principles that guide the four hundred elect of France. These gentlemen are envious of every office-holder; they pare down the salaries of ministers, that tells the story!—go and ask them for money for an old servant!—What is one to expect from people who pay in such niggardly fashion as they pay the magistracy to-day? who give thirty sous a day to mechanics in the port of Toulon, when it's a physical impossibility to live there for less than forty sous for a family? who do not reflect on the atrocity of paying clerks six hundred, a thousand, and twelve hundred francs a year in Paris, and who want our places for themselves when the salary is forty thousand?—lastly, who refuse to give up to the crown a parcel of crown-property, confiscated to the crown in 1830,—and a purchase made with Louis the Sixteenth's money at that!—when they were asked to do it for the benefit of a needy prince!—If you had no fortune, prince, they would leave you, as they have my brother, high and dry, with nothing but your salary, without remembering that you saved the *Grande Armée*, with me by your side, in the marshy plains of Poland."

"You have robbed the State! you have put yourself in a position where you're liable to be dragged before the Assize Court, as the cashier of the Treasury was," exclaimed the maréchal, "and you take it as flippantly as this?"

"But what a difference, monseigneur!" cried

Hulot. "Have I plunged my hands in a treasure-chest that was placed in my charge?"

"When a man commits such infamous crimes," said the maréchal, "he is guilty twice over, occupying the position you occupy, if he does things bunglingly. You have compromised most shamefully, the responsible administration of our department, which hitherto has been the purest in Europe! —And that, monsieur, for two hundred thousand francs and a strumpet!—" roared the maréchal in a voice of thunder. "You are a Councilor of State, and the private soldier who sells the property of his regiment is punished with death. Listen to what Colonel Pourin of the Second Lancers told me one day. At Saverne one of his men fell in love with a little Alsatian girl, who was very anxious to have a shawl; the hussy was so persistent that the lancer, who was on the point of being promoted to be sergeant-major after twenty years' service, and was the pride of his regiment, sold the company property in order to give her the shawl. Do you know what the lancer did, Baron d'Ervy? He pounded up the glass out of his window and ate it, and died of the trouble in the hospital, in eleven hours.—Do your best to die of apoplexy, so that we can save your honor."

The baron looked at the old war-horse, with haggard eyes; and the maréchal, observing his expression, which betrayed a coward, felt the color mount to his cheeks, and his eyes gleamed.

"Would you abandon me?" stammered Hulot.

At that moment Maréchal Hulot, having learned that his brother and the minister were closeted together, took the liberty of walking in, and went as a deaf man would, straight to the prince.

"Oh!" cried the hero of the Poland campaign, "I know what you have come for, my old comrade!—But it's all useless."

"Useless?—" repeated Maréchal Hulot, who heard only the last word.

"Why, yes, you have come to speak in your brother's behalf; but do you know what your brother is?"

"My brother?—" demanded the deaf man.

"Well, he's a damned scoundrel, unworthy of your affection!" cried the maréchal.

And his wrath caused his eyes to send forth lightning-like glances, similar to those with which Napoléon shattered men's minds and brains.

"You lie, Cottin!" retorted Maréchal Hulot, pale as death. "Throw away your bâton as I do mine! —I am at your service."

The prince walked up to his old comrade, gazed earnestly in his face, and said in his ear as he pressed his hands:

"Are you a man?"

"You shall see."

"Well then, be strong! for you have to endure the greatest misfortune that can happen to you."

The prince turned, took a bundle of papers from his table, and put it into Maréchal Hulot's hands.

"Read!" he shouted.

The Comte de Forzheim read the following letter, which was within the package:

"TO HIS EXCELLENCY THE PRESIDENT OF THE COUNCIL.

"*Confidential.*

"ALGIERS, * * * *

"MY DEAR PRINCE:

"We have an extremely unpleasant business on our hands, as you will see by the documents I send you herewith:

"In brief, Baron Hulot d'Ervy sent one of his uncles to the province of Oran to dabble in grain and forage, and furnished him with a storekeeper for confederate. This storekeeper confessed, in order to make himself notorious, and ended by running away. The king's attorney pushed the affair somewhat roughly, seeing only two subordinates concerned; but Johann Fischer, your director-general's uncle, finding that he was on the point of being brought before the Court of Assizes, stabbed himself in prison with a nail.

"That would have been the end of the incident, had not that upright and respectable man, who was probably deceived both by his nephew and his confederate, undertaken to write to Baron Hulot. His letter, which fell into the hands of the prosecuting authorities, so astounded the king's attorney, that he came to me. The arrest and prosecution of a Councilor of State, a director-general, who has such a record of faithful and valuable service,—for he saved us all after the Bérésina by reorganizing the administration,—would be such a terrible blow, that I caused all the papers to be sent to me.

"Must the affair take its course? Or, the principal apparent culprit being dead, shall we stifle the prosecution by convicting the storekeeper by default?

"The *procureur-général* consents that the papers be sent to you; and as Baron d'Ervy has his domicile at Paris, the prosecution will properly be carried on in your Royal Court.

We have invented this method, somewhat devious, I admit, of getting rid of the difficulty for the moment.

"But, my dear maréchal, make up your mind promptly. There is already too much gossip about this deplorable business, which would be a vastly more serious matter for us, if the complicity of the principal culprit, who is as yet known only to the king's attorney, the examining magistrate, the *procureur-général* and myself, should be bruited abroad."

The paper fell from Maréchal Hulot's hands; he glanced at his brother and saw that it was useless to examine the other papers; but he took out Johann Fischer's letter, and handed it to him after running his eye over it.

"FROM THE PRISON AT ORAN.

"My nephew, when you read this letter I shall have ceased to live.

"Have no fear, for they will find no evidence against you. With me dead and your jesuit of a Chardin out of the way, the prosecution will come to an end. The face of our Adeline, made happy by you, makes death very sweet to me. You need not send the two hundred thousand francs. Adieu.

"This letter will be handed you by a prisoner whom I think I can trust.

"JOHANN FISCHER."

"I beg your pardon," said Maréchal Hulot, with touching pride, to the Prince de Wissembourg.

"Come, come, let things be as always between us, Hulot!" replied the minister pressing his old friend's hand.—"The poor lancer killed nobody but himself," he added, with a withering glance at Hulot d'Ervy.

"How much have you taken?" the Comte de Forzheim sternly demanded of his brother.

"Two hundred thousand francs."

"My dear friend," said the comte, addressing the minister, "you shall have the two hundred thousand francs within forty-eight hours. It shall never be said that a man bearing the name of Hulot cheated the public out of a sou."

"What childish nonsense!" said the maréchal. "I know where the two hundred thousand francs are, and I propose to compel restitution.—Send in your resignation, and ask to be placed on the retired list!" he continued, tossing a double sheet of foolscap across the table to where the Councilor of State had taken a seat, for his legs refused to support him. "Your prosecution would disgrace us all, so I have obtained the consent of the Council of Ministers to act as I am acting. As you accept life without honor, without my esteem, a life of degradation, you shall have the retiring pension which is your due. But blot yourself out of everybody's memory."

He rang.

"Is Marneffe here?"

"Yes, monseigneur," said the usher.

"Send him to me."

"You and your wife," cried the minister as Marneffe entered, "have designedly ruined Baron d'Ervy here."

"Monsieur le Ministre, I beg your pardon, but we are very poor; I have only my salary to live on, and I have two children, the last one of whom will have been brought into my family by Baron Hulot."

"What a gallows-bred face!" said the prince to Maréchal Hulot.—"Enough of your snivelling," he continued; "you will return two hundred thousand francs, or go to Algeria."

"But, *Monsieur le Ministre*, you don't know my wife; she has spent it all. Monsieur le Baron invited six people to dinner every day.—They spent fifty thousand a year at my house."

"Go," said the minister in the thundering tone with which he sounded the charge in the midst of a battle; "you will receive notice of your transfer in two hours. Go."

"I prefer to resign," said Marneffe impudently; "for it's too much to be what I am, and be beaten; I shouldn't be satisfied."

And he left the room.

"What an impudent rascal!" said the prince.

Maréchal Hulot, who had remained standing throughout this scene, motionless as a statue and pale as a corpse, covertly glancing at his brother, took the prince's hand, and said again:

"In forty-eight hours the material wrong will be repaired; but honor!—Adieu, maréchal! it's the last blow that kills.—Yes, it will kill me," he whispered.

"Why the devil did you come this morning?" replied the prince, deeply moved.

"I came on his wife's account," replied the comte, pointing to Hector; "she is without bread,—now more than ever."

"He has his retiring pension!"

"It's assigned!"

"He must have the very devil in him!" said the prince, with a shrug. "What sort of a love draught do these women give you to take your mind away?" he asked the baron. "How could you, knowing as you do the minute exactness with which the French government makes a record of everything, requires reports of everything and uses up reams of paper in verifying the receipt or disbursement of a few centimes,—you, who used to deplore the necessity of obtaining a hundred signatures for the merest trifles, to liberate a soldier, or buy a curry-comb,—how could you hope to conceal such a theft for any length of time? And the newspapers? And the men who envy you? And the men who'd like a chance to steal? Do the hussies take away your common sense? do they put walnut-shells over your eyes? or are you made differently from us? You should leave the government the minute you cease to be a man, and become a mass of sentiment! If you have been guilty of so many idiotic performances in addition to your crime, you'll end,—I don't want to tell you where."

"Promise me to look out for her, Cottin, won't you?—" said the Comte de Forzheim, who heard nothing of what was said, and was thinking of his sister-in-law alone.

"Never fear!" said the minister.

"Very well; thanks, and adieu!—Come, monsieur," he said to his brother.

The prince cast an apparently unmoved glance at the two brothers, so strongly contrasted in attitude, in build and character, the brave man and the coward, the man of rigid virtue and the voluptuary, the upright man and the peculator,—and he said to himself:

"That dastard will not know enough to die! and my poor, incorruptible Hulot has death in his pocket!"

He sat down at his desk and resumed his perusal of the despatches from Africa, with a gesture which expressed at once the sang-froid of the brave captain, and the profound pity caused by the sight of a battle-field; for there is no class of men so tender-hearted in reality, as are the soldiers, who seem so unfeeling, because familiarity with war imparts to them the cold, unmoved demeanor that is so essential on the battle-field.

The next morning some of the newspapers contained the following articles under various headings:

"Monsieur le Baron Hulot d'Ervy has asked to be retired. The irregularities in the accounts of the Algerian administration, which have been disclosed by the death of one clerk and the flight of another, had much to do with the step taken by this prominent member of the administration. Upon being informed of the crimes committed by employés, in whom unfortunately he had placed his confidence, Monsieur le Baron Hulot was stricken with paralysis in the minister's cabinet.

"Monsieur Hulot d'Ervy, the brother of the maréchal, has been in the service of the nation forty-five years. His present resolution, which he has been urged to reconsider, but to no purpose, is viewed with much regret by all those who know

Monsieur Hulot, whose private qualities equal his administrative talents. No one has forgotten the devoted service of the Commissary-in-Chief of the Imperial Guard at Warsaw, nor the marvelous activity with which he organized the different branches of the army hastily got together by Napoléon in 1815.

"Another of the glories of the Imperial era is about to leave the stage. Since 1830 Monsieur le Baron Hulot has constantly been one of the indispensable luminaries in the Council of State and the Ministry of War."

"ALGIERS.—The affair known as the forage affair, to which certain newspapers have attributed an absurdly disproportionate importance, is concluded by the death of the principal culprit. Monsieur Johann Wisch committed suicide in prison, and his confederate has fled; but he will be convicted by default.

"Wisch, formerly an army contractor, was an honest man and highly esteemed, and could not endure the thought that he had been the dupe of Chardin, the fugitive storekeeper."

And among the Parisian news appeared the following:

"Monsieur le Maréchal, Minister of War, to avoid all future irregularity, has determined to create a bureau of subsistence in Africa. Monsieur Marneffe, chief of one of the bureaus, is appointed to organize this new department."

"The question of the succession to Baron Hulot excites the keenest rivalry. The directorship has been promised, so it is said, to Monsieur le Comte Martial de la Roche-Hugon, a deputy and brother-in-law of Monsieur le Comte de Rastignac. Monsieur Massol, Master of Requests, will be appointed Councilor of State, and Monsieur Claude Vignon Master of Requests."

Of all varieties of *canards*, the most dangerous to opposition newspapers is the official canard. However shrewd journalists may be, they are sometimes the dupes, voluntary or involuntary, of the skill of those men, who have risen, like Claude Vignon, from the newspaper office to the exalted regions of power. The newspaper, it may be said, can be put down by the newspaper man, and by no one else. So we might say, paraphrasing Voltaire:

The news of Paris is simply what a vain people think.

*

Maréchal Hulot drove back to his own house with his brother, who sat in the front seat of the carriage, respectfully leaving the back seat to his elder. The two did not exchange a word. Hector was completely crushed. The maréchal sat in deep thought, like a man who was collecting all his forces and binding them together to sustain a crushing weight. When they reached the house he led the way to his study, without a word but with an imperative gesture. The comte had received from the Emperor Napoléon a superb pair of pistols from the factory at Versailles; he took the case, on which this inscription was engraved: *Presented by the Emperor Napoléon to General Hulot,* from the secretary in which he kept it, and showed it to his brother.

"There's your doctor," he said.

Lisbeth, who was peeping through the half-opened door, ran out to the carriage, and ordered the coachman to drive at full speed to Rue Plumet. In about twenty minutes she brought back the baroness, telling her on the way of the maréchal's threat to his brother.

The comte, meanwhile, without looking at his brother, rang for his factotum, the old soldier who had been in his service thirty years.

"Beau-Pied," said he, "bring my notary here, also Comte Steinbock, my niece Hortense, and the transfer clerk from the Treasury. It is half-past ten and I must have them all here at noon. Take carriages,—and go *quicker than that!*"—he added, resorting to a republican phrase which at one time was often in his mouth.

And he made the awe-inspiring grimace which used to keep his soldiers attentive to their duties when he was searching the thickets of Brittany in 1799.—See *The Chouans.*—

"You shall be obeyed, maréchal," said Beau-Pied, putting the back of his hand to his forehead.

Without paying any heed to his brother, the veteran returned to his cabinet, took a key that was concealed in a secretary, and opened a casket made of malachite laid upon steel, a present from the Emperor Alexander. By order of the Emperor Napoléon, he had gone to return to the Russian Emperor certain private property taken at the battle of Dresden, in exchange for which Napoléon hoped to obtain Vandamme. The Czar rewarded General Hulot handsomely by the gift of this casket, and said to him that he hoped to be able some day to perform a similar act of courtesy to the Emperor of the French,—but he kept Vandamme. The Imperial arms of Russia in gold were on the cover, and all the trimmings of the box were gold. The maréchal counted the bank-notes and gold, which the casket contained; he possessed one hundred and fifty-two thousand francs! He allowed a gesture of satisfaction to escape him. At that moment Madame Hulot entered in a state to move even political judges to compassion. She threw herself upon Hector, glancing from the box of pistols to the maréchal, with a wild look in her eyes.

"What have you against your brother? What has my husband done to you?" she demanded in so piercing a voice that the maréchal heard it.

"He has disgraced us all!" replied the veteran of the Republic, reopening one of his wounds by the effort. "He has stolen from the State! He has made my name odious; he makes me long to die, he has killed me.—I have strength enough left to make restitution and no more!—I have been humiliated before the Condé of the Republic, before the man whom I esteem above all others, and to whom I unjustly gave the lie,—the Prince de Wissembourg!—Is all that nothing? That's his account with his country!"

He wiped away a tear.

"And now for his family!" he continued. "He snatches from your mouths the bread I was saving for you, the fruit of the savings of thirty years, the hoard amassed by the old soldier's privations! There's what I intended for you!" he added, pointing to the bank-notes. "He has killed his uncle Fischer, a noble, worthy son of Alsace, who could not, as he can, endure the thought of a stain upon his peasant's name. And last of all, God with unspeakable kindness allowed him to make choice of an angel among all the women in the world! he had the incredible good fortune to take for his wife an Adeline! and he has betrayed her, he has made her drink the cup of sorrow, he has deserted her for strumpets, for street-walkers, for dancing-girls, actresses, Josephas, Cadines, Marneffes!—And that's the man whom I looked upon as my child, who was my pride!—Begone, unhappy man, if you accept the infamous life you have made for yourself, leave this house! I haven't the strength to curse a brother I have loved so dearly; I am as weak where he is concerned as you are, Adeline; but let me never see his face again. I forbid him to attend my funeral, to follow my coffin. May he have the shame of crime, if he has no remorse."

The maréchal, deadly pale, fell upon the couch in his study, exhausted by this solemn harangue. And, for the first time in his life perhaps, two tears fell from his eyes and made a furrow down his cheeks.

"My poor uncle Fischer!" cried Lisbeth with a handkerchief at her eyes.

"Brother!" said Adeline, kneeling at the maréchal's feet, "live for me! Help me in the task I will undertake of reconciling Hector to life, of making him atone for his sins!"

"He!" cried the maréchal; "if he lives, he's not at the end of his crimes yet! A man who has failed to appreciate an Adeline, and who has extinguished in his heart those sentiments which make the true republican, the love of country, of his family, and of the poor, which I strove to inculcate in him,—that man is a monster, a hog.—Take him away if you still love him, for I hear a voice within me crying to me to load my pistols and blow his brains out! By killing him I should save you all, and I should save him from himself."

The old maréchal sprang to his feet with such an alarming gesture that poor Adeline, crying "Come, Hector!" seized her husband, and left the house, almost dragging the baron, whom she was obliged to put in a carriage to transport him to Rue Plumet, where he took to his bed. He remained there several days without speaking, completely prostrated and refusing all nourishment. Adeline, by dint of much weeping, induced him to swallow a little soup; she nursed him, sitting constantly by his bedside, and feeling, of all the sentiments that formerly filled her heart, naught but profound pity.

At half-past twelve Lisbeth, who dared not leave her dear maréchal, so terrified was she by the change that had taken place in him, ushered in the notary and Comte Steinbock.

"Monsieur le Comte," said the maréchal, "I beg you to sign the necessary document to authorize my niece, your wife, to sell a certificate of stock, in which she now has a reversionary interest only.—Mademoiselle Fischer, you will surrender your interest in the income and acquiesce in this sale?"

"Yes, dear comte," said Lisbeth without hesitation.

"Very well, my dear," said the veteran. "I hope to live long enough to reward you. I did not doubt you; you are a true republican, a daughter of the people."

He took the old maid's hand and deposited a kiss upon it.

"Monsieur Hannequin," he said to the notary, "prepare the necessary document in the form of a power of attorney, so that I may have it two hours hence and be able to sell the stock on the Bourse to-day. My niece, the comtesse, holds the title; she is coming, and will sign the power when you bring it, as will mademoiselle. Monsieur le Comte will go with you to your office to affix his signature."

The artist, at a signal from Lisbeth, bowed respectfully to the maréchal and went away.

The next morning at ten o'clock the Comte de Forzheim sent in his name to the Prince de Wissembourg, and was at once admitted.

"Well, my dear Hulot," said Maréchal Cottin offering his old friend the newspapers, "we have saved appearances, you see. Read."

Maréchal Hulot laid the papers on the minister's desk, and held out the two hundred thousand francs.

"Here's the amount my brother took from the State," said he.

"What folly" cried the minister. "It's impossible," he added, taking the ear-trumpet the maréchal handed him, and speaking into his ear, "for us to manage a restitution. We should be compelled to admit your brother's peculations, and we have done everything under heaven to conceal them."

"Do what you choose with it; but I don't propose that there shall be a liard that has been stolen from the State in the coffers of the Hulot family," said the comte.

"I will take the king's orders on this subject. Let us say no more about it," replied the minister, realizing the impossibility of overcoming the old man's sublime obstinacy.

"Adieu, Cottin," said he, taking the prince's hand, "I feel as if my heart were frozen."

He took a step or two, then turned and looked at the prince, and seeing that he was deeply moved, opened his arms, and the two veterans embraced.

"It seems to me that I am bidding adieu to the whole *Grande Armée* in your person. Farewell, my dear old comrade!" said the minister.

"Yes, farewell, for I am going where all our old comrades for whom we have wept have gone."

At that moment Claude Vignon came in. The two old relics of the Napoleonic phalanxes bowed gravely, banishing all traces of emotion.

"You ought to be satisfied with the tone of the newspapers, my prince," said the future master of requests. "I arranged matters so as to make the opposition sheets believe that they were publishing our secrets."

"Unfortunately, it's all of no avail," replied the minister looking after Hulot, as he walked away through the salon. "I have just bade that man adieu for the last time, and it has nearly broken my heart! Maréchal Hulot hasn't three days to live; I saw it yesterday plainly enough. That man, whose sturdy honesty is almost divine, a soldier respected by the cannon-balls; despite his gallantry —see! in that chair, yonder—received his death-blow, at my hand, from a paper!—Ring and order my carriage. I am going to Neuilly," he said, placing the two hundred thousand francs in his ministerial portfolio.

Notwithstanding Lisbeth's devoted care, Maréchal Hulot died three days later. Such men are the honor of the parties they espouse. To republicans the maréchal was the ideal of patriotism; so they were all at his funeral, which was followed by an immense crowd. The army, the government, the court, the people, all ranks and classes assembled to do homage to his exalted virtue, his unswerving probity, his spotless renown. May not any man who desires it have the people at his funeral? These obsequies were signalized by one of those outbursts of delicacy, good taste, and kindness of heart, which come at long intervals, to recall the great virtues and the glory of the nobility of France. Behind the coffin of the maréchal walked the aged Marquis de Montauran, brother of the man, who, when the Chouans took up arms in 1799, was the adversary, and the unsuccessful adversary, of Hulot. The marquis, when dying from wounds received at the hands of the Blues, entrusted his young brother's interests to the soldier of the Republic—See *The Chouans*.—

Hulot accepted the nobleman's verbal legacy in good faith, and succeeded in saving the property of the young man, then an *émigré*. So it was that the homage of the old French nobility was not wanting at the obsequies of the soldier, who, nine years before, had vanquished MADAME.

The maréchal's death, happening as it did four days before the last publication of her marriage, was to Lisbeth the lightning stroke which burns the crop after it is safely housed, with the barn that contains it. The Lorrainer, as often happens, had succeeded too well. The death of the maréchal was due to the blows aimed at the family by herself and Madame Marneffe. The old maid's hatred, which seemed to have been glutted by success, became more intense with the defeat of all her hopes. Lisbeth went to weep out her rage at Madame Marneffe's; for she was without a home, the maréchal having limited the duration of his lease to that of his life. Crevel, to console Valérie's friend, took her savings, increased them considerably, and invested the whole amount at five per cent in Célestine's name, the income to be paid to Lisbeth. By virtue of this transaction Lisbeth had two thousand francs a year for her life. When the inventory of the property of the maréchal was taken, they found a line addressed to his sister-in-law, his niece Hortense, and his nephew Victorin, charging them to pay, between them, twelve hundred francs a year for life to her who was to have been his wife, Mademoiselle Lisbeth Fischer.

Adeline, seeing that the baron was between life and death, succeeded in concealing the death of the maréchal from him for several days; but Lisbeth came to see him, dressed in mourning, and the fatal truth was revealed to him eleven days after the funeral. This terrible blow restored the sick man's energy, he left his bed and found all his family assembled in the salon, dressed in black; they all ceased speaking when he appeared. Hulot had become as thin as a ghost in the fortnight that had passed, and appeared to his family as but a shadow of his former self.

"We must come to some resolution," he said in a weak voice, sitting down in an armchair and looking around upon the family party, from which Crevel and Steinbock were missing.

"We can stay here no longer," Hortense was saying just as her father appeared, "the rent is too high.—"

"As far as lodgings are concerned," said Victorin, breaking the painful silence, "I offer *my mother*—"

At these words, which seemed to exclude him, the baron raised his eyes, which were gazing at the flowers in the carpet without seeing them, and cast a piteous glance at the advocate. A father's rights are always so sacred, even when he is an infamous scoundrel and bereft of honor that Victorin stopped short.

"Your mother—" the baron repeated. "You are right, my son!"

"The suite above ours in our pavilion," said Célestine, finishing her husband's sentence.

"Am I a burden to you, my children?" said the baron with the gentle manner characteristic of those who are convicted by their own consciences. "Oh! have no anxiety for the future; you will have no more cause to complain of your father, and you will never see him again until the time when you will not have to blush for him."

He went to Hortense and kissed her on the brow. He opened his arms to his son, who threw himself into them despairingly, divining his father's intentions. The baron made a sign to Lisbeth, who came to him, and he kissed her on the brow. Then he withdrew to his bed-room, whither Adeline followed him in the keenest of anxiety.

"My brother was right, Adeline," said he, taking her by the hand. "I am unworthy to live with my family. I did not dare bless, otherwise than in my heart, my poor children, whose whole conduct has been noble; tell them that I could do nothing more than kiss them; for the blessing of a dishonored man, of a father who becomes the assassin, the scourge of his family, instead of being its protector and its glory, might bring misfortune upon them; but I will bless them from afar every day. As for yourself, God alone, for He is omnipotent, can reward you in proportion to your deserts!—I ask you to forgive me," he said, kneeling at his wife's feet, taking her hands, and wetting them with his tears.

"Hector! Hector! your sins are great; but the Divine pity is infinite, and you can atone for everything by remaining with me.—Stand erect in the faith of a Christian, my dear.—I am your wife and not your judge. I am your chattel, do with me whatever you choose, take me wherever you go, for I feel that I have the strength to comfort you and to render life supportable to you, by my love and care and respect.—Our children are taken care of, they no longer need me. Let me try to be your diversion, your amusement. Allow me to share the hardships of your exile, of your poverty, so that I may lighten them. I shall always be good for something, if it were nothing more than to save the expense of a servant."

"Do you pardon me, my dear, beloved Adeline?"

"Yes; but pray get up, my dear!"

"With your forgiveness I shall be able to live!" he continued, rising to his feet. "I came into our room so that our children should not witness their father's abasement. Ah! it's a frightful thing, it degrades the paternal authority, and destroys the family, for children to have before their eyes every day a father who is a criminal like myself. So I can not stay among you, I leave you to spare you the hateful spectacle, of a father bereft of a father's dignity. Do not urge me not to go, Adeline. It would be equivalent to loading the pistol for me to blow my brains out. Lastly, do not follow me in my flight, or you will deprive me of my only remaining source of strength,—remorse."

Hector's earnestness imposed silence on the heartbroken Adeline. Great amid so much ruin and desolation, she derived her courage from her happy reunion with her husband; she thought that he was hers again, she assumed the divine mission of consoling him, of wooing him back to live contentedly with his family, of reconciling him to himself.

"Hector, do you mean to leave me to die of despair and anxiety?" said she, seeing that the main source of her strength was about to be withdrawn.

"I will come back to you, my angel, sent from heaven expressly for me, I verily believe; I will return to you, in comfortable circumstances at least, if not rich. Listen, dear Adeline; I cannot stay here for a multitude of reasons. In the first place, my pension, which will be six thousand francs, is assigned for four years, so that I have nothing. That is not all! in a few days I shall be subjected to arrest, on a suit upon certain notes of hand held by Vauvinet.—So I must go away until my son, with whom I shall leave precise instructions, has taken them up. My disappearance will assist greatly in that operation. When my retiring pension is free, and Vauvinet paid, I will come back to you. You would disclose the secret of my hiding-place. Have no fear, Adeline, don't weep.—It's only a matter of a month."

"Where will you go? what will you do? what will become of you? who will take care of you, for you're no longer young? Let me disappear with you, and we will go abroad together," said she.

"Well, we'll see about it," he replied.

The baron rang, and ordered Mariette to get his things together, and pack them secretly and quickly. Then he begged his wife, after kissing her with a demonstration of affection to which she was not accustomed, to leave him alone a moment to write out the instructions Victorin required, promising not to leave the house until night and with her. As soon as the baroness returned to the salon, the cunning old fellow went through the dressing-room to the reception-room and left the house, handing Mariette a scrap of paper on which he had written: "Send my trunks to Monsieur Hector, *bureau restante*, Corbeil, by the Corbeil railroad." The baron had taken a fiacre, and was already driving rapidly through Paris, when Mariette entered the salon and showed the baroness the paper, telling her that monsieur had gone. Adeline darted into the bed-room, trembling more violently than ever; her children heard a piercing shriek and followed her, in terror. They found the baroness unconscious; she was at once put to bed, for she was taken with a nervous fever which kept her hovering between life and death for a month.

"Where is he?" were the only words they could induce her to utter.

*

Victorin's search for his father was without result. For this reason. The baron was driven to the Place du Palais-Royal. In possession once more of all his faculties, which were restored to him for the accomplishment of a plan thought out during the days he had passed in bed, worn out with sorrow and chagrin, he passed through the Palais-Royal and hired a magnificent hackney carriage, on the Rue Joquelet. Following the orders given him the coachman turned into Rue de la Ville-l'Évêque, in the rear of the mansion occupied by Josépha, whose gates were thrown open for this superb equipage at the call of the coachman. Josépha's curiosity brought her to the window; her footman informed her that a feeble old man, who was unable to leave his carriage, entreated her to come down to him for an instant.

"Josépha! it's I!—"

The famous cantatrice recognized Hulot by his voice alone.

"What, you, my poor old man!—On my word you look like the twenty-franc pieces clipped by German Jews, that bankers won't accept!"

"Alas! yes," Hulot replied; "I am just out of the arms of death! But you are still lovely! will you be kind to me?"

"That depends, everything is relative," said she.

"Listen," rejoined Hulot. "Can you put me up in one of your servant's rooms under the eaves for a day or two? I am without a sou, without hope, without bread, without a roof to cover me, without a wife, without children, without a place of refuge, without honor, without courage, without a friend, and worse than all! I have certain notes hanging over me."

"Poor old man! there's a fine lot of *withouts!* Are you without breeches—*sans-culotte*—also?"

"You laugh at me, I am lost!" cried the baron. "And yet I relied upon you, as Gourville did upon Ninon."

"It's a society woman, so I've been told, who's brought you into this condition," said Josépha. "The *pulcinellas* know how to pluck a turkey better than we do!—Why, you're like a carcass abandoned by the crows,—I can look right through you!"

"Time flies, Josépha!"

"Come in, old boy! I am alone and my people don't know you. Send your carriage away. Is it paid for?"

"Yes," said the baron, stepping down, leaning on Josépha's arm.

"You shall pass for my father if you choose," said the singer compassionately.

She led Hulot to the superb salon where he had seen her before, and bade him be seated.

"Is it true, old man," said she, "that you have killed your brother and your uncle, ruined your family, mortgaged your children's house beyond its value, and fed on the government frogs in Africa with the princess?"

The baron bowed sadly.

"Well, do you know, I like that!" cried Josépha, springing to her feet, overflowing with enthusiasm. "It's a general *conflagration!* It's Sardanapalus! it's great! it's complete! You may be a sad dog, but you have heart, for my own part I prefer a spendthrift, mad after women as you are, to those cold heartless bankers, supposed to be virtuous, who ruin thousands of families with their railroads, which are gold for them, but iron for the *gogos!* You ruined nobody but your own people, you made way with none but yourself! and then you have an excuse, both physical and moral.—"

She assumed a theatrical pose and exclaimed:

"'Tis Venus herself who has seized her prey.' And here she is!" she added, with a pirouette.

Thus Hulot received absolution from vice, vice smiled upon him from the midst of its boundless luxury. There, as in the eyes of jurors, the magnitude of the crime was an extenuating circumstance.

"Your society woman is pretty, at least?" queried the singer, trying to begin her alms-giving by distracting Hulot's attention, for his grief tore her heart.

"Faith, almost as pretty as you!" the baron cunningly replied.

"And—very cunning, so I've been told. Pray what did she do to you? Is she more amusing than I am?"

"Let's not talk about her any more," said Hulot.

"They say she has trapped my Crevel, and little Steinbock, and a magnificent Brazilian?"

"It's very possible."

"She lives in a house as pretty as this, given her by Crevel. The hussy is my provost, she finishes off the men I've taken the first slice of! That's the reason I'm so curious to find out about her; I saw her in a calèche at the *Bois,* but at a distance. She's *a shrewd thief,* so Carabine told me! She tried to swallow Crevel, but she could only get a nibble at him. Crevel's a skin-flint! a good-humored one, who always says *yes*, but acts only with his head. He is vain and passionate, but his money's cold. One can get no more than one to three thousand francs a month from such duffers, and they draw back from any considerable expenditure like a donkey when he comes to a river. You're not that kind, old man; you're the slave of your passions, and a woman could make you sell your country! So you see I'm ready to do anything for you. You are my father, you gave me my start in life! that makes you sacred to me. What do you want? A hundred thousand francs? we'll pull the skies down to get them for you. As to giving you the grub and the nest to lie in, that's nothing. You shall have a cover laid for you every day, you can have a fine room on the second floor, and a hundred crowns a month in your pocket."

The baron, touched by this reception, exhibited a last spark of noble feeling.

"No, little one, no, I didn't come here to have you keep me," said he.

"At your age it's quite a triumph!"

"This is what I do want, my child. Your Duc d'Hérouville has vast estates in Normandy, and I would like to be his manager under the name of Thoul. I am capable and honest,—for though a man may take money from the government it doesn't follow that he'll steal private property."

"What's that?" exclaimed Josépha; "who has drunk will drink!"

"Well, I simply ask to be enabled to live out of sight for three years."

"That will take but a moment to arrange; to-night, after dinner," said Josépha, "I need do no more than mention it. The duke would marry me if I chose; but I have his fortune and I want something more!—his esteem. He's a duke of the old school. He is noble, distinguished, great as Louis XIV. and Napoléon, placed one on top of the other, although he's a dwarf. And then I have done as the Schontz did with Rochefide: by following my advice he has made two millions. But, look you, my old pistol. I know you; you are fond of women, and you'd run about down yonder after the little Normans, who are fine girls; you'd get your bones broken by their sweethearts or their fathers, and the duke would be forced to turn you off. Don't you suppose I can see by the way you look at me that *the young man* isn't dead within you yet, as Fénelon says! That sort of business isn't the thing for you. A man can't break with Paris and with us women at will, old fellow! You would die of ennui at Hérouville!

"What can I do?" demanded the baron, "for I only want to stay with you long enough to settle my plans."

"Well, do you want me to pick out a place for you according to my ideas? Listen, old satyr!—You can't get along without women. They can console for everything. Now attend to what I say. At the foot of the Courtille, Rue Saint-Maur-du-Temple, I know a poor family possessing a rare treasure: a little daughter prettier than I was at sixteen!—Aha! your eye begins to sparkle already!—She works sixteen hours a day embroidering rich stuffs for silk merchants, and earns sixteen sous a day, one sou an hour, a wretched pittance!—And she eats potatoes, like the Irish, but fried in rat-grease, bread five times a week, and drinks Ourcq water from the city pipes, because Seine water is too dear; and she can't set up in business on her own account for lack of six or seven thousand francs. She would do the *hundred horrors* to get seven or eight thousand francs. Your wife and family bore you, don't they?—Besides you can't stand it to be nobody where you used to be a god. A father without money or honor should be stuffed and put in a glass-case."

The baron could not help smiling at this irreverent pleasantry.

"Well, little Bijou is coming to-morrow to bring me an embroidered dressing-gown, a perfect love; they have spent six months on it, nobody will have anything like it. Bijou is fond of me, for I give her nice things to eat and my old dresses. Then I send presents of bread and wood and meat to the family, who would break both legs for me at a wink, if I chose. I try to do a little good. Ah! I remember what I suffered when I was hungry! Bijou has poured her little secrets into my heart. There's the making of a *figurante* at the Ambigu-Comique in that little creature. Bijou dreams of wearing lovely dresses like mine, and above all things, of riding in a carriage. I'll say to her: 'Little one, would you like a gentleman—' How old are you anyway?" she asked, interrupting herself,—"seventy-two?"

"I haven't any age!"

"'Would you like a gentleman of seventy-two,' I'll say to her, 'neat as a pin, who doesn't use tobacco, sound as my eye, and worth any young man of them all? you'll be married to him in the thirteenth arrondissement*; he'll do the handsome thing by you, give you seven thousand francs to do what you please with, and furnish apartments for you in mahogany throughout; then, if you're a good girl, he'll take you to the play now and then. He'll give you a hundred francs a month for yourself and fifty for expenses!' I know Bijou, she's just myself at fourteen over again. I jumped for joy when that disgusting Crevel made these same shocking propositions to me! Well, old man, you'll be

*"To be married in the thirteenth arrondissement" was an expression used at the time Paris had but twelve arrondissements as a synonym for taking a mistress.

packed away there for three years. It's a wise plan, and honest, and the illusion will last three or four years, not more."

Hulot did not hesitate, he had made up his mind to refuse; but he pretended to waver between vice and virtue in order to thank the kind-hearted, good-natured songstress who was doing the best she knew.

"Come, come! you're as cold as the pavement in December!" she continued in amazement. "Just think! you will bring happiness to a family that consists of an old tottering grandfather, a mother who's wearing herself out with work, and two sisters, one very ugly, who earn thirty-two sous a day together, by murdering their eyes. That will make up for the harm you've done at home, you can atone for your sins, and at the same time enjoy yourself like a lorette at the Mabille."

Hulot, to put an end to these seductive suggestions, went through the motion of counting money.

"Have no fear as to ways and means," Josépha went on. "My duke will loan you ten thousand francs: seven thousand for an embroidery establishment in Bijou's name and three thousand to furnish her apartment; and every three months you will find six hundred and fifty francs here with a note. When your pension is free again you must pay back the seventeen thousand francs. Meanwhile you'll be as happy as a pig in clover, and out of sight in a hole where the police can't possibly find you! You can wear a great beaver overcoat, and you'll look like a well-to-do householder of the quarter. Call yourself Thoul if that suits you. I'll turn you over to Bijou as an uncle of mine come from Germany after failing in business there, and you'll be looked up to as a god. There you are, papa!—Who knows? perhaps you won't find reason to regret anything. If by chance you do get bored, keep one of your dress suits, and then you can come here and ask me to keep you to dinner and to pass the evening."

"And I intended to become a virtuous, reformed man!—Come, arrange a loan of twenty thousand francs for me, and I'll go off to America and make my fortune, like my friend d'Aiglemont when Nucingen ruined him."

"You!" cried Josépha; "for God's sake leave morals to the grocers, the simple clodhoppers, the Fr-r-rench citizens, who have nothing but their virtue to travel on! You! Why, you were born to be something better than a simpleton; as a man you are just what, as a woman, I am, a *vagabond* genius!"

"The night brings counsel, we'll talk of all this to-morrow."

"You'll dine with the duke to-night. My d'Hérouville will receive you as cordially as if you had saved the State! and to-morrow you can make up your mind. Come, cheer up, old man! Life's a suit of clothes; when it's dirty, we brush it; when it's torn we mend it; but we stay clothed as long as we can!"

This philosophy of vice and the enthusiasm with

which it was put forward madc Hulot forget his poignant suffering.

The next day, at noon, after a succulent breakfast, Hulot's eyes were attracted by the appearance of one of those living chefs-d'œuvre which Paris alone, in all the world, can produce, because of the incessant concubinage of luxury and poverty, of vice and virtue, of repressed desire and recurring temptation, which makes that city the legitimate heir of Nineveh and Babylon and imperial Rome. Mademoiselle Olympe Bijou, a young girl of sixteen, possessed the same sublime countenance that Raphaël conceived for his Virgins; innocent eyes, made melancholy by overwork, black, dreamy eyes, provided with long lashes, and in which the natural moisture was dried up by the wearing labors of the night,—eyes clouded with fatigue; a complexion like porcelain, almost unhealthy in its whiteness; a mouth like a half-opened pomegranate; a throbbing bosom, well-rounded figure, pretty hands, beautiful white teeth, luxuriant black hair,—the whole enveloped in calico at seventy-five centimes the metre, adorned with an embroidered neckerchief, her feet encased in leather shoes without nails, and her hands in gloves at twenty-nine sous. The child, who was ignorant of her worth, had made her finest toilet to visit the great lady's house. The baron, seized anew by the claw-like hand of lust, felt that all his life was escaping through his eyes. He forgot everything in the presence of this sublime creature. He was like the hunter when he catches sight of the game; even in an emperor's presence, he takes aim at it.

"And its warranted fresh," said Josépha in his ear, "and virtuous! and no bread. That's Paris! I've been there!"

"It's agreed," rejoined the old man, rising and rubbing his hands.

When Olympe Bijou had taken her leave, Josépha cast a mischievous glance at the baron.

"If you don't want to have trouble, papa," said she, "be as stern as a *procureur-général* on his bench. Keep the little one in leash; be another Bartholo! 'Ware the Augustines and Hippolytuses, the Nestors and Victors and all the other *ors.*—Damme, when, she is once well clothed and well-fed, if she raises her head, you'll be led by the nose like a Russian.—I am going to see about furnishing your rooms. The duke does things handsomely; he loans you, that is to say he gives you, ten thousand francs, and he will place eight thousand in his notary's hands, who will be instructed to pay you six hundred francs every quarter, for I'm afraid of you.—Am I a good girl?"

"Adorable!"

Ten days after his desertion of his family, when they stood, a tearful group, about the bedside of the dying Adeline, who constantly asked in a feeble voice: "What is he doing?" Hector, under the name of Thoul, was with Olympe at the head of an embroidery establishment on Rue Saint-Maur, under the absurd firm-name of Thoul and Bijou.

*

The unremitting ill-fortune of his family was to Victorin Hulot the last touch that perfects or demoralizes a man. He became perfect. In the great storms of life man imitates the sea-captain who lightens his ship in a hurricane by throwing the more cumbersome freight overboard. The advocate lost his internal pride, his palpable self-conceit, his oratorical pomposity, and his political pretensions. In short he became, as a man, what his mother was as a woman. He determined to make the best of his Célestine, who certainly did not come up to his dreams; and reached the sound, sensible conclusion that the common law of life requires man to content himself with an *almost* in everything. He took a solemn oath to himself that he would fulfil his duty, so horrified was he by his father's conduct. These sentiments acquired new strength at his mother's bedside on the day that her life was saved. This first stroke of good fortune did not come alone. Claude Vignon, who came every day on behalf of the Prince de Wissembourg to inquire for Madame Hulot's health, requested the newly re-elected deputy to accompany him to the minister's office.

"His Excellency," he said, "desires to confer with you touching your family affairs."

Victorin Hulot and the minister had been long

acquainted; so the former was welcomed with characteristic and auspicious affability. "My friend," said the veteran, "in this very room I swore to the maréchal, your uncle, that I would have an eye to your mother's welfare. That noble woman is convalescent, I am told, and the time has come to cure your wounds. I have two hundred thousand francs here for you and I am going to turn them over to you."

The advocate made a gesture worthy of his uncle the maréchal.

"Don't be alarmed," said the prince with a smile. "It's a trust-fund. My days are numbered; I shall not always be here, so do you take the money, and take my place as trustee in your family. You can use this money to pay off the mortgage with which your house is burdened. These two hundred thousand francs belong to your mother and sister. If I should give such a sum to Madame Hulot, I should be afraid, on account of her devotion to her husband, that it would be squandered; and it is the intention of those who give it that it should be used for the support of Madame Hulot and her daughter Comtesse Steinbock. You are a discreet man, the worthy son of your noble mother, the true nephew of my friend the maréchal, and you are as thoroughly appreciated here as elsewhere, my dear friend. So be the guardian angel of your family, accept our uncle's legacy and mine."

"Monseigneur," said Hulot, taking the minister's hand and pressing it, "men like you know that verbal thanks mean nothing, and that gratitude is proved by deeds."

"Prove yours!" said the old soldier.

"What must I do?"

"Accept my propositions," was the reply. "We propose to appoint you to take charge of all matters in litigation in the War Department, which is overburdened with law-suits, in the engineering branch, growing out of the fortifications of Paris; also consulting advocate of the prefecture of police, and counsel for the Civil List. These three appointments will be worth eighteen thousand francs a year to you, and will not take away your independence. You will vote in the Chamber according to your political opinions and your conscience.—Act with perfect freedom, my boy! we should be much embarrassed if we had no national opposition! The fact is that a line from your uncle, written only a few hours before he breathed his last, marked out the line of conduct he wished me to adopt toward your mother, of whom the maréchal was very fond! —Mesdames Popinot, de Rastignac, de Navarreins, d'Espard, de Grandlieu, de Carigliano, de Lenoncourt and de la Bâtie have created for your mother a position as inspector of benevolent work. These presidents of benevolent associations cannot do everything themselves; they need a reliable lady to support them energetically, to visit the unfortunate, find out whether charity is misplaced in any instance, make sure that the money or supplies have been delivered to those who asked for them, seek out those poor people who are ashamed to ask alms, etc. Your mother will perform the mission of an angel on earth; she will come in contact with none but the curés and the ladies engaged in the charitable work; they will give her six thousand francs a year and her carriages will be paid for. You see, my young friend, that the pure man, the virtuous, noble-hearted man, even from the grave looks out for the welfare of his family. Such names as your uncle's are, and should be, an ægis against misfortune in all properly-constituted society. Follow in your uncle's footsteps; or rather continue in your present course, for you are now following in his footsteps, I know."

"So great delicacy, prince, does not surprise me in my uncle's friend," said Victorin. "I will strive to fulfil all your hopes."

"Go at once and comfort your family!—By the way," added the prince, exchanging a grasp of the hand with Victorin, "your father has disappeared?"

"Alas! yes."

"So much the better. The unhappy man showed his wit in that; indeed, he doesn't lack that quality."

"There were some notes hanging over him."

"Aha!" said the maréchal; "you will receive six months' salary for your three offices in advance. This will assist you no doubt to take up the notes from the usurer who holds them. I will see Nucingen, too, and perhaps I may be able to release your father's pension, without it's costing you or the Department a sou. The peer of France hasn't buried the banker; Nucingen is insatiable and he's now after some concession or other, I don't know what."

Thus on his return to Rue Plumet Victorin was able to carry out his plan of taking his mother and sister home with him.

The young and famous lawyer's whole fortune consisted in one of the finest pieces of real estate in Paris, a house purchased in 1834, in anticipation of his marriage, and located on the boulevard between Rue de la Paix and Rue Louis-le-Grand. A speculator had built two houses, one on the street and one on the boulevard. Between the two with a courtyard and garden on either side stood a handsome pavilion, the last remnant of the splendors of the magnificent De Verneuil mansion. Hulot junior, sure of Mademoiselle Crevel's dowry, purchased this fine property at auction for a million and paid five hundred thousand down. He established himself on the ground floor, expecting to make up the balance of the purchase-money by renting the other floors; but, although real-estate speculation in Paris may be sure, it is slow and capricious, for it depends upon many circumstances that cannot be anticipated. As Parisian *flâneurs* may have noticed, the boulevard between Rue Louis-le-Grand and Rue de la Paix was built up very slowly; so much care was taken to clean it up and beautify it that it was not until 1840 that commerce began to be in evidence there in the shape of gorgeous shop-fronts, the unrivaled magnificence of the shops themselves, the fairy-like devices of fashion, and the gold of the money-changers. Notwithstanding the two hundred thousand francs presented to his daughter by Crevel at a time when his self-love was tickled by the marriage and before the baron had taken Josépha from him; notwithstanding the fact that Victorin had paid two hundred thousand francs in seven years, he still owed five hundred thousand francs on the house because of his devotion to his father. Luckily the continual advance in rents and the desirable situation made it possible for him at this time to rent both houses for all they were worth. At the end of eight years the speculation was justified, and meanwhile the advocate had exhausted his resources in paying interest and insignificant instalments of the principal. The tradespeople themselves made advantageous offers for the shops, on condition that they were allowed to take leases for eighteen years. The apartments gained in rental value by the change of the business centre, which was at this time between the Bourse and the Madeleine, thenceforth the centre of political power and of finance in Paris. The sum turned over by the minister, added to the year's rents paid in advance, and the good-will agreed to by the tenants, would reduce Victorin's debt to two hundred thousand francs. The two buildings he did not occupy, being entirely let, would bring in a hundred thousand francs a year. Two years more, during which Victorin's professional income would be doubled by the places the maréchal had offered him, and he would be in a most enviable position. It was like the manna falling from heaven. Victorin was able to give his mother the whole first floor of the pavilion and his sister the second, on which Lisbeth would have two rooms. With Cousin Bette for housekeeper the threefold household would be able to pay all expenses, and maintain an honorable position in the eyes of the world, as befitted the celebrated advocate. The stars of the Palais are soon eclipsed; and Hulot junior, being endowed with the art of discreet speech, and a reputation for the strictest probity, had the ear of the judges and councilors; he made a careful study of his cases, he made no statements that he could not prove, he did not accept a retainer in all cases indiscriminately,—in short he did honor to the bar.

Her home on Rue Plumet was so hateful to the baroness that she consented to change her abode to Rue Louis-le-Grand. Thus, through her son's means, Adeline was installed in handsome apartments; she was spared all concern about the material details of existence, for Lisbeth undertook the duty of performing once more the economical miracles she had performed at Madame Marneffe's, seeing an opportunity of wreaking her vengeance upon these three noble creatures, her unrelenting hatred for them being embittered by the overthrow of all her hopes. Once a month she went to see Valérie, being sent to her by Hortense who sought news of Wenceslas, and by Célestine who was extremely anxious about her father's avowed and recognized liaison with a woman to whom her husband's mother and sister owed their ruin and their unhappiness.

As may be imagined, Lisbeth took advantage of their anxiety to see Valérie as often as she desired.

About twenty months passed, during which the baroness's health constantly improved, although the nervous trembling did not leave her. She made herself familiar with her duties, which afforded a noble means of forgetting her grief for the moment, and food for the divine aspirations of her heart. She saw in it, moreover, a possible means of recovering her husband, as her duties took her to every part of Paris. During this time the Vauvinet notes were paid, and the pension of six thousand francs, awarded to Baron Hulot, was almost freed from incumbrance. Victorin paid all his mother's expenses as well as Hortense's with the ten thousand francs interest on the fund handed over to him by the maréchal in trust. As Adeline's salary was six thousand francs, that sum, added to the six thousand of the baron's pension would ere long afford the mother and daughter an income of twelve thousand a year, free of all charges. The poor woman would have been almost happy, except for her never-ending anxiety as to the fate of the baron, whom she would have liked to have by her side to enjoy the good fortune which was just beginning to smile upon the family; except for the sad spectacle of her deserted daughter, and the terrible blows *innocently* dealt her by Lisbeth, whose infernal disposition was no longer under the slightest restraint.

A scene that occurred in the beginning of the month of March, 1843, will serve to explain the effect produced by the persistent though concealed hatred of Lisbeth, always seconded by Madame Marneffe. Two great events had happened at Madame Marneffe's. In the first place, the latter had brought into the world a premature child, whose death was worth two thousand francs a year to her. Then as to Monsieur Marneffe, eleven months previously Lisbeth had imparted the following information to the family on her return from a visit of exploration to the Marneffe mansion:

"This morning," she said, "that horrible Valérie sent for Doctor Bianchon to ask if the doctors who had given her husband up the day before, were not mistaken. This doctor said that, before this night is over, that beast of a man will have gone to the hell that awaits him. Père Crevel and Madame Marneffe went to the door with the doctor, and your father, my dear Célestine, gave him five pieces of gold for the good news. When they returned to the salon Crevel capered about like a ballet-dancer; he kissed that woman, and cried: 'At last then you will be Madame Crevel!'—And when she left us alone to resume her place by the bedside of her husband, who had the death-rattle in his throat, your honorable father said to me: 'With Valérie for my wife, I shall be a peer of France! I'm going to buy an estate I've got my eye on, the estate of Presles which Madame de Sérizy wants to sell. I shall be Crevel de Presles, I shall become a member of the General Council of Seine-et-Oise, and a deputy. I shall have a son! I shall be whatever I choose to be.'—'Very good,' I replied, 'and your daughter?'—'Bah! she's a girl,' he exclaimed, 'and she's become altogether too much of a Hulot, and Valérie has a horror of all those people.—My son-in-law has never been willing to come here; why does he play the mentor, the Spartan, the Puritan, the philanthropist? Besides, I've settled accounts with my daughter, and she has received all her mother's fortune with two hundred thousand francs more! So I am at liberty to go my own way. I shall pass judgment on my daughter and son-in-law when I am married; as they do, so will I do. If they are kind to their mother-in-law, I'll see! I am a man!' All such nonsense as that! and he struck an attitude like Napoléon on the column!"

The ten months of widowhood, formally enjoined by the Code Napoléon, had expired some days. The estate of Presles had been purchased. Victorin and Célestine had sent Lisbeth on the morning in question to Madame Marneffe's in quest of news touching the marriage of that fascinating widow to the Mayor of Paris, now a member of the Council General of Seine-et-Oise.

Célestine and Hortense who had become much more attached to each other since they had lived under the same roof, were almost always together. The baroness, impelled by her unswerving honesty of purpose, which led her to exaggerate the duties of her position, sacrificed herself to the benevolent work in which she was the intermediary, and was away from home almost every day from eleven o'clock till five. The two sisters-in-law, drawn together by their maternal duties, for they took care of their children in common, remained at home and worked side by side. They had acquired the habit of thinking aloud, a touching instance of perfect harmony between two sisters, one of a happy, the other of a melancholy disposition. Beautiful, full of overflowing life, animated, bright and smiling, the unfortunate sister seemed to give the lie to her real situation by her external bearing; just as the melancholy one, gentle and calm, as even-tempered as reason itself, habitually thoughtful and reflecting, would have led one to believe in some secret trouble. Perhaps this contrast contributed to their warm friendship. They loaned to each other whatever either lacked. Seated in a little kiosk, in the middle of the garden which the trowel of speculation had spared by a whim of the builder, who counted upon retaining the hundred square feet for himself, they feasted their eyes upon the first blooming of the lilacs, a spring festival which is enjoyed to its fullest extent only in Paris, where the Parisians have lived for six months in total forgetfulness of all vegetation, amid the stone cliffs against which their living ocean beats.

"Célestine," said Hortense, replying to an observation of her sister-in-law, who was complaining because her husband had to be in the Chamber in such fine weather, "it seems to me that you don't appreciate your good fortune as you ought. Victorin is an angel, and sometimes you worry him."

"My dear, men love to be teased! Certain fault-finding ways are a proof of affection. If your poor mother had been, not exacting, but always on the point of being, I am sure you wouldn't have had so much misery to deplore."

"Lisbeth doesn't come back! I am going to sing *Malbrouck's* song," said Hortense. "How I long for news of Wenceslas!—What is he living on? he has done nothing for two years."

"Victorin saw him the other day with that hateful woman, so he told me, and he fancies that she's supporting him in idleness.—Ah! if you chose, dear sister, you could bring your husband back to you even now."

Hortense shook her head.

"Believe me, your position will soon become intolerable," continued Célestine. "At first, wrath, indignation and despair gave you strength. The incredible disasters which have since overwhelmed our family: two deaths, the ruin and disappearance of Baron Hulot, have filled your mind and heart since; but, now that you are living in tranquillity and peace you will not find it easy to endure the emptiness of your life; as you can not, as you will not deviate from the path of honor, the time will come when you must be reconciled to Wenceslas. Victorin, who loves you so dearly, is of that opinion. There is something stronger than our feelings, and that is nature!"

"Such a coward!" cried the proud Hortense. "He loves that woman because she supports him.—So she has paid his debts, has she?—My God! night and day I think of that man's plight! He is the father of my child, and he is dishonoring himself—"

"Look at your mother, dear—" rejoined Célestine.

Célestine belonged to that class of women who, when you have given them reasons strong enough to convince a Breton peasant, begin upon their original argument again for the hundredth time. Her somewhat expressionless, cold and uninteresting face, her light chestnut hair disposed in stiff plaits, her complexion, everything in her appearance, in short, indicated the woman of good sense, without the power to charm, but also without weakness.

"The baroness would love dearly to be with her disgraced husband, to comfort him and conceal him in her heart from all eyes," continued Célestine. "She has had a room arranged for him upstairs as if she might find him any day, and bring him home."

"Oh! my mother is sublime!" Hortense replied; "she has been sublime every minute in every day for twenty-six years; but I haven't her disposition.—What can I do? sometimes I lose my head when I know I ought not. Ah! Célestine, you don't know what it is to have to palter with infamy!"

"What about my father?" rejoined Célestine calmly. "He is certainly on the road where yours came to grief. My father is ten years younger than the baron, and he's been a business man, to be sure, but how will it end? This Madame Marneffe has made my father her dog, she does as she pleases with his fortune and his ideas, and no one can make him realize what he's doing. Indeed, I am trembling with apprehension lest I hear that the banns are published! My husband is making one last effort, he looks upon it as his duty to avenge society and his family, and to call that woman to account for all her crimes. Ah! dear Hortense, noble minds like Victorin's and hearts like ours learn too late the world and its methods! This is a secret, dear sister; I tell it to you, for it concerns you; but do not reveal it by word or gesture, either to Lisbeth or your mother or anyone else, for—"

"Here's Lisbeth!" said Hortense.—"Well, cousin, how goes the hell on Rue Barbet?"

"Badly for you, children.—Your husband, Hortense, my love, is more intoxicated than ever with that woman, who seems to have a mad sort of passion for him, I admit.—Your father, dear Célestine, is as blind as a king. That's nothing; that's what I see every fortnight, and upon my word I think I'm fortunate never to have known what a man is.—They're absolute beasts! Five days hence you and Victorin, little one, will have lost your father's fortune!"

"Are the banns published?" Célestine asked.

"Yes," replied Lisbeth. "I have pleaded your cause. I said to the monster, who is walking in the footsteps of another, that, if he would relieve you from your embarrassment, by paying off the incumbrance on your house, you would be grateful to him and would receive your mother-in-law—"

Hortense made a gesture of horror.

"Victorin will decide for us," rejoined Célestine coldly.

"Do you know what Monsieur le Maire answered?" continued Lisbeth: "'I prefer to leave them in trouble; you can't subdue a refractory horse except by hunger, lack of sleep and sugar!' Baron Hulot's a better man than Crevel.—So, my poor child, put on mourning for your inheritance. And such a fortune! Your father paid three millions for Presles, and he has thirty thousand francs a year left! Oh! he has no secrets from me. He talks of buying the Hotel de Navarreins, Rue du Bac. Madame Marneffe has forty thousand a year herself. —Ah! here's our guardian angel, here's your mother!—" she cried as she heard the rumbling of a carriage.

A moment later the baroness ascended the steps and joined the family group. At fifty-five years, Adeline, though she had been so sorely beset by trouble and sorrow, and trembled incessantly as if she were always suffering from fever, though she was pale and wrinkled, still retained a beautiful figure, superb in its outlines, and her natural nobility of carriage. People who saw her would say: "She must have been very beautiful!" Consumed by the misery of knowing nothing of her husband's fate and of his being unable to share the good fortune the family was about to enjoy in the retirement and silence of this Parisian oasis, she resembled one of those majestic ruins upon which the eye loves to dwell. As each gleam of hope faded away, as each new quest proved fruitless, Adeline would have an attack of black melancholy which drove her children to despair. As she had left home on this particular morning, with a fresh clue to follow, her return was impatiently awaited. A certain *intendant-général*, being under obligations to Hulot, to whom he was indebted for his official position, said that he had seen the baron in a box at the Ambigu-Comique, with a woman of magnificent beauty. Adeline therefore had gone to call upon Baron Vernier. That exalted functionary informed her that he did see his former patron, and asserted that his bearing toward the woman during the performance seemed to indicate a clandestine marriage; but he told Madame Hulot that her husband left the theatre before the end of the performance to avoid meeting himself.

"He acted like a family man, and his dress bespoke the straitened condition he sought to hide," he added in conclusion.

"Well?" said the three women in one voice to the baroness.

"Monsieur Hulot is in Paris; and it's a gleam of happiness for me simply to know that he is near us," Adeline replied.

"He doesn't seem to have mended his ways!"

said Lisbeth when Adeline had told the story of her interview with Baron Vernier; "he must have taken up with some little work-girl. But where does he get his money? I'll wager that he goes to his former mistresses for it, Mademoiselle Jenny Cadine or Josépha."

The constant agitation of the baroness's nerves redoubled in intensity; she wiped away the tears that came to her eyes, and raised them piteously toward heaven.

"I don't believe that a grand officer of the Legion of Honor can have fallen so low," said she.

"What wouldn't he do for his own pleasure?" retorted Lisbeth; "he has stolen from the State, he'll steal from private individuals, he'll commit murder perhaps—"

"Oh! Lisbeth!" cried the baroness, "keep such thoughts to yourself."

At that moment Louise approached the family group, which had already been increased by the two little Hulots and little Wenceslas, curious to know if there were any sweetmeats in their grandmother's pockets.

"What is it, Louise?—"

"A man asking to see Mademoiselle Fischer."

"What sort of a man is he?" said Lisbeth.

"He's all in rags, mademoiselle, and he's covered with wool like a mattress-maker; he has a red nose, he smells of wine and brandy. He's one of the workmen that hardly works half the week."

This unalluring description had the effect of

sending Lisbeth in a great hurry out into the courtyard of the house on Rue Louis-le-Grand, where she found the man smoking a pipe, the coloring of which made it clear that he was an artist in the matter of smoking.

"Why do you come here, Père Chardin?" said she. "It was agreed that you should be at the door of the Hôtel Marneffe, on Rue Barbet-de-Jouy on the first Saturday of every month. I have just come from there after waiting five hours, and you didn't come!—"

"I have been there, my respected and charitable young lady!" replied the mattress-maker; "but there was a big pool up at the Café des Savants, Rue du Cœur-Volant, and every man to his passions. Mine's billiards. Without billiards I should eat off silver-plate; for just you mark this!" he continued, feeling for a paper in the pocket of his dilapidated breeches, "billiards lead to brandy drinking. It ruins a fellow by the things that go with it, like everything else that's decent. I know my orders, but the old man's in such a pickle that I ventured to step on the forbidden ground.—If our horsehair was all horsehair you could lie down and go to sleep on it; but it's a mixture! God isn't the same to everybody, as they say; He has His preferences; that's His right. Here's the hand-writing of your estimable relative, a good friend to the mattress.—That's his political opinion."

Père Chardin tried to draw zigzag lines in the air with the forefinger of his right hand.

Lisbeth, paying no heed to him, read these two lines:

"Dear cousin, be my providence! Give me three hundred francs to-day.

"HECTOR."

"What does he want so much money for?"

"The *landlord!*" said Père Chardin, still trying to design arabesques. "And then my son has come back from Algeria, by way of Spain, Bayonne and—he didn't take anything, contrary to his custom; for he's a finished rascal, is my son, saving your presence. What's he to do? he's half-starved; but he'll return you what we let him have, for he means to get himself talked about; he has ideas that may carry him a great way—"

"Into the police court!" retorted Lisbeth. "He's my uncle's murderer, I'll not forget that!"

"He! why he couldn't bleed a chicken, respected young lady!"

"Here are three hundred francs," said Lisbeth, taking fifteen gold pieces from her purse. "Off with you now, and never come here again."

She escorted, to the door, the father of the keeper of the forage store-houses at Oran, and called the concierge's attention to the drunken old man.

"Whenever that man comes, if by any chance he does come again, you won't let him in, and you'll tell him that I'm not here. If he should try to find out whether Monsieur Hulot junior or

Madame la Baronne Hulot lives here, you will reply that you don't know any such persons."

"Very well, mademoiselle."

"Your place will be in danger in case of any blunder, even if it's involuntary," said the old maid in the concierge's ear.—"Cousin, you are threatened with a great calamity," she said to the advocate, who came in at that moment.

"What is it?"

"Your wife will have Madame Marneffe for a step-mother within a few days."

"We'll see about that!" said Victorin.

*

For six months Lisbeth had been paying, and paying with great promptitude, a small pension to her former protector, Baron Hulot, whose protectress she had become; she knew the secret of his abiding-place, and she gloated over Adeline's tears, saying to her when she found her in good spirits and filled with hope: "Wait a while and some day you'll read my poor cousin's name in the police court news." In this, as on previous occasions, she went too far in her thirst for vengeance. She had put Victorin on his guard. Victorin had determined to do away with this sword of Damocles constantly held over their heads by Lisbeth, and with the female demon to whom his mother and the family owed so much misery. The Prince de Wissembourg, who was made acquainted with Madame Marneffe, supported the advocate in his secret undertaking; he promised him, as a president of the Council promises, the secret intervention of the police to enlighten Crevel, and to save a large fortune from the claws of the diabolical courtesan, whom he had not forgiven for the death of Maréchal Hulot nor for the total ruin of the Councilor of State.

Lisbeth's words: "He goes to his former mistresses for money!" filled the baroness's mind during the whole night. Like those invalids given up by their physicians who put themselves in the hands of charlatans, like those persons who have reached the last Dantesque stage of despair, or like the drowning man who clutches at a straw for support, she ended by believing in the degradation, the mere suggestion of which had aroused her ire, and she conceived the idea of calling upon one of those odious creatures for aid. The next morning, without consulting her children, without a word to anyone, she drove to the house of Mademoiselle Josépha Mirah, *prima donna* at the Royal Academy of Music, seeking the fulfilment or the death of the hope which gleamed before her eyes like a will-o'-the-wisp. Just at noon the famous songstress's maid handed her Baroness Hulot's card, saying that the lady was waiting at her door, having sent up to ask if mademoiselle could receive her.

"Are the rooms in order?"

"Yes, mademoiselle."

"Have you put fresh flowers about?"

"Yes, mademoiselle."

"Tell Jean to take a look round and see that everything's all right, before showing the lady in, and tell him that she's to be treated with the greatest respect. Go! then come back and dress me, for I want to look my loveliest!"

She went and looked at herself in her mirror.

"I must put on my Sunday best," she said to herself. "Vice must be under arms to face virtue! Poor woman! what can she want of me?—It makes me nervous to see

"*The August Victim of Misfortune.*"

She was just finishing that famous air, when her maid returned.

"Madame," said she, "the lady has an attack of nervous trembling."

"Give her some orange water, rum, a cup of soup—"

"I have done so, mademoiselle, but she refused them all; she says it's a little trouble she's subject to,—nervous excitement—"

"Where did you take her?"

"To the large salon."

"Hurry with me, my girl! Quick, my prettiest slippers, my flowered robe de chambre by Bijou, with all its fluttering lace on it. Dress my hair so as to astonish any woman.—This lady plays a part the exact opposite of mine! And let some one tell her—for she's a great lady, my girl! that's still better; that's something you will never be; a woman whose prayers release souls from your purgatory!—let some one tell her that I acted last night and was in bed, but am getting up."

The baroness took no heed of the time she passed in the grand salon of Josépha's apartments, although she waited there a long half-hour. This salon, which had already been redecorated and refurnished since Josépha's installation in the little palace, was now done in *massaca*-colored silk and gold. The magnificence which great noblemen formerly displayed in their *petites maisons*, and of which so many examples still bear witness to those *follies* that fully justify the name applied to them, shone resplendent with the greater perfection due to more modern methods in the four rooms opening into one another, where an equable temperature was maintained by concealed heating apparatus. The bewildered baroness examined each object of art in the utmost astonishment. She found therein the explanation of the melting away of great fortunes in the crucible, beneath which licentiousness and vanity kindle a consuming fire. This woman who, for twenty-six years, had lived amid the faded relics of the splendor of the imperial régime, whose eyes were accustomed to carpets on which the flowers had become invisible, worn bronzes, and silk hangings as dilapidated as her own heart, caught a glimpse of the seductions of vice as she gazed upon its results. It was impossible not to look with envious eye upon these lovely things, these admirable creations to which the great unknown artists who make Paris what it is to-day, and the renown of its productions,European, had all contributed. One's wonder was aroused by the perfection of each individual object. The models being broken, the figures, the sculptures, the shapes were all original. That is the culmination of the luxury of the present day. To possess things which are not vulgarized by two thousand wealthy ex-tradesmen, who think they are living luxuriously when they make a parade of the treasures with which the shops are filled,—that is the stamp of genuine luxury, the luxury of modern great noblemen, ephemeral stars in the Parisian firmament. Upon examining the jardinières filled with the rarest exotic flowers,—jardinières made of bronze with carved ornaments of the so-called Boulle pattern,—the baroness was actually dismayed at the treasures the room contained. Necessarily that sentiment extended to the person upon whom they were showered in such profusion. Adeline concluded that Josépha Mirah, whose portrait by Joseph Bridau beamed upon her from the boudoir adjoining, was a cantatrice of great talent, a Malibran, and she waited in the expectation of seeing a real lioness. She regretted having come. But she was impelled by so powerful and natural a feeling, by a devotion so utterly free from calculating self-interest, that she summoned all her courage to go through with the interview. Then, too, she was to have an opportunity to satisfy the curiosity, which she had felt so keenly, to study the charm possessed by women of this class, which enabled them to extract so much gold from the miserly deposits in the Parisian soil. The baroness looked herself over to see if her appearance did not make a blot upon all this magnificence; but she carried herself nobly in her velvet dress, with a lovely neckerchief of superb lace, and her velvet hat of the same color as her dress was most becoming. Realizing that she was still as imposing as a queen, always a queen even when she is dethroned, she concluded that the nobility born of misfortune might hold its own against the nobility of talent. She heard doors opening and closing, and at last Josépha stood before her. The famous singer resembled Allori's *Judith,* a masterpiece that remains graven for ever on the memory of all who have seen it in the Pitti Palace, near the door of one of the great salons; the same haughty pose, the same sublime features, black hair twisted carelessly into a knot, and a yellow robe de chambre with thousands of embroidered flowers, an exact reproduction of the brocade in which the immortal homicide created by Bronzino's nephew is dressed.

"Madame la Baronne, I am abashed by the honor you confer upon me in coming here," said the cantatrice, who had promised herself to play the rôle of a great lady to perfection.

With her own hand she drew forward an easy chair for the baroness and sat down herself upon a folding-chair. She detected the traces of her visitor's vanished beauty, and was conscious of a feeling of profound compassion when she saw how her whole frame was shaken by the nervous trembling which the least emotion made convulsive. At a glance she read the whole story of the saintly life which Hulot and Crevel had long before described to her; and not only did she thereupon abandon all thought of a contest with her, but she humbled herself before this grandeur of soul, which she could understand. The divine artist admired that of which the courtesan made sport.

"Mademoiselle, I am brought hither by despair, which leads one to resort to any expedient—"

A gesture on Josépha's part gave the baroness to understand that she had wounded her from whom she expected so much, and she looked up into the artist's face. This supplicating glance extinguished the fire in Josépha's eyes, and she smiled. There was a thrilling eloquence in this dumb by-play between the two women.

"It is now two years and a half since Monsieur Hulot left his family, and I do not know where he is, although I know he is living in Paris," said the baroness in a trembling voice. "A dream gave me the idea, an absurd idea perhaps, that you might have interested yourself in Monsieur Hulot. If you could put me in the way of seeing him again if nothing more, oh! mademoiselle, I would pray for you every day so long as I remain on earth."

Two great tears glistened in the singer's eyes as she replied.

"Madame," said she, in a tone of deep humility, "I injured you when I did not know you; but, now that I am fortunate enough to see you, and in you the most perfect image of virtue upon earth, pray believe that I realize the magnitude of my sin, and that I most sincerely repent; you may therefore be sure that I am ready to do anything to repair it!"

She took the baroness's hand before she had time to resist, kissed it most respectfully and carried her self-abasement so far as to bend the knee before her. Then she stood erect again as proudly as when she came upon the stage in the part of Mathilde, and rang.

"Take a horse," she said to her footman, "and founder him if necessary, but find little Bijou for me, Rue Saint-Maur-du-Temple; bring her to me, put her into a carriage and pay the driver to come at a gallop. Don't lose a minute,—or I'll dismiss you.—Madame," she continued, returning to the baroness and addressing her in a most respectful tone, "you must forgive me. As soon as the Duc d'Hérouville became my protector I dismissed the baron, having learned that he was ruining his family for me. What more could I do? To all of us who adopt a theatrical career a protector is necessary when we make our first appearance. Our salaries do not pay half of our expenses, so we take temporary husbands.—I had no great regard for Monsieur Hulot, who induced me to leave a rich man, a conceited idiot. Père Crevel would certainly have married me—"

"He told me so," the baroness interrupted.

"Well, you see, madame! I should be an honest woman to-day, having but one lawful husband!"

"You have excuses, mademoiselle," said the baroness, "and God will give you due credit for them. But I, far from reproaching you, have come to incur a debt of gratitude to you."

"Madame, nearly three years ago I provided for Monsieur le Baron's necessities—"

"You did!" cried the baroness, her eyes filling with tears. "Oh! what can I do for you? I can only pray."

"Monsieur le Duc d'Hérouville," continued the

G. Cain del. — Gaujean sc.

cantatrice, "a noble-hearted, true gentleman, and myself,—"

And Josépha told the story of Père Thoul's establishment and marriage.

"And so, mademoiselle, my husband, thanks to you, has had all that he needed?" said the baroness.

"We did all we could, madame, to see that he had."

"And where is he?"

"Monsieur le Duc told me about six months ago that the baron, who was known to his notary under the name of Thoul, had exhausted the eight thousand francs, which were to be handed him in equal quarterly payments," Josépha replied. "Since then neither Monsieur d'Hérouville nor myself has heard of him. Our life, you know, is so full, so busy, that I couldn't run after Père Thoul. It so happens that for the last six months Bijou, who does my embroidering, his—what shall I say?—"

"His mistress," said Madame Hulot.

"His mistress," Josépha repeated, "has not been here. Mademoiselle Olympe Bijou may well have left him. Divorce is very common in our arrondissement."

Josépha rose, looked over the rare flowers in her jardinières, and picked a lovely, fragrant bouquet for the baroness, whose anticipations, we ought to say, were entirely falsified. Like the good bourgeois who look upon men and women of genius as monsters who eat, drink, walk and talk differently from the rest of mankind, the baroness had expected to see Josépha the siren, the cantatrice, the clever and voluptuous courtesan; and she found a calm and sedate woman, with the noble bearing suited to her talent, the simple manners of an actress who knows that she will be queen when night comes, and, better than all, a frail woman, who, by her look, her attitude and her whole manner did full and unqualified homage to the virtuous woman, *à la Mater Dolorosa* of sacred song, and who strewed flowers upon her wounds, as the Italian peasants deck their Madonnas.

"Madame," said the footman, returning after an absence of half an hour, "Mère Bijou's on the way; but you can not count upon seeing little Olympe. Madame's embroiderer has become a good bourgeoise, she is married.—"

"With the left hand?" asked Josépha.

"No, madame, really married. She's at the head of a magnificent establishment, she has married the proprietor of a great emporium of novelties on which millions have been spent, on the Boulevard des Italiens, and she has left her embroidery establishment to her sister and mother. She's Madame Grenouville. The rich merchant—"

"Another Crevel!"

"Yes, madame," said the footman. "He acknowledges to thirty thousand a year in Mademoiselle Bijou's contract. Her elder sister, they say, is going to marry a rich butcher."

"Your matter doesn't seem to look very promising," said Josépha to the baroness. "Monsieur le Baron isn't where I located him."

Ten minutes later Madame Bijou was announced.

Josépha took the precaution to ask the baroness to go into her boudoir, and drew the portière.

"You would frighten her," said she; "she wouldn't let out anything if she guessed that you were interested in what she might say, so let me confess her! Conceal yourself there, where you will overhear everything. This scene is played as often in real life as on the stage.—Well, Mère Bijou," said she to an old woman enveloped in a dress of the material called *tartan*, and who resembled a concierge in her Sunday clothes, "so you're all in luck, are you? your daughter has had her chance!"

"Oh! in luck!—my daughter gives us a hundred francs a month and she rides in her carriage and she eats off silver; she's a *miyonaire*!—Olympe might have put me out of want. To work, at my age!—Is that a kindness?"

"She does wrong to be ungrateful, for she owes her beauty to you," said Josépha; "but why hasn't she been to see me? I was the one who made life easy for her by marrying her to my uncle."

"Yes, madame, Père Thoul!—But he's pretty old, all used up—"

"What have you done with him, pray? Is he with you?—She did very wrong to leave him, for here he is worth his millions."

"Ah! *Dieu de Dieu!*" exclaimed Mére Bijou; "that's what I used to say to her when she didn't treat him well, and him gentleness itself, poor old man! Ah! she made him step round! Olympe was led astray, madame!"

"How?"

"Saving your presence, madame, she got acquainted with a *claqueur*, grand-nephew of an old mattress-maker of Faubourg Saint-Marceau. This *loafer*, for that's what all these pretty boys are, a paid *applauder* of plays, you know! is the darling of the Boulevard du Temple, where he works for the new pieces, and *looks after the entrées* of the actresses, as he says. In the morning, he takes his breakfast; before the play he dines so's to get a little mellow; indeed he's been fond of liquors and billiards ever since he was born. 'That's no business at all!' I used to tell Olympe."

"Unfortunately it is a business," said Josépha.

"At last Olympe lost her head over this scamp, who kept bad company, madame, for didn't he come near being arrested in the tavern where the thieves go? but, for that once, Monsieur Braulard, the head of the *claque*, got him off. The creature wears gold earrings and lives by doing nothing, at the expense of women who go mad over such doll-faced men! He used up all the money Monsieur Thoul gave the little one. The business got in a very bad way. What embroidery brought in went for billiards. The boy, madame, had a pretty sister who was in the same business as her brother, on a small scale, in the students' quarter."

"A lorette of the Chaumière," said Josépha.

"Yes, madame," said Mère Bijou. "So Idamore, —he calls himself Idamore but that's a *nom de guerre*, his real name's Chardin,—Idamore imagined your uncle must have more money than he'd admit, and he found a way to send his sister Élodie—he gave her a stage name—to us, without my daughter's suspecting it, as a workgirl; *Dieu de Dieu!* how she did turn the place upside down! she debauched all the poor girls and they're all past soiling, saving your presence.—She did so much that she took Père Thoul for herself and carried him off, we don't know where, and that put us in a mess on account of all the notes that were out. We ain't able to pay them to this very day; but my daughter, who's on hand, looks out for them when they come due.—When Idamore saw that he had the old man, through his sister, he let my poor girl drop, and now he's with a *jeune première* at the Funambules.—And that's how my daughter came to be married, as you'll see—"

"But do you know where the mattress-maker lives?—" interposed Josépha.

"Old Père Chardin? Do you call what he does living?—He's drunk at six o'clock in the morning, he makes one mattress every month, he spends the whole day in low tap-rooms, he plays pool—" *

"What! he makes chickens?—he's a fine sort of rooster!"

"You don't understand, madame; I mean pool (*poule*) at billiards; he wins three or four games every day, and he drinks—"

"Chicken's milk!—" *Des laits de poule!*—said

* *Il fait des poules.* This may mean, "he plays pool," or "he makes chickens"—the word *poule* having both meanings.

Josépha. "But Idamore carries on his business on the boulevard, and we can find him by applying to my friend Braulard."

"I don't know, madame, seeing that this all happened six months ago. Idamore's one of the fellows who's sure to get into the police court, from there to Melun, and then—damme!—"

"To the penitentiary!" said Josépha.

"Ah! madame knows it all," said Mère Bijou with a smile. "If my daughter'd never known that creature, she'd be—But she's had a good chance all the same, you'll tell me; for Monsieur Grenouville got so dead in love with her that he married her."

"How did the marriage come about?"

"Because Olympe was in despair, madame. When she saw that she was deserted for the *jeune première* who she'd often spanked! ah! she boxed her ears!—and that she'd lost Père Thoul who adored her, she swore she'd have no more to do with men. Then Monsieur Grenouville, who used to buy a lot of stuff at our place—two hundred embroidered China sashes a quarter—undertook to console her; but, true or not, she wouldn't hear to anything unless the mayor's office and the church were included. 'I mean to be an honest woman!' she always said, 'or may I die!' And she stuck to it. Monsieur Grenouville agreed to marry her on condition that she gave us up, and we consented—"

"For a money consideration?" inquired the sharp-witted Josépha.

"Yes, madame, ten thousand francs, and a little income for my father, who can't work."

"I asked your daughter to make Père Thoul happy, and she's thrown him into the mud! It isn't fair. I'll never interest myself in anybody again! That's what it is to be guided by a charitable instinct!—Charity's no good except as a speculation, that's sure. Olympe ought at least to have let me know about this muddle! If you find Père Thoul within a fortnight, I'll give you a thousand francs."

"It's a very hard thing to do, my good lady, but there's a many hundred-sou pieces in a thousand francs, and I'll try to earn your money.'

"Adieu, Madame Bijou."

Upon returning to her boudoir the singer found Madame Hulot in a dead swoon; but, although she was unconscious, her nervous affection made her tremble still, just as the fragments of a snake that has been cut in pieces continue to wriggle. Strong salts, fresh water and all the usual remedies, being applied in profusion, restored the baroness to life, or, if you please, to the consciousness of her suffering.

"Oh! mademoiselle, how low he has fallen!" she said as she recognized Josépha and saw that they were alone.

"Have courage, madame," said Josépha, who had seated herself on a cushion at the baroness's feet and was kissing her hands; "we'll find him; and if he's in the mire, why, he'll wash himself clean. My word for it, with well-bred men it's a matter of clothes. Let me undo the wrong I have done you, for I see how much you must be attached to your husband, notwithstanding his conduct, to have come here! Damme! the poor man! he does love women.—Now, you see, if you'd had a little of our *chic*, you could have prevented his running riot so; for you would have been what we have the secret of being: *all sorts of women* for one man. The government ought to set up a school of gymnastics for virtuous women! But governments are so prudish!—they are managed by men whom we lead by the nose! For my part, I pity the people! —But the point now is to work for you, and not to joke.—Have no fear, madame, return home, and don't worry any more. I'll bring your Hector back to you as he was thirty years ago."

"Oh! mademoiselle, let us go to this Madame Grenouville!" said the baroness; "she must know something; perhaps I shall see Monsieur Hulot today, and I may be able to rescue him at once from want and shame.—"

"Madame, I will prove to you in advance the profound gratitude with which I shall always think of you for the honor you have done me, by not exhibiting Josépha the actress, the Duc d'Hérouville's mistress, beside the most beautiful, the most saintly image of virtue. I respect you too deeply to show myself by your side. It is not the humility of an actress, but my homage to you. You make me regret, madame, that I did not follow your path, despite the thorns that have torn your feet and hands!

But what would you have? I belong to art as you belong to virtue—"

"Poor girl!" exclaimed the baroness, deeply touched, amid her own sorrows, by a strange feeling of sympathetic commiseration. "I will pray for you, for you are the victim of society, which is sadly in need of plays. When old age comes upon you, repent—you will be forgiven if God will deign to listen to the prayers of a—"

"Of a martyr, madame," said Josépha, kissing the hem of the baroness's dress with deep respect.

But Adeline took her hand, drew her to her side and kissed her on the forehead. Blushing crimson with pleasure, the cantatrice escorted Adeline to her carriage, with demonstrations of almost servile humility.

"It's some one of those charitable women," said the footman to the maid, "for *she* isn't like that to anyone, not even her good friend, Madame Jenny Cadine!"

"Wait a few days, madame," said Josépha, "and you shall see *him*, or I will deny the God of my fathers; and for a Jewess, you know, that's a promise of success."

*

About the time that the baroness arrived at Josépha's home, Victorin received in his office an old woman of some seventy-five years, who, in order to gain access to the celebrated advocate, made use of the awe-inspiring name of the chief of the secret police. The servant announced:

"Madame de Saint-Estève!"

"I have taken one of my *noms de guerre,*" said she as she took a seat.

Victorin felt an internal shudder, so to speak, at the sight of this horrid old woman. Although richly dressed she was a terrifying object on account of the indications of cold-blooded depravity on her hard, deeply-wrinkled, dead-white muscular face. Marat, if a woman, would have been, at that age, like Saint-Estève, a living image of the Terror. The sinister old hag's sharp little eyes gleamed with the bloodthirsty cupidity of the tiger. Her broad flat nose, with nostrils like oval-shaped cavities in her face exhaling the flaming breath of hell, reminded one of the beak of the fiercest of birds of prey. The genius of intrigue was written upon her low, cruel forehead. The long hairs which grew at random in all the furrows of her face betrayed the virility of her mind. One who looked upon the woman might well have thought that every painter who ever essayed to portray the face of Mephistopheles had missed his mark.

"My dear monsieur," she began in a patronizing tone, "I haven't had a hand in a job—I have not mixed myself up with anything for a long time. What I am going to do for you I do out of consideration for my dear nephew, whom I love better than I should love my son if I had one.—Now, the prefect of police, after the President of the Council had said a couple of words in his ear, referring to you, upon conferring with Monsieur Chapuzot concluded that the police ought not to appear at all in any matter of this kind. So they gave my nephew carte blanche; but my nephew won't take any part except to give advice, for he can't afford to compromise himself."

"You are the aunt of—?"

"You've hit it, and I'm a little bit proud of him," she replied, cutting the advocate short, "for he's my pupil, a pupil who soon became the master.—We have looked into your matter, and *gauged* it! Will you give thirty thousand francs to be rid of it all? I'll do the business for you, and you needn't pay till it's done."

"Do you know the persons concerned?"

"No, my dear monsieur, I await information from you. They told us: 'There's an old simpleton who's got into the clutches of a widow. This widow, twenty-nine years old, has plied her trade as a *thief* so successfully that she has forty thousand a year wormed out of two fathers of families.

She's on the point of raking in twenty-four thousand a year more by marrying an old fellow of sixty-one; she will ruin a whole virtuous family; she will soon get rid of her old husband and will give that immense fortune to her child by some lover.' There's the problem."

"You have it just right!" said Victorin. "My father-in-law, Monsieur Crevel,—"

"Formerly a dealer in perfumery, now a mayor; I live in his arrondissement under the name of *Mame* Nourrisson," said she.

"The other person is Madame Marneffe."

"I don't know her," said Madame de Saint-Estève, "but within three days I'll be able to count her chemises."

"Could you prevent the marriage?" the advocate inquired.

"How far along is it?"

"The second publication."

"We should have to kidnap the woman. It's Sunday to-day, and we have only three days, for they'll be married Wednesday; no, it can't be done. But we can kill her for you—"

Victorin Hulot started back with the horror of an honest man at these seven words, uttered with perfect sang-froid.

"Kill her!" said he. "How will you go about it, pray?"

"For forty years, monsieur, we have taken the place of destiny," she replied with aggressive pride, "and have done whatever we chose in Paris.

More than one family, and in the Faubourg Saint-Germain, too, has told me its secrets. I have made and broken many marriages, I have torn up many wills, I have saved many reputations, I have stowed away here," she said, pointing to her head, "a whole flock of secrets, worth thirty-six thousand francs a year to me; and you will be one of my lambs, you know! Would a woman like me be what I am if she chattered about her methods? I act! Everything that happens, my dear master, will be the work of chance, and you needn't have the slightest remorse. You'll be like people cured by sleepwalkers; who at the end of a month think nature did it all."

The cold sweat stood on Victorin's forehead. The sight of the executioner would have moved him less than this sententious and pretentious sister of the galleys; as he looked at her dress of the color of wine-lees, he fancied that she was dressed in blood.

"Madame, I cannot accept the assistance of your experience and zeal, if success is to be attained at the cost of a life, or if anything in the nature of a crime is to result."

"You're a great baby, monsieur!" replied Madame de Saint-Estève. "You want to remain virtuous in your own eyes, and at the same time you want to see your enemy go under."

Victorin made a sign of dissent.

"Oh! yes," she continued; "you propose that this Madame Marneffe shall release the prey she has in her jaws! And how would you make a tiger let go his piece of beef? By patting him on the back, and saying: 'Pretty puss!—pretty puss!' —You're not logical. You order a battle, but you won't have any wounds! Very good; I'll make you a present of the innocence you have so much at heart. I have always looked upon virtue as the stuff of which hypocrisy is made! Some day, in the course of three months, a poor priest will come and ask you for forty thousand francs for some pious cause, a ruined convent in the East or in the desert! If you are satisfied with your lot, give the good man the forty thousand francs! you'll pay many times that amount into the exchequer. It will be a small matter, God knows, in comparison with what you'll reap."

She stood up on her enormous feet, which her satin shoes could so ill-contain that the flesh overhung them, bowed smilingly to the advocate, and withdrew.

"The devil has a sister," said Victorin to himself, as he rose.

He walked to the door with the horrible unknown, evoked from the caverns of espionage, as a hideous monster rises from the depths below the stage at the opera, in obedience to the magic wand in a fairy ballet.

Having concluded his duties at the Palais, Victorin, in search of information touching his unknown visitor, called upon Monsieur Chapuzot, who was at the head of one of the most important departments in the prefecture of police. Finding Monsieur

Chapuzot alone in his office, Victorin thanked him for his assistance."

"You sent me," said he, "an old woman who might serve to personify Paris, as seen on its criminal side."

Monsieur Chapuzot placed his spectacles on his papers, and stared at the advocate in amazement.

"I should not allow myself to send any person whatsoever to you without notifying you, or without a word of introduction," said he.

"Then it must have been Monsieur le Préfet."

"I don't think it," said Chapuzot. "The last time the Prince de Wissembourg dined with the Minister of the Interior he saw Monsieur le Préfet, and talked with him about the plight you were in, a truly deplorable plight, and asked him if he could not obligingly come to your assistance. Monsieur le Préfet, deeply interested by his Excellency's evident feeling on the subject of this family affair, was kind enough to consult me concerning it. When Monsieur le Préfet took the reins of this department, which is so maligned and at the same time is so useful, he first of all forbade our taking part in any family broils. He was right, both in principle and morally; but he was wrong in practice. The police, during the forty-five years I have been in the department, has rendered services of immense value to families, from 1799 to 1815. Since 1820 the press and the constitutional government have totally changed the conditions of our existence. So my advice was against meddling with an affair of this sort, and Monsieur le Préfet was so kind as to coincide with my opinion. The chief of the secret police received in my presence orders to take no steps; and if, by any chance, you have received a visit from any one sent by him, I shall reprimand him. It would be a case for dismissal. It's easy to say: 'The police will do thus and so!' The police! The police! But, my dear sir, the maréchal and the Council of Ministers have no idea what the police is. Only the police itself knows. The kings, Napoléon and Louis XVIII., knew what their police were about; but in our day, only Fouché, Monsieur Lenoir, Monsieur de Sartines, and some few clever prefects ever suspected.—Now all is changed. We are reduced in numbers, disarmed! I have seen many private disasters sprout and blossom that I might have prevented with five grains of arbitrary power. We shall be regretted by the very men who have wiped us out, when they are brought face to face, as you are now, with some moral monstrosity, which we should be empowered to put out of the way as we remove the mud from the streets! In politics the police are expected to anticipate everything when the public welfare is at stake; but the family is sacred. I would do anything to discover and defeat a plot against the king's life; I would make the walls of a house transparent; but to poke our noses into private households, into family affairs!—never so long as I sit in this office, for I am afraid—"

"Of what?"

"Of the press, Monsieur le Député of the Left Centre!"

"What ought I to do?" said Hulot after a pause.

"Eh! you call yourself the family!" retorted the chief of division; "that's all right, act as you see fit; but to come to your assistance, to make the police the instrument of private passion and private interests,—is such a thing possible?—Therein, you see, lies the secret of the inevitable persecution, which the magistrates deemed illegal, aimed at the predecessor of our present chief of the secret service. Bibi-Lupin ran the police for the benefit of private individuals. This concealed an immense social danger! With the means at his disposal that man would have been formidable, he would have been a sort of *sub-destiny*—"

"But, in my position—?" said Hulot.

"Oh! you, who sell consultations, come and ask for a consultation with me!" retorted Monsieur Chapuzot. "Go to, my dear master, you're laughing at me."

Hulot bowed to the chief of division and took his leave without noticing the almost imperceptible shrug which escaped that official when he rose to show him out.

"And that man claims to be a statesman!" said Monsieur Chapuzot to himself, taking up his reports once more.

Victorin returned home, concealing his perplexity, which he could confide to no one. At dinner the baroness joyfully announced that, within a month, their father might be sharing their good fortune, and finishing his days in peace in the bosom of his family.

"Ah! I would gladly give my thirty-six hundred francs a year to see the baron here!" cried Lisbeth. "But, dear Adeline, I beg of you, don't count too much upon such happiness beforehand."

"Lisbeth is right," said Célestine. "Dear mother, do wait until he's here."

The baroness, all heart and hope, told of her visit to Josépha, dilated upon the unhappiness of such poor creatures in all their good-fortune, and spoke of Chardin, the mattress-maker, the father of the store-keeper at Oran, thus proving that she was not following a false clue.

At seven o'clock the next morning Lisbeth was on the Quai de la Tournelle, in a fiacre which she stopped at the corner of Rue de Poissy.

"Go to Number 7 Rue des Bernardins," said she to the driver; "it's a house on a court, with no concierge. You will go up to the fourth floor and ring at the door on the left, on which you will read: 'Mademoiselle Chardin, laces and cashmeres repaired.' When your ring is answered you will ask for *the chevalier*. The answer will be: 'He has gone out.'—You will say: 'I know it, but go and find him, for his *bonne* is down on the quay in a fiacre, and wants to see him.'"

Some twenty minutes later an old man, who seemed quite eighty years of age, with snow-white hair, a nose reddened by the cold wind set in a pallid face as wrinkled as an old woman's, his back bent double, dressed in an old alpaca overcoat, with list slippers on his feet, with the sleeves of a knitted waist-coat protruding at his wrists, an alarmingly yellow shirt, and wearing no decoration, timidly made his appearance, dragging one foot after the other, looked at the fiacre, recognized Lisbeth, and came to the door.

"Oh! what a state you're in, my dear cousin!" said she.

"Élodie takes all the money for herself!" said Baron Hulot. "These Chardins are a stinking canaille—"

"Do you want to come back with us?"

"Oh! no, no," said the old man; "I'd like to cross to America."

"Adeline's on your track."

"Ah! if they could only pay my debts," said the baron suspiciously, "for Samanon is after me."

"We haven't yet been able to pay up your arrears; your son still owes a hundred thousand francs."

"Poor boy!"

"And your pension won't be free for seven or eight months to come.—If you are willing to wait, I have two thousand francs here!"

The baron put out his hand with an eager gesture of awful significance.

"Give it to me, Lisbeth! May God reward you! Give it to me! I know where to go!"

"But you'll tell me, old monster?"

"Yes, I can wait eight months, for I've discovered

a little angel, a dear, innocent creature who isn't old enough to be depraved yet."

"Look out for the Assizes," said Lisbeth, who flattered herself that she should see Hulot there some day.

"Oh! it's Rue de Charonne," said Hulot, "a neighborhood where there's no noise made about anything that happens. No one will ever find me there. I'll disguise myself as Père Thorec, Lisbeth, and people will take me for an old cabinet-maker; the little one is fond of me, and I shall not have to eat the clothes off my back."

"No, that's already done!" said Lisbeth with a glance at his overcoat. "Suppose I drive you there, cousin?"

Baron Hulot jumped into the carriage, abandoning Mademoiselle Élodie without saying adieu to her, as one tosses aside a novel when it is read.

After a drive of half an hour, during which the baron talked of nothing but little Atala Judici, for he had arrived by degrees at the horrible passions which sap the lives of old men, his cousin deposited him, with two thousand francs in his pocket, on Rue Charonne, Faubourg Saint-Antoine, at the door of a house of very suspicious and ominous appearance.

"Adieu, cousin; now you will be *Père Thorec,* is that it? Don't send anybody to me but regular messengers, and never engage them twice in the same place."

"All right. Oh! I'm a lucky man!" exclaimed

the baron, whose face lighted up in joyful anticipation of the happiness in a new form which awaited him.

"She'll not find him there," said Lisbeth to herself, as she dismissed her cab on Boulevard Beaumarchais, whence she returned to Rue Louis-le-Grand in an omnibus.

*

The next morning Crevel was announced at his children's home, just as the whole family had assembled in the salon after breakfast. Célestine ran and threw herself on her father's neck, and ushered him into the room as if he had been there the day before, although it was his first visit in two years.

"Good-morning, father!" said Victorin, offering him his hand.

"Good-morning, my children!" said the consequential Crevel.—"Madame la Baronne, I offer you my profoundest respect. Heavens! how these children grow! they drive us about! they say: 'Grandpapa, I want my place in the sunlight!'—Madame la Comtesse, you are still wonderfully lovely!" he added, looking at Hortense.—"Ah! there's the balance of our crowns Cousin Bette, the wise virgin. Why, how comfortable you all are here,"—he continued, after this individual distribution of greetings, accompanied by roars of laughter which with difficulty moved the repose of the ruddy masses of his immense cheeks.

He glanced around his daughter's salon with something like disdain.

"My dear Célestine, I give you all the furniture on Rue des Saussayes; it will do very well here. Your salon needs to be furbished up.—Ah! there's that little rascal of a Wenceslas! Well, do we behave ourselves, my little dears? you must look after your morals."

"For those who haven't any," said Lisbeth.

"That sarcasm, my dear Lisbeth, doesn't concern me now. I am going to put an end, my children, to the false position I have occupied so long; and like a good paterfamilias I have come to-day to announce my approaching marriage, without any ifs or buts."

"You have the right to marry," said Victorin, "and so far as I am concerned I give you back the promise you made me when you consented to give me my dear Célestine's hand."

"What promise?" demanded Crevel.

"That you would not marry again," replied the advocate. "You will do me the justice to admit that I asked for no such promise, that you gave it voluntarily despite my remonstrances, for I urged upon you at the time that you ought not to bind yourself so."

"Yes, I remember, my dear boy," said Crevel shamefacedly. "And on my word,—ah! my children, if you choose to live on good terms with Madame Crevel you shall have no reason to repent it.—Your delicacy touches me, Victorin.—No man can be generous to me with impunity. *Sapristi!* come, receive your mother-in-law kindly, come to my wedding"

"You don't tell us who your *fiancée* is, father," said Célestine.

"Why, that's the secret of the play," said Crevel. "Let's not play at hide-and-seek! Lisbeth must have told you—"

"My dear Monsieur Crevel," retorted the Lorrainer, "there are names one can not pronounce here."

"Well, then, it's Madame Marneffe!"

"Monsieur Crevel," rejoined the advocate sternly, "neither my wife nor myself will attend your wedding, not from any interested motives, for I spoke to you just now with perfect sincerity. Yes, I should be very happy to know that you have found happiness in this union; but I am guided by motives of honor and delicacy which you must understand, and which I can not express, for I should reopen wounds which are still bleeding here."

The baroness made a sign to the countess, who took her child in her arms and said:

"Come, Wenceslas, come and have your bath!—Adieu, Monsieur Crevel."

The baroness bowed to Crevel without a word, and that worthy could not repress a smile as he saw the child's amazement at being threatened with this unexpected bath.

"You propose to marry, monsieur," cried the advocate when he was alone with Lisbeth, his wife and his father-in-law, "a woman who is laden with my father's spoils, and who with utter unconcern led him into his present plight; a woman who is living with the son-in-law, after ruining the father-in-law; a woman who is the cause of my sister's mortal suffering.—And you fancy that I will sanction your madness by my presence? I sincerely pity you, my dear Monsieur Crevel! you have no idea of the family, you do not understand the powerful bond of honor which binds its different members together. One can't reason with the passions—unfortunately I have had too much experience in that direction. Men who are ruled by their passions are as deaf as they are blind. Your daughter Célestine is too fully sensible of her duty to utter a single word of reproach."

"That would be a fine thing for her to do!" said Crevel, trying to cut short this lecture.

"Célestine would not be my wife if she said one word to you on the subject," rejoined the advocate; "but I can try to stop you before you put your foot over the precipice, especially after I have proved my disinterestedness. It certainly is not your fortune, but you yourself, that I am concerned about.—And, to leave you in no doubt as to my feelings, I may add, were it only to set your mind at rest concerning your marriage-contract, that my pecuniary situation is such that we have nothing to wish for."

"Thanks to me!" cried Crevel, whose face had become purple.

"Thanks to Célestine's fortune," retorted the advocate; "and if you regret having given your daughter, as a marriage-portion coming from yourself, a sum which does not represent the half of what her mother left her, we are all ready to return it to you."

"Do you know, my good son-in-law," said Crevel, striking his attitude, "that, when I give Madame Marneffe the protection of my name, she will not be answerable to the world for her conduct, except as Madame Crevel?"

"That may be very noble," said the advocate; "it's very generous so far as affairs of the heart and the errors due to passion are concerned; but I know no name, no laws, no title which can cover up the theft of the three hundred thousand francs vilely extorted from my father!—I tell you plainly, my dear father-in-law, that your intended wife is unworthy of you, that she is deceiving you, that she is madly in love with my brother-in-law Steinbock, whose debts she has paid—"

"It was I who paid them!"

"Very good," retorted the advocate; "I am very glad for Comte Steinbock, who may be able to pay you some day; but she loves him, she loves him very dearly, and loves him often—"

"She loves him!" said Crevel, whose face bore witness to his great agitation. "It's a cowardly, dirty, mean, vulgar thing to slander a woman!—When one makes such statements as that, monsieur, one must prove them."

"I'll give you your proofs."

"I await them!"

"Day after to-morrow, my dear Monsieur Crevel, I will tell you the day, hour and moment when I shall be prepared to lay bare the shocking depravity of your future wife."

"Very well, I shall be charmed," said Crevel, recovering his self-possession.—"Adieu, my children, au revoir.—Adieu, Lisbeth."

"Pray go with him, Lisbeth," said Célestine in Cousin Bette's ear.

"Well, well, how you go on!" cried Lisbeth to Crevel.

"Ah!" said Crevel, "he's become a very great man, has my son-in-law; he's presumptuous. The Palais, the Chamber, the wiles of the law and the wiles of politics are making a very pretty fellow of him. Ah! he knows that I'm to be married next Wednesday, and on Sunday my gentleman proposes to tell me, three days after, the time when he will prove that my wife's unworthy of me. That's very clever. I am going back to sign the contract. Come, Lisbeth, come with me! They'll know nothing about it! I intended to leave Célestine forty thousand francs a year, but Hulot has acted in a way to alienate my heart forever."

"Give me ten minutes, Père Crevel; wait ten minutes for me in your carriage at the door, while I invent an excuse for going out."

"Very well, I'll do it."

"My dears," said Lisbeth returning to the family in the salon, "I am going with Crevel; the contract's to be signed to-night, and I may be able to tell you its provisions. It will probably be my last visit to that woman. Your father's in a furious rage. He means to disinherit you."

"His vanity will prevent him from doing it,"

replied the advocate. "He was anxious to own the Presles estate, and he'll keep it; I know him. Even if he should have children, Célestine will get half of what he leaves; the law forbids him bequeathing his whole fortune away from her.—But those questions have no weight with me; I am thinking solely of our honor.—Go, cousin," he said, pressing Lisbeth's hand, "and listen closely to the contract."

Some twenty minutes later Lisbeth and Crevel entered the house on Rue Barbet, where Madame Marneffe was awaiting in mild impatience the result of the step she had ordered to be taken. Valérie had, in the end, conceived a violent passion for Wenceslas, of the sort which assails a woman's heart but once in a lifetime. In her hands the unsuccessful artist had become so perfect a lover, that he was to her what she had been to Baron Hulot. Valérie had her slippers in one hand, and the other was in Steinbock's, against whose shoulder her head was resting. It might well be said of the disconnected conversation in which they had been engaged since Crevel's departure, as of the bulky literary productions of our day, which bear the legend on their title-pages: *Reproduction prohibited.* This delicious hour of poetic privacy naturally brought to the artist's lips a regret, which he expressed not without bitterness.

"Ah! how unfortunate it is that I married!" he said; "for, if I had waited, as Lisbeth advised, I might marry you now.'

"One must be a Pole to long to make one's devoted mistress his wife!" cried Valérie. "To exchange love for duty! pleasure for ennui!"

"I know you to be so fickle!" Steinbock replied. "Haven't I heard you talking with Lisbeth about Baron Montès, that Brazilian?"

"Do you want to rid me of him?" said Valérie.

"That would be the only way of preventing you from seeing him," replied the ex-sculptor.

"Understand, my darling," said Valérie, "that I was playing him to make a husband of him, for I tell you everything—the promises I made this Brazilian,—oh! long before I knew you, she said in reply to a gesture from Wenceslas—"those promises, which he is using now as weapons to torment me with, force me to marry almost in secret; for if he learns that I am to marry Crevel he is just the man to—to kill me!"

"Oh! as for any fear of that!—" exclaimed Steinbock, with a disdainful gesture which signified that that danger was quite insignificant for a woman who was beloved by a Pole.

Take notice that in the matter of personal courage the Poles are not to be accused of bravado, they are so truly and unequivocally brave.

"And that idiot of a Crevel, who insists upon giving a party, and is displaying his taste for magnificence—economical magnificence—in connection with our wedding, places me in an embarrassing position that I can't see my way out of!"

Could Valérie confess to the man she adored that

Baron Henri Montès, after Baron Hulot's dismissal, had inherited the privilege of visiting her at all hours of the night, and that, notwithstanding her address, she was still in imminent danger of a dispute in which the Brazilian would believe that she was entirely in the wrong? She was too well acquainted with the baron's quasi-savage disposition, which closely resembled Lisbeth's, not to tremble as she thought of her Moor from Rio-de-Janeiro. When they heard the carriage-wheels, Steinbock, whose arm was about Valérie's waist, moved away from her, and took up a newspaper in which he seemed to be deeply absorbed. Valérie was embroidering, with painstaking attention, a pair of slippers for her intended spouse.

"How they slander *her!*" said Lisbeth in Crevel's ear, pointing to the picture before them as they stood in the doorway.—"Look at her hair! is it tumbled? To hear Victorin talk, you might have expected to surprise a pair of turtle-doves in their nest."

"My dear Lisbeth," replied Crevel, in his favorite pose, "to make a Lucretia of an Aspasia, you see, all you need do is to inspire her with a real passion!"

"Didn't I always tell you," retorted Lisbeth, "that women love fat old libertines like you?"

"She'd be mighty ungrateful if she didn't," said Crevel; "for how much money have I laid out here? Nobody knows but Grindot and myself!"

And he went up stairs.

In the renovation of this mansion, which Crevel

looked upon as his own, Grindot had tried to measure his strength with Cleretti, the architect then in vogue, to whom the Duc d'Hérouville had entrusted the decoration of Josépha's house. But Crevel, who was utterly unable to understand art, determined, like all men of his class, to spend a fixed sum, decided upon in advance. Restricted as he was by an iron-clad estimate, it was impossible for Grindot to realize his architectural dream. The principal difference between Josépha's mansion and the one on Rue Barbet was the same difference that exists between any object that has an individuality of its own and one that is utterly commonplace. The things that one admired in Josépha's rooms one saw nowhere else; the glittering ornaments of Crevel's salons could be bought anywhere. These two different varieties of luxury are separated from each other by the broad stream of the million. A mirror of which there is no duplicate is worth six thousand francs, the mirror invented by a manufacturer who sells as many as he can of the same pattern, costs five hundred. An authentic Boulle chandelier sells as high as three thousand francs at public auction; the same chandelier remoulded can be made for a thousand or twelve hundred; one is in archæology what a genuine Raphaël is in painting, the other is its copy. What value do you attach to a copy of a Raphaël? The Crevel mansion therefore was a magnificent specimen of the splendor of fools, as Josépha's was the most beautiful type of an artistic habitation.

"The war is on," said Crevel, walking toward his fiancée.

Madame Marneffe rang.

"Go for Monsieur Berthier," she said to the footman, "and do not come back without him.—If you had succeeded," said she, winding her arms about Crevel, "we would have postponed my happiness, my little father, and we would have given a feast to make people open their eyes; but when a whole family opposes a marriage, my dear, decency requires that it should be celebrated quietly, especially when the bride is a widow."

"On the contrary I propose to have it celebrated on a scale of magnificence worthy of Louis XIV.," said Crevel, who had long since concluded that the eighteenth century was beneath contempt. "I have ordered new carriages: there's monsieur's carriage and madame's, two pretty little coupés, a calèche, and a state berlin, with a magnificent box which shakes like Madame Hulot."

"Aha! *I propose!*—So you won't be my lamb any longer? No, no, my buck, you'll do as I wish. We will sign our contract here, between ourselves, to-night. Then, on Wednesday, we'll be married formally, a genuine marriage, on the sly, as my poor mother used to say. We will go on foot, dressed very simply, to the church, where we will hear low mass. Our witnesses are Steinbock, Stidmann, Vignon and Massol, all clever fellows who will be at the mayor's office as if by chance, and who will make the sacrifice of listening to mass for our sake. Your colleague will make an exception in our case and marry us at nine o'clock in the morning. Mass is at ten o'clock and we shall be back here to breakfast at half-past eleven. I have promised our guests that we would not leave the table till evening. We shall have Bixiou, your former comrade Du Tillet, Lousteau, Vernisset, Léon de Lora, Vernou, the élite of the entertaining men of the day, none of whom need know that we are married; we will mystify them, we will get just a shade tipsy, and Lisbeth will be on hand; I want her to know of the marriage, Bixiou is to make some proposals to her, and teach her—a little something."

For two hours Madame Marneffe poured forth a flood of playful talk, which suggested to Crevel's mind this sage reflection:

"How can a woman so light of heart be depraved? Frolicsome, if you please! but wicked—nonsense!"

"What did your children say about me?" Valérie asked Crevel at a moment when she drew him close to her on her sofa; "horrible things, I suppose!"

"They declare," Crevel replied, "that you have a criminal passion for Wenceslas; you, virtue itself!"

"I should say that I do love my little Wenceslas!" cried Valérie, calling the artist to her side, taking his head in her hands, and kissing him on the brow. "Poor boy, without friends or fortune! thrown aside in disdain by a carrot-colored giraffe! What do you expect, Crevel? Wenceslas is my poet, and I love him in broad daylight as if he were my child! These virtuous women see evil everywhere and in everything. Ah well! so they couldn't be content without trying to injure me about a man? I am like a spoiled child who has never been refused anything; bonbons no longer cause me any emotion. Poor women, I pity them!—Who was it, pray, who maligned me like that?"

"Victorin," said Crevel.

"Well, why didn't you close his beak, the magisterial parroquet, with his *mamma's* two hundred thousand francs?"

"Ah! the baroness ran away," said Lisbeth.

"Let them beware, Lisbeth!" exclaimed Madame Marneffe with a frown; "either they will receive me under their roof, and civilly, too, and will call on their step-mother, every one of them! or I'll sink them lower than the baron is now; tell them so from me.—I propose to become wicked at last! On my word, I believe evil is the reaping-hook with which men gather in this world's goods."

At three o'clock Monsieur Berthier, successor to Cardot, read the marriage-contract, after a brief conference with Crevel, for certain articles depended upon the decision of Monsieur and Madame Hulot junior. Crevel made over to his future wife a fortune consisting of:

1. Forty thousand francs a year, to be derived from securities which were named;

2. The house on Rue Barbet and everything contained therein; and

3. Three millions in cash.

Over and above this he gave his future wife all that the law allowed him to give; he provided that she need furnish no inventory; and in the event that there should be no children of the marriage, they agreed that the one who should die first should give to the other the whole of his or her property, real and personal. This contract reduced Crevel's fortune to two millions. If he had children by his new wife, it would cut down Célestine's share to five hundred thousand francs, because of the income provided for Valérie. That sum represented about one-ninth part of his present fortune.

Lisbeth returned to Rue Louis-le-Grand to dinner, with despair depicted on her countenance. She explained and dilated upon the marriage-contract, and found Célestine no less indifferent to the disastrous news than Victorin.

"You have angered your father, my children! Madame Marneffe has sworn that you shall receive Monsieur Crevel's wife, and that you shall call upon her," she said.

"Never!" said Hulot.

"Never!" said Célestine.

"Never!" cried Hortense.

Lisbeth was seized with an ardent longing to put down the haughty pride of all the Hulots.

"She seems to have some weapon to use against you!" she replied. "I don't know what it is, but I will know.—She spoke vaguely of some story about two hundred thousand francs, which has some connection with Adeline."

Madame Hulot quietly fell over on the couch where she was sitting, and a frightful attack of convulsions followed.

"Go to her, my children!—" cried she. "Receive the woman here! Monsieur Crevel is an infamous man! he deserves the greatest of all punishments. —Obey that woman.—Ah! she's a monster! *She knows all!*"

After she had uttered these words, mingled with tears and sobs, she summoned sufficient strength to go up to her own room, leaning on her daughter's arm and Célestine's.

"What does all this mean?" cried Lisbeth, when she was left alone with Victorin.

The advocate, rooted to the spot, in a state of stupefaction that can readily be conceived, did not hear Lisbeth.

"What's the matter, dear Victorin?"

"I am terrified!" said the advocate, whose face assumed a threatening expression. "Woe to her who injures my mother; my scruples have vanished! If I could do it, I would crush that woman as one would crush a viper.—Ah! she aims a blow at my mother's life and honor!"

"She said, but don't repeat this, my dear Victorin, she said that she would sink you all lower than your father.—She reproached Crevel roundly for not having closed your mouth with this secret which seems to frighten Adeline so."

A physician was sent for, for the baroness's condition grew worse. He ordered a draught containing a large amount of opium, and Adeline fell into a deep sleep as soon as she had taken it; but the whole family was alarmed beyond measure. The next day, the advocate started at an early hour for the Palais; he called at the prefecture of police on his way, and besought Vautrin, the chief of the secret service, to send Madame de Saint-Estève to him.

"We are forbidden, monsieur, to take any part in your affair, but Madame de Saint-Estève is in business on her own account, and she's at your service," replied the famous officer.

On his return the poor fellow learned that his mother's reason was in danger. Doctor Bianchon, Doctor Larabit and Professor Angard, in consultation, had decided to resort to heroic methods to check the flow of blood to the brain. While Victorin was listening to Doctor Bianchon giving his reasons for hoping that the crisis would end favorably, although his associates despaired of any such result, the footman announced Madame de Saint-Estève. Victorin left Bianchon in the middle of a sentence, and ran down stairs like a madman.

"Can there be a germ of contagious insanity in the family?" said Bianchon turning to Larabit.

The physicians went away, leaving an assistant to watch Madame Hulot.

"A whole lifetime of virtue!" were the only words the invalid had pronounced since her seizure.

Lisbeth did not leave Adeline's bedside; she had sat up all night with her and was looked upon with admiration by the two younger women.

"Well, my dear Madame Saint-Estève!" said the advocate, showing the horrible old woman into his study, and carefully closing the doors, "how far have we got?"

"Well, my dear friend," she replied, looking at Victorin with a coldly ironical eye, "have you reflected on what I said?"

"Have you done anything?"

"Will you give fifty thousand francs?"

"Yes," replied Hulot, "for we must go ahead. Do you know that that woman has endangered my mother's life and reason with a single sentence? So, go on!"

"We have gone on!" said the old woman.

"Well?—" said Victorin convulsively.

"Well, do you stick at any expense?"

"On the contrary."

"The expenses already mount up to twenty-three thousand francs."

Hulot stared at the Saint-Estève with an idiotic expression.

"Well, well! can you be such a gull, you, one of the shining lights of the Palais?" said the old woman. "For that sum we have procured a lady's maid's conscience and a picture by Raphaël; that's not a high price.—"

Hulot still stood stupidly by with his eyes opened to their fullest extent.

"Well," continued La Saint-Estève, "we have purchased Mademoiselle Reine Tousard, a young lady from whom Madame Marneffe has no secrets."

"I understand."

"But if you're going to be stingy, say so!"

"I will pay you and trust to you," he replied; "go on! My mother told me that these people deserved the most severe of all punishments."

"They don't break people on the wheel any more," said the old woman.

"You will answer for the success of your plan?"

"Let me alone," said La Saint-Estève. "Your vengeance is simmering."

She looked at the clock; it was just six.

"Your vengeance is dressing, the ovens at the *Rocher de Cancale* are lighted, the horses in the carriages are stamping, my irons are being heated. Ah! I know your Madame Marneffe by heart. Everything is ready! There is bait in the trap, and I'll tell you to-morrow if the mouse will be poisoned. I think so! Adieu, my son."

"Adieu, madame."

"Do you know English?"

"Yes."

"Did you ever see the play of Macbeth, in English?"

"Yes."

"Well, my son, you shall be king! that is to say, you shall inherit!" said the frightful hag, whom Shakespeare imagined, and who seemed familiar with Shakespeare.

She left Hulot dumfounded on the threshold of his study.

"Don't forget that the case is on for to-morrow,"

said she graciously with the air of an experienced litigant.

She saw two people coming and was anxious to pass in their eyes for a *Comtesse de Pimbèche.*

"What assurance!" muttered Hulot, as he bowed to his pretended client.

*

Baron Montès de Montejanos was a lion, but a lion shrouded in mystery. Fashionable Paris, the Paris of the turf and the lorettes, admired the foreign nobleman's ineffable waistcoats, the irreproachable polish of his boots, his matchless canes, his much admired fine horses, his carriage, driven by perfectly trained and well-controlled negroes. The amount of his fortune was known; he had a credit of seven hundred thousand francs with Du Tillet the famous banker; but he was always alone. If he went to a first performance, he sat in an orchestra stall. He frequented no salon. He had never offered his arm to a lorette! It was impossible to connect his name with that of any charming woman in society. For pastime, he played whist at the Jockey Club. People were reduced to the necessity of attacking his manners, or, what seemed infinitely more amusing, his personal appearance; they called him Combabus!—Bixiou, Léon de Lora, Lousteau, Florine, Mademoiselle Héloïse Brisetout and Nathan, when supping one evening with the illustrious Carabine, with lions and lionesses galore, invented this most absurd appellation. Massol, in his capacity of Councilor of State, and Claude Vignon, who had once been a professor of Greek, had told the ignorant lorettes the famous anecdote, related in Rollin's Ancient History, concerning

Combabus, that voluntary Abelard to whom was entrusted the custody of the wife of a king of Assyria, Persia, Bactriana, Mesopotamia, and other divisions of the private geography of old Professor Du Bocage, who completed the work begun by D'Anville, the creator of the ancient Orient. This nickname, which furnished food for laughter to Carabine's guests for a quarter of an hour, was the subject of a multitude of decidedly broad jests in a work to which the Academy could not award the Montyon prize, but among them was noticed the name which clung to the bushy mane of the handsome baron, whom Josépha called a *magnificent Brazilian,* as one speaks of a magnificent *catoxantha!* Carabine, most illustrious of lorettes, whose refined beauty and witty sallies had wrested the sceptre of the thirteenth arrondissement from the hands of Mademoiselle Turquet, better known by the name of *Malaga,*—Carabine, or Mademoiselle Séraphine Sinet—such was her real name—was to the banker Du Tillet what Josépha Mirah was to the Duc d'Hérouville.

Now, on the morning of the very day when La Saint-Estève predicted success to Victorin, Carabine had said to Du Tillet about seven o'clock:

"If you were a good fellow, you'd give me a dinner at the *Rocher de Cancale,* and bring Combabus; we mean to find out whether he has a mistress.—I've bet on —and I want to win."

"He's always at the Hôtel des *Princes,* and I'll drop in and see him," replied Du Tillet; "we'll have some sport. Have all the boys there: Bixiou, Lora, the whole gang in fact!"

At half-past seven in the evening, the table was laid for dinner in the finest salon of the establishment where all Europe has dined; upon the table shone a magnificent service of silver-plate made expressly for use at dinner-parties where vanity liquidated the bill in bank-notes. Torrents of light caused cascades of brilliancy to play along the edges of the chasing. Waiters, whom a provincial would have mistaken for diplomatists, barring their age, moved sedately about like men who knew that they would be handsomely tipped.

Five persons had arrived and were awaiting the arrival of nine others. First of all there was Bixiou, the salt of every intellectual feast, still on his feet in 1843, with a whole armor of jokes, always new,—a phenomenon as rare in Paris as virtue itself. Then there was Léon de Lora, the greatest landscape and marine painter living, who had the advantage over all his rivals of never having fallen below the level of his first work. The lorettes could not do without these kings of witticism. No supper, no dinner, no party of any sort was complete without them. Séraphine Sinet, alias Carabine, as titular mistress of the Amphitryon of the feast, had been one of the first to arrive, and was exhibiting beneath the waves of light in all their glory a pair of shoulders unrivaled in Paris, a neck as faultless in outline as if turned on a lathe, and without a wrinkle! a saucy face, and a dress of figured satin, blue upon blue, trimmed with English lace in sufficient quantity to support a whole village for a month. Pretty Jenny Cadine, who was not acting at her theatre and whose portrait is too well known to make any description necessary, arrived in a costume of fabulous splendor. To these ladies a party is always a Longchamp in the matter of toilettes, where each seeks to win the prize for her particular millionaire, saying, as it were, to her rivals:

"See how much I am worth!"

A third woman, doubtless just at the beginning of her career, was looking on, almost shamefacedly, at the magnificence of her two wealthy and established companions. She was simply dressed, in white cashmere trimmed with blue lace; her hair had been dressed with flowers by a hairdresser of the *merlan* type, whose unskilful hand had, unwittingly, imparted the charm of simplicity to her lovely blonde locks. Embarrassed as she still was by her costume, *she had the shyness inseparable from a first appearance*, according to the time-worn phrase. She came from Valognes to find employment in Paris for a despairingly-blooming freshness, innocence calculated to arouse the passions of a dying man, and beauty worthy to take rank with all those that Normandy has already furnished to the different theatres of the capital. The perfect lines of her face fulfilled one's ideal of angelic purity. The milky whiteness of her skin reflected the light so perfectly that you would have said you were looking in a mirror. The delicate colors were laid upon her cheeks as with an artist's pencil. She was called Cydalise. She was, as we shall presently see, a necessary pawn in the game *Mame* Nourrisson was playing against Madame Marneffe.

"You haven't an arm in keeping with your name, my dear," said Jenny Cadine, to whom Carabine had introduced this sixteen-year chef-d'œuvre, and who had brought her to the dinner.

In truth Cydalise presented for public admiration a pair of lovely arms, compact and of fine texture, but reddened by the vigorous current of blood that flowed beneath.

"How much is she worth?" Jenny Cadine asked Carabine in an undertone.

"A fortune."

"What do you propose to make of her?"

"Madame Combabus of course!"

"And for that transaction you are to have—?"

"Guess!"

"A handsome service of plate?"

"I have three!"

"Diamonds?"

"I sell them."

"A green monkey?"

"No, a Raphaël!"

"What rat has got into your brain?"

"Josépha puts my nose out of joint with her pictures," replied Carabine, "and I propose to have finer ones than hers."

Du Tillet brought with him the hero of the

dinner, the Brazilian; the Duc d'Hérouville followed them with Josépha. The cantatrice wore a simple velvet dress; but about her neck gleamed a necklace worth a hundred and twenty thousand francs, of pearls which could hardly be distinguished from her white camelia-like skin. She had thrust among the black tresses of her hair a single red camelia—a *patch!*—with stunning effect, and she had amused herself by piling up eleven pearl bracelets on each arm. As she pressed Jenny Cadine's hand, the latter said to her:

"Pray lend me your mittens, will you?"

Josépha removed her bracelets and offered them to her friend upon a plate.

"What style!" said Carabine; "she must be a duchess! Pearls, too! You've stripped the sea to adorn your girl, eh, Monsieur le Duc?" she added, turning to the little Duc d'Hérouville.

The actress took but two bracelets and replaced the other twenty on the singer's arms, on which she deposited a kiss.

Lousteau, the literary parasite, La Palférine and Malaga, Massol and Vauvinet, and Théodore Gaillard, part-proprietor of one of the leading political journals, completed the number of guests. The Duc d'Hérouville, courteous, as a great nobleman always is, to everybody, exchanged with the Comte de la Palférine that special form of salutation which, without suggesting esteem or intimacy, says to all the world: "We are of the same family, of the same race, we know each other's worth."

That salutation, the *shibboleth* of the aristocracy, was invented to carry despair to the wits of the upper middle-class.

Carabine seated Combabus at her left and the Duc d'Hérouville at her right. Cydalise flanked the Brazilian and Bixiou was placed on the other side of the young Norman. Malaga was next the duke.

At seven they attacked the oysters. At eight, between two courses, they discussed frozen punch. Everybody knows the menu of such banquets. At nine o'clock they were chattering away as people will chatter after forty-two bottles of different kinds of wine have been emptied by fourteen persons. The dessert, the horrible dessert of the month of April, was served. The heady atmosphere had intoxicated none but the Norman girl, who was singing a Christmas carol. With the exception of that poor creature no one had lost his wits, for the drinkers, men and women, were the élite of supping Paris. Spirits were gay, eyes, although brilliant were still full of intelligence, but lips were tending to satire, anecdote and indiscretion. The conversation, which had thus far been confined within the vicious circle of racing and horses, Bourse operations, the different merits of the reigning lions compared with one another, and well-known scandalous anecdotes, threatened to become more private, and to be divided among groups of two hearts.

At this juncture, in obedience to divers meaning

glances bestowed by Carabine upon Léon de Lora, Bixiou, La Palférine and Du Tillet, the subject of love was brought forward.

"The best doctors never talk about medicine, real noblemen never talk about their ancestors, talented people never talk about their works," said Josépha; "why should we talk about our profession?—I made them close the doors at the opera so that I could come, and it certainly wasn't for the purpose of *working* here. So let's not *pose*, my dear friends."

"They're talking about real love, my dear!" said Malaga, "the love that makes a man throw himself overboard, and his father and mother, sell his wife and children and go to Clichy—"

"Talk away, then!" rejoined the singer. "Not up to it!"

"Not up to it." This phrase, adopted into the lorette's vocabulary from the slang of the Paris gamin, becomes with the assistance of their eyes and expression, a whole poem upon their lips.

"Don't I love you, Josépha?" said the duke in a low voice.

"You may love me truly," the cantatrice whispered in his ear, with a smile; "but as for myself, I don't love you with the kind of love they're talking about, the love that makes the world all black without the man one loves. You are very agreeable to me, and useful, but you're not indispensable; and if you should desert me to-morrow, I should have three dukes for one—"

"Does love really exist in Paris?" said Léon de

Lora. "No one here has the time to make his fortune, and how can one yield to the true love which takes possession of a man as water does of sugar? One must be enormously rich to love, for love nullifies a man, as it has our dear Brazilian baron here. I have said for a long time that *extremes stop each other up.* A true lover resembles a eunuch, for women no longer exist on earth so far as he is concerned! He's a mysterious creature, he's like the true Christian, alone in his desert! Just look at our gallant Brazilian yonder!"

The whole table turned to look at Henri Montès de Montejanos, who was abashed to find himself the cynosure of every eye.

"He's been feeding there an hour without any more idea than an ox would have, that he's sitting beside the—I won't say in this presence the loveliest, but the freshest young woman in Paris."

"Everything is fresh here, even the fish; that's the reputation of the house," said Carabine.

Baron Montès de Montejanos looked across at the landscape-painter with an affable expression, and said:

"Very good! I drink to you!"

And he nodded to Léon de Lora, put his full glass of port to his mouth and drank with great dignity.

"So you are in love?" said Carabine to her neighbor, putting this interpretation upon the toast.

The baron ordered his glass refilled, bowed to Carabine and repeated the toast.

"To madame's health!" then said the lorette, in so waggish a tone that the painter, Bixiou and Du Tillet roared with laughter.

The Brazilian maintained the gravity of a bronze statue. His indifference vexed Carabine. She was perfectly well aware that Montès was in love with Madame Marneffe; but she did not look for this uncompromising fidelity, the obstinate silence of a man whose mind is made up. We so often judge a woman by the attitude of her lover that we are accustomed to judge a lover by the bearing of his mistress. Proud of his love for Valérie and of being beloved by her, there was a tinge of irony in the smile the baron bestowed upon these accomplished connoisseurs; moreover he was superb to look upon; the wine had not changed his color, and his eyes, bright with the brilliancy peculiar to burnished gold, kept the secrets of his heart.

"What a woman!" said Carabine to herself; "how she has sealed up that heart!"

"He's a stone!" said Bixiou half-aloud, looking upon it all as a bit of fooling, and without a suspicion of the importance attached by Carabine to the demolition of this fortress.

While this discussion, apparently trivial, was going on at Carabine's right, the discussion concerning love was continued at her left by the Duc d'Hérouville, Lousteau, Josépha, Jenny Cadine and Massol. They were trying to decide whether these infrequent phenomena were produced by passion, by obstinacy, or by true love. Josépha, bored to death by their theories, tried to change the subject of conversation.

"You're talking about something of which you are absolutely ignorant! Is there any one of you who ever loved a woman enough, and a woman unworthy of him, to throw away his fortune and his children's, sell his future, besmirch his past, run the risk of the galleys by stealing from the State, kill his brother and uncle, and allow his eyes to be blindfolded so completely that he never thought it was being done to prevent him from seeing the pit, into which he was pushed, as a final jest? Du Tillet has a strong-box under his left breast, Léon de Lora has his wits there, Bixiou would laugh at himself if he loved anybody but himself, Massol has a minister's portfolio in place of a heart; Lousteau has nothing but a muscle there, for he allowed Madame de la Baudraye to leave him; Monsieur le Duc is too rich to be able to prove his love by ruining himself; Vauvinet doesn't count; I draw the line at the discounter of mankind. So you have never loved, any of you, nor have I, nor Jenny, nor Carabine.—For my own part I never have seen the phenomenon I have just described but once. That was our poor Baron Hulot," she said to Jenny Cadine, "whom I'm going to advertise for like a lost dog, for I want to find him."

"Oho!" said Carabine to herself with a meaning glance at Josépha; "has Madame Nourrisson two of Raphaël's pictures, that I find Josépha playing my game?"

"Poor man!" said Vauvinet, "he was very tall and stately. What style! what a figure! He had the carriage of François I. What a volcano he was! and what cleverness, what downright genius he displayed in raising money! Wherever he is he's on the look out for it, and he ought to be able to get some out of the walls built of bones that you see in the suburbs of Paris, near the gates, where he's in hiding, no doubt—"

"And all for that little Madame Marneffe!" said Bixiou. "There's a female roué for you!"

"She's going to marry my friend Crevel!" observed Du Tillet.

"And she's mad over my friend Steinbock!" said Léon de Lora.

These three remarks were like three pistol shots received by Montès full in the chest. He turned pale as death, and was in such agony that it was difficult for him to rise.

"You're *canaille!*" he exclaimed. "You've no right to mingle a virtuous woman's name with the names of all your abandoned creatures! nor, above all things, to make her a target for your low jokes!"

Montès was interrupted by bravos and unanimous applause. Bixiou, Léon de Lora, Vauvinet, Du Tillet and Massol gave the signal. It was a grand chorus.

"Vive l'Empereur!" said Bixiou.

"Crown him!" cried Vauvinet.

"A *groan* for Médor! *hurrah* for Brazil!" cried Lousteau.

"Aha! my copper-colored baron, you love our Valérie, do you?" said Léon de Lora; "you're not easily disgusted!"

"What he said wasn't parliamentary, but it was magnificent!" observed Massol.

"But, my love of a client, you have recommended me, I am your banker, your innocence will be a bad thing for me."

"Ah! you're a serious-minded man, do you tell me—" said the Brazilian to Du Tillet.

"Thanks for us all," said Bixiou, bowing.

"Tell me something positive," continued Montès, disregarding Bixiou's interruption.

"Well, my boy," replied Du Tillet, "I have the honor to tell you that I am invited to Crevel's wedding."

"Aha! Combabus assumes the defense of Madame Marneffe!" exclaimed Josépha rising solemnly from her chair.

She walked up to Montès with a tragic air, gave him a friendly little tap on the head, looked at him for a moment with an expression of amused admiration in her face, and shook her head.

"Hulot is the first example of love *in spite of all*, and here's the second," she said; "but he ought not to count, for he comes from the tropics."

As Josépha dealt Montès the above gentle tap upon the forehead, he fell back upon his chair, and appealed with a look to Du Tillet.

"I am the victim of one of your Parisian jokes," he said; "if your object was to wrest my secret from me—"

He enveloped the whole table with a circle of fire, embracing all the guests in a glance in which blazed the Brazilian sun.

"In God's name, tell me so," he went on in a supplicating, almost childlike tone; "but do not slander a woman whom I love."

"Ah!" said Carabine in his ear, "but suppose you were shamefully betrayed, deceived, played with by Valérie, and I should prove it to you within an hour at my house, what would you do?"

"I can't tell you before all these Iagos," said the Brazilian baron.

Carabine understood him to say *magots*—coxcombs—

"Well, keep quiet!" she replied with a smile; "don't give the brightest men in Paris a chance to laugh at you, but come to my house; we will talk—"

Montès was completely crushed.

"Proofs!—" he faltered; "reflect—"

"You shall have only too many," said Carabine, "and since the mere suspicion goes to your head so, I'm afraid for your reason."

"What an obstinate creature it is, he's worse than the late King of Holland!—I say, Lousteau, Bixiou, Massol, ohé! and you others! aren't you all invited to breakfast by Madame Marneffe for day after to-morrow?" asked Léon de Lora.

"*Ya.*" replied Du Tillet. "I have the honor to

tell you once more, baron, that if by any chance you intended to marry Madame Marneffe, you are rejected like the draft of a law by a ball in the name of Crevel. My friend, my old comrade Crevel, has eighty thousand a year, and you probably haven't exhibited as much as that or you'd have had the preference, I fancy."

Montès listened with a half-dreamy, half-smiling expression, which had a terrifying effect upon everybody present. The head waiter at this juncture approached Carabine and whispered that a relation of hers desired to speak with her in the salon. The lorette rose, left the room, and found Madame Nourrisson veiled in black lace.

"Well, am I to go to your house, my child? Has he bitten?"

"Yes, little mother, the pistol is so heavily loaded that I'm afraid it will go off," Carabine replied.

An hour later Montès, Cydalise and Carabine had returned from the *Rocher de Cancale* to Rue Saint-Georges, and entered Carabine's little salon. The lorette espied Madame Nourrisson ensconced in an easy-chair by the corner of the hearth.

"Ah! there's my good aunt!" said she.

"Yes, my child, I have come myself for my little allowance. You might forget me, although you have such a kind heart, and I have notes to pay to-morrow. A dealer in ladies' wardrobes is always hard up. Who's that you're dragging after you?—The gentleman seems to have had something to annoy him.—"

The repulsive Madame Nourrisson, who was completely metamorphosed and had the appearance of a respectable old lady, rose to kiss Carabine, who was one of the hundred and odd lorettes she had launched in their horrible career of vice.

"He's an Othello who makes no mistakes, and whom I have the honor to present to you: Monsieur le Baron Montès de Montejanos—"

"Oh! I know monsieur, I've heard so much said about him; they call you Combabus because you love only one woman; in Paris that's the same thing as having none at all. Well, does it happen by any chance that something's wrong with your beloved? with Madame Marneffe, Crevel's wife?—My dear monsieur, you should bless your fate, 'stead of cursing it.—She's a nobody, that little woman. I know her tricks!"

"Nonsense!" said Carabine, into whose hands Madame Nourrisson had slipped a letter when she kissed her; "you don't know the Brazilians. They're a quarrelsome lot, and believe in stabbing to the heart!—The more jealous they are, the more they want to be. *Môsieur* talks about massacring everybody, and he won't massacre anybody because he's in love. By the way, I've brought Monsieur le Baron here to furnish him with the proofs of his hard luck, which I got from little Steinbock."

Montès was drunk, and listened as if he were not himself concerned in what was going on. Carabine went to throw off her velvet cape, and read the following letter in fac-simile:

"My pet, *he* is going to dine at Popinot's to-night, and will come to the opera for me at eleven. I will leave the house about half-past five, and shall expect to find you at our paradise, where you will have a dinner sent from the *Maison d'Or*. Dress yourself as though you were going to take me to the Opera. We shall have four hours to ourselves. You must return this little note to me, not that your Valérie distrusts you, for I would give you my life, my fortune, my honor, but I am afraid of the tricks chance may play us."

"There, baron, there's the love-letter sent to Comte Steinbock this morning; read the address! The original has been burned."

Montès turned the paper over and over in his hand, recognized the hand-writing, and was struck with a shrewd idea, which goes to prove how far his mind was disturbed.

"Tell me," said he, "what interest you have in tearing my heart to pieces, for you must have paid a high price to get this note into your hands long enough to have it lithographed?" said he, looking at Carabine.

"You great idiot!" said Carabine at a sign from Madame Nourrisson; "don't you see poor Cydalise here—a child of sixteen who's loved you so for three months that it's taken away her appetite, and who's in despair because she hasn't yet been honored even with one of your most absent-minded glances?"

Cydalise put a handkerchief to her eyes, and seemed to be weeping.

"She's furious, for all her demure looks, to see that the man she's mad over is the dupe of a villain," continued Carabine, "and she would kill Valérie—"

"No, no," said the Brazilian, "that's my business!"

"Kill her!—you, my dear?" said the Nourrisson. "That sort of thing isn't done any more here."

"Ah!" retorted Montès, "I'm not of this country! I live in a jurisdiction where I laugh at your laws; and if you give me proofs—"

"Proofs! is this note of no account?"

"No," said the Brazilian. "I don't believe in the handwriting, I want to see."

"Oh! to see!" said Carabine, marvelously quick to understand a second gesture on the part of her pretended aunt; "well, we will let you see everything, my dear tiger, on one condition.—"

"What is that?"

"Look at Cydalise."

At a signal from Madame Nourrisson Cydalise gazed affectionately at the Brazilian.

"Will you love her? will you set her up in life? A woman as beautiful as that is well worth a house and a carriage! It would be a crying shame to leave her to go on foot. And she has—debts.—How much do you owe?" said Carabine, pinching Cydalise's arm.

"She's worth what she's worth," said the Nourrisson. "It's enough that there's someone to buy!"

"Listen!" cried Montès, becoming conscious at last of the existence of this glorious chef-d'œuvre of womankind; "you will show me Valérie—"

"And Comte Steinbock, *parbleu!*" said Madame Nourrisson.

For ten minutes past the old lady had been watching the Brazilian closely, and she saw in him the instrument that she needed, tuned to the pitch of murder; most important of all she saw that he was so far blinded by passion that he would no longer care by whom he was guided, and so she interposed.

"Cydalise is my niece, my dear Brazilian, so I am somewhat interested. This whole business can be cleared up in ten minutes; for it's one of my friends who lets Comte Steinbock the furnished room where your Valérie is at this moment taking her coffee—a queer kind of coffee, but that's what she calls it. So, let us understand each other, Brazil! I love Brazil, it's a hot country. What will you do about my niece?"

"Old ostrich!" said Montès, whose attention was attracted by the feathers on the Nourrisson's hat, "you interrupted me. If you show me—show me Valérie and this artist together—"

"As you'd like to be with her," said Carabine, "that's understood."

"Well then, I will take this young Norman and carry her—"

"Where?—" queried Carabine.

"To Brazil!" the baron replied; "I'll make her my wife. My uncle left me ten square leagues of unsalable land; that's why I still own the estate; I have a hundred negroes there, nothing but negroes, negresses, and little negroes bought by my uncle—"

"A slave-dealer's nephew!—" exclaimed Carabine with a wry face, "that's to be considered.—Cydalise, my child, are you a negrophile?"

"Come, come, let's have no more *blaguing*, Carabine," said La Nourrisson. "What the devil! Monsieur and I are talking business now."

"If I take another Frenchwoman, I propose that she shall be all mine," continued the Brazilian. "I give you fair warning, mademoiselle, I'm a king, but not a constitutional king; I am a czar, I have bought all my subjects, and no one can leave my kingdom, which is a hundred leagues from any human habitation; it is bounded by a country of savages on the interior, and separated from the coast by a desert as great as the whole of France.—"

"I prefer an attic here!" said Carabine.

"That's what I thought," rejoined the Brazilian, "as I sold all my estates and everything I owned at Rio-de-Janeiro, to come over and join Madame Marneffe."

"One doesn't take such voyages for nothing," said Madame Nourrisson. "You are entitled to be loved on your own account, especially as you are so handsome.—Oh! he is handsome," she said to Carabine.

"Very handsome! handsomer than Longjumeau's postilion," retorted the lorette.

Cydalise took the Brazilian's hand, but he disengaged it as politely as possible.

"I returned to carry off Madame Marneffe!" he said, resuming his argument, "and do you know why I didn't return for three years?"

"No, savage," said Carabine.

"Well, she had told me so many times that she longed to live with me, alone, in a desert—"

"He's not a savage any longer," said Carabine, with a great burst of laughter, "he belongs to the tribe of civilized gulls."

"She had told me that so many times," continued the baron, insensible to the lorette's raillery, "that I prepared a delightful home for her in the centre of that vast property. I returned to France in quest of Valérie, and the night I inspected her for the first time,—"

"Inspected is a good word," said Carabine; "I'll remember it!"

"She told me to wait for that vile Marneffe's death, and I consented, at the same time forgiving her for receiving attentions from Hulot. I don't know whether the devil caught her skirts, but from that moment the woman has gratified all my whims, all my demands; in fact she has not given me reason to suspect her for a single moment!"

"That's very clever!" said Carabine to Madame Nourrisson.

Madame Nourrisson nodded her head assentingly.

"My faith in that woman," said Montès allowing his tears to flow freely, "equals my love. I was within an ace of fighting the whole party at table just now."

"So I saw!" said Carabine.

"If I am deceived, if she is to be married, if she is at this moment in Steinbock's arms, that woman deserves a thousand deaths, and I will kill her as one crushes a fly.—"

"And the gendarmes, my dear?" said Madame Nourrisson with the smile of an old hag trying to make her hearer's flesh creep.

"And the commissioner of police, and the magistrates, and the Assizes, and all the rest of the horrors?" said Carabine.

"You are a fool, my dear boy!" continued Madame Nourrisson, who was determined to know the Brazilian's plan of vengeance.

"I will kill her!" repeated Montès coldly. "Ah! you called me a savage. Do you suppose I will copy the idiocy of your compatriots who go and buy poison at a druggist's?—I thought, while we were driving to your house, of my vengeance in case your charges against Valérie were just. One of my negroes carries about him the most deadly of animal poisons; a terrible malady which works much better than a vegetable poison, and can be cured only in Brazil. I will give it to Cydalise to take, and she will give it to me; then, when death is planted in the veins of Crevel and his wife, I shall be beyond the Azores with your cousin, whom I will cause to be cured, and will make my wife. We savages have our way of doing things!—Cydalise," said he with a glance at the Norman, "is the creature I need. What does she owe?"

"A hundred thousand francs!" said Cydalise.

"She talks little, but well," said Carabine under her breath to Madame Nourrisson.

"I shall go mad!" cried the Brazilian in a hollow voice, falling back upon a sofa. "It will kill me! But I must see, for it's impossible! A lithographed note!—who says that it isn't the work of a forger? —Baron Hulot love Valérie!" he exclaimed recalling Josépha's harangue; "why the bare fact that she still lives proves that he didn't love her!—I won't allow her to live for anybody else, if she's not all mine!"

Montès was frightful to look at and more frightful to hear! He roared and writhed; everything he touched was broken; the violet-wood seemed as fragile as glass.

"How he is smashing things!" said Carabine, looking at Madame Nourrisson.—"My dear," she continued, touching the Brazilian on the arm, "Roland in a rage was very well in a poem, but in a room he's very prosaic and costly."

"My son," said the Nourrisson, rising and taking her stand in front of the crushed Brazilian; "I am of your religion! When one loves in a certain way, when one is *hooked till death*, the life is answerable for the love. The one who goes away tears up everything by the roots! its a general demolition. You have my esteem, my admiration, my consent, especially for the touch which makes me negrophile. But you're in love! perhaps you'll draw back?"

"Draw back!—if she's an infamous wretch, I—"

"Come, you talk too much after all!" rejoined the Nourrisson, herself once more. "A man who wants to be revenged, and who claims to be so fierce in his dealings, is apt to act differently. In order that you should see your charmer in her paradise, you must take Cydalise, and enter the room as if you had been shown in there with your partner, through the mistake of a maid; but no commotion! If you want to be revenged, you must cheat and pretend to be in despair, and induce your mistress to discard you.—Isn't that the way?" she said, noticing the Brazilian's surprise at so subtle a scheme.

"Go on, ostrich," he replied, "go on!—I understand."

"Adieu, my love," said Madame Nourrisson to Carabine.

She motioned to Cydalise to go with Montès, and remained a moment alone with Carabine.

"Now, my darling, I am afraid of one thing, and that is that he'll strangle her. I should be in a bad fix, for all our business must be done quietly, I think that you've earned your Raphaël, but they say it's a Mignard. Don't be alarmed, it's much finer; they tell me that the Raphaëls are all black, while this is as pretty as a Girodet."

"All I care about is to beat Josépha!" cried Carabine, "and it's all the same to me whether it's with a Raphaël or a Mignard.—No, that thief wore pearls to-night—pearls one would willingly be damned for!"

Cydalise, Montès and Madame Nourrisson entered

a fiacre which was waiting at Carabine's door. Madame Nourrisson gave the driver orders in a low voice to drive to a house •in the Block des Italiens where they might have arrived in a few moments, for it is a drive of only seven or eight minutes from Rue Saint-Georges; but Madame Nourrisson ordered him to go by Rue Le Peletier, and to drive very slowly so as to pass in review the carriages stationed there.

"Brazilian!" said La Nourrisson, "see if you recognize your angel's servants and her carriage."

The baron pointed to Valérie's equipage just as the fiacre passed.

"She told her people to come at ten o'clock, and drove in a fiacre to the house where she now is with Comte Steinbock; she has dined there and will go to the opera in half an hour. It's very well done!" said Madame Nourrisson. "That explains how she succeeded in cheating you so long."

The Brazilian did not reply. Transformed into a tiger, he had resumed his imperturbable sang-froid, so much admired during the dinner. In short he was as calm as a bankrupt the day after making an assignment.

At the door of the fatal house a closed carriage with two horses was standing—one of those called *Compagnie Générale* from the name of the company that owns them.

"Stay where you are," said Madame Nourrisson to Montès. "You can't go in here as you'd enter a tavern; we'll come and call you."

*

The paradise of Madame Marneffe and Wenceslas could hardly be said to resemble Crevel's *petite maison,* which he had sold to Comte Maxime de Trailles, it having, in his opinion, become useless. This paradise, the paradise of a great many persons, consisted of a single room opening on the landing on the fourth floor of a house in the Block des Italiens. On each floor, opening upon each landing of the house in question, was a room originally intended to serve as a kitchen for the suite of which it formed a part. But as the house had become a sort of inn, in which rooms were let to clandestine lovers at exorbitant prices, the principal tenant, the real Madame Nourrisson, dealer in ladies' apparel on Rue Neuve-Saint-Marc, had conceived a just idea of the great value of these kitchens, and had converted each of them into a sort of dining-room. Each room, flanked on both sides by thick party-walls, was lighted from the street, and was totally isolated by means of very heavy folding-doors, which afforded a double protection on the landing. The occupants, therefore, could discuss important secrets at dinner, without running the risk of being overheard. For greater security the windows were provided with blinds without and shutters within. These rooms, because of the privacy thus afforded, cost three hundred francs a month. The house, pregnant with the mysteries of paradise, was let for twenty-four thousand francs to Madame Nourrisson I., who made twenty thousand out of it, taking good years and bad together, after paying her agent—Madame Nourrisson II.—for she did not manage the property herself.

The particular paradise let to Comte Steinbock had been furnished in chintz. The hard, cold, and mean red-tiled floor, could not be felt beneath a luxurious carpet. The furniture consisted of two dainty chairs and a bed in an alcove, at this time half hidden by a table laden with the remains of a choice dinner, on which two long-necked bottles, and an exhausted champagne bottle in its envelope of ice marked the bounds of the fields of Bacchus cultivated by Venus. One saw, sent without doubt by Valérie, a comfortable easy-chair beside a low fireside-chair, and a pretty rosewood commode with a mirror in a lovely Pompadour frame. A lamp hanging from the ceiling shed a sort of half-light, increased to some extent by the wax-candles on the table and those which adorned the mantel-piece.

This sketch will serve to depict, *urbi et orbi*, the pitiful surroundings in which clandestine love-affairs were carried on in the Paris of 1840. How immeasurably far removed, alas! from the unholy love symbolized by Vulcan's fillets, three thousand years ago!

As Cydalise and the baron ascended the stairs, Valérie was standing in front of the fireplace, where a few sticks were burning, while Wenceslas laced her corsets. It was the moment of all others, when the woman who is neither too stout nor too thin, like the slender and graceful Valérie, appears supernaturally lovely. The pink, moist flesh craves a glance from the sleepiest eyes. The lines of the body, so imperfectly concealed at such a time, are so plainly marked by the clinging folds of the skirt and the tight-fitting corset, that the woman is irresistible, like everything one is obliged to leave. The happy, smiling face reflected in the mirror, the foot tapping impatiently on the floor, the hand raised to arrange the disordered locks of the badly readjusted head-dress, the eyes overflowing with gratitude, and the flame of satisfied desire, which, like the rays of the setting sun, lights up every detail of the countenance,—everything, at that hour, makes an impression to be long remembered! —Certain it is that, whoever, as he looks back over the first errors of his life, recalls some of these delicious details, will understand perhaps, though he do not excuse, the follies of the Hulots and Crevels. Women are so well aware of their power at that moment, that they always gather then what we may call the aftermath of the assignation.

"Well, well! after two years, don't you know how to lace a woman yet? You're too much of a Pole! Here it is ten o'clock, my Wences—las!" laughed Valérie.

At that moment a mischievous maid, with the aid of a knife-blade, adroitly threw back the hook of the folding-door, which afforded Adam and Eve their only protection. She threw open the door without warning, for the tenants of these Edens have all too little time to themselves, and disclosed one of the charming *genre* paintings after Gavarni, so often exhibited at the salon.

"This way, madame!" said the girl. And Cydalise entered, followed by Baron Montès.

"Why there's somebody here!—Excuse me, madame," said the Norman in dismay.

"What's this! why, it's Valérie!" cried Montès, closing the door with violence.

Madame Marneffe, overcome by emotion too keen to be dissembled, fell back upon a low chair in the corner of the fireplace. Two tears glistened in her eyes, but immediately vanished. She looked at Montès, espied the Norman, and uttered a forced laugh. The dignity of the injured woman effaced all thought of the inelegance of her unfinished toilet; she went up to the Brazilian and looked him in the face so haughtily that her eyes gleamed like sword-blades.

"So this," said she, taking her stand in front of him, and pointing to Cydalise, "this is what you mean by fidelity, is it? You who have made me promises that would convince an atheist in love! you for whom I have done so much, even committed crime!—You are right, monsieur, I am nothing compared to a girl of her age and beauty!—I know what you are going to say," she continued, pointing to Wenceslas, whose disordered clothing was too convincing a proof to be denied. "That's my business. If I could love you, after such infamous treachery, for you have put spies on me, you have bought every step of this staircase, and the mistress of the house, and the maid, and perhaps Reine herself—Oh! how noble it all is!—if I had a spark of affection left for such a dastard, I could give him reasons of a nature to redouble his love!—But I leave you, monsieur, with all your suspicions, which will some day change to remorse.—Wenceslas, my dress!"

She took her dress and put it on, looked at herself in the mirror, and tranquilly finished dressing without looking at the Brazilian, precisely as if she were alone.

"Wenceslas, are you ready? Go out first."

She had watched the Brazilian's face in the mirror and out of the corner of her eye, and she fancied that she could detect in his pallor an indication of the weakness which renders the strongest man the slave of a woman's fascination; she took his hand, standing so near him that he could inhale those potent well-loved perfumes, which intoxicate lovers; and, feeling his heart beat fast, she looked into his face with a reproachful expression:

"I give you leave to go and tell Monsieur Crevel of your expedition; he'll never believe you, so I have a right to marry him; he will be my husband day after to-morrow—and I shall make him very happy!—Adieu! try to forget me—"

"Ah! Valérie," cried Montès throwing his arms about her, "it's impossible!—Come to Brazil!"

Valérie glanced at him and recovered her slave.

"Ah! Henri, if you still loved me, in two years I would be your wife; but your face at this moment looks very sly—"

"I swear to you that they made me drunk, that false friends left this woman on my hands, and that it's all the work of chance!" said Montès.

"Might I still venture to forgive you then?" she asked with a smile.

"And you persist in being married?" demanded the baron in heartrending suspense.

"Eighty thousand francs a year!" she exclaimed with half-comic enthusiasm. "And Crevel loves me so dearly, that he will soon die of it."

"Ah! I undertsand you," said the Brazilian.

"All right, in a day or two, we'll have an understanding," said she.

And she went down stairs in triumph.

"I have no more scruples!" thought the baron, standing still for a moment. "What! the woman thinks of making use of her love to get rid of that old fool, just as she calculated on Marneffe's death! —I shall be the instrument of divine wrath!"

Two days later those of Du Tillet's guests who had torn Madame Marneffe to pieces most mercilessly, were sitting about her table an hour after she had donned a new skin by changing her name for the glorious name of a mayor of Paris. This tongue treachery is one of the most ordinary varieties of fickleness in Parisian life. Valérie had had the pleasure of seeing at the church the Brazilian nobleman, whom Crevel, now a lawful husband, invited from sheer bravado. Montès' presence at the breakfast surprised no one. All these men of genius had long since become familiar with the cowardice of passion and the bargaining of lust. The profound melancholy of Steinbock, who was beginning to despise her of whom he had made an angel, seemed in the best of taste. It was as if the Pole took this method of saying that all was at an end between Valérie and himself. Lisbeth came in to embrace her dear Madame Crevel, apologizing for not attending the breakfast, on the ground of Adeline's lamentable condition.

"Have no fear," said she to Valérie as she took her leave, "they will receive you there and you will receive them here. The baroness is at death's door simply from having heard the four words: *two hundred thousand francs!* Oh! you have them all in your power by that anecdote; but won't you tell it to me?"

A month after her marriage Valérie had arrived at her tenth quarrel with Steinbock, who insisted upon an explanation from her respecting Henri Montès; he reminded her of her remarks during the scene in their paradise; and, not content with withering Valérie with scornful epithets, watched her so closely that she could not obtain a single moment of liberty, so closely pressed was she by Wenceslas' jealousy and Crevel's devotion. As Lisbeth, whose advice was always most judicious, was no longer with her, she lost her head so far as to taunt Wenceslas bitterly about the money she had loaned him. The Steinbock pride was thereupon awakened and he came no more to the Crevel mansion. Valérie's object was attained; she wanted to keep Wenceslas away for a time in order to recover her freedom of action. She awaited the opportunity afforded by a visit Crevel paid to Comte Popinot in the country to make arrangements for Madame Crevel's presentation, and was thus enabled to make an appointment with the baron, whom she desired to have to herself for a whole day in order to supply him with explanations calculated to redouble his love. On the morning of the day in question, Reine, estimating the extent of her crime by the magnitude of the sum she received, tried to warn her mistress, in whose welfare she was naturally more interested than in that of strangers; but as they had threatened to make her out a madwoman and send her to the Salpêtrière, in case of any indiscretion, she was timid.

"Madame is so happy now," said she; "why should she bother any more with this Brazilian?—I don't trust him myself!"

"You are right, Reine," Valérie replied; "so I mean to dismiss him."

"Oh! madame, I am so glad; he frightens me, the black-a-moor! I believe he's capable of anything—"

"What a fool you are! He's the one to be alarmed for, when he's with me."

At that moment Lisbeth appeared.

"My dear, sweet little kid, it's a long time since I saw you!" said Valérie—"I am very unhappy.—Crevel bores me to death, and I haven't any Wenceslas; we've had a row."

"I know it," replied Lisbeth, "and it's on his account that I've come here. Victorin met him about five in the evening just as he was going into a twenty-five-sous restaurant on Rue de Valois; he caught him fasting, worked on his feelings and brought him to Rue Louis-le-Grand.—When Hortense saw him, thin and sick and poorly-clothed, she gave him her hand.—That's the way you go back on me!"

"Monsieur Henri, madame!" said the footman in Valérie's ear.

"Leave me, Lisbeth; I'll explain it all to you to-morrow."

But, as we shall see, Valérie was soon to be in a condition in which she could explain nothing to anybody.

*

Toward the close of the month of May, Baron Hulot's pension was entirely freed from encumbrance by virtue of the successive payments made by Victorin to Baron de Nucingen. Everyone knows that the semi-annual payments of pensions are not made except upon presentation of a certificate of life, and as Baron Hulot's residence was unknown, the semi-annual payments assigned to Vauvinet had accumulated at the Treasury. Vauvinet having executed a release of his claim, it was indispensable to find the pensioner in order to collect the arrears. The baroness, thanks to the devoted care of Doctor Bianchon, had recovered her health. Kind-hearted Josépha contributed materially to her complete recovery by a letter, the orthography of which betrayed the collaboration of the Duc d'Hérouville. This is what the famous singer wrote the baroness after forty days of unremitting activity:

"MADAME LA BARONNE,

"Monsieur Hulot, two months ago, was living on Rue des Bernardins with Élodie Chardin, the lace-mender, who had stolen him from Mademoiselle Bijou; but he went away, leaving everything he owned behind him, without a word, and without a hint as to where he has gone. I am not discouraged, and I have put a man on his track, who thinks that he has seen him already on Boulevard Bourdon.

"The poor Jewess will keep her promise to the Christian.

May the angel pray for the devil! that must sometimes happen in Heaven.

"I am with profound respect, and forever, your humble servant,

"JOSÉPHA MIRAH."

Mâitre Hulot d'Ervy, hearing no more of the terrible Madame Nourrisson, seeing that his father-in-law was safely married, having induced his brother-in-law to return to the family fireside, finding that his new mother-in-law showed no disposition to attack him, and that his mother's health was improving from day to day, devoted himself to his legal and political labors, borne on by the swift current of Parisian life in which hours count for days. Having a report to prepare for the Chamber of Deputies, he was obliged, toward the close of the session, to work on it throughout the entire night. He was in his office about nine o'clock waiting for his servant to bring his shaded lamps, and was thinking of his father. He reproached himself for leaving the cantatrice to prosecute the search, and was thinking that he would see Monsieur Chapuzot on the subject the next day, when he saw at his window, in the fading twilight, a venerable bald head, fringed with white hair.

"My dear monsieur, tell them to let me come in; I am a poor hermit from the desert, seeking alms to assist in rebuilding a sacred place of shelter."

This apparition, which took to itself a voice, and suddenly recalled to the advocate's mind a prophecy of the horrible Nourrisson, made him shudder.

"Admit this old man," he said to his footman.

"He'll breed the plague in monsieur's office," the servant replied; "he has on a brown frock that he hasn't changed since he left Syria, and no shirt—"

"Admit this old man," the advocate repeated.

As he entered the room Victorin scrutinized with a suspicious eye this soi-disant hermit on a pilgrimage, and saw that he had before him a superb specimen of those Neapolitan monks whose frocks are true sisters to the rags of the lazzaroni, whose sandals are rags of leather, as the monk himself is a rag of humanity. His make-up was so complete, that, although his suspicions remained, the advocate reproached himself for having believed in Madame Nourrisson's sorcery.

"How much do you want?"

"Whatever you think you ought to give me."

Victorin took one hundred sous from a pile of change, and handed the coin to the stranger.

"That's very little on account of fifty thousand francs," said the beggar from the desert.

This remark banished all Victorin's uncertainty.

"Has Heaven kept its promises?" he said with a frown.

"Doubt is an insult, my son!" rejoined the recluse. "If you prefer not to pay me until the funeral is over, you are within your right; I will come again in a week."

"The funeral!" cried the advocate, rising.

"We have been at work," said the old man,

leaving the room, "and deaths come quickly in Paris!"

When Hulot, who hung his head at these words, attempted to reply, the old man had disappeared.

"I don't understand a word of it," said Hulot to himself. "But, a week hence, I will ask him about my father if we haven't found him. Where does Madame Nourrisson—yes, that's what she calls herself—find such actors?"

The next day Doctor Bianchon allowed the baroness to go down to the garden, after he had examined Lisbeth, who had been compelled, by a slight bronchial trouble, to keep her room for a month past. The learned doctor, who did not dare express his whole opinion concerning Lisbeth until he had detected some more decisive symptoms, accompanied the baroness to the garden in order to study the effect of the fresh air, after two months' confinement, upon the nervous trembling which he was seeking to overcome. The cure of this nervous disorder called forth all Bianchon's talent. When they saw the great and famous physician sitting beside them and giving them a few moments of his valuable time, the baroness and her children politely opened a conversation with him.

"Your life is very fully occupied, and very sadly!" said the baroness. "I know what it is to spend one's days looking constantly upon poverty or physical suffering."

"Madame," the physician replied, "I know something of the sights which your charitable work obliges you to witness; but you will get accustomed to them in time as we all do. It is the law of society. The confessor, the magistrate, the lawyer, would be impossible if the *good of the State* did not subdue the *heart of the man.* Could we live except for the happening of this phenomenon? The soldier, in time of war, is doomed, is he not, to witness sights even more cruel than ours? and all soldiers who have seen fire are kind-hearted. We have the pleasure of successfully effecting a cure, as you have the pleasure of rescuing a family from the horrors of hunger, depravity, misery, by providing them with work, and restoring them to social life; but what satisfaction have the magistrate, the commissioner of police and the lawyer, who pass their lives investigating the most villainous schemes of self-interest, that social monster which knows the regret of failure, but which will never know repentance? One-half of society passes its life watching the other half. I have long had for a friend a lawyer, now retired from practice, who told me that, for the last fifteen years, the notaries and lawyers were as suspicious of their clients as of their clients' adversaries. Your son, madame, is a lawyer—has he never been compromised by the man whose defence he undertook?"

"Oh! often," said Victorin with a smile.

"What is the source of this deep-seated evil," the baroness asked.

"Absence of religious feeling," replied the physician, "and the invasions of finance, which is nothing else than selfishness solidified. In the old days money was not everything; other forms of superiority were admitted, which took precedence of it. There were nobility, talent, and services rendered the State; but to-day the law makes money the universal standard, and has adopted it as the basis of political capacity! Certain magistrates are not eligible, Jean-Jacques Rousseau would not be eligible! The constant division of inheritances compels everyone to think for himself as soon as he is twenty years old. Well, between the necessity of making money and the depravity of the various combinations effected there is no obstacle, for religious sentiment is lacking in France, notwithstanding the praiseworthy efforts of those who are striving to bring about the restoration of the Catholic faith. That is what everyone says, whose occupation, like mine, gives him an insight into the very bowels of society."

"You have little relaxation?" said Hortense.

"The true physician," replied Bianchon, "is passionately devoted to science. He is sustained by that sentiment as well as by the certainty of his usefulness to society. For instance, at this moment I am experiencing a sort of scientific joy, and yet many superficial observers would take me for a man without a heart. I am going to announce a new discovery to the Academy of Medicine to-morrow. I am watching at the present time the progress of a long-lost disease; a fatal disease, too, against which we are helpless in temperate climates, although it is curable in the Indies—a disease which was prevalent in the Middle Ages. It's a noble struggle—the struggle of the physician with such a malady. For ten days past I have thought of little but my patients, for there are two of them, the husband and wife! By the way are they not kinsfolk of yours? I believe you are Monsieur Crevel's daughter, madame?" he added, addressing Célestine.

"What! can it be that this patient of yours is my father?" exclaimed Célestine. "Does he live on Rue Barbet-de-Jouy?"

"He does, indeed," replied Bianchon.

"And the disease is fatal?" said Victorin in dismay.

"I am going to my father!" cried Célestine, rising.

"I positively forbid you to do it, madame," said Bianchon tranquilly. "The disease is contagious."

"But you go there, monsieur," retorted the young woman. "Don't you think that a daughter's duty is more imperative than a physician's?"

"Madame, a physician knows how to protect himself from contagion, and your unreflecting devotion is sufficient proof to my mind, that you could not have my prudence."

Célestine returned to her room and dressed to go out.

"Monsieur," Victorin asked Bianchon, "do you hope to save Monsieur and Madame Crevel?"

"I hope to, but hardly expect to," replied Bianchon. "It's a most inexplicable case to me.—The disease is one peculiar to the negroes in the American colonies, whose cutaneous system differs from that of the white races. Now, I am unable to establish any connection between the negroes, the Indians or the half-breeds and Monsieur or Madame Crevel. Although it is a very interesting disease from our point of view, it's a most frightful one to everybody else. The poor creature, who, they tell me, was very pretty, is well punished in the same direction in which she sinned, for to-day she is shockingly ugly, if indeed she can be said to be anything!—Her teeth and her hair are falling out, she looks like a leper, and her aspect is horrifying to herself; her hands are a fearful sight, they are badly swollen and covered with greenish pustules; her nails are loosened and remain in the sores that she scratches; in fact, all her extremities are being destroyed by the sanies which is consuming them."

"But what is the cause of it all?" queried the advocate.

"Oh!" said Bianchon, "the cause is the rapid degeneration of the blood; it is decomposing with frightful rapidity. I hope to attack the blood; I have had it analyzed, and I am now going home to learn the result of the labors of my friend Professor Duval, the renowned chemist, preparatory to undertaking one of those desperate strokes we sometimes play against death."

"The finger of God is in it!" said the baroness in a tone of deep feeling. "Although that woman has been the cause of all my misery, which has led me in moments of madness, to invoke divine justice against her, I most earnestly hope, God knows! that you may succeed, Monsieur le Docteur."

Victorin's head swam, he looked alternately at his mother, his sister and the doctor, trembling lest they should divine his thoughts. He considered himself a murderer. Hortense, for her part, deemed God most just. Célestine reappeared to beg her husband to accompany her.

"If you go there, madame, and you, monsieur, remain a foot away from the sick-bed; that is the only precaution you need take. Neither your wife nor yourself must entertain the thought of kissing the dying man! You had better go with your wife, Monsieur Hulot, to see that she doesn't disobey this order."

Adeline and Hortense, being left to themselves, went up to sit with Lisbeth. Hortense's hatred of Valérie was so bitter that she could not refrain from an explosion.

"Cousin, my mother and I are avenged!—" she cried. "That poisonous creature must have bitten herself, she's in a state of decomposition!"

"Hortense," said the baroness, "you are not a true Christian now. You ought to pray God that he will deign to bring the wretched woman to repentance."

"What are you saying?" cried Bette, rising from her chair, "are you talking about Valérie?"

"Yes," Adeline replied, "she is doomed; she is

dying of a horrible disease, the mere description of which is enough to make one shudder."

Cousin Bette's teeth chattered, the cold sweat stood upon her forehead, she experienced a terrible shock, which disclosed the depth of her passionate affection for Valérie.

"I am going there!" she said.

"But the doctor forbade your going out."

"No matter! I am going!—Poor Crevel! what a state he must be in, for he loves his wife!"

"He is dying too!" rejoined Countess Steinbock. "Ah! all our enemies are in the devil's hands—"

"In God's hands, my child."

Lisbeth put on her famous yellow cashmere, her black velvet cape, and her boots; and in defiance of the remonstrances of Adeline and Hortense started off as if she were impelled by a power not to be resisted. She reached Rue Barbet a few moments after Monsieur and Madame Hulot, and found seven physicians there whom Bianchon had summoned to watch this unique case; he himself had just joined them. The doctors stood in the salon discussing the case, and sometimes one of them, sometimes another entered Valérie's room or Crevel's, and returned with an argument based upon the results of his rapid observation.

These princes of science were divided between two opinions. One of them stood alone in the belief that it was a case of poisoning, and talked about private vengeance, denying that it was a reappearance of the disease known in the Middle

Ages. Three others insisted that it was a case of decomposition of the lymph, and humors in the blood. The second party, which included Bianchon, maintained that the disease was caused by degeneration of the blood which was poisoned by some unknown noxious principle. Bianchon brought the result of the analysis of the blood made by Professor Duval. The curative methods, although desperate and altogether experimental, depended upon the solution of this medical problem.

Lisbeth stood as if turned to stone three feet from the bed on which Valérie was dying, for she saw the vicar of Saint-Thomas d'Aquin at her friend's pillow, and a sister of charity in attendance upon her. Religion found a soul to save in a putrefying mass which retained, of the five senses of the human being, that of sight alone. The sister of charity,—nobody else could be found to undertake the task of attending Valérie,—stood at a distance. Thus the Catholic Church, that divine body, always animated by the spirit of self-sacrifice in everything, came to the assistance, in its double essence of spirit and flesh, of this infamous, tainted dying woman, pouring out upon her its infinite gentleness and its inexhaustible treasures of pity.

The terrified domestics refused to enter monsieur's room or madame's; they thought only of themselves and considered that their masters were justly smitten. The decomposition was so rapid that, although the windows were wide open, and the most powerful perfumes were scattered broadcast, none could remain long in Valérie's room. Religion alone kept constant watch there. How could a woman of so superior an intellect as Valérie's have failed to ask herself what interest those two representatives of the Church could have in remaining by her side? So it was that the dying woman had listened to the voice of the priest. Repentance had laid hold of that perverse heart with an ardor proportioned to the inroads the malignant disease had made upon her beauty. The delicate Valérie had offered less resistance to the disease than Crevel, and she was likely to be the first to die,—indeed she was attacked first.

"If I hadn't been sick I would have come and nursed you," said Lisbeth at last, after exchanging a glance with her friend's mournful eyes. "I have kept my room for fifteen or twenty days; but as soon as I learned of your condition from the doctor I hurried to you."

"Poor Lisbeth, you still love me, I see that," said Valérie. "Listen to me! I have but a day or two more to think, for I can't say *to live*. As you see I haven't any body, I am a mass of filth.—They don't let me look at myself in the mirror.—I have no more than I deserve. Ah! I would like to undo all the harm I have done, so that I might be admitted to pardon."

"Oho!" said Lisbeth, "if you talk that way, you must be as good as dead!"

"Don't interfere with this woman's repentance; leave her to her Christian thoughts," said the priest.

"Nothing left!" said Lisbeth to herself in dire dismay. "I don't recognize her eyes or her mouth! Not a single one of her features remains! And her mind is unhinged! Oh! it's horrible!—"

"You don't know," rejoined Valérie, "what death is, what it is to be compelled to think of the day after one's last day, and of what one will find in the grave; worms for the body, but what for the soul?—Ah! Lisbeth I feel that there is another life! —and I am in the grasp of a deadly terror which prevents me from feeling the torture of my decomposing flesh!—I whc said laughingly to Crevel, while making sport of a saint, that God's vengeance assumed the shape of all varieties of misfortune! Oh! well, I was a prophet!—Don't joke about sacred things, Lisbeth! If you love me, follow my example. Repent!"

"I repent!" said the Lorrainer; "I have seen vengeance everywhere in nature, insects die to satisfy the thirst for vengeance when they are attacked! And don't these gentlemen," she added, pointing to the priest, "tell us that God wreaks vengeance, and that his vengeance is eternal!"—

The priest cast a glance overflowing with gentleness at Lisbeth and said to her:

"You are an atheist, madame."

"But consider what has come to me then?" said Valérie.

"Where did you get all this corruption?" asked the old maid, persisting in her peasant-like incredulity.

"Oh! I received a note from Henri which left me in no doubt as to my fate.—He has killed me. To think of dying just when I had made up my mind to live an honest life, and to die an object of horror!—Lisbeth give up all idea of vengeance! Be kind to your family, to whom I have already, in my will, bequeathed all that the law allows me to dispose of! Go, my child, although you are the only being to-day who doesn't shrink from me in horror—go, I beg you, leave me; I have no time to do anything more than give myself up to God!—"

"She has lost her wits!" said Lisbeth to herself on the threshold.

The most violent sentiment known to mankind, a woman's love for a woman, had not the heroic constancy of the Church. Lisbeth, suffocated by the noisome fumes, left the room. She saw the doctors still discussing. But Bianchon's opinion carried the day, and they were simply considering the method of performing the experiment.

"It will be a magnificent autopsy at all events," said one of the dissentients, "and we shall have two subjects for purposes of comparison."

Lisbeth went back with Bianchon, who approached the sick-bed without seeming to notice the fetid exhalations.

"Madame," said he, "we propose to try the effect of a powerful preparation upon you, which may save your life."

"If you save my life," she said, "shall I be as beautiful as I was?"

"Perhaps," said the eminent physician.

"I understand your *perhaps!*" said Valérie; "I shall look like a woman who has fallen into the fire! Leave me entirely to the Church! I can please nobody but God now! I am going to try and reconcile myself with him; that will be my last flirtation! Yes, I must take the sacrament.

"There's my poor Valérie's last word, I recognize her there!" said Lisbeth, weeping.

The Lorrainer thought it her duty to go on to Crevel's bedroom, where she found Victorin and his wife sitting three feet away from the plague-stricken man's bed.

"Lisbeth," said he, "they are concealing my wife's condition from me; you have just seen her—how is she?"

"She is better, she says that she is saved," replied Lisbeth, permitting herself this pun in order to set his mind at rest.

"Ah! that is well," said the mayor, "for I was afraid that I was the cause of her illness. I haven't been a druggist's traveling salesman for nothing. I have been reproaching myself. If I should lose her what would become of me? On my word of honor, my children, I adore that woman."

Crevel sat up in bed and tried to strike his attitude.

"Oh! papa," said Célestine, "if you could only get well, I would receive my step-mother. I make that vow!"

"Poor little Celestine!" said Crevel, "come and kiss me!"

Victorin restrained his wife, who was darting to the bed.

"You are not aware, monsieur," said the advocate gently, "that your disease is contagious."

"True," replied Crevel; "the doctors are congratulating themselves that they have discovered in me some pest or other of the Middle Ages which they thought lost for ever, and they're making a great noise about it in their Faculties.—It's very amusing!"

"Papa," said Célestine, "have courage, and you will triumph over the disease."

"Never fear, my children; death looks twice before striking down a mayor of Paris!" he said with comical sang-froid. "And even if my arrondissement is so unfortunate as to be deprived of the man whom it has twice honored with its suffrages —Hem! see how gracefully I express myself!—why I shall know how to pack my trunks. I'm an old commercial traveler and I'm used to breaking camp. Ah! my children, I'm an atheist."

"Papa, promise me to let the Church come to your bedside."

"Never!" replied Crevel. "What would you have? I have sucked the milk of the Revolution; I haven't the mind of Baron d'Holbach, but I have his strong heart. I am the Regent, Gray Guardsman, Abbé Dubois, and Maréchal de Richelieu more than ever! *Sacrebleu!* my poor wife, who's out of her mind, just sent a man in a frock to me—to me, the admirer of Béranger, the friend of

Lisette, the child of Voltaire and Rousseau.—The doctor said to me, to try me, to find whether the disease was abating; 'Did you see Monsieur l'Abbé?'—And I followed the example of the great Montesquieu. Yes, I looked at the doctor, see, like this," he exclaimed, turning three-quarters round as in his portrait, and putting forth his hand magisterially, "and I said:

"'The slave arrived,
His order showed, but naught derived.'

"*His order* is a pretty play upon words which proves that in his death agony Monsieur le President de Montesquieu preserved all the charm of his genius, for they had sent him a Jesuit!—I love that passage—one cannot say of his life, but of his death. Ah! the passage! another pun! the passage—or passing—of Montesquieu!"

Hulot gazed sadly at his father-in-law, wondering if folly and vanity do not possess a power equal to that of true grandeur of soul. The causes which put in motion the mechanism of the soul seem to be entirely foreign to the results. Can it be that the courage displayed by a great criminal is of the same nature as that which enables a Champcenetz to walk proudly to the scaffold?

At the end of the week Madame Crevel was buried after suffering untold torture, and Crevel followed his wife two days later. Thus the disastrous effects of the marriage-contract were averted, and Crevel inherited from Valérie.

On the day following the burial the advocate saw the old monk once more, and received him without a word. The monk silently put out his hand, and Master Victorin Hulot silently handed him eighty bank-notes of one thousand francs each, taken from the money found in Crevel's secretary. Madame Hulot the younger inherited the estate of Presles and thirty thousand francs a year. Madame Crevel had bequeathed three hundred thousand francs to Baron Hulot. The scrofulous Stanislas was to have, at his majority, the Crevel mansion on Rue Barbet and twenty-four thousand francs a year.

*

Among the numerous and praiseworthy associations founded by the charitable Catholics of Paris, there is one, founded by Madame de la Chanterie, the purpose of which is to bring about the marriage, civil and religious, of couples who are living together in good faith. Our legislators, who are much interested in swelling the proceeds of registration, and the reigning bourgeoisie, who covet notarial honors, feign to be ignorant of the fact that three-fourths of the common people are unable to pay fifteen francs for their marriage-contract. In this respect the Chamber of Notaries stands on a lower plane than the Chamber of Advocates. The advocates of Paris, a much slandered body, undertake gratuitously the conduct of causes for those who are unable to pay, while the notaries have not yet decided to draw contracts of marriage for the poor without charge. As for the Treasury the whole governmental machine must be set in motion in order to obtain any relaxation of its rigor in that direction. The registrar's office is deaf and dumb. The Church, too, levies taxes upon marriages. The Church in France is excessively mercenary; it lowers itself so far as to countenance in the very house of God, a despicable traffic in little benches and chairs, at which strangers wax wroth, although it can not have forgotten the Saviour's wrath when he drove the money-changers forth from the Temple. If the Church is so loath to abandon its fees we must conclude that its fees,—called property—constitute to-day one of its main sources of revenue, and the fault of the churches would then become the fault of the State. The combination of these various circumstances, at a time when people are busying themselves far too much with negroes and petty police court offenders to pay any heed to the sufferings of honest men, leads to this result,—that a great number of well-meaning couples go on living in concubinage, for lack of thirty francs, the lowest price at which the notary, the registrar, the mayor and the Church can make two Parisians one. Madame de la Chanterie's society, instituted for the purpose of giving such needy couples a fair start upon a legal and religious path, is constantly seeking them out, and unearths them the more easily in that it relieves their poverty, before it interferes to regulate their unlawful mode of life.

When Madame Hulot was fully restored to health, she resumed her former occupations. Then it was that the estimable Madame de la Chanterie urged her to add the legalizing of natural marriages to the other charitable undertakings in which she acted as agent.

One of the baroness's first essays in this direction took place in the unsavory quarter, formerly called *Little Poland,* bounded by Rue du Rocher, Rue de la Pépinière and Rue de Miroménil. It is a sort of branch of Faubourg Saint-Marceau. To describe the neighborhood it will suffice to say that the owners of certain houses occupied by mechanics without work, by dangerous ruffians, by beggars engaged in nefarious trades, dare not demand their rents and can find no bailiffs who will undertake to expel their insolvent tenants. At the present moment, speculation, which is bent upon changing the aspect of this corner of Paris, and upon building up the unoccupied space which lies between Rue d'Amsterdam and Rue du Faubourg-du-Roule, is almost certain to change the character of its population, for the trowel is more of a civilizing instrument in Paris than one would imagine. By building handsome, stylish houses, with concierges, laying sidewalks in front of them, and arranging shops on the street-floor, the speculator places rents at so high a figure as to exclude vagabonds, families without belongings and undesirable tenants generally. Thus the quarters in question are gradually ridding themselves of their unsavory inhabitants, and of the dens in which the police never set foot except by special orders from the powers above.

In June, 1844, the aspect of Place de Laborde and its neighborhood was still by no means reassuring. The fashionable lounger, who happened to stray from Rue de la Pépinière into one of those disreputable streets, was amazed to see that aristocracy was jostled there by the dregs of Bohemia. In these districts, where ignorant indigence and want vegetate in the last stages of wretchedness, the lowest public writers to be found in Paris live and flourish.

Wherever you see the two words: *Public writer*, in coarse running hand, upon a white paper pasted on the window of the entresol or ground-floor of some disreputable looking den, you may safely conclude that the quarter contains many illiterate people, and consequently much misery and vice and crime. Ignorance is the mother of all crimes. A crime is, first of all, a lack of reasoning power.

Now, during the baroness's illness, this quarter, to which she was a second providence, had made an acquisition in the shape of a public writer, who had established himself on the Passage du Soleil; the name being one of those antitheses familiar to Parisians, for that "Sun" passage was more than ordinarily dark. This writer, suspected of being a German, was named Vyder, and was living in concubinage with a girl, of whom he was so jealous that he would allow her to visit nowhere except at the house of certain honest flue-builders on Rue Saint-Lazare, Italians like all flue-builders, and for many years settled in Paris. These people had been saved from inevitable failure, which would have reduced them to want, by Baronne Hulot, acting for Madame de la Chanterie. In a few months comparative ease had succeeded poverty, and religion had entered the hearts, which formerly cursed Providence, with the ardor peculiar to Italian flue-builders. So it was that one of the baroness's first visits was paid to this family. She was overjoyed by the spectacle which met her eyes in the house occupied by these good people on Rue Saint-

Lazare near Rue du Rocher. Above the workshop, now well-furnished and swarming with journeymen and apprentices, all Italians from the valley of Domo d'Ossola, the family occupied a small suite of rooms to which sufficient work had brought material abundance. The baroness was welcomed as if she were the Blessed Virgin returned to earth. After a quarter of an hour passed in looking about, Adeline, who was obliged to await the husband's return, in order to ascertain how his business was prospering, took advantage of the interval to carry on her blessed work by inquiring as to any people needing help whom the flue-builder's family might know.

"Ah! my kind lady, who would save the damned from hell," said the woman, "there's a young girl close by to be saved from perdition."

"Do you know her well?" inquired the baroness.

"She's the grand-daughter of a former employer of my husband named Judici, who came to France at the time of the Revolution, in 1798. Père Judici was one of the first flue-builders in Paris, under the Emperor Napoleon; he died in 1819 leaving his son a handsome fortune. But young Judici has squandered it all on bad women, and ended by marrying one of them, cleverer than the others, who bore him this poor little daughter, who's just past fifteen."

"What has happened to her?" asked the baroness, deeply impressed by the resemblance between this Judici's character and her husband's.

"Well, madame, the little creature—her name is

Atala—left her father and mother to come and live near by with an old German, at least eighty years old, named Vyder, who attends to everything for folks who can't read or write. If the old libertine, who, they say, bought the little one from her mother for fifteen hundred francs, would only marry her, as he undoubtedly hasn't long to live and as they say he's likely to have a few thousand francs, why the poor child, who's a little angel, would come to no harm, and would escape poverty, which will be her ruin."

"I thank you for having told me of this opportunity to do a good deed," said Adeline; "but we must act with prudence. Who is this old man?"

"Oh! madame, he's a good man; he makes the little one happy, and he doesn't lack good sense; for he left the quarter where the Judicis live, to save the child from her mother's claws, I suppose. The mother was jealous of her daughter, and she may have had an idea of making the most of her beauty, of making the child a *mademoiselle!*—Atala thought of us and advised *her gentleman* to set up in business near our house; and as the good man saw what sort of people we are he lets her come here; but marry them, madame, and you will do a deed worthy of you.—Once married, the little one will be free, in that way she will escape from her mother, who keeps an eye on her, and would like to see her go on the stage, or make a success in the horrible career she started her in, so that she could make something out of her."

"Why hasn't the old man married her?"

"It wasn't necessary," said the Italian, "and although goodman Vyder is not downright wicked, I think he's crafty enough to prefer to be the little one's master, whereas if he marries her, lady! he dreads, poor old fellow, what constantly threatens all old men."

"Can you send for the girl?" said the baroness; "I will see her here and find out if there's any way."

The woman made a sign to her eldest daughter, who at once left the room. Ten minutes later she returned, holding by the hand a girl of some fifteen years and a half, beautiful after the Italian style of beauty.

Mademoiselle Judici inherited from her father the complexion, which sallow by daylight, at night, by artificial light, becomes as white as the lily, eyes whose size and shape and brilliancy were worthy of the Orient, thick, drooping eyelids which resembled little black feathers, hair as black as ebony, and that majestic bearing, innate in the Lombard, which leads the foreigner who walks through the streets of Milan on Sunday, to imagine that the porter's daughters are so many queens. Atala, informed by the flue-builder's daughter of the presence of the great lady of whom she had often heard, had hastily donned a pretty silk dress, a stylish cape and laced boots. A cap with cherry colored ribbons increased ten-fold the effect of her shapely head. The little creature stood in an attitude of artless curiosity, looking askance at the baroness, whose nervous trembling astonished her much. The baroness heaved a deep sigh to see such a masterpiece of female loveliness wallowing in the slough of prostitution, and she swore to lead her back into the paths of virtue.

"What is your name, my child?"

"Atala, madame."

"Do you know how to read or write?"

"No, madame; but that makes no difference, since *monsieur* knows."

"Did your parents ever take you to church? Have you had your first communion? Do you know your catechism?"

"Madame, papa tried to make me do things like what you say, but mamma wouldn't have it."

"Your mother!" cried the baroness. "Tell me is your mother very cruel?"

"She was always whipping me! I don't know why, but my father and mother were continually quarreling about me."

"Did they never talk to you about God?" cried the baroness.

The child opened her eyes to their fullest extent.

"Oh! mamma and papa often said: 'Holy name of God! God's thunder! God damn!—'" she replied with refreshing innocence.

"Have you never seen any churches? did it never occur to you to go into one?"

"Churches?—Oh! yes, Notre-Dame and the Pantheon,—I saw them in the distance when papa took me into Paris, but that didn't happen often. There are no churches like that in the faubourg."

"In what faubourg were you?"

"In the faubourg."

"What faubourg?"

"Why, Rue de Charonne, madame."

The denizens of Faubourg Saint-Antoine never call that celebrated quarter anything but the faubourg. To them it is *the* faubourg *par excellence,* the king of faubourgs, and the manufacturers understand by that word when used alone, the Faubourg Saint-Antoine.

"Did they never tell you what was good and what was bad?"

"Mamma beat me when I didn't do things according to her idea."

"But didn't you know you were doing a wrong thing when you left your mother and father to go and live with an old man?"

Atala Judici looked at the baroness with a haughty air and did not reply.

"She's a totally uncivilized child!" said Adeline to herself.

"There are many like her in the faubourg, madame," said the flue-builder's wife.

"But she knows nothing at all, not even what wrong is, *mon Dieu!*—Why don't you answer me?" the baroness asked trying to take Atala by the hand.

But Atala was angry and drew back.

"You're an old fool!" said she. "My father

and mother had been fasting for a week! Mother wanted to make something very bad of me, because father beat her and called her a thief. Then Monsieur Vyder paid all father's and mother's debts, and gave them money—oh! a whole bagful!—And he took me away, and my poor papa wept. But we had to part!—There, is that wicked?" she demanded.

"And do you love this Monsieur Vyder dearly?"

"Do I love him?—" said she. "I should think so, madame! He tells me fine stories every evening!—and he has given me lovely dresses and linen and a shawl. Why, I'm rigged out like a princess, and I don't wear wooden shoes any more! For two months I haven't known what it is to be hungry. I don't eat potatoes now! he brings me bonbons and sugared almonds! Oh! how good almond-chocolate is! I do everything he wishes for a bag of chocolate. And then, my old Père Vyder is very kind; he takes care of me so nicely and neatly that I can see what mother should have done.—He's going to get a good old woman to help me, for he doesn't want me to soil my hands cooking. A month ago about, he began to earn money pretty fast; he brings me three francs every night and I put them in a money-box. Only he won't let me go out except to come here.—That's a man's love! so he does what he pleases with me. He calls me his little darling, and my mother never called me anything but little b—, f— p— or thief, or vermin, or I don't know what!"

"Well, then, my child, why don't you make Père Vyder your husband?"

"Why, it's all done, madame!" said the girl looking proudly into the baroness's face, without a blush, calm-eyed and with unclouded brow. "He told me I was his little wife; but it's very tiresome to be a man's wife!—That is, without the almonds, I mean!"

"My God!" murmured the baroness, "who is the monster who could take advantage of such perfect, holy innocence? Might one not atone for many sins by leading this child into the straight path?—I knew what I was doing!" she said to herself thinking of her scene with Crevel; "but she knows nothing at all!"

"Do you know Monsieur Samanon?—" asked Atala coaxingly.

"No, my dear; but why do you ask me that?"

"Honor bright?" said the innocent creature.

"Don't be afraid of madame, Atala," said the flue-builder's wife, "she's an angel!"

"You see my old pet is afraid of being found by this Samanon; he's in hiding, and I would like very much to have him free."

"Why?"

"Damme! he'd take me to Bobino! perhaps to the Ambigu!"

"What a fascinating creature!" said the baroness, throwing her arms about the child.

"Are you rich?" asked Atala, playing with the baroness's lace ruffles.

"Yes and no," she replied. "I am rich for good little girls like you, when they are willing to allow a priest to teach them the duties of a Christian, and to walk in the right road."

"In what road?" said Atala. "I'm a good one on my legs."

"The road of virtue!"

Atala glanced at the baroness with a sly, mocking expression.

"Look at madame," said the baroness pointing to the flue-builder's wife; "see how happy she is since she was received into the bosom of the Church. Your marriage is like the pairing of animals!"

"Marriage?" replied Atala; "why, if you choose to give me what Père Vyder gives me, I should be satisfied not to be married. He's a nuisance! do you know what that means?"

"When one has once been united to a man, as you are," observed the baroness, "virtue demands that you should remain faithful to him."

"Till he dies?—" said Atala cunningly. "I shan't have him long. If you knew how Père Vyder coughs and how he blows!—Peuh! peuh!" she exclaimed, imitating the old man.

"Virtue and good morals require that the Church, which represents God, and the mayor, who represents the law, shall legalize your marriage," rejoined the baroness. "See madame, she is lawfully married."

"Will that be more fun?" queried the child.

"You will be happier," said the baroness, "for

none can blame you for that marriage. You will please God! Ask madame if she was married without receiving the sacrament of marriage."

Atala looked at the flue-builder's wife.

"What has she got that I haven't?" she asked. "I'm prettier than she is."

"Yes, but I'm an honest woman," interposed the Italian, "and anyone can call you a vile name."

"How can you expect God to protect you if you trample divine and human laws under foot?" said the baroness. "Do you know that God holds paradise in reserve for those who obey the commands of His church?"

"What is there in paradise? theatres?" queried Atala.

"Oh! paradise contains all the delights you can imagine," said the baroness. "It is full of angels, with snow-white wings. There we shall see God in His glory, we shall share His power, and be happy always and forever!"

Atala Judici listened to the baroness as she would have listened to music; and Adeline, realizing that she had gone beyond her powers of comprehension, concluded that she must adopt a different plan and appeal to the old man.

"Return home, my dear, and I will come and talk with Monsieur Vyder. Is he a Frenchman?"

"He's an Alsatian, madame; but he'll be rich by-and-by! If you would only pay what he owes that villain Samanon, he would pay you back! for in a few months, he says he shall have six thousand francs a year, and then we're going to live ever so far away in the country, in the Vosges."

The word *Vosges* caused the baroness to fall into a deep reverie. She seemed to see her native village once more. She was aroused from her sorrowful abstraction by the greetings of the flue-builder himself, who was anxious to exhibit the evidence of his prosperity.

"In a year, madame, I shall be able to return the money you loaned us, for it belongs to the merciful Lord, to the poor and unfortunate! If I prosper, some day you shall draw upon our purse, and I will repay to others by your hands the assistance you brought to us."

"Just now," said the baroness, "I do not ask you for money, but for your co-operation in a work of charity. I have just seen little Judici, who is living with an old man, and I want to have them married in accordance with law and religion."

"Ah! Père Vyder is a very worthy and excellent man, and his advice is always good. The poor old man has made friends in the quarter already in the two months he's been here. He makes out my bills in fine shape. He's a gallant colonel, I think, who served the Emperor faithfully—Ah! how he loves Napoléon! He is decorated, but he never wears any decoration. He is waiting till he's square again, for he has debts, poor dear man!—Indeed I think he's in hiding, and the bailiffs are after him."

"Tell him that I'll pay his debts, if he chooses to marry the girl."

"Ah! that will be soon done!—Come, madame, let us go there; it's only a step away, in the Passage du Soleil."

The baroness and the flue-builder set out together for the Passage du Soleil.

"This way, madame," said the Italian, turning into Rue de la Pépinière.

The Passage du Soleil begins at Rue de la Pépinière and runs into Rue du Rocher. About half-way along the passage, which is of recent creation, the shops therein being rented at a very modest figure, the baroness espied, above a window screened with green taffeta to a sufficient height to prevent passers-by from casting inquisitive glances within: PUBLIC SCRIVENER, and upon the door:

BUSINESS OFFICE.

Petitions drawn up here, Accounts adjusted, etc.

Secrecy and Dispatch.

The interior resembled the waiting-rooms provided by the omnibus companies of Paris for the convenience of their patrons. An interior stairway led doubtless to the apartments on the entresol, lighted from the gallery, and which were let in connection with the shop. The baroness noticed a desk of blackened whitewood, some cards, and a shabby second-hand easy-chair. A cap with a vizor, and a shade of green taffeta strung on an iron wire, both filthy, indicated precautions taken for disguise or else an infirmity of the eyes not to be wondered at in an old man.

"He is upstairs," said the flue-builder; "I'll go up and tell him and send him down."

The baroness lowered her veil and sat down. A heavy step shook the little wooden staircase, and Adeline could not restrain a piercing cry as she recognized her husband, Baron Hulot, in a gray knitted vest, gray swanskin trowsers much worn, and slippers.

"What can I do for you, madame?" said Hulot courteously.

Adeline rose, seized Hulot's arm, and exclaimed in a voice trembling with emotion:

"At last I have found you!"

"Adeline!" cried the stupefied baron, securing the shop-door.—"Joseph!" he cried to the Italian, "go out into the hall."

"My dear," said she, forgetting everything else in her exuberant joy, "you can come back to your family, for we are rich! your son has a hundred and sixty thousand francs a year! your pension is free, and there are arrears to the amount of fifteen thousand francs simply awaiting a certificate that you are living! Valérie is dead and has left you three hundred thousand francs. Your name is forgotten, you can return to the world, and you will find a fortune awaiting you beneath your son's roof. Come, our happiness will be complete. For nearly three years I have been looking for you, and I was so hopeful of falling in with you, that I have a room all ready to receive you. Oh! come away, come away from this horrible place I find you in!"

"I am very willing to go," said the bewildered baron; *"but can I take the little one?"*

"O Hector, give her up! do this for your Adeline, who has never asked the slightest sacrifice from you! I promise to find a good husband for the child, to provide a suitable *dot* for her, and to have her educated. Let it be said that one of those who have made you happy is happy herself, and do not fall back again into vice, into the mire!"

"So it was you who wanted me to marry?" rejoined the baron with a smile.—"Stay here a moment," he added, "I will go and dress upstairs, where I have some decent clothes in a trunk."

When Adeline was alone, and looked once more about the horrible place, she burst into tears.

"He has been living here," she said, "and we are living in opulence!—Poor man! how he has been punished, he who was always refinement itself!"

The flue-builder returned to say adieu to his benefactress, who told him to call a carriage. When he returned the baroness begged him to take little Atala Judici home with him, to take her away at once.

"You may say to her," she added, "that if she chooses to put herself under the direction of the curé of the Madeleine, on the day when she goes to communion for the first time, I will give her a *dot* of thirty thousand francs, and a good husband, some clever young man!"

"My eldest son, madame. He is twenty-two, and he worships the child."

The baron came down at this moment, his eyes wet with tears.

"You are taking me away," he said in his wife's ear, "from the only creature who ever approached your love for me! The little creature is crying her heart out and I can't leave her so.—"

"Never fear, Hector! she will be taken into a virtuous family, and I will answer for her morals."

"Ah! then I can go with you," said the baron, escorting his wife to the carriage.

Hector, become Baron Hulot d'Ervy once more, had donned a blue cloth frock coat and trowsers, white waistcoat, black cravat and gloves. When the baroness had taken her seat in the carriage Atala glided in with a snake-like movement.

"Oh! madame," said she, "let me go with you. See, I will be polite and obedient, I will do whatever you want me to; but don't part me from Père Vyder, my benefactor, who gives me such nice things. I shall be thrashed!"

"Come, come, Atala," said the baron, "this lady is my wife, and we must part."

"Your wife! as old as that!" replied the child; "why she trembles like a leaf! Oh! what a head!"

And she mischievously imitated the baroness's trembling. The flue-builder, who was looking for her, came to the carriage door.

"Take her away!" said the baroness.

He took Atala in his arms and carried her home with him by force.

"Thanks for this sacrifice, my dear," said Adeline, taking her husband's hand and pressing it with delirious joy. "How changed you are! How you must have suffered! Think what a surprise for your daughter and for your son!"

Adeline talked, as lovers talk when they meet after a long separation, of a thousand things at once. In ten minutes the baron and his wife reached Rue Louis-le-Grand, where Adeline found the following letter:

"MADAME LA BARONNE,

"Monsieur la Baron d'Ervy remained a month on Rue de Charonne, under the name of Thorec, an anagram of Hector. He is now on the Passage du Soleil under the name of Vyder. He calls himself an Alsatian, is a writer and lives with a young girl named Atala Judici. Be wary, madame, for active search is being made for the baron, I don't know in whose interest.

"The actress has kept her word, and subscribes herself, as always,

"Madame la Baronne,

"Your humble servant,

"J. M."

*

The baron's return aroused transports of joy which made him a convert to the delights of family-life. He forgot little Atala Judici, for the excessive indulgence of his passions had brought him to a point where his emotions were as fickle as those of a child. The happiness of the family was somewhat clouded by the change that had taken place in the baron. When he left his children he was still strong and well, and he returned almost a centenarian in appearance, bent and broken, his features bearing the stamp of vice. A splendid dinner improvised by Célestine recalled to the old man's mind the dinners given by Josépha; he was fairly dazzled by the family splendor.

"You are celebrating the return of the Prodigal Father!" he said in Adeline's ear.

"Hush!—everything is forgotten," she replied.

"And what of Lisbeth?" queried the baron, noticing that the old maid was not present.

"Alas!" Hortense replied, "she is in bed; she will never leave it again, and we shall soon have to endure the grief of losing her. She expects to see you after dinner."

The next morning at sunrise Victorin Hulot was informed by his concierge that his house was entirely surrounded by soldiers of the Municipal Guard. The officers of the law were in quest of Baron Hulot.

The bailiff, who followed close upon the concierge's heels, presented judgments in proper form to the advocate, and inquired if he proposed to pay, for his father, the amount due thereon. It was a matter of ten thousand francs in notes of hand, discounted by a usurer named Samanon, who had probably given the baron some two or three thousand francs. Victorin requested the bailiff to send his people away, and paid the amount of the judgment.

"Will this be the last?" he said to himself with some anxiety.

Lisbeth, who was wretched enough over the good fortune which was shining upon the family, could not endure this last happy event. She grew worse so rapidly that Doctor Bianchon announced that she would die within a week; vanquished at last after a long struggle marked by so many victories for her. She kept the secret of her hate amid the horrible agony of the last stages of phthisis. Moreover she had the supreme satisfaction of seeing Adeline, Hortense, Hulot, Victorin, Steinbock, Célestine and their children all in tears around her bed, weeping for her as the good angel of the family.

Baron Hulot, having his fill of substantial and nourishing food, a thing unknown to him for almost three years, recovered his strength, and eventually almost resembled his old self. This change for the better made Adeline so happy that her nervous trembling decreased sensibly in intensity.

"She will end by being perfectly happy!" said Lisbeth to herself on the day before her death, noticing the sort of veneration in which the baron held his wife, whose sufferings had been described to him by Hortense and Victorin.

This feeling hastened Cousin Bette's end, and her funeral was attended by a whole family in tears.

Baron and Baronne Hulot, having reached the age when absolute repose is most desirable, gave up the magnificent apartments on the first floor to Comte and Comtesse Steinbock, and took up their own quarters on the second floor. The baron, through the efforts of his son, obtained a place on a railroad in the early part of 1845, with a salary of six thousand francs, which, added to his retiring pension of six thousand and the fortune bequeathed to him by Madame Crevel, gave him an income of twenty-four thousand francs. Hortense having had a separate estate from that of her husband during the three months of their estrangement, Victorin no longer hesitated to transfer to his sister the two hundred thousand francs held by him in trust, and he gave Hortense an allowance of twelve thousand. Wenceslas, finding himself the husband of a rich wife, was guilty of no further infidelity; but he idled his time away, unable to make up his mind to undertake any work, however trifling. An artist *in partibus* once more, he had much success in salons and was consulted by many amateurs; in short, he became a critic, as all incapables do whose beginnings give promise that is not fulfilled. Each of these various households therefore possessed its own private fortune, although they lived together as one family. Learning wisdom from her many misfortunes the baroness left the care of the whole property in her son's hands, and thus restricted the baron to his salary, hoping that the slender proportions of that source of revenue would prevent him from falling back into his former errors. But, by a strange stroke of good fortune, upon which neither the mother nor the son had calculated, the baron seemed to have renounced the fair sex. His quiescence in this respect, which was credited to the account of nature, so reassured the family that at last they could enjoy, unreservedly, the restored amiability and charming qualities of Baron d'Ervy. He was unflagging in his attentions to his wife and children, accompanied them to the theatre, reappeared in society with them, and did the honors of his son's salon with exquisite grace. In short, this prodigal father, restored, afforded the liveliest satisfaction to his family. He was an agreeable old man, completely broken down physically, but clever and witty, and had retained of his vice only those elements which tended to make it a social virtue. Naturally, they felt at last perfectly secure. The baroness and her children held the head of the family in great regard, forgetting the death of the two uncles. Life cannot go on without examples of noble forgetfulness!

Madame Victorin, who managed this enormous household and displayed great talents as a housekeeper, due to the teaching of Lisbeth, had been compelled to hire a male cook. The cook made it necessary to have a scullery-maid. Scullery-maids are in these days ambitious creatures, intent upon prying into the chef's secrets, and they become cooks as soon as they know how to stir gravies. Therefore, they changed scullery-maids very frequently. Early in December, 1845, Célestine hired in that capacity a stout Norman girl from Isigny, short, with fine red arms and a very ordinary face, and as stupid as an impromptu play; so stupid that she could hardly be induced to lay aside the classic cotton cap which is the ordinary head-dress of the damsels of Lower Normandy. This damsel, endowed with the figure of a wet-nurse, seemed as if she were always on the point of bursting the cotton goods in which her waist was enveloped. One would have said that her ruddy face was cut out of flint, so immovable were its yellow outlines. Naturally no heed was paid to the addition to the household of this Agathe, the genuine sophisticated girl sent daily to Paris from the provinces. Agathe tempted the cook but very little, her language was so vulgar, for she had been waiting upon wagoners, she came from a suburban tavern, and instead of making a conquest of her superior and inducing him to instruct her in the great art of cooking, she became the object of his contempt. The cook was courting Louise, Countess Steinbock's maid. So it was that the Norman, finding that he treated her badly, complained of her lot; she was always sent outside upon one pretext or another when the chief was preparing some new dish, or putting the finishing touches to a sauce.

"It's certain that I have no chance here," she said, "I'll go to some other house."

Nevertheless she remained, although she had already asked twice to go.

One night Adeline, awakened by a strange sound, found that Hector was not in the bed he occupied beside hers, for they slept in twin beds, as it becomes old people to do. She waited an hour, but the baron did not return. Seized with terror, dreading some horrible catastrophe, apoplexy or the like, she went first of all to the upper floor, to the attics where the servants slept, and was attracted to Agathe's room as much by the bright light that streamed out through the half-open door as by the murmur of voices. She paused in dismay as she recognized the baron's voice; fascinated by Agathe's charms, he had been led on so far by the shameless coarse woman's premeditated resistance as to say these odious words:

"My wife hasn't long to live, and, if you choose, you shall be a baroness."

Adeline shrieked, dropped her candle and fled.

Three days later the baroness, who had received the last sacraments the night before, was at the point of death, surrounded by her family, all in tears. A moment before she died she took her husband's hand, pressed it, and whispered to him:

"My dear, I had nothing else but my life to give

G. Cain del.

Gaujean sc.

you; in a moment you will be free, and you can make a Baroness Hulot."

And they saw, what must indeed be rare, tears starting from the eyes of a corpse. The ferocity of vice had conquered the patience of the angel, from whose lips, on the brink of eternity, escaped the only reproachful word she had uttered in her whole life.

Baron Hulot left Paris three days after the burial of his wife. Eleven months later Victorin learned indirectly of his father's marriage to Mademoiselle Agathe Piquetard, which was celebrated at Isigny, on the first of February, 1846.

"Parents may oppose the marriage of their children, but children can not prevent the follies of their parents in their dotage," said Master Hulot to Master Popinot, the second son of the former Minister of Commerce, who mentioned this marriage to him.